Advance Pr

"A terrific read that not only perfectly captures the New York City of the 1970s but, in its page-turning plotting, has resonance with some of today's scandal headlines. If you lived through that era, this book will bring it back to you in a rush; for younger readers, it's a perfect time capsule of a time that nostalgia has deceptively disguised as more innocent."
–Peter Bloch, *Saturday Evening Post*, Contributing Editor

"Having grown up attending Bronx Catholic schools, *Fallout Shelter* really hits home for me. Schindler excels at re-creating that environment, and the joys and sorrows of childhood relationships in the inner city. Steven Schindler is up there with great Bronx authors Richard Price and Avery Corman in telling wonderful stories in this much-maligned borough!"
-James Hannon, Author, *Lost Boys of the Bronx: The Oral History of the Ducky Boys Gang*

"Glimmers of hope and happiness shine through all the way to the end… An extraordinary tale of the tribulations on the road to adulthood."
-*Kirkus Reviews*

FALLOUT SHELTER

FALLOUT SHELTER

A NOVEL

STEVEN SCHINDLER

San Diego

Fallout Shelter is a work of fiction.

All incidents and dialogue are products of the author's imagination and are not to be construed as real.

Where real-life places and public figures are mentioned, they are fictional situations and not intended to depict actual events.

Any other resemblance to persons living or dead is entirely coincidental.

COPYRIGHT© 2022 STEVEN SCHINDLER

ALL RIGHTS RESERVED, INCLUDING THE RIGHT TO REPRODUCE THIS BOOK OR PORTION THEREOF IN ANY FORM WHATSOEVER.

FOR INFORMATION AND REQUESTS CONTACT:

The Elevated Press

747 S. Mission Rd.

#1422

Fallbrook, CA 92088

www.TheElevatedPress.com

ISBN-13   978-0-9662408-3-2

ISBN-10   0-9662408-3-9

LIBRARY OF CONGRESS CONTROL NUMBER: 2021947708

THE ELEVATED PRESS ORIGINAL TRADE PAPERBACK

FIRST EDITION, SEPTEMBER 2022

PRINTED IN THE USA

EDITOR BRIAN MC KERNAN

COVER DESIGN BY THE ELEVATED PRESS

COVER PHOTO BY M.V. STANTON

Praise for Steven Schindler's Novels

The Last Sewer Ball - Grand Prize Winner, NY Book Festival

High Desert High- "A provocative physical and emotional trip" —*Publishers Weekly*

From the Block - Best Fiction, Hollywood Indie Book Festival

From Here to Reality (Simon & Schuster/Pocket Books) "Required Reading" -*NY Post*

Sewer Balls- "Probably the best novel produced by the small presses in 1999" —*Small Press Review*

On the Bluffs - "Captivating" -*Glendale News Press*

With love to Sue-
My wife, coach, and traveling partner
on this big blue ball
somewhere in the universe

AUTHOR'S NOTE

I attended 12 years of Catholic school and would like to thank the wonderful nuns, priests, brothers and teachers who guided and taught us.

However, I hope that the cruel, sadistic, abusive, and criminal ones get what they deserve in this life, and the next.

But whoever causes one of these little ones who believe in me

to stumble,

It would be better for him to have a great millstone fastened

around his neck

And be drowned in the depth of the sea.

Matthew 18:6

PART ONE
∽ Chapter 1 ∾

They could tell something was up. Sister Ignatius kept nervously pulling back her long, thick black sleeve to look at her wristwatch and then jerking her head to check the clock on the wall. Nervous was her natural state, but when she also twitched like a chicken in a slaughterhouse, she was obviously getting ready to hatch some kind of surprise on this the very last day of grammar school for the class of 1972. Forever.

Sister Ignatius was probably in her fifties, but to the eighth-grade class in St. Gall's Grammar School she might as well have been a hundred. Her face and her hands were the only parts of her body that were exposed. Her black *Little House on the Prairie* bonnet was pulled tight around her face with a black satin ribbon tied in a neat bow just below her chin. Her skin seemed whiter than white. Almost transparent. With thin veins of red and purple trying to come to the surface. Somehow flakes of dandruff would find their way on to the black shawl that covered her shoulders. And occasionally a white strand of hair would peek from under the bonnet, having escaped their life sentence of confinement.

"No talking!" She shrieked, even though no one was even whispering.

The clock on the wall didn't have a second hand and when the minute hand advanced it would make a loud click. It was one minute before ten.

Then...*THUNK!*

Followed immediately by the deafening alarm bells clanging in the classroom and in the hall and an announcement on the speaker fixed to the wall just above the clock. It was the principal, Sister Agnes.

"This is not a fire drill. This is an atomic bomb drill. This is not a fire drill. This is an atomic bomb drill. Proceed as instructed by your teachers."

Eight years ago, when most of these same students were together in first grade, teachers didn't even tell them why they were to go into a darkened hallway in complete silence, squat on the floor and put their heads between their legs. The year then was 1964 at the height of the cold war. President Kennedy was assassinated the year before, so there was always a sense of dread that anything could happen. Kids knew it was a drill for an atomic bomb attack by the Russians, because it was all over the TV news. People were building bomb shelters in their backyards, and apartment buildings had to designate a room in the cellar, which used to be where tenants stored baby carriages, bicycles, and Christmas decorations, but was now magically transformed into a nuclear fallout shelter.

Most of the schools in the Bronx had abandoned the atomic bomb drills several years earlier. But old traditions were hard to let go of at St. Gall's in 1972. So the nuns, almost invisible in their black head to toe get-ups, slowly walked up and down the hall, as the four classes on the second floor of the school lined the long dark hallway in silence, squatted with heads tucked low.

The only light that appeared was from two eighth-grade boys holding flashlights who also walked up and down the hall, shining a light on any troublemakers who might dare utter a syllable. One boy was Ignatius Cottle. Of course he was forever doomed to ridicule and bullying for two reasons; his first name forever linked him to the most reviled nun in St. Gall's history, and the fact that his second name reminded everyone that he was a coddled teacher's pet. The other boy holding a flashlight was William Manzilla, known to everyone, except the teachers, as Chili.

Chili was an unusual boy for his class because he didn't fall into the two distinctly divided factions of teacher's pets and class clowns. Even though teachers liked him, he still had a bit of the devil in him.

Chili was approaching the squatting eighth-grade class from down the hall, flashlight beam scanning the fifth, sixth, and seventh-graders randomly. But when he arrived next to the eighth-grade class, his beam of light found a controversial target. Or rather, two targets. Like a Hollywood Boulevard opening-night searchlight, Chili's light was shining bright on the well-developed breasts of Pamela Hinderlap. The eighth-grade boys who were not teacher's pets immediately began discreetly laughing while most of the girls gasped. All except for Pamela, who made no attempt to hide her breasts or her broad toothy smile adorned with braces.

"What's all the noise over there?" Sister Ignatius asked in a loud stage whisper from down the hall.

"Nothing, Sister," Chili replied, restoring order as he pointed his flashlight to the ceiling, at the same time getting the big "A-Okay" hand signal from his two best friends, Angel Rodriguez and Mikey McGowan.

Chili was liked by all ever since the very first day of first grade. That day in 1964 was a drizzly, windy day, and William Manzilla sat in the row next to the open windows that faced Van Cortlandt Park. The first-grade teacher, Sister Joan, was having each child say their name. When they got to *William*, the first thing out of his mouth was, "I'm chilly," which forever branded him as Chili. From that day on, that's how he was known, not only to his classmates and every student in the school, but to everyone in his building, on the block, and in the entire neighborhood, including his little brother. Only his father still called him William. His deceased mother used to call him Willy. And in tender moments, called him Chilly Willy, like the cartoon character. His father, George Manzilla, never ever showed moments of tenderness.

Mr. Manzilla worked for the New York City subway system as a maintenance worker. He sometimes worked nights, which meant he would get home from work, stinking from eight hours slogging through the garbage, filth, slime, piss, and worse from human and animal vermin that use the almost 700 miles of ancient tunnels where upwards of 5 million people and ten times as many rats use every day. Chili was the big brother to Jamie, who was four years younger.

Those mornings when their father came home at 8:30am were dreaded. Besides the putrid stench of the subway still on his grimy uniform, there was also lingering smell of rotgut whiskey and a beer chaser gulped down at the corner bar, The Terminal, right under the el, that never seemed to close as long as you knew which knock to use on which window. Chili, being an eighth-grader and the oldest, felt a strong sense of responsibility to try and protect Jamie from his father's tirades without getting into an actual fistfight. He had one of those last year, just before his mother died from cancer. Chili confronted his father with both fists up and ready, like a statue of John L. Sullivan, demanding his father "shut the fuck up!" and stop yelling at their mom, who was trying to keep up with her household duties despite being weeks from death. You wouldn't think a kid who stood at five foot eight inches and a hundred twenty pounds soaking wet would be intimidating, but when the father is five foot three and one hundred ten pounds and half in the bag most of the time, the father did shut the fuck up. But his father was never the same to him. And after the missus died he was as rotten as he was before that awful time, but barely even looked at Chili. He didn't yell anymore when Chili was present. He just seethed.

Chili and Jamie slept in the same bedroom. It was the only bedroom. Jamie by the wall next to the door, and Chili on the other side of the room, between the window that his mom used to hang out the clothes to dry and the window that led out to the fire escape. Mom and dad used to sleep on the Castro convertible pullout sofa in the living room. But since his mom died, sometimes he didn't even bother opening it, but just slept on the couch without blankets or a sheet in his underwear.

Chili would get Jamie out of bed, serve breakfast, help him dress, and get him off to school. Now that he was graduating from grammar school, he worried if he'd still be able to perform these duties as well once he'd be in high school and

Fallout Shelter

probably needing to leave an hour earlier in the morning. He'd be attending Archbishop Corrigan High School for boys, which would mean a bus ride and a subway ride all the way to the South Bronx, just a pop fly beyond Yankee Stadium. Younger brother Jamie would just have to step up and be more responsible next fall. After all he'll be in sixth grade for chrissakes!

Sister Agnes clanged her giant hand-held bell that would befit an Eighteenth Century town crier, as would her nun's habit.
"The drill is over. Please return to your classrooms. In silence!"
But the louder she rang her bell, the louder the chatter got. Chili got in line next to Angel and Mikey, who held out their hands to be slapped five.
"That was wicked cool," Angel said, patting his own chest.
"Pamela liked it! Did you see the smile across her face? Her braces shot light beams across the hall!" Mikey said, excitedly.
Chili, Angel, and Mikey weren't always best friends. Back in sixth grade when Mikey McGowan was left back and landed in Chili and Angel's class, he acted like he was Mr. Big Shot. He bullied the weak teacher's pets, like Ignatius Cottle and Joel Hanrahan, who were easy marks. Then one day in sixth grade, when Sister Aloysius was at the door talking to another teacher in the hall, Mikey held Chili's head down from behind and started twisting his arm for no good reason. Or even a bad one. Chili was helpless in that position and it took one roundhouse swing from Angel coming to Chili's defense and Mikey was bleeding from the mouth on the floor. When Sister Aloysius rushed over and asked what happened, Mikey said he slipped and fell. That was the moment the three of them became best friends.
St. Gall's Parish was an unusual one for the Bronx. Situated in the northwest Bronx it encompassed the usual block

after block of dreary brick apartment buildings built in the early 1900s that were roach-infested one- and two-bedroom lead-painted apartments that housed poor people who had the wherewithal to escape the worse-off slums of upper Manhattan and the South Bronx.

But also included in the gerrymandered map of the parish were several blocks, literally on the other side of the tracks; the number 1 train, elevated subway tracks, that is. The Archdiocese probably realized when drawing up the map that it would help the Sunday collections baskets if they drew the red line a little further west to include the first few blocks of Riverdale, one of New York City's wealthiest neighborhoods. Riverdale was home to diplomats, professional athletes, Wall Street titans, mobsters, and normal people with money like doctors, lawyers, city managers, and business owners.

Angel Rodriguez lived on the first street up the hill from the Kingsbridge lowlands that was part of Riverdale. His father owned three bodegas and his mother didn't even work part-time like most of the kids' mothers in class did. Their home was no Riverdale mansion, but it had an upstairs and downstairs, a front and back yard, trees, and a two-car garage that was larger than most of the apartments his classmates lived in. Angel was a happy, beefy kid who was the smartest boy in the class and despite his short stature and chunky size was adept at all competitive sports, from curb ball to basketball to baseball, football and everything else that required excellent eye-hand coordination.

As every nun in the school declared on the first day of class in each grade he passed through, Mikey McGowan was "bold." Having been left back, of course he was a year older than everyone else in the class, so he was the tallest, strongest, but certainly not the smartest. If he attended a school that had any kind of organized athletic program, he undoubtedly would be a valued and pampered athlete who would certainly lead the baseball, basketball, and football teams to championships. But since the only school sponsored athletic competition at St. Gall's was a once a year "field day" held at the nearby Gaelic Park Irish football field where kids raced each other in potato sacks and carried eggs in spoons, Mikey was just another classroom disrupter who very often got the rough edge of an enraged nun's tongue, and sometimes the back of her boney hand across his face.

Chili, Angel, and Mikey were inseparable from the day Angel punched Mikey out in defense of Chili. They met before school, during lunch, after school, and weekends. They began their friendship as children playing curb ball, stick ball, and scully, and progressed as young teens to enjoy sports, poker, smoking, *Playboy* centerfolds, chasing girls and even experimenting with drinking beer and cheap fortified wine. Well, Angel and Mikey anyway. They were still working on Chili in several of those categories.

After graduating they knew they'd be attending different high schools, and another constant in their friendship was about to change: being altar boys. Chili, Angel, and Mikey had been altar boys since third grade, the last generation of Latin-speaking altar boys. Mikey was especially relieved when the Latin prayers and responses were finally retired in favor of English after many centuries. In fact, most of Mikey's Latin responses sounded like a cross between the Three Stooges-as-surgeons pig-Latin doubletalk and pure blather. Through Mikey's lips, the Latin version of the prayer, The Confiteor, which started, *Confiteor Deo, omnipotenti, beatae Mariae semper Virgini, beato Michaeli Archangelo, beato Joanni Baptistae,* etc. became something sounding like *You can feed your dog omni alpo, bocce marty sampler Virginia beat up michaelangelo, b.o. salami bopster* when properly mumbled.

But being an altar boy did have its advantages. There were the school day mornings when altar boys were pulled out of the classroom to serve at a nine or ten o'clock funeral mass. Or the weekends where one could serve at a wedding and get tipped in cash for as much as twenty-five bucks. And of course the sheer fun of dressing up in long, black, priest-like robes with a white fluffy pirate shirt over it as if you were in a play.

To a certain degree it was like a Shakespearean play. Altar boys get into their period costumes backstage, prepare their props of wine and water-filled cruets, bells, books, and candles. And of course they are supposed to have their lines committed to memory. And just as in any theatrical presentation, when there's a screw-up on stage, the director gets pissed off! In their case, the director being the priest, or heaven forbid, the monsignor saying mass.

The only four eighth-grade boys who were still altar boys fell into the teacher's pet category, except for Chili, who remained neutral between the two camps. Mikey had quit during seventh grade and Angel followed his lead, as did most of the boys who valued cool over school. But Chili was hanging in there. In fact, he took his role quite seriously. He knew all his lines, and his timing for cues to ring bells, opening books for priests, and presenting props was impeccable.

This classroom crammed with 23 boys and 32 girls started out eight years ago as humans barely past the toddler stage. They were essentially testosterone- and estrogen-free, stumbling and mumbling, just past baby-hood, afraid of most things when mommy wasn't next to them. But now as young teens? They were like festering cakes of yeast, exuding so much effluvia that there seemed to be a cloud of mysterious odors and pheromones that varied from row to row of students. Was it sweat? B.O.? Or secretions from newly discovered body parts sprouting by the hour like mushrooms on damp sod. Most girls seemed to want to hide their budding breasts with sweaters even though they already wore thick cotton blouses with plaid jumpers despite the warm June heat. Boys had to cross their legs to hide erections that seemed to jump into action for any reason, whether a picture of Pocahontas in a text book, or perhaps a girl in class saying a provocative word such as "pajamas." But some girls, like Pamela Hinderlap, were thrilled with their newly sprouted breasties. They loved to yawn and stretch and push their elbows back, making their boobs protrude like Mamie Van Doren in a 1950's B-movie. And there were a few boys, led by Freddie Gastrich, who would poke other kids for attention and point to his crotch every time an unexpected urge caused a pointy thing in his pants. It didn't matter where he was; standing in line for cookies, sitting during a test, or kneeling in a church pew. He wanted whoever was nearby to take a peek. He now knew better than attempting to show his bulge to a girl. This was strictly a guy thing. He found that out when he tried to get Pamela Hinderlap to take a gander at his manly mound during music class, and she screeched at the top of her lungs as if somebody put a scorpion down her bra. Luckily for Freddie, she said she was just singing loudly to "Ave Maria" and didn't rat him out. If Pamela Hinderlap couldn't handle looking at such a thing, another girl might have a heart attack or call the cops.

This being the last day of class before summer vacation, Chili, Angel, and Mikey knew where to meet after school as they always did before special occasions, or on rainy days, cold days, or pretty much any day they wanted to just hang out: in the fallout shelter. They needed to plan their hijinks for the most important day of the entire eight years of grammar school. The graduation boat ride to Rye Beach Playland.

    The fallout shelter in the basement of Chili's ancient early Twentieth Century apartment building was really an old storage room hidden down a creepy, dark tunnel by the boiler with walls of stone like an ancient dungeon. But about eight years ago, the super made everybody move their bicycles, baby carriages, and boxes of Christmas decorations to another smaller room by the elevator where almost everything immediately got robbed. Once the stuff was out they filled it with large barrels and cardboard boxes. The empty barrels, marked with civil defense symbols and government instructions were to be filled with water. The cardboard boxes were filled with, of all things, saltines. This was supposed to save everybody in the building, all 85 families living in apartments, in case of nuclear annihilation. In the meantime, it made a great hidden hangout, now that nobody ever came for their stuff anymore. Chili had figured out how to cut off the old padlock, and replace it with a similar-looking one. Even the super didn't bother going in the forgotten chamber anymore.

Mikey brought a pack of Marlboros, Angel had a *Playboy* he stole from his father's hidden stash in the garage, and Chili brought three 16 ounce Cokes and a bag of pretzel rods. It was a celebration of anticipation.

"I'm gonna sneak some Night Train Express on the boat ride, I swear!" Mikey said, taking a cigarette from the box, and waving it slowly around in case anybody didn't notice. He lit it, inhaled deeply, and then desperately tried to stifle a coughing fit. "I'm still shaking a cold," he explained.

"If you bring the Night Train, I'll bring cigarettes!" Angel added enthusiastically, also lighting up a cigarette and taking baby puffs.

"Oh man, if you guys get caught!" Chili said, following the others by lighting up a Marlboro but not inhaling at all. He sort of puffed some smoke, opened his mouth and turned his head so as not to get any up his nose or in his mouth.

Mikey looked at Chili, eyes bugged out, lips scrunched up all crooked. "*You* guys? You're going too, right? We're in this together, right?"

Chili, looked at Angel, who was usually the voice of reason mediating between the two extremes of Mikey and Chili.

"Chili, c'mon," Angel said rising from his perch on an empty water barrel. "You don't have to stand on the poop deck swilling wine from a bottle and blowing smoke rings, but this is it! It's our graduation boat ride! It's what we've been waiting for! Pranks! Getting high! Seeing Pamela in a bikini!"

"L.S.M.F.T.!" Mikey proclaimed.

"Lucky Strike means fine tobacco?" Chili asked. "We only smoke Marlboro."

"No! Loose straps mean flabby tits!" Mikey shouted with glee.

Chili shook his head. "This isn't a party at the Playboy Club! Nuns and priests will be watching us like undercover cops looking for pick pockets in Times Square."

"Priests?" Mikey asked, shocked. "I thought it was just the sister Mary Ferris wheel brigade."

"You didn't hear? There's a new priest assigned to the parish. He's a teacher at Archbishop Corrigan and he's going to say mass at St. Gall's on the weekend."

"Is that the young hippie priest I heard about?" Angel chimed in.

Chili nodded. "Yes, he's got longish hair, wears bell-bottoms and sneakers! He's part of the new youth ministry."

"How do you know?" Angel asked.

"Mrs. Madigan told me," Chili replied, referring to the long-time parish worker who takes care of the rectory and the church.

Mikey shook his head and scoffed. "That sounds like a plainclothes cop to me. I don't care if he's got love beads and a VW bus. He's a priest and he'll be watching us."

"I'll know more this Sunday. I'm serving with him at 9 a.m.," Chili said, followed by snuffing out his cigarette and taking a gulp of Coke.

"I like it! Our spy, spying on their spy!" Angel said gleefully, holding up his bottle of Coke for a toast. They clinked their bottles together in solidarity.

Sunday mass at 9 a.m. was the mass for the kids who attended St. Gall's School. It wasn't different from any of the other half-dozen or so Sunday masses, but it was a way for the nuns to keep an eye on the kids all in one place and observe who was and who wasn't putting envelopes in the collection basket. Chili had good memories of saying mass with Mikey and Angel.

They'd meet before and hang out, or arrange to get together afterwards for baseball, basketball, softball, or touch football in Van Cortlandt park right across the street. But now that Mikey and Angel retired from being altar boys, Chili was basically the elder statesman for the under classmen. He planned to hang up his cassock for good at the end of August, just before he started high school.

This day was extra nerve-wracking for Chili. Not only would he be meeting the new hippie priest Father Palmer for the first time, he'd also be serving mass with his little brother Jamie for the first time in ages. Monsignor Shannon, the pastor, had complained to Chili that Jamie was at risk of being dropped from the altar boys. He was showing up late, missing his cues for bells and presenting the water and wine, and not saying his prayer responses loudly enough. Chili hoped Jamie would be on his best behavior on this of all days.

"Where have you been?" Chili asked Jamie who was fifteen minutes late and wearing shoes that hadn't been polished since he stomped through a mud puddle in the last rain storm two weeks ago.

"I don't know. I lost track of the time," Jamie mumbled.

Jamie was small for his age, and was very unlike Chili. Whereas Chili could be seen talking to Louie the shoemaker in his store with a bunch of old geezers, or hanging out with the older teenagers who openly drank beer by the see-saws in the park, or helping third- and fourth-grader altar boys get the hang of ringing the bells at mass on cue, Jamie didn't seem to get along with anyone in particular. His grades weren't great, he didn't play curb ball or stickball with the kids in his class, and Chili had no idea who his best friends were.

"Well hurry up and get ready. Mass starts in fifteen minutes," Chili said, trying to find him a cassock that would fit in the server's closet. Suddenly, Chili almost screamed when he felt two sharp jabs in his side. "What the fu...," Chili said, stopping the "*ck*" just in the nick of time when he saw a priest standing behind him. "Oh, excuse me, father."

"Excuse me father, for I have sinned? Close, but not quite," the gangly, youthful priest said through a broad smile. Chili knew it was the new hippie priest.

"Hi, I'm Father Palmer," the priest said extending his hand to shake with Chili.

Chili couldn't remember if he had ever shaken hands with a priest before. "Hi, I'm Chi... William Manzilla. And this is my little brother, Jamie."

"Hello, William and Jamie," Father Palmer said warmly. "What grades are you boys in?"

"I'm in eighth and Jamie is in fifth."

"And where are you going to high school next year, William?"

"Archbishop Corrigan."

"Good choice! Did you know I was a teacher there?"

"I heard that."

"Oh! Did you hear anything else about me? I hope it wasn't anything bad?!" Father Palmer said, laughing a little too hard.

"No, father."

"I think you'll find I'm very fair and also fun!"

Chili immediately knew this priest was different. A poke in the ribs? That's something a drunk uncle might do at a barbecue, but a priest? Plus he seemed to talk to him almost as though he was trying to impress him. The priests Chili knew over the years at St. Gall's were far from exuberant in their friendliness. A few were polite, cordial, and marginally friendly at best, and several were as mean as Riker's Island prison guards forced to work on Christmas Eve. There weren't any priests who were teachers in St. Gall's grammar school. The only time priests appeared in a classroom setting were those who once a year would drop into class to pitch the priesthood during vocation week. They extolled the bliss of being God's chosen servant, with free room and board and no vow of poverty. But the priests

Chili was really familiar with were the ones in charge of the altar boys. Over the years, those priests varied from cantankerous drill sergeants trying to get third-graders to memorize prayers and replies in perfect Latin, to bulbous-nosed alcoholic old Irish priests who thought mumbles that sounded like "dominoes and biscuits" and jokes about the pope's phone number being Et Cum Spiri 2-2-0 were just fine as long as you were on time and didn't spill the water and wine on the newly cleaned church carpet.

"And Jamie! Come over here!" Father Palmer said motioning for Jamie to get closer. Once in front of him, the priest tousled Jamie's hair and gave him a playful pat on the head. "You listen to your big brother! And listen to me, too!"

Jamie looked at Chili, then back at the priest. "Yes, father."

"Chop chop! Let's get ready. We're on in five minutes!" Father Palmer said, rallying the two perplexed altar boys.

Suddenly, the door swung open and a wiry, angular, wisp of a woman in her fifties, wearing a flowered kitchen apron, entered and brought everything to a grinding halt.

"Father! No need for you today. The monsignor is saying the mass, thank you," she said, waiting for the priest's smile to neutralize. "I'll be calling you at your residence when we need you next," she continued, pushing the two boys away from the priest. "Boys! Look at you! Did your mother iron the surplices, like I told you?"

Father Palmer left the room and quietly closed the door behind him.

"I tried my best to do it like my mom used to, but it's hard," Chili said, trying to flatten the long white garment for his little brother.

"Oh, yes. I forgot," Mrs. Madigan said softly, recalling that her friend, Chili's mom, was in fact dead. "On second thought, you did a fine job. Leave them for me after mass, and I'll clean and iron them for you."

Fallout Shelter

Mrs. Madigan's job title was Sacristy Custodian, but her duties included everything from being the den mother to altar boys, wrangler of priests, polisher of ancient, valuable shiny objects, keeper of the candles, and guardian of all things that needed protecting, whether dead-saint body parts known as *relics* or the living.

She felt ashamed that she briefly forgot that her close friend and neighbor Mrs. Manzilla had passed away. It's easy to do when you know someone for decades. Mrs. Madigan and Mrs. Manzilla were like so many of the mothers fighting for their children day by day, hour by hour. They are all that stands between the kids and the dangerous world of the streets, and even the dangers behind closed steel apartment doors and in altar boy dressing rooms. St. Gall's didn't have a P.T.A. but they did have a Mother's Club. Of course they had the usual bake sales and novenas and rosary recitations. But Mother's Club meetings, held in the St. Gall's basement lunchroom in the quiet early evenings, were also coffee- and cigarette-fueled communication sessions with no kids, priests, nuns or husbands around. It was their opportunity to share their unfiltered perspective on the aforementioned groups. Mrs. Madigan knew all about Mr. Manzilla's ways, and every other father in the parish. They knew who were the drunks, the fighters, the flirters, the gamblers, the druggies, and the deadbeats. But also, there was equal time given to the saints among them. The men with a firm but fair hand. The ones who could tenderly pat a child on the head one moment and punch in the face anyone who would threaten the family in any way shape or form. The men who studied for promotional exams after 12 hours at grueling jobs. Fathers who had the same pair of shoes re-soled and heeled for decades so the children could have school shoes, sneakers, ice skates, and roller skates each year.

Mrs. Madigan's husband was one of those saints. He fought evil in World War II and fought similar evil under the streets of New York as a subway cop. He helped raise three children who had no idea of the horrors his soft blue eyes had seen. He put food on the table and a soft touch into each of their hearts. But Mrs. Madigan knew. She knew what he did "over there" and "under ground" here.

"The Monsignor is in a hurry today with his blasted tee time at the golf course, so Chili I want you to do everything quickly. No slow bell-ringing and no dilly-dallying!"

"Yes, Mrs. Madigan," Chili said, pushing Jamie out of the door to the rear of the church where they would meet Monsignor Shannon.

This was the first Sunday since school ended and Chili wasn't quite sure where Angel and Mikey might be hanging out. The baseball fields, the lake, the alley, the fallout shelter? Those decisions were always made during lunch recess or walking home after school. It wouldn't take long to drop off Jamie, put on some shorts, and check out the usual spots.

After noting the fallout shelter in his cellar was locked, he headed to the Vannie basketball courts where a lot of the older kids would play, and sometimes even drink beer on the sidelines. He entered through a hole in the chain-link fence and saw Angel mixing with the high-school-aged players trying to get into a game. But on the adjacent court was another group of younger kids, with Father Palmer laughing and carrying on among them like he was a teenager.

"How long has Father P. been over there?" Chili asked after slapping Angel five.

"Who?" Angel asked, intently watching the game action.

"Father Palmer. He's over there with the fifth- and sixth-graders."

"Got me. I didn't notice. Hey, I got next!" Angel shouted, running over to try and get picked for the next game.

"Yeah, me too!" Chili said, following Angel, but getting there too late.

"Stick around for the next game!" Angel yelled, dribbling the ball up-court.

Chili took a walk to the drinking fountain that was between the two basketball courts. He leaned over to drink from it, while keeping an eye on Father P. interacting with the younger kids on the sidelines. Father P. noticed him, smiled broadly, and waved. Chili threw a weak wave back without smiling and returned to the older kid's game. He thought about the Monsignor rushing through the mass to get to his golf game just up the park path in the golf course. He was sure if he went to the golf course clubhouse, he'd find him at the snack bar with a few old codgers with similar beer bellies and poor posture eating hamburgers and potato chips and drinking Cokes. That's normal. But something about Father P. was weird, and it shows.

Mikey darted through the hole in the fence carrying a basketball and dribbled over to Chili at the fountain.

"I need a drink of water! I just ran all the way from my house! You're not playing?"

"I think I'll get in the next game," Chili said, still watching Father P.

"Let's get over there and get in a game. Hey, how was mass with the new priest? I see he's over there hanging with the munchkins."

"Shannon bumped him 'cause he had a tee time at the golf course. I could barely keep up with him! He was rushing through mass like it was an auction."

"So what's he like? The hippie."

"He's...I don't know. Friendly."

"Yeah, he looks it, with those midgets over there. Come on! Angel's waving us into the next game!"

Angel, Mikey, and Chili were on the same team, and their personalities were reflected in how they played. Angel, although short and chunky, was deceptively agile, and worked to set up Mikey under the basket. Mikey, tall and lanky, knew how to go where Angel wanted him to for an easy basket. And Chili stayed quietly around the perimeter, observing everything, putting himself in a position if plan A didn't work, so that he could nail a long bank shot from the left side, which was his trademark move.

As the sun set over high rises to the west, kids began slowly drifting away from the park in all directions. Some to a fun extended Italian family Sunday dinner around a Formica table in a cramped walk-up apartment kitchen with endless plates of pasta, roast beef, and then pastries. Other kids to dark basement hovels to grab whatever was wrapped in wax paper in the refrigerator while a mom napped on a couch with a TV blaring and dad was down the block on his regular creaky red bar stool with an ashtray full of Chesterfield butts in front of him, working on emptying a quart of Dewar's a shot glass at a time.

Ever since his mom died, Chili kept the Sunday family dinner tradition alive, even though usually it was just he and Jamie. He always had a place setting on the kitchen table for his father, but he was rarely there. For the first time in ages, there was a fourth place setting at the table. This was for Mikey, who never turned down an invitation to a meal, a game of anything, or a fight.

"You sit there, Mikey. I'm almost finished with the salad. You can wash up in the bathroom."

Mikey had been to Chili's many times. He had fun with Mrs. Manzilla, who was quick to laughter and slow to anger. But he had only seen Mr. Manzilla a few times, and each of those were memorable. Mr. Manzilla was the opposite of Mrs. Manzilla. Mikey was washing his hands with the door open, and saw young Jamie appear in the mirror behind him. He stood there, staring at him with his dark, doe like eyes.

"Hi, Jamie! You need to take a whizz?"

"No."

"A dump?"

"No."

"Choke the chicken?"

Fallout Shelter

"No. What's that?"

"Never you mind. Just make sure you wash your hands before eating no matter what goes on in there," Mikey said, drying his hands and heading back to the kitchen table to plop down on a folding chair in front of a neat place setting of Woolworth's-issue china and silverware.

Chili placed an oversized bowl of steaming spaghetti with meatballs floating in red sauce on top in the middle of the oilcloth tablecloth adorned with farm animals.

"Do you have to call your mom to tell her you're having dinner here?"

"Nah," Mikey said, dismissively, his eyes as large as the meatballs he was ogling. "Last week I went to Angel's for dinner. My brother said they were happy at home because there was more for them."

Jamie appeared in the kitchen doorway and just stood there as if in a daze. Mikey tilted his head in Jamie's direction to get Chili's attention.

"Hey, Jamie. Go put on a clean shirt, please. I just put clean clothes in your drawer."

Jamie did an about face and went to his room.

Mikey knew that since Mrs. Manzilla died, Chili did almost everything: cook, clean, laundry, pay bills, make the beds, and help Jamie with his homework. He didn't bother asking about why he got stuck with everything. He knew the answer.

"Is your father eating with us?"

"I don't know. He's usually out around now."

Mikey knew what that meant: out at a bar. The bars were full Sundays after noon, which is when they could legally serve alcohol. Oh, there were men in there drinking since the early morning, some even from the night before, but those alkeys needed to know the bartender and maybe a secret window knock. Sometimes the regulars wore out their welcome with bartenders, if they didn't leave good tips, or demanded too many buy-backs, or caused a ruckus. That's why Chili never knew where his dad would be. His charms, or lack thereof, were well-known in every gin mill from the Puerto Rican owned bars on 207th Street in Inwood, to the Irish pubs under the El at end of the No. 1 train at 242nd, and every druggy bar, old man bar, minors-with-fake-id's bar, Chinese restaurant, and steak house bar in-between.

Chili served spaghetti and meatballs to Jamie, "You eat all of this! Then some salad. Then you can have some Stella D'Oro cookies if you finish."

"I'll take that deal," Mikey said to Chili, piling on the spaghetti, meatballs, and red pepper. "What's that contraption?"

"You don't have one of these?" Chili said picking up the parmesan cheese grater. "You flip this over, put in a chunk of fresh parmesan, cut to fit in here just right, flip this back over, put pressure on the handle like this, and rotate slowly for a shower of deliciousness."

Mikey's jaw dropped as curly strings of cheese floated onto his mound of spaghetti and meatballs, melting as they landed. "That's better than sprinkles on a sundae!"

All three were busy slurping spaghetti, chomping mounds of meat balls, and dipping Italian bread into cheesy sauce when a familiar sound froze them mid-mouthful. It was the clicking of the four locks on the front steel door.

The door opened, and a disheveled Mr. Manzilla, wearing his grimy work uniform entered. He didn't say a word and made a quick turn into the bathroom. The three boys continued eating at a much slower pace as they heard a pee stream, toilet flush, sink faucet water, some gargling and toilet seat slam. Then Mr. Manzilla approached the kitchen doorway. He stood there, a little wobbly for several seconds in his boxer shorts and undershirt.

Fallout Shelter

"Save some… food for me. I'm going to…nap… in the bedroom. Be quiet. I have to be at work at midnight," he said, trying hard not to sound inebriated.

"Dad works very hard," Chili said quietly to no one in particular, or perhaps to himself, as the three of them continued their food fest, trying not to chew too loudly.

∽ Chapter 2 ∾

As expected on many such nights, Chili slept on some cushions on the living room floor while Jamie slept on the couch. They didn't dare wake up dad from his nap in the bedroom. And like vampires who instinctively know when the sun has set, hearing the sounds of the four front-door locks clank into position, signaling that their father has left for work, they rise from their positions and sleepwalk to their beds. Chili has gotten used to the unpleasant smells that his father has left behind. He's just glad there's nothing moist or soaking wet on the sheets.

Passing cars create moving blades of light as they pass through venetian blinds and cut across the wall and Jamie's face on the other side of the room in his juvenile-sized bed, which he barely fits in. Jamie doesn't complain because he knows that if he has a normal size bed, like Chili's, there's a fifty-fifty chance his father will be napping there a few nights a week. The bright streaks of shifting light are keeping Chili awake. Or at least that's what he's telling himself. More than likely it's not the light at all. He's dealt with the outside lights and sounds of the Bronx streets making their way into the apartment since he was brought home from Montefiore Hospital on the No. 38 bus a few days after being born. Being only a block from the elevated subway, a few hundred feet from a highway, and across the street from a row of stores, including a bar, sounds and smells from the outside are part of the inside.

It begins with the pre-dawn sounds of the newspaper bundles and bread deliveries being tossed from trucks onto the sidewalk outside Snooky's candy store and luncheonette, with AM radios blasting. Followed by milk trucks, garbage trucks, and of course the loud, lousy brakes on the No. 38 bus directly outside their windows. The squeals of the No. 1 train's steel wheels reverberate in the early morning darkness, sometimes causing bright bursts of light one would think would be lightning or the flash of an explosion. But exploding in Chili's head was none of those things but the anticipation of what lies ahead in days, weeks, and months. Graduating eighth grade was the just the start of it all. There was the boat ride to Rye Beach Playland, which was fraught with danger not the least of which was Angel and Mikey pledging to sneak booze in. Then there was the pressure of committing to be a mentor to all the younger altar boys and being the only altar boy left that wasn't in grammar school. And the fact that he would have to secure a full-time job for the summer, which would hopefully convert to part-time once high school started. Plus taking care of Jamie and then there was high school itself.

Archbishop Corrigan High School for Boys was a Catholic high school about a few Mickey Mantle home runs from Yankee Stadium. It was big for a Catholic school, with over two thousand students. A far cry from St. Gall's grammar school, which had approximately three hundred sixty students for all eight grades. Chili would be going solo, as Angel was going to Fordham Prep, another boys-only school, which was located on the Fordham University campus. And Mikey was going to Our Lady of the Reservoir aka DeWitt Clinton High School, which is where the Catholic school boys who didn't make it into Catholic high schools because of grades and/or their financial situation. DeWitt C. was across the street from the Jerome Reservoir, hence the moniker.

The students at Archbishop Corrigan were called "wrong wayers" not because of the reputation of Archbishop Corrigan himself, but because of the infamous "Wrong Way Corrigan," the early Twentieth Century aviator who took off in a fog in New York, headed for California, only to land twenty eight hours later in Dublin. Chili knew he'd face ridicule among the neighborhood guys with constant "wrong way" admonitions on the basketball court, the baseball diamond, the football field, traveling on the subway, or anywhere else where direction is an important factor, like… with everything in life. But that was minor compared to worries he had about being a loner in a gigantic hodgepodge of New York City kids who aren't exactly known for welcoming those who aren't the first picks for sports, or loud-mouthed class clowns, or cool ladies' man types, brainiacs who don't mind you looking over their shoulder, or fast-talking dudes with some kind of scam in the works. Chili was going to Corrigan for one reason: it was the cheapest Catholic high school in the city.

    Chili also knew why he wasn't bullied much. It was because he knew just about every kid in the neighborhood since they were pooping their diapers. Even the really bad, glue-sniffing, hubcap-stealing, Alexander's Department Store-shoplifting kids left him alone. But in a school with a couple thousand of teenagers from every corner of New York including the hippie- and drug-infested lower east side, the guido gangs of the northeast Bronx, Black Harlem, Spanish Harlem, Hell's Kitchen, and pocket neighborhoods of Albanians, Dominicans, and other ethnicities Chili had no idea even existed, he knew he'd have a tough time fitting in. Especially without Angel and Mikey by his side.

Jamie still had school, so like every morning Chili helped him, or rather forced him, to put on clean clothes and underwear, brush his teeth, comb his hair, eat some Sugar Pops, and push him out the door. Now he could concentrate on this momentous day of all momentous days in grammar school history: the eighth-grade graduation boat ride to Rye Beach Playland! Chili grabbed his St. Gall's Day Camp tote bag and stuffed it with his bathing suit, towel, extra underwear, and his rarely used Roy Rogers wallet he got as a first Communion gift with thirteen dollars in it, and he darted out the door and down the stairs to the lobby. He paused in front of the doorway that led to the basement stairway until he was sure no one was watching and slipped through. He had to get to the fallout shelter before Mikey and Angel because he

Fallout Shelter

was the keeper of the key. Past the hot vents of the boiler-room door, and the stench of the garbage-can room, past the super's back door, turn left at the FALLOUT SHELTER sign down a dark corridor, and he knew he was home free to enter their rendezvous site without detection. He took the key from its hiding place on the top of the door frame, opened the padlock, and entered the forgotten pitch-black room. He carefully sensed his way to the center of the room, minding the crates and barrels of nuclear-war sustenance, and pulled on a string, switching on the ceiling light bulb. He hated this part of their get-togethers; sitting there alone in a room some official deemed good enough to possibly insulate one from an atomic bomb. The walls weren't brick or concrete but were actual hewn large black stones with rough chiseled surfaces. They were probably mined from the great Harlem River ship canal excavation in the 1890's, which joined the Harlem and Hudson Rivers on the northern tip of Manhattan only a few miles from the building. The five- and six-story apartment buildings in the neighborhood were mostly built around 1910, right after the No. 1 subway train was extended in an elevated line over Broadway from Dyckman Street in upper Manhattan to 242nd Street. They say a lot of the workers who dug out the Harlem River, the subway tunnels, and the swamps around here were off-the-boat Irish and Italian immigrants, many of whom died in their labors and awful working conditions. Little did they know the rocks they blasted and carried on their backs would be foundations of the apartment buildings their children and grandchildren would be living in for generations.

KNOCK KNOCK knock knock KNOCK KNOCK.

Chili knew that was the secret knock and opened the inside latch to let Mikey and Angel in.

Mikey carried a rumpled brown-paper grocery bag, which still had prices written in pencil on it. Angel had a gym bag with FORDHAM PREP written in gold letters. They placed their bags on the top of a barrel. Mikey reached into his bag first.

"I had to give Murph the bum an extra dollar to buy us this, so we'll have to include that in the price when we split it,"

Mikey said, pulling out a large bottle of Night Train Express fortified wine, holding it high by the dangling light bulb. Chili was terrified. *He really did it.* "Um, are you, I mean, we going to drink that here? Or when we get there or what?"

Angel reached into his gym bag. "Both!" he said proudly pulling out a pint-sized plastic flask. "We can drink some here. Pour the rest into this. And finish it off when we get there. I got a pack of Marlboro's, too."

Chili rooted around in his tote bag. "I got a pack of matches… some Sen-Sen… and three cups," he said, nervously placing the three cups on one of the empty barrels.

Mikey poured a half-cup of the cheap wine into each cup, and screwed the metal cap back on. "Well, here we go!" Mikey picked up his cup, followed by Angel, and finally after a couple of false starts, Chili.

Angel lifted his cup up. "First, a toast. Here's to us! We made it to our first big accomplishment: graduation! Let's celebrate this and all future achievements!"

"Hey," Chili interjected, "and let's do it here, each time. Even if we graduate different schools or even if one of us moves away. Let's come back here to mark the occasion!"

"Let's just hope it's not because of a nuclear war," Mikey added. "Through the lips, past the gums, look out liver here it comes!" Mikey downed his in one gulp, followed by an ear-to-ear smile. It took Angel two gulps, but he also was pleased with his accomplishment. They both looked at Chili with his arm extended in mid-air.

"It's not cyanide, Chili!" Mikey said, urging him on.

Angel grabbed Chili's wrist and began pushing the cup to Chili's mouth.

"Okay, okay," Chili said, giving in and bringing the cup closer and closer to his trembling lips. He finally took a small sip, and reacted as though he just tasted a cup of sick. "That stuff is awful! Yuk! It tastes like piss!"

"Well you should know!" Mikey yelled with glee.

"Drink it!" Angel shouted.

Chili looked at his friends, both in hysterics, held his nose and finished off the wax-coated paper cup. "That's worse than accidentally swallowing Listerine! Where's the Sen-Sen?"

Mikey poured himself a second cup. "You just need to get a taste for it," he said, swilling it and smacking his lips afterwards.

Angel also took a second cup and drank it with far less enthusiasm than the first. He put the cup down, and grabbed at his chest. "Whoah. It just landed in my gut like a depth charge. Chili have a second."

Chili shook his head. "No, that's it for me! One more taste and I'll be leaving sidewalk pizzas on the way to the bus. Which, by the way, is leaving," Chili said looking at his watch, "in twenty minutes!"

After carefully pouring the remainder of the Night Train into Angel's flask, while passing around a Marlboro as if in a ceremonial ritual, they exited the cellar into blinding daylight. They stuck close together, thinking how cool they were compared to the rest of the class as they stood in line in the schoolyard to get on the bus to City Island where they would board the boat to Rye Beach. It was a strange sight to see all the kids in summer street clothes while Sister Ignatius, Sister Agnes, and Sister Aloysius were still lording over everyone in their usual heavy black habits from head to toe as they carefully observed each student entering the bus. Each nun was equipped with a device to ensure control. Sister Ignatius had a yardstick for measuring girl's shorts and skirts, Sister Agnes a bell to get everyone's attention, and Sister Aloysius a heavy-duty pointer, which the boys knew as a painful weapon. The students, especially the girls, must adhere to the dress code; shorts and skirts could not be more than two inches above the knee. And bathing suits must be "modest."

As Sister Ignatius pulled Pamela Hinderlap out of line to see if she adhered to the legal knee to shorts mandate, Mikey pulled Chili and Angel close, and said softly, "I can't wait to see if that yardstick can measure how much of her tits are hanging out of her bikini." Everyone within earshot either gasped in shock or laughed hysterically as it became quite clear that Mikey was feeling the effects of his Night Train.

"Shut up, you goon!" Chili said sternly as he jabbed Mikey in the ribs with his exposed bony elbow.

DING DING DING DING went Sister Agnes' bell at full fire-drill volume.

"Uh oh," Angel said. "Here it comes. I hope this Sen-Sen works."

Sister Agnes slowly walked down the length of the line. "What's going on down here?" She pointed the pointy black handle of the bell at the three of them. "There will be no shenanigans today. I'm watching you," she seethed as she stopped a few feet in front of them.

"Yes, sister," Chili said.

She turned and went back to the front of the line.

"Now shut up, Mikey," Angel said sternly. "They'll call the freakin' F.B.I. if they catch us with booze. And that's after they beat us with the yardstick, the pointer, and that damn bell!"

Mikey just laughed quietly, shuffling along, then blurted, "L.S.M.F.T." pointing at Pamela Hinderlap.

"Shush!" Chili said, with another elbow jab.

They smiled at the three nuns as they stepped onto the bus and headed to the back row of seats. A few minutes later, the bus was full, all the kids were on, and so were the three nuns.

"Hey, there's no priest!" Chili said as the bus pulled out of the schoolyard.

They each slapped each other five, in anticipation of not having a priest tailing them on the boat and at the amusement park.

"We are home free!" Angel added. "Those nuns can't be keeping up with us in those get-ups. We'll leave them in the dust."

Fallout Shelter

The bus arrived at the City Island docks after a 20 minute ride across the Bronx. There was no scrutiny from the bonneted chaperones as they walked up the ramp onto the boat. Mikey, forgetting to keep it down, exclaimed, "Next stop, the beach, bikinis, and boo…." Another elbow from Chili, in anticipation of either the words *boobs* or *booze*, stopped Mikey just in time.

"Books! Yes, I brought some books!" Said Mikey, much to the relief of Angel and Chili.

It was obvious that the fortified wine was doing its job with both Mikey and Angel. Both were laughing and making ridiculous faces as they passed by kids from the class.

"You guys better simmer down or we'll be in big trouble," Chili said, pulling them into a corner. "Don't forget the same kids, like Ignatius Cottle, who've been squealing on us since first grade, can't wait to get us thrown out."

"We're on a freakin' boat! How can they do that?" Mikey said falling down laughing with Angel.

Chili was getting serious. "Really guys. We'll get slaughtered if they find out. Wait until we arrive at Rye Beach before we… uh oh. Straighten up and fly right. Here comes Sister Agnes."

All three composed themselves, pretending to have a casual conversation. "Yes, the Yankees are doing bad, but they're rebuilding," Angel said loudly as Sister Agnes passed by giving them the stink eye the whole way. She took a turn and was out of sight. "Yeah, let's wait 'til we get off the boat to drink the rest. It's too dangerous here," Angel added.

"Speaking of dangerous. Here she comes," Mikey said, eyes bulging, lips smacking with glee. Pamela Hinderlap was sashaying towards them, all alone, slowly, with purpose, knowing full well that the silky blouse she was wearing clearly displayed her newly forming voluptuous shape, with her premature ample breasts bouncing with each step. The three watched in awe.

Chili grabbed Angel and Mikey as they attempted to follow her. "Oh my God! It's true. L.S.M.F.T." Chili said, still holding them back.

By the time the boat landed at the Rye Beach Playland docks, kids were lined up and clambering in anticipation, like puppies about to be freed from their crates after a long car ride. Angel, Mikey and Chili kept their pledge not to drink or attract attention during their journey, but were anxious to cut loose as they waited to go down the ramp to unchaperoned freedom in the large amusement park, complete with a swimming beach. But at the bottom of the ramp, there was a crowd gathering. The three nudged each other as they inched forward.

"Oh shit. Here comes real trouble," Chili said his voice filled with dread. "It's Father Palmer! He must have driven up here to spy on us."

"Let's not act suspicious. Sister Agnes probably tipped him off that Mikey could be trouble," Angel said, laying out a plan.

"Why me?"

Angel and Chili smirked at Mikey.

"Okay, what's the plan?" Mikey said, in defeat.

Angel pointed his finger at Mikey. "You need to be quiet. Chili, you already met Father P. When we pass, we ask him if he wants to go on the Dragon roller coaster with us. He'll turn us down, and then it looks like we want to be around him and have nothing to hide."

"What if he says *yes*?" Chili responded.

"Then, we go on the ride, say goodbye and that's the last we'll see of him."

Father Palmer was greeting each of the students as they walked down the ramp and entered the park through the turnstile. He was dressed in a short-sleeved black shirt with an attached priest collar, and black bell-bottoms. He was also wearing sandals with black socks and on his head was a silly souvenir cheap red fedora with a blue feather. His sandy blonde

Fallout Shelter

hair was sticking straight out by his ears making look like a goofy tourist in the Alps.

"Go ahead," Angel said, poking Chili from behind.

"Hi Father!"

Father Palmer paused for a moment. "Oh, hello there… Soupy."

"It's Chili."

"Of course!"

"Want to come on the Dragon roller coaster with us?"

"Who's us?"

"Me, Angel and Mikey."

"Um, sure! Let's go! There's only a few kids left for me to greet. Wait for me when you go through the turnstile."

"Great." Chili said, unenthusiastically.

The three of them stood next to the large clown head whose open mouth was the portal for the garbage can. "Should we dump our stuff into the trash?" Chili asked nervously.

"Nah," Mikey said confidently. "But smell my breath. Do I need more Sen Sen?"

Angel obliged. "No. Any more would be too obvious. Here he comes."

Father Palmer waved as he pushed his way through the crowd. "Let's go. This should be fun! I haven't been on a roller coaster since I was a child. Actually, it was a kiddie roller coaster," he said as they walked together towards the Dragon Coaster entrance. Mikey smiled broadly, but keeping his lips tightly sealed, not wanting either Sen-Sen or Night Train to give him away.

"You've never been on a big roller coaster?" Chili asked.

"Nope. It should be fun!"

"Yeah, big time fun," Angel added.

The Dragon coaster was known as one of the scariest roller coasters in the New York area, since Palisades Amusement Park closed last year, shutting down forever. The Atom Smasher roller coaster at Rockaways' Playland was also wooden, ancient, and rickety, as was the Cyclone at Coney Island. But the Dragon

Coaster was built in 1929 and as the legend goes, hasn't been maintained since. And when it goes through the dragon tunnel you are plunged into total darkness because the turn it takes is too terrifying to watch, so they say.

    Mikey, Angel, Chili, and Father Palmer were next on the platform for the ride and as the empty coaster screeched to a halt, Mikey and Angel jumped into the front two-seater car, leaving Chili and Father Palmer for the second seat. As they waited for the attendant to push the safety bars into place, Mikey leaned in to Angel and whispered, "That's as close to a priest I'd ever want to get."

    "At least Chili's only next to him and not in front of him," Angel replied.

    When the coaster jerked to a start Father Palmer's smile disappeared and his face turned serious as they chugged up the giant incline. "This thing… really gets… up there," he said, adjusting his collar.

    "Yeah, it's freakin'… I mean, yes it's thrilling," Chili said noticing Father Palmer's change in mood.

    Angel, Mikey, and Chili threw their hands up in the air, as Father Palmer's knuckles turned white, gripping the safety bar as they plummeted straight down the first hill. Girls shrieked and boys screamed as they jostled back and forth, up and down, and their stomachs turned inside out. Then suddenly, they were plunged into the dark abyss of the dragon tunnel.

    "What the fuck?" Chili said under his breath, when a hand grabbed his thigh and squeezed tight for the entire duration in blackness. Once out of the Dragon's butt and into daylight, Chili strained to catch a glimpse of Father Palmer without turning his head only to see him still frozen in terror. The roller coaster came to a sudden stop at the platform and all exited with much cheering and excitement. Except for Chili.

    "That was fantabulously utterly wickedly boss!" Angel said, slapping Mikey's hands.

"Right arm!" Mikey replied. "Look behind us. Father P. looks like he's about to lose his cookies and Chili looks like he saw the ghost of Christmas past, present, and future."

Father Palmer was a whiter shade of pale, white collar crooked, and goofy fedora gone. Chili walked in front of him, with a confused look of shock across his face. He rushed up to Angel and Mikey. "You wouldn't believe what happened!" He blurted just out of earshot of Father P. who was a few slow paces behind him.

"Hey Father! Where's your lid?" Mikey yelled as Father P. joined the group.

"Oh yeah, my hat," Father P. said, both hands reaching up to his messy locks. "That was gone on the first hill. That was nothing like the Tom Thumb ride I took the last time I was on a roller coaster."

Angel deadpanned, "The Tom Thumb ride? At Lake Hopatcong? That's a kiddie ride."

Father P. didn't respond.

"Well, nice to see you Father, but um, we have to get going. We're supposed to meet some kids...."

"Mind if I join you?" Father P. said, perking up.

Mikey leaned over and said with a stage whisper into his ear. "Look Father, we're actually going to meet some girls and...."

"'Nuff said! Have your fun, guys! I'll meander and check in on the rest of gang!"

"See ya, Father! Bye! Adios!" the three barked as they rushed off into the nearest crowd to disappear as quickly as their Chuck Taylor's could take them.

"We need to find somewhere to finish off the wine," Mikey said a little too loud, prompting punches in his shoulder from both.

"Shut up, doofus!" Chili said. "Don't say that word! Say something else. A code word."

"Potatoes!" Angel suggested. Guffaws ensued.

Mikey pushed through the crowd, picking up where he left off, proclaiming for all to hear, "We need to find where so we can finish off the…," he then cupped his hands to mouth and shouted, "Potatoes!"

"Follow me," Chili said through laughter, "I know a place from when we were kids and my mom took us over to this lake and they had paddle boats that looked like swans." As they went past each of the rides towards the lake they were frothing at the mouth with anticipation of riding every one of them. There was the terrifying Derby Racer, a carousel for adults, where the horses go 25 miles per hour and if you fall off on your head, you're dead. Bumper Cars, where head-on collisions were supposed to be forbidden according to the signage, but were the one and only goal of every teenage boy in the park. And The Whip, where in the 1920's a guy was killed and flung so far, people thought he might have dropped out of an airplane that flew nearby.

Along the way, they were careful to keep an eye out for nuns, Father P., and any kids from class they thought would rat them out. But in scrutinizing the crowds, there was also the discovery of interesting students from other schools. Namely, girls!

Mikey nearly sprained his neck, whipping it around so fast. "Look at that red head in those short shorts! Oh my God, she makes Pamela Hinderlap look like Olive Oyl!" He then jerked the other way, as a little blonde cutie caught his eye, "It's Gidget! Let's go surfing!"

"Shut uppa you mouth!" Angel said, pulling him through the throngs.

The placid lake was only across a road from the amusement park, but it seemed a world away from the nearby hurly burly. A few rowboats were slowly cruising along, but Chili noticed there were no Swan paddleboats. And that of course reminded him of the real void in his life; his mom.

Fallout Shelter

    Rose Manzilla was the one who took Chili and Jamie past the same rides, carnival game booths, and cotton-candy stands, holding each by the hand as they skipped through the park like three best friends to the quiet joy of gliding across the lake in their white swan. Her husband was left at the outdoor snack bar by the seaside casino, where they served beer. She didn't need to wonder if he'd still be there when they returned. He was sure to be in his normal life position; close to a full ashtray and a nearly empty glass. Thank goodness they always took the bus.

    Chili kept a photo of his mom in his wallet and he instinctively reached for it when he spotted the picnic table where he, Jamie, and his mom had lunch only a few summers ago, but now seemed like so many lifetimes in the past. He was relieved when he felt it. Also in his wallet was the memorial card from the funeral home with Psalm 23 printed on it. Like the Latin and English altar boy responses, he knew Psalm 23 by heart. Since his mother's death, all the prayers, psalms, devotions, even quotes from his favorite saint, St. Francis of Assisi, became more than just phonetic rote barked back at nuns and priests. The words were real to him. He studied them. Visualized them. Internalized them. Well, he tried. He also knew the trials and tribulations the saints went through, including St. Francis. Francis was a pampered, rich young man living a life of luxury and sensual pleasure, whose life was changed after a mystical vision of Jesus appeared to him, just as Saul was transformed into St. Paul after a blinding light on the road to Damascus. Chili thought that one day he would see an apparition, a vision, a sign, something, that would lead him to saintly devotion and dedication he thought could possibly be his destiny. His mom thought the same thing.

    "Break open that flask!" Mikey shouted as they plopped on the picnic table bench.

    Angel fished through his bag and revealed the plastic bottle filled with Night Train Express fortified wine followed by three paper cups.

"I'll keep an eye out. You guys go ahead," Chili said, scanning the area for trouble, hoping they wouldn't pressure him to join them to partake in the illegal libations. Besides, they needed somebody to babysit them if they crossed the line from tipsy to toasted.

Angel carefully poured the syrupy elixir into one cup, then the next one. He paused for the third cup and gave a sly smile to Chili. "You're in, right?"

"I think I've had it for today. My stomach didn't feel good after that first taste this morning. Plus, I think it might be a good idea for one of us to keep his head screwed on straight for the rest of the day."

Angel and Mikey nodded in agreement, then gulped down their drinks. Their expressions morphed from shock to elation as the stuff coursed down their gullet. "Again," Mikey implored Angel. He complied with glee.

"You better slow down or you'll be sorry," Chili said with concern. "We'll be whipping around, shot into the air, rolling down a magic carpet, and bouncing along Long Island Sound before the day is done."

"And this will make sure we enjoy every single moment!" Angel said, followed by gulp number two.

Chili watched as Mikey and Angel quickly began displaying the effect of the wine infused with extra alcohol deeming it not just wine, but fortified wine. "The Night Train Express is ready to leave the station!" Mikey shouted, raising one arm in the air as if ready to pull on a train whistle, with Angel following suit. "Woooot Wooot!" Angel and Mikey blasted several times. Their breathy blasts were so obviously charged with cheap wine, Chili began to realize his job of keeping the trio out of major trouble might be an impossible task.

The trek from the secluded lakeside picnic area began all right. They threw their trash in the garbage can, including the forever-stained with purple-wine plastic flask, and began walking normally. For about ten paces. "Look!" Mikey shouted, dropping his bag, and in a decent imitation of his favorite cartoon character he shrieked, "Thufferin' thucotash! It's Daffy Duck in person!" as he ambled across the grass towards a pair of ducks on the bank of the lake. "Wabbit season! Duck season! Wabbit season! Duck season!" he squawked running towards the mellow mallards who merely flew off when Mikey got within their danger zone of about ten feet away. But Mikey continued towards them anyway, right up to the lake's slippery edge. His feet went out from under him and he landed ass first into the muck, causing uncontrollable hysterics from all three. Mikey sat in the several inches of water and began splashing. "I guess duck season is over!" He stood up and saw that the seat of his shorts were covered in brown mud. "Aww shit."

"That's what it looks like to me!" said Chili.

But the playful plunge didn't dampen their spirits. In fact, Mikey and Angel seemed even more crocked as they made a detour towards a lakeside men's room where Mikey changed into his boxy bathing suit, which looked like shorts anyway.

As they crossed the road, and headed back into the amusement park, Chili knew there could be big trouble ahead. After all, although classes were over, graduation was still a few days away, which meant nothing was official yet. Until you had that diploma in your hand, you were still at the mercy of the nuns who relish retribution and inflicting pain on those who violate their strict code of conduct. If snickering in class is enough to get a three-pointed ruler across the knuckles, being drunk and unruly at the graduation class outing might be cause for a being hung by the neck off the Ferris wheel.

Just inside the park, Chili pulled Angel and Mikey off to the side, next to the entrance of the Magic Carpet Ride fun house. "Listen to me. You guys are gonna have to pull yourselves together and not act drunk. We'll get slaughtered if we're caught," Chili said, giving each of them some extra doses of Sen Sen. They both nodded in agreement.

"Chili's right, Mikey," Angel said, his arm around Mikey. "We've got to act normal. So, let's just be ourselves, and... go check out some girls in bikinis!"

Chili chased after them as they tore-ass down the path that headed towards the swimming beach, carrying both their bags, which flopped about as he tried to keep up. To make matters worse, Mikey, who was not displaying his usual coordination due to the Night Train factor, started kicking off his shoes, socks, and flinging off his shirt as he sped through the crowded beach, darting between blankets and umbrellas, and finally running into the calm waters of the Long Island Sound far enough until he could do a clumsy leap in the air and belly-flop into the water, which sent people of all ages in every direction away from the mini tidal wave he created. Angel and Chili stood at the water's edge in hysterics. Mikey stood up in the knee-high water, shook his body like a Labrador after getting out of pond, put his hands on his hips, and let out a huge belch, causing equal amounts of laughter and disgust from nearby bathers.

"Let's find a spot by some new chicks," Mikey said, drying off and leading them by zig zagging around beachgoers. "Oh my my! Over there."

They put their three towels together and plopped down between two groups of young teenage girls around their age in bathing suits. Mikey and Angel immediately began poking and nudging each other with their discoveries of surprisingly nubile girls adorned with goofy sailor hats and souvenir fedoras. With their alcohol intake probably at full effect at this point, they were both about as subtle as Godzilla chasing Japanese pedestrians. Chili could hear their breathy whispers; "Check out the red head's head lights! I think the blonde's got water balloons in there! That little one ain't so little where it counts!"

"Keep it down guys! They'll hear you!" Chili said through clenched teeth, emphasized with shoulder punches. This wasn't the first time Chili had to deal with drunk friends on the verge of falling off a ledge into a vat of deep doo-doo. Slaps from girls, sucker punches from older kids, climbing fences fleeing cops, and beatings from parents were just a few of the minor outcomes when thirteen- and fourteen-year-old boys think they can imitate their fathers gulping down tumblers, bottles, and cans of beer, wine, and booze. Or there were the even worse offenders who thought it was cool to smoke pot, sniff glue, and drink cough syrup with codeine. Some of those kids didn't just get in trouble. They got killed; falling off moving subway cars, out of trees, and drowned in rivers after diving off rocks, which all were preceded by raucous fun and big laughs. Chili knew of those horrific stories of neighborhood deaths and disasters, but he never sensed he, Mikey, and Angel would go that route.

All Chili could do was watch and hope for the best as Angel and Mikey started talking to the aforementioned blondes, redheads, brunettes, little ones, big ones, black, brown, and white ones. He heard the girl's laughter, as Mikey went into assorted Curly of the Three Stooges routines, egged on by Angel's applause. Chili noticed one of the girl's had an Our Lady of Mercy tote bag, which was another Bronx Catholic parish. He wondered why girls from other schools seemed so much more desirable than the girls from their own class. The girls Angel and Mikey were losing their minds over were no more cute than their classmates. And not one of them could compare with Pamela Hinderlap, who Chili noticed was back at the Whip with the other girls from the class. Maybe it was just difficult to get worked up over a girl who you remember as six-year-old crying over a broken crayon in first grade.

Suddenly the laughs were overwhelmed by a girl's shrill scream. Chili, jolted to attention, saw a girl pushing away Mikey as he barked like a dog on all fours and pretended to bite her feet. Out of nowhere, three boys from a nearby group of towels came charging over, and without a word of warning started wailing away at Mikey and Angel. Shrieks and screams from girls, accompanied the boy's shouts of "Get the fuck out of here! Asshole! I'll kick your ass!" as fists, slaps, and sand flew and girls fled. Chili ran to the defense of his overmatched pals, only to be met with one punch to the side of his face by his ear that sounded like thunder inside his head. He was down. Lifeguard whistles were heard, followed by four huge college-aged kids in Speedos, with athletic adult physiques and white zinc across their noses like Indian war paint. They grabbed all the boys by the arms and shook some sense into them. All was quiet.

"What's going on here?" One of the lifeguards yelled. "I'm ready to call the cops on you jerks!"

Chili rose up, "Sorry sir, but it was only a misunderstanding between rival Catholic schools. We recently played each other in a baseball game and some of that competitive spirit spilled over here today."

"Okay. Knock it off. Or you'll wind up locked up in the jail under the roller coaster."

"Yes, sir," Chili said calmly, despite the ringing in his ear. "We understand. We have to meet Father Palmer for lunch now anyway." He led them back to their towels, picked up their stuff and headed for the locker rooms. "Shut up and let's get out of here."

After cleaning up and licking their wounds, the first person they saw upon exiting the locker room was Father P. "Hey fellas!" Father P. shouted as he waved. "You guys want to go on that Ferris wheel?"

Chili, pulled Angel and Mikey closer. "Let's take a breather and hang with Father P. Those kids that just kicked our asses might be on the lookout for us."

"If I see that fat freckle-faced dick...," Mikey seethed.

"That other little prick with the Beatle haircut suckerpunched me," Angel added.

"Simmer down. We need to just hang with Father P. for one ride to give us some time and let things cool off," Chili said, pushing them towards Father P.

"Good to see you guys! The girls took me on the Whip, the Derby Racer, the Mouse; I need a rest. But I do want to check out the Ferris wheel. But let's grab a snack first. It's on me! How about it?"

"Yes Father!" All three cheered.

The three exhausted friends sat in the hot mid-day sun at a wooden picnic table and chowed down with gusto plates of corn dogs, French fries, and onion rings, plus jumbo sodas, popcorn, cotton candy, and little buttons of hard candy on long reams of paper. Father P. sipped on a lemonade and nibbled on a hot dog with nothing on it.

The four finished off their fried feast and meandered through the midway. Mikey steered them away from the Ferris wheel, and towards the Rock-O-Plane, which is a Ferris wheel with a twist. Instead of sitting in gondola type open seats, you sit in a cage, and the riders are turned totally upside down for most of the ride as they spin around on the giant wheel. Just as with the roller coaster, Angel and Mikey jumped into the first cage, again leaving Chili to sit with Father P.

"I don't think this will be as extreme as the Dragon Coaster. I'm looking forward to seeing the Long Island Sound from the top. After all it's only a Ferris wheel," Father P. stated calmly.

"Not exactly, Father," Chili said turning to his caged companion. "It's the Rock-O-Plane. We're in a cage, because it turns us upside down."

"Oh," was all Father P. could muster, as a teenage ride operator clanked the safety bar and the cage door shut.

The ride jerked to begin its climb, and Chili observed that each time they reached to apex of the wheel, Mikey and Angel would be upside down directly over them. "Hey, Mikey!" Chili shouted, before the screams started. "How is your lunch feeling?"

"I think you'll know soon enough!" Mikey said, shaking his head.

"What's that supposed to mean?" Father P. asked.

"I just hope it's not what I think it means," Chili said as their cage whipped upside-down and the screaming and yelling began from all the boys, girls, and one priest.

They cruised into the down side of the wheel, and momentarily were right side up. Father P. sighed in relief. Chili knew the worst was yet to come. And it did, as the speed increased precipitously as they rose up higher and higher and turned upside down.

Suddenly, amidst the screams of the girls directly below them, Chili heard a sound he dreaded he might hear from directly above.

BLAAAAACHHH BIUUUULLLLKKK BLOOOOOFFFF!

"Oh shit!" Chili yelled, as he let go of the safety bar, trying to shield himself from the putrid liquids raining down on them from Mikey and Angel's cage. "What the fuck is going on up there? Sorry Father."

"Mikey's lunch, breakfast, and last night's desert are making an escape!" Angel laughed, pushing Mikey away from himself.

Father P. was in stunned silence, with bits of Mikey's vomit on his head and shoulders. His eyes were closed, possibly in prayer. But the rain of terror continued for a few more seconds.

Thankfully, the ride came to a halt and Chili's car was the first to depart, which meant Angel and Mikey would be the last to get out. Father P. didn't say a word and slowly headed for the rest room, strategically within eyesight of the exit. Subsequent cages of boys and girls shouted curse words as they also ran to the rest rooms to wipe off the stink.

Finally Mikey and Angel, the last cage to unload, stopped. Angel jumped out first, and Mikey, smiling ear to ear, leapt after him.

"I feel a lot better now!" Mikey announced to all, cleaning himself up as he walked. "I need to use the bathroom."

Fallout Shelter

Chili and Angel pushed him towards the bathroom. "Yeah, and so does everybody else on the freaking ride," Chili chortled.

"It think it was that last onion ring that put me over the edge," Mikey said.

"Oh, it couldn't have been the half of bottle of Night Train!" Angel groaned, giving him a final shove into the men's room.

The sinks were busy with boys washing up and wiping their clothes with wet paper towels. Sounds were heard coming from one of the bathroom stalls, where someone was throwing up and dry-heaving. It wasn't a kid. The door to the stall slowly opened, and an ashen-faced Father P. exited and weakly waved at the trio as he walked past and out into the park.

Angel put his arm around Mikey. "I've seen kids make priests curse, throw temper tantrums, punch kids in the face, and clutch their rosaries, but I've never seen a kid make a priest throw up!"

"This is going to do wonders for me in high school," Chili said, throwing the last of his paper towels in the trash.

Angel and Mikey began laughing. "Oh yeah!" Mikey said gleefully. "You'll be in high school with Father P.! Well, he won't forget who you are!"

"I don't think he'll forget this day for the rest of his life," Chili said, dejectedly. "And neither will I. The boat leaves in an hour. Let's head back to the dock."

⋄§ Chapter 3 ⋄§

This was the first time ever that the three of them converged in the dusty fallout shelter wearing suits. And of course it would be the only time in their lives that they would also have their caps and gowns with them. Each wiped off a barrel top with a rag before sitting.

Chili hung up the hanger that contained his cap and gown on a hook where the family's bag of assorted Christmas decorations used to hang. They were to meet in the school auditorium an hour before the ceremony was to begin, but meeting in the basement first was a certainty.

"Look what I got," Mikey said, pulling three mini-bottles out of his jacket pocket. "The good stuff. Southern Comfort."

"Are you nuts?" Chili asked in disbelief.

"Not me. No way. Not now," Angel added.

"Sheesh. You guys. All right, I'll leave them here for later," Mikey said stashing them behind his barrel. "I have an idea for a celebration. It's a good one!"

"Does it involve throwing up on people?" asked Chili.

"You never know, but look at this ad I got out of my brother's hidden copy of *Screw* magazine." Mikey said handing the crumpled paper to Angel.

"This I gotta see," Angel said unfolding it. "Live sex show. Private booths. Open twenty four hours. What is this?"

"It's a peep show!" Mikey said, throwing his arms upward in excitement.

"Peep show?" Chili questioned him.

"You go to the place and you can sit in the audience to watch strippers get totally nude or go in another room where you go in a private booth and watch people have raw sex."

"You have to be eighteen to get in those places," Angel said.

"Not to mention, be a degenerate pervert," Chili chimed in.

"My brother told me he got in when he was fifteen. It'll be a gas! It's in Times Square. We just jump on the number 1 train, go to 42nd Street, and it's right upstairs!"

"I'm game," Angel affirmed.

They both looked at Chili.

"Oh, it's up to me? Well, I'll burn in hell, but I'll give it a try I guess," Chili said shaking his head in disbelief of what he was agreeing to. "In the meantime, let's go to graduation mass and maybe get enough grace points to count towards purgatory time off."

It was disconcerting to see the parents of every kid in eighth grade sitting, kneeling, and standing on cue like students in their Sunday best, although many of the outfits were ill-fitting and showed signs of wear. Some of the men could barely fit into what was probably their only suit, buttons stretched to the limit, shoulders and bellies tightly constricted. Other men were swimming in dress shirts and jackets that used to fit their muscular bricklayer and steamfitter bodies on their wedding day. But after three packs of Lucky's and a quart of Dewar's daily, decomposing and rigor mortis seemed to be already setting in to their boney frames. The women's clothing were less obvious in their shabbiness. With so many discount stores, such as Alexander's and John's Bargain Store, it was relatively easy to cobble together a presentable outfit, even though it was a style from a decade or so ago. Dresses printed with giant flowers seem to be the most deeply discounted frocks available on the Fordham Road or 231st Street shops.

But regardless of their attire, these parents were beaming with pride. Many of them were born in Ireland, Puerto Rico, Italy, or in some New York City ghetto and didn't even finish grammar school. Some fathers were in World War II and weren't sure whether they would return home to raise a family or wind up fertilizing a French farm field after they were blown to bits. And some mothers who finished grammar school didn't attend high school. Yet, here they were, attending the graduation of their children from a Catholic school in the greatest city, in the greatest country on God's green earth.

    Despite being told to keep their heads forward and not turn around, most of the kids couldn't help but try and sneak a peek at their parents and grandparents, who would give a small wave of acknowledgement in return. Chili fidgeted and strained his neck around to finally see his father, sitting with Jamie in the last pew of the church. *At least he made it*, Chili thought to himself.

    Angel, Mikey, and Chili, being different in size, didn't sit next to one another, but would shoot each other goofy faces to try and crack each other up. Sister Ignatius of course caught Mikey in the act and gave him the death stare. He hoped the statute of limitations would exempt him from any punishment.

    After mass, Maryanne Marino, the first-ranking student in the class since first grade, gave a speech that nobody could hear as she whispered far from the microphone. Then Monsignor Shannon called each student to the altar and handed them a diploma. After receiving the diploma the students sat back down until the last one was issued. The Monsignor dipped a golden baton into a bucket of holy water and started spritzing everyone as he walked down the aisle. Mrs. Weiner the organist began "Pomp and Circumstance" for the second time and the students stepped slowly out of the church under the watchful eye of the nuns and the monsignor for the last time. Chili noted that Father P. was outside greeting everyone and shaking hands, and expected Father P.'s presence was just beginning to be a part of his life.

    Photos were being taken with friends, teachers, family members, priests, and nuns. Chili handed Angel a small Brownie camera that Jamie had around his neck and asked him to take a picture of him with his father and Jamie. But while Angel was saying "cheese" and imploring the three of them to smile, and not blink, and look at the camera, Chili was thinking about his mother. About how she wasn't here to see him graduate. She was the one who practiced his multiplication tables with him and asked him questions about the Declaration of Independence and followed along the page as he tried to memorize a poem by Henry Wadsworth Longfellow. She dried his tears, held his head over the toilet when he was sick, and laughed at his riddles from *Boy's Life* magazine. She told him to always be a good boy even when it was fun to do something bad.

Angel snapped a few shots and handed the camera back to Jamie. "Do you like taking pictures, Jamie?"

"Yeah."

"Hey Chili, come over to my house tonight for a graduation party. Around seven. See ya!" Angel said as he ran across the parking lot and jumped into his family's Cadillac.

"Let's get going," Mr. Manzilla said, walking in front of the kids, who followed behind. "I've got to work tonight. I need a nap."

Luckily Mikey noticed the note on Chili's front door just in time. It read, KNOCK VERY SOFTLY! Mikey knew why. He tapped on the door with his fingernail, and it opened. "Good idea putting that note there. Last thing I need to do is get in trouble with another parent," he said softly. "Hey, Jamie," Mikey said waving to Jamie sitting on the floor in front of the television with his camera still around his neck.

"There's food in the refrigerator for dinner. Eat all your salad, not just the chicken. Don't stay up all night watching the boob tube," Chili said as he waved good-bye.

Although Angel's house was only a few blocks away, it was in another world. Mikey, Chili, and just about every kid in the class lived in a one- or two-bedroom apartment in a building that was at least 60 years old, stifling hot in the summer, freezing in the winter, and infested with cockroaches. A few kids lived in private houses stuck between some apartment buildings, but those homes were also built in the early 1900's and similarly lacking in the basic necessities of comfortable living amidst cramped quarters. To get to Angel's house, you had to work your way around gangs of kids clogging the sidewalks, playing their games or hanging out, pass rows of busy mom-and-pop stores, tenements with old men on the front stoops, cross Broadway, going under the el, and continue several blocks to a dead end. It was there that you had to walk up a massive set of stairs, known as City Steps, because on a map they were actually considered to be a street. And once you climb up the 120 steps to the top, it's quite evident you are no longer in the same neighborhood. Here the streets and sidewalks are under a canopy of leafy green trees. The cars parked on the street aren't twenty-year-old banged-up Chevy and Fords like down the hill; here they're newer Oldsmobiles, Buicks, and even Caddies. There are two and even three-story homes, with expansive front lawns, long driveways, two-car garages, white picket fences, and—weirdly—hardly anybody on the street!

"It's hard to believe this is still the Bronx," Chili said, breathing in the sweet air.

"It is? I thought this was Riverdale?" Mikey said, tearing a small red rose off a bush and sticking it in his suit-jacket buttonhole.

"Riverdale *is* in the Bronx."

"It doesn't look it."

"Mark Twain, JFK, Lou Gehrig, and Theodore Roosevelt's father used to live around here."

"Lou Gehrig! Wicked!"

"I guess we go around the back," Chili said as they walked past the garage and opened the gate to the back yard.

"A two-car garage? You think they have two cars? We don't even have a car. Did your father get one?"

"No. He works for transit, so we get free passes for the bus and trains."

"Man! You're lucky!"

Angel's father, a chubbier, hairier version of Angel, gave them both big bear hugs. "It's so good to see you boys! Now the three musketeers are complete! Maria, Angel, it's Chili and Mikey!" He shouted across the patio, illuminated with strings of Christmas lights.

Angel and his mom rushed over to meet them, passing through several couples dancing to Latin music playing on a large record player console that was moved outside.

"Hey guys!" Angel said.

His mom then gave them both hugs and kisses on the cheek. "Mikey and Chili, the three musketeers are together again!"

"Ha, I just said that!" Angel's dad laughed. "Chili with a name like yours, are you sure you're not Puerto Rican? Then maybe we could call you the Tres Amigos!"

"No, Italian both sides."

"Oh, Chili Willy. That's what you're beautiful mama called you. I miss her so much. She would be so proud of you," Angel's mom said, pulling Chili close to her as she teared-up.

So did Chili. "Yeah."

"Have some food and drinks!" Angel's dad said, joyfully. "All you want! Tacos, tamales, hamburgers, hot dogs, ever have flan?"

Mikey's eyes widened. "I will tonight! What is it?"

"It's like a sweet soft custard with syrup…," Angel's dad said.

"I'll start with that!" Mikey said, cracking everybody up as he headed to the food tables.

There was lively music and dancing, colorful lights, smiling happy friends, neighbors and relatives. But anytime someone mentioned his mother, Chili couldn't help but feel sad. Especially when so many mothers in attendance were doting over precious children of all ages. He remembered the many times they went to one of his aunt's or uncle's homes. His mom was the youngest of five, so parties very much like these were frequent. Sometimes in similar backyards in Flushing or Bay Ridge, or in cramped apartments in the East Bronx or Inwood. But since she died, his father didn't want to attend those parties. He never explained why. But Chili could figure it out. He wasn't stupid.

"I'm gonna get a hot dog," Chili said, excusing himself from the others.

Chili shuffled his way over to the barbeque, which was on the other side of the large patio and away from the dancing and merriment. There were a couple of people already on line, waiting to be served, and Chili stood there alone, unable to stop thinking about his mom. Then he received a sharp jab in that fleshy area between one's rib cage and hip, which when jabbed properly makes you wobbly. Thinking it was Mikey, Chili swung around to flip him the bird, until he realized it wasn't Mikey. It wasn't a guy. It was a girl. And what a girl! It was probably the first time Pamela Hinderlap noticed him since fifth grade.

"Oh! I didn't see you," said Chili, shocked as he quickly turned his two middle finger salutes into an ordinary two-handed wave hello.

"Gotcha!" Pamela smiled. "I saw you and Mikey arrive. Me and a few other girls from class were inside hanging out. Are there other boys coming?"

They were standing directly under a low-hanging strand of multi-colored light bulbs that were most likely Christmas lights hung on a tree or in the front yard last December. Chili wasn't sure if it was the way the unusual subdued lighting illuminated her face, or the fact that she was standing closer to him at that moment than any other time in their eight years of being crammed into a classroom with 60 or so other kids, but it was as though Chili was looking at Pamela for the first time ever. Sure, she was slightly hunched over like many girls who develop and grow tall so much sooner than the boys in the class. Her braces were now reflecting blue, green, and red sparkles, making her already large lips seem even more fleshy and round. And of course, there were those grown-up woman-sized breasts. Chili knew that this was the closest he had ever been to a full-sized bosom except for hugging his mom and his aunts. But he sure felt different about these breasts than he ever did hugging those Italian relatives.

"Um, what?"

"Are there other boys from class coming?"
"I don't know. I guess."
"I hope so. It's your turn."
"Excuse me?"
"It's your turn. Do you want a hot dog or what?"
"Oh."

Chili told the smiling man who looked like he could be Angel's dad's twin brother how he wanted his hot dog, but couldn't help thinking about Pamela standing so closely right behind him. He got his hot dog and moved to the table with the soft drinks. He watched and listened as Pamela ordered her hot dog, and he made a big decision: to wait at the soda table for Pamela to arrive.

"Oh, you got a hot dog, too?"
"Yeah, like Patty Duke; a hot dog makes me lose control!"
"Can I pour you a soda?"
"Yes! Ginger ale, please."

Chili tried not to shake as he poured two paper cups of ginger ale to the brim. Now came the real moment of truth for him. He wasn't sure if he could muster the courage as he slabbed a little more mustard on his dog.

"Want to sit over there. And. Eat?"
"Okay."

They stepped across a lawn and sat on a concrete bench under a towering oak tree with lights strung across its lower limbs in the far corner of the large yard. In the soft light, Chili saw Pamela in a completely different way. She sat very straight on the backless bench with dainty hands holding both sides of her hot dog bun. He felt ashamed that he joined in with the boys and constantly commented on her larger-than-average boobs, and shined the flashlight on them. But looking around at the other females at the party, he noticed that her breasts weren't freakishly large, but just normal-sized for a teenager or young woman. In his mind's eye, Pamela was her class picture; crooked, toothy smile, nose a little too large, squinting eyes, too much hairspray on clumps of hair protruding from a graduation hat. It was hard to believe that the gentle, ladylike, softly featured girl was the same person. Her nose wasn't large at all. It just wasn't a turned-up tiny nose like many of the Irish girls in the class. Her hair was thick, and tied back in a wide braid that went half way down her back. She wore a red, silk blouse with only one button undone, but even that made Chili feel something come over him. Mocking Pamela was the furthest thing from his mind.

"It's a fun night," Chili said, immediately knowing it was a stupid thing to say.

"Yes, it is! I wasn't going to come, but my mother said to mingle with people outside of class is an important part of growing up. And going to high school will mean a lot more of socializing with girls *and* boys in different settings."

Chili nearly choked on his hot dog, as he tried to comprehend what Pamela said and how intelligently she said it. "Yeah, it seems like it's always been boys doing one thing and girls doing another in our own little groups."

"I know!" Pamela said smiling broadly.

Chili noticed that yes, her smile was a little crooked, but it was endearing and gave her a deep dimple on the left side of her face. "In fact, me, Mikey, and Angel used to make fun of the guys that hung out with girls."

"Would they make fun of you now?" Pamela said, with a red twinkle in her eye from the Christmas light bulb dangling overhead.

"That's a good question." Chili responded, pondering the thought. "You know, I don't think they would. Not at all."

"Why is that?"

Chili froze. How could he answer that? He couldn't tell the truth. And tell her that for the first time in his life, his heart was about to explode with something he didn't even understand. His pulse was racing, his palms were sweaty, he was fidgeting nervously. Pamela was without a doubt the most beautiful, sensuous, delightful, amazing girl in the world.

Fallout Shelter

"Um. How could they make fun of me for sitting, um, next to you? I mean, you're...great." Chili again regretted how stupid he must sound. Why couldn't he just say something intelligent?

"That's sweet," Pamela said, putting her hot dog on the paper plate next to her, and briefly holding Chili's hand for about two seconds, then picking up her hot dog again.

Chili thought about jumping up and down and doing a touchdown dance, but instead mustered enough self-control to put his hot dog down.

"Pamela?"

"Yes, William?"

She called him William, which sent Chili even deeper into a brain-spinning whirlwind of a hormone cyclone. "Um, would you like to...." Chili was stumped. Like to what? Get another hot dog? Make out? Trip the light fantastic? Get married? "Um, would you like to go for a walk?"

"Okay William."

The mere fact that Pamela called him William made him melt inside. Anytime anyone outside of school called him William or Willy, it reminded him of his mom.

"And you can call me Chili."

"Okay Chili."

They took their empty paper plates and plastic cups to the trash, and Chili tilted his head in the direction of a gate on the other side of the garage that led out to the street. No one noticed as they walked down the sidewalk under a canopy of oaks and chestnut trees towards the darkness a couple of blocks away.

"Where would you like to go?" Chili asked, wondering if he should hold her hand and what that might mean. Then it hit him! The Beatle song, *I want to hold your hand*. He finally got it after all these years!

"Anywhere."

"Have you been to the Indian Pond?" Chili said still thinking about going for her hand.

"What's that?"

"It's a pond that they say is haunted by Indians. It's only a few blocks away."

"That sounds neat."

Chili felt like running away and hiding. Instead, looking straight ahead, without even missing a stride or moving an eyeball, he reached out for her hand and held it. Pamela did not pull her hand away. They were holding hands.

It was hard to believe this was the Bronx. They were only a few blocks from the traffic, noise, dirt, and clatter of the number 1 train El on Broadway, yet it was country-quiet. The few cars that drove by went slowly and only a few people were walking dogs. They turned down a couple of streets and each time the houses and yards became larger and the streets even emptier.

"We go down here, now," Chili said leading Pamela by the hand.

"It looks scary. There are no lights."

"That's okay," Chili said, giving her hand a reassuring squeeze that made her smile.

They passed under a stone arch where a gravel path began and sure enough a pond could be seen in the moonlight, which was visible now with the lack of street lamps.

"Oh my goodness! I've never heard about a pond over here," Pamela said excitedly. "It's called the Indian Pond?"

"Yup. Legend has it that two young Indian lovers died when the girl fell in, and the boy dove in after her, and they both drowned. They say it used to be a lot bigger; actually a large lake. But it got smaller and smaller as they built more homes. Want to sit on the bench?"

"I guess so." Pamela whispered.

They sat on the wooden bench, still holding hands and took in the silence for several minutes.

"It sure is quiet," Pamela said with a slight quiver in her voice. Suddenly there was a splash somewhere in the water. "What was that?" she said excitedly.

Fallout Shelter

Chili didn't want to reveal his own astonishment at the unusual noise. "I guess it could be a fish."

"There are fish in there?"

"I guess so. Or maybe a bird flew down to get a bug."

"In the dark?"

"Probably not. Or maybe an acorn fell from the tree and blew over there landing in the water," Chili said reassuringly.

"Maybe. Chili, I'm going away for the summer. And when I come back in September, I won't have braces anymore."

"Oh," Chili said, trying to contain his disappointment. He finally almost has a girlfriend and she's leaving for the whole summer. Well, at least she won't have braces when she returns, he thought to himself.

They sat in silence again. Shards of light from the full moon cut through the trees and danced on the ripples in the water. Chili imagined this is what it would be like to not live in the Bronx, but somewhere in the country. And even have a girlfriend and go for long walks and just be silent. And maybe even make out? He turned his head towards her, and now that his eyes were used to the darkness he could see with the little bit of ambient light there was, that Pamela had that look in her eye. A girl had never given him that look before, although he heard about it. And he wasn't sure what it was supposed to look like. But he knew this was it. He leaned closer, and felt Pamela also leaning in. He closed his eyes, then an eternity later, he felt Pamela's moist lips against his. Their lips pressed together and their heads made a circular motion in unison as if they were doing rotating neck exercises.

PLOPPSPLASH!

Another, larger object seemed to land somewhere on the pond. Their heads jolted apart. They looked at the large ripples in the pond and at each other.

"That was no acorn," Chili said shaking his head slowly.

KERPLOPSPLASH!

Something that must have been the size of bowling ball dropped from a high diving board landed on the other side of the pond.

"I think we should go," Pamela said, taking Chili by the hand and standing upright as if at attention. They began to walk swiftly towards the stone arch with the pond behind them, keeping their eyes straight ahead.

Then there was a blood curdling shriek, and rustling of branches followed by the typical hoots and hollers of attacking Indians as you might hear in an episode of *The Lone Ranger*.

"*Woo woo woo woo woo, ahh ahh ahh ahh!*" came from somewhere above and behind them.

They ran hand-in-hand under the arch and down the streets as quickly as possible.

Back at the pond, two teenage boys, climbed down an oak tree, laughing hysterically. They went over to the bench, pulled out packs of Kool cigarettes, and lit up. Just behind the bench in some bushes one of them reached in and pulled out a bottle of Boone's Farm Apple wine.

"Did you see them run?" A shorter skinny kid asked.

"Yeah. That little twerp and Pamela Hinderlap. I know that chick. She lives by my cousin. Next time, we'll shoot some arrows at the tree next to the bench." The fatter kid said.

Chili and Pamela slowed down when they got to the block where the party was still going on. They were both out of breath.

"I guess, no matter how quiet and nice things seem to be around here, you can never forget you're still in the Bronx," Chili said, giving Pamela one last quickie kiss before heading back into the party. Just before entering the back gate, they dropped each other's hand.

Angel popped up from behind a barbecue grill with a kebab in hand. "Hey, Chili! Where you been?"

The party seemed louder and more crowded than when Chili and Pamela went for their first holding-hand jaunt about an hour earlier. And the parents seemed to be the ones making most of the noise.

"I, I mean, we went for a walk," Chili said, trying to keep a straight face to hide the fact that he just experienced the most grown-up thing he has ever experienced in his life.

"Oh," Angel said, as one side of his face scrunched together in confusion. "Let me get Mikey. We wondered where you disappeared to." Angel rushed off to the other side of the yard, cutting through a conga line. As he dodged the moms reaching for him to join the drunken dance line, he thought to himself, *Chili and Pamela Hinderlap? Could it be? Chili with the sexiest, most developed and grown-up-looking girl in the class? Maybe they just went for a walk. Maybe nothing happened.*

Mikey was on a hammock, swinging slowly over a pile of empty soda cans, Dixie cups, ketchup- and mustard-stained napkins, and crumbs from assorted churros, donuts, graduation cake, and Italian bread.

"Hey Mikey, 'ten hut!" Angel shouted, tugging on the hammock, almost knocking him out of it. "You're not gonna believe this!"

"I'll bite."

"From the looks of it, you've already bitten into everything in sight. Chili and Pamela Hinderlap are a thing."

"A thing? The only *thing* I know is on the *Addams Family* and lives in a box," Mikey said, pulling a Mallomar out of his top pocket.

"I just saw Chili and Pamela and he looks like he just got back from a trip to the moon! He's spacier than Dobie Gillis chasing after Tuesday Weld! Come see for yourself!"

"Chili and Pamela? Oh, she's too freakin' hot for him to handle! This I gotta see."

"You're not gonna leave that mess there, are you?"

"Oh yeah," Mikey said sheepishly

"I'll help." Angel said, as they both picked up the flotsam and jetsam of Mikey's hearty appetite. A few handfuls of garbage in, they heard a scream and shouts over the music of Xavier Cugat's Rhumba.

Without saying anything, Mikey and Angel rushed to the source of the commotion, which Angel knew was exactly where he left Chili and Pamela.

There was a group of people tending to someone on the ground, while Pamela sat on a nearby chair sobbing. Chili was on the ground and bleeding from his nose and mouth.

"What happened?" Angel said to his dad.

"That little fat shit Murphy from down the block came in here and started insulting Pamela. Chili stood up to him, and then the skinny jerk sucker-punched him."

"Let's go get them!" Mikey yelled, taking a few steps towards the gate until he was grabbed by the arm.

"No! It's over!" Angel's dad said forcefully. "That will solve nothing. What's done is done. Mama, take Chili inside and help him to clean up."

Angel's mom led Chili into the house, followed by Angel, Mikey. And Pamela.

"Anybody get the license plate of that truck?" Chili joked, lightening up the mood, but still feeling the pain and a little wobbly as they walked to the kitchen.

As Angel's mom tenderly wiped the blood and dirt away, her face was only a few inches away from his. He couldn't help but think of all the times his own mother wiped dirt, blood, and tears from his eyes. She reminded him so much of his mom; the olive skin, the dark soulful eyes that squinted with each careful pat with a dampened kitchen dish towel, thick raven hair that from that close proximity revealed the gray roots beginning to be exposed. He felt weary and closed his eyes. But instead of darkness there were splotches of light that burst behind his eyelids from different corners. Then they all came together in the center and there she was: his mother. Clear as day. She looked worried.

And she began to speak to him... *Oh, Chilly Willy, my baby. You are so brave. Continue to do what is right. And don't forget to look to*

Fallout Shelter

the Virgin Mary for guidance. She's always there and will always lead you to Jesus. She's always there. Look for her. And pray.

Shouts of "Chili! Chili! Chili!" made Chili open his eyes, with the help of an ice-cold wet cloth being patted on his cheeks.

"What? What?" Chili asked, opening his eyes to see the concerned looks of Pamela, Angel and his mom, and couple of other ladies he didn't know. "What's the matter?"

Angel's mom sighed in relief. "Oh Jesus, Mary, and Joseph, praise their holy names, you must have passed out for a moment. Your eyes rolled back into your head, and oh, my Lord! You're sure you're okay?"

"Yes, in fact, I feel a lot better than I did before." He felt someone grab his hand and squeeze it. He turned to see that it was Pamela, who had a weak smile trying to mask her concern.

By the time Chili was patched up, the party was pretty much emptied out. Angel's dad was using a wire brush on the grill, and assorted kids and ladies were picking up the trash, and folding up tables and chairs.

Chili walked over to Mikey and Angel who were folding up and stacking the tables. "I can help."

"Where's Pamela?" Angel asked.

"Oh, her dad picked her up out front."

"How's the kisser?" Mikey asked.

"How's the kissing? What?" Chili asked, confused. "Oh, you mean my face after the punch, ha ha ha.. Yeah, it's okay."

"Hey, Mikey and Chili, come over here!" Angel's dad yelled, still scraping the charred meat from the grill. "It's getting late and we can finish this up. You guys better head home." He wiped his hands on his apron, and reached into his pocket. "Here you go, this is for helping out, and for graduation," he said handing each of them a bill.

"Twenty dollars!" Mikey said in awe.

"Oh Mr. Rodriguez! Thanks!" Chili said, also amazed.

"You boys be good, listen to your parents and your teachers, and your priests, and you'll do good on your journey to manhood. Okay, promise?"

"Yes, Mr. Rodriguez," they said in unison.

"And be careful going home now."

"Yes, Mr. Rodriguez."

"C'mon Angel, let's finish up here," Mr. Rodriguez said, patting Angel on the shoulder, as Mikey and Chili walked away. "Listen, Angel. If your friends can't find summer jobs, let me know and we can find something for them at one of the stores, okay?"

"That would be great, Dad."

It was only in the last year or so that Angel was aware that Mikey and Chili's home life wasn't the same as his. He had no idea that the other guys had problems at home. They just played games, goofed around, got into trouble, and hung out. The sudden jolt of reality was when Chili's mom died. It seemed like everybody got a little more serious and grew up a little faster. High school would definitely keep that trend going. But first there was a summer to get through!

∞ Chapter 4 ∂

It had been a while since Chili, Angel, and Mikey got together in the fallout shelter in the cellar of Chili's building. Angel and Mikey were busy working in Angel's father's bodegas. There were three grocery stores, so they didn't always work together in the same store. One was in Inwood, in upper Manhattan, next to Gary Owens bar on Dyckman Street. Another was near Alexander's Department store on Fordham Road. And the third was on 161st Street, just up the block from Yankee Stadium and not far from Archbishop Corrigan High School. They didn't like the long ride on the No. 1 bus to 161st Street, which took an hour or more, but there were some amazing advantages when the Yankees were home. The Yanks were a long way from the glory years of Mickey Mantle, Yogi Berra, Roger Maris, and Whitey Ford, but they were still the Yankees! One time Felipe Alou came in with Bobby Murcer before a game and bought homemade tamales that Angel's mother made fresh daily. And some of the neighborhood kids showed Angel and Mikey how to sneak in to Yankee Stadium where they took out the garbage. The store in Inwood also had its benefits. It was a few doors over from the bar Gary Owens, which was a popular hangout for mostly young people, including kids as young as 15 years old. The drinking age was 18, so a 15-year-old boy over five-foot-nine or so with sideburns would usually get in, or a 15-year-old girl with ample boobs, or at least adorned with decent falsies, was also allowed entry. If they worked late at night after closing, they'd get a taste of what was in store for them in just a year of two when they would attempt to hang out there or in one of the other gin mills that turned a blind eye to underage kids. They would peek through the front window and witness drunken fist fights between guys and sometimes girls. Guys pissing between parked cars was an almost every night sight, but they even saw a few blotto girls squatting there. One time, in the middle of some kind of gang free-for-all rumble, a guy got stabbed and bled all over the front of the store. After cleaning that up, neither were anxious to work at that location.

    Chili's summer working experience was quite different. He was a counselor at St. Gall's Day Camp. His days were spent taking camp buses to Rockaway Beach, or some pools in the suburbs, or on rainy days trips to downtown Manhattan museums like the Museum of Natural History. Most of the other counselors were college kids, but Chili was the only junior counselor that was hired. The camp director, Mr. Black, lived in Chili's building, so he knew him well. He was well aware that Chili's mom had died and that his father was not a candidate for the parish father of the year. And he knew that Chili took care of his younger brother Jamie, who was a camper. Mr. Black also knew that Chili was the oldest altar boy, who was using this summer to make sure the altar boys under his tutelage took their duties seriously, including Mr. Black's young son. Chili was a model young Catholic boy.

    But today was the day Chili, Mikey, and Angel would finally meet in the fallout shelter for a get-together in preparation for a big bash that was happening that weekend in the stands of Van Cortlandt Park. It was called Midsummer Night's Madness, a tradition started by the older guys of the neighborhood who still slicked-back their hair and listened to doo-wop on CBS FM. This would be the first year that the three of them would attempt to be part of that big bash, which had been happening the first weekend in August for the past dozen or so years. They had heard stories about gang fights, police raids, multi-ambulance visits, and fathers coming for their daughters, and wanted to see for themselves.

    Camp was over for the day, and Chili opened the door to the fallout shelter hangout. He was repelled by the stench and sight of a dead rat lying belly up in the middle of the concrete floor. He looked around for something to scoop it up with and found an old coffee can on shelf. He was in the process of kicking it into the can, when Mikey and Angel entered.

"Oh my God! Chili you better start using deodorant!" Mikey said, laughing.

"What's in the can?" Angel asked.

"Oh, I brought you guys some delicious nuts. Wanna see?" Chili said, holding the can o' dead rat up to them.

"Shit!" Mikey said, slapping the can across the room. "Meeting adjourned! Let's make like a tree and get the fuck outta here!"

"Wait for me I have to lock up!" Chili said, fumbling with the padlock and the hasp.

In the bright light of the summer afternoon they didn't even have to discuss where they were headed. Like worker ants that instinctively meander about the neighborhood around their underground nest, they walked up the block to their warm-weather backup hang out: "The Rocks."

"The rocks" was one of the few empty lots in the neighborhood, which was a good isolated location due to its unusual topography. On the west side, Fort Independence Street, there were huge granite boulders you had to negotiate in order to gain entry by climbing up. It wasn't like climbing a sheer rock face in the order of El Capitan, but you needed sneakers to traverse from cut boulder to boulder as you made your way up. Once you got to the top of the rocks, you had to fight your way through some thorny bushes and bramble. If you tried to enter from the east side at the top of the lot along Cannon Place, you had a very steep cliff going downward consisting of more granite, loose dirt, and rocks. The reason this was one of the last remaining lots in the area was exactly those features. It would take a lot of dynamite to tame this hillside enough to construct another crappy apartment building or row of bodegas and laundromats. Plus the fact that it was positioned between Fort Independence Street and Cannon Place supposedly also was a reason. It had some historical significance. This spot was near the Revolutionary War location of Fort Independence, and

Cannon Place was the location of the cannons, the highest eastern position looking down on the valley below. And like General Washington and his officers, Angel, Mikey, and Chili were sitting on their favorite rocks in the middle of the lot under the shade of probably the same giant oak tree that George sat under as they plotted the rest of their summer campaign.

Now that all three of them had summer jobs, each had their own cigarettes, sodas, and snacks. No more need to share. There was a new air of confidence as Angel and Mikey lit up and then each of them took long gulps from their 16 ounce Coke bottles and munched on pretzels, Yankee Doodles, and jawbreakers.

"How's camp going?" Angel asked Chili.

"It's great. We went to Orchard Beach today."

"You mean, horse shit beach." Mikey said, punctuated by a long, wet burp.

"How do you guys like working in the stores?"

Angel placed his cigarette, bottle, and package of jaw breakers beside him on the rock, and pulled out a thin wallet. He opened the wallet and pulled out a piece of paper that looked like a bubble gum wrapper. "Check this out, Chili."

"Bazooka Joe. Big Deal."

"Look closely, doofus! It's autographed by Felipe Alou! He comes in the store on 161st."

"Oh man! I see it," Chili said, examining the waxy piece of paper closely.

"I know it's hard to see, but that's all I had handy," Angel said, gingerly folding it and putting it back in his wallet.

"That's not all, we saw a girl's tits last week."

"What?" Chili was dumbfounded. "How?"

Mikey closed his eyes, recalling the delicious moment. "We were at the store on Dyckman, next to Gary Owens, and all our lights were out. Mr. Rodriquez was doing the books in the back 'til late. It must have been midnight and we were just mopping up and eating churros, when this guy and girl started making out, right against the front window. And next thing you know, he's feeling her up and unbuttons her blouse and we saw the whole thing. Actual naked tits and nipples right there in full view!"

"Totally true, Chili. For real." Angel said wistfully.

"Which reminds me," Mikey said seriously. "We have to plan a trip to a Times Square peep show. Before we know it, the summer will be over and we'll be in high school with not as much time to kid around."

"Yup. It's time. Are you in Chili?" Angel asked pointedly.

"Hey, hey, guys. Gimme a little time here to decide. You think we can get in? I think the age limit is 21," Chili said halfheartedly. His brain scrambled as he tried to come up with other excuses not to go on this sleazy adventure. Time Square was a disgusting pit of porno movie theatres, pimps, prostitutes, junkies, bums, and hicks from sticks. It was hard core, but the hardest of the hard core were the peep shows where sleaze balls sat in booths to watch nude women do… stuff that Chili couldn't even imagine. How did he know? From sitting in Louie the shoemaker's store and listening to the old men talk about what Times Square used to be, and what it had become. Mr. Bonelli even had the red outline of a boot heel on the side of his face from when a mugger knocked him to the ground and stomped on his face before stealing his wallet, watch, and pinky ring. You could actually see the outline of the heel brand's logo, Cat's Paw. On the rare occasions when Chili's father would talk about work, he would mention the "scrotes, scum, skells, and pukes" he'd see in the Time Square subway station when as he working on the tracks. His dad didn't talk much about the job, but when he did it was always some horrible smell, mess, crime scene, or pathetically sad situation that he had to let out of his brain like the steam out of a radiator.

"Chili, look," Angel said playing the middle man, "we'll go down there and check out the scene. If it's something that's not cool, we'll drop it, get a dollar-ninety nine steak at Tad's, and head back home."

"Well, okay," Chili caved.

Mikey sprang into action. It was obvious he and Angel had been planning this for a while. He laid out the day, the time, where they would go first, second, third, fourth, as if detailing a military reconnoiter.

"Mikey, where did you find all this stuff out?" asked Chili.

"Well, my oldest brother took me down there last week. He was getting tickets for a Broadway show for a date, and he said I needed to see some stuff about, you know, sex, because I'm at that age. Just reading the movie titles and looking through the holes they left in the windows of the porno stores so you could peek into, showed me more than all the *Playboy*s I've ever seen. I saw kids our age getting into the porno movies. They don't care down there. A girl even approached us wearing a mini skirt up to her ass and asked if we wanted a triple date."

Now Chili was terrified. The three of them would be on their own. No six-foot-three 19-year-old construction worker by their sides. "What did your brother say to her?"

"He said he was an undercover cop and she thanked him and ran away down into the subway."

"Okay, I'll go along with this but I get to pick the next outing."

"You got it! Alright!" Mikey and Angel said with gusto.

The plan was set. Saturday at 6 they would meet by the 238th Street el station. Mikey even gave them a dress code: no shorts, shirts with a collar, no sneakers. It will make them look older. And if they had any facial peach fuzz, let it grow. They'd kick around Times Square until dark, then pick a peep show, or at least a porno movie. Mikey had a plan to give Angel and Mikey fake IDs made up from a copy of his brother's draft card.

Once the doors of the No. 1 train opened and they took their seats, Chili felt like an infantryman in a Higgins boat on D-Day. Yeah, he worried about getting mugged, beat up, busted by cops, embarrassed, and bamboozled. But more importantly, he also had images of himself getting a pitchfork shoved up his butt while burning in hell. And that was why he sat there terrified.

The three were standing at the front of the first car so they could look out the window as the train rumbled along the ancient elevated tracks. When they crossed the 225th Street Bridge, which connected the Bronx with Manhattan, they always looked to the west to see if anyone was on the "Big C." That was the huge, 110-foot slab of granite with a giant Columbia University logo "C" painted on it next to the treacherous waters of Spuytin Duyvil, where the waters of the Harlem River and the Hudson came together in a deadly swirl of currents and pollution. They were on the lookout for two possibilities. One, there could be kids on the top of the rock jumping the 100 feet into the water, which was even more dangerous than jumping off a cliff in Hawaii. In Hawaii there's an almost zero chance you might hit a shopping cart or '63 Cadillac submerged below. The second possibility was that they might recognize kids hanging out on top of the rock, drinking beer.

"Look! There's the Circle Line!" Mikey announced.

The Circle Line was a tour boat that circled Manhattan every few hours on the weekend, and if there were kids drinking beer on "The Cut" as it was also called, there was a near 100 percent chance that the tourists were in for a surprise.

"Here it comes!" Mikey said, knowing what was next.

First the kids waved to the hicks as they slowly passed by, then they all dropped their pants, mooned them, gave them the finger, and shouted obscenities at them.

"Like clockwork," Angel said, slapping Mikey and Chili five as they laughed.

Some of the other passengers had their heads twisted towards the windows to take a peek, and were smiling. While others had their normal subway faces on: staring at a book or newspaper with a blank expression, pretending they were invisible.

"I want to do that this summer," Mikey said, as the three took their seats.

Chili worried that was another thing he might be coaxed into attempting as the summer days heated up.

In a few stops the bright daylight was sucked out of the car and only darkness was evident outside the windows as they plunged into the descending subway tunnel at Dyckman Street. Dim light bulbs flickered, as they were in one of the last subway cars that still had incandescent bulbs, cane seats, and overhead fans. But like every subway car in the city, even the new ones, it was covered with ugly graffiti from floor to ceiling, inside and out. One didn't notice it quite so much when there was daylight present, but in the dim 40-watt atmosphere the "fuck yous," "suck my dicks" and "Taki 183s" appeared more ominous.

The subway car became crowded as they went along the local line down Broadway and Seventh Avenue in Manhattan through Inwood, Washington Heights, and Harlem. Mostly weary working people and out-of-town college students from Columbia, CCNY, and other schools on the line. They didn't see any kids their age, which made Chili a little more nervous. Once they hit 96th Street on the upper West side, well-dressed men in suits, women in dresses, and teenage hippies started filling the car. Not your typical, B.B.Q. hippies. *B.B.Q.* meant Bronx, Brooklyn, and Queens. That's how the Manhattan hippies disparaged the hippies from the outer boroughs. The hippies in the Bronx, Brooklyn, or Queens didn't wear $100 Jordache jeans, Saks Fifth Avenue leather vests, and Bloomingdale beads. The BBQs wore Army-Navy store discount jeans that got their knees ripped from too many washes, not by the corner alteration shop. They wore vests, army shirts, and old neckties as bandanas, bought at the Salvation Army thrift store. Sandals were bought at Alexander's or John's Bargain Stores, not Pierre's Leather Emporium on Madison Avenue.

"Times Square. Change for all trains and the 42nd Street shuttle," a conductor announced from between cars.

Fallout Shelter

"This is it!" Angel said, leading Mikey and Chili through the crowded car onto the platform. People were rushing everywhere like kitchen cockroaches when the light is turned on at midnight. "We go up the stairs over there."

It was still daylight, but the sun had already set behind the tall buildings, putting all the streets west of 10th Avenue into a grey twilight shadow. The dazzling lights of Times Square, which were blazing 24 hours a day, began to take effect on the pedestrians and sidewalks below, showering the grease-soiled, ranting-and-raving bums with multi-colored sparkles of light from enormous electronic signage. The Winston Cigarette man blew giant smoke rings from ten stories high. A battleship-sized bottle of Gordon's gin poured into a porno marquee below. Bonds Clothing Store, Camel cigarettes, Buitoni pasta, and even newcomers Sony and JVC splashed their lights onto the human circus below. The ubiquitous Howard Johnson's had a hefty neon sign just above street level, but directly above it the flashing lights for the Gaiety Theatre and the Pussycat were beckoning those below going into HoJo's for the all-you-can-eat fried clam platters.

Angel, Mikey and Chili, mouths agape, were in awe of all the signs for sin that were every which way and loose. THE BODY RUB PARLOR, WHIRLY GIRL REVUE with daily matinees, PEEP LAND, THE ZOO, ADULT ACTIVITY SWINGERS CLUB, and PINKS used wide-lapelled males in skin-tight bell-bottoms of every ethnicity, snapping cards and pamphlets at passersby by the hundreds, whether families from Banjo City, Iowa, sorority sisters from Upper Montclair, New Jersey, up-and-coming street hustlers from Philly, or wide-eyed Catholic school kids from the Bronx.

"Hey kid, here, take this. Use it to get a discount at the door," a pock-faced junkie in a black velour jacket said to Mikey, handing him a card with a lousy drawing of a nude woman with a hairy bush.

Mikey took one look at it and stuffed it into his back pocket. "Over here!" He said, leading the others to a relatively quiet spot next to a dilapidated corner newsstand in front of Nathan's. "Check this out. Peep Land," he said, shielding the lewd invite so only the three of them could get a good look at it. "Live, nude women, private booths, swingers welcome, special intimate bonus booth. Sanitary conditions. Present this coupon for one dollar off admission. Two dollars off matinees."

"Sanitary conditions?" Chili said shaking his head. "Did you get a look at that place? I wouldn't want to change a flat tire in that pit!"

Angel patted Chili on the shoulder. "Chill, Chili. First of all, he wouldn't have given us the card if he thought we were too young to get in. And if we hurry, we'll get the two-dollar discount. But we only have a half-hour to the last matinee it says here in the fine print," taking the card from Mikey.

"Let's do it. That's what we're here for!" Mikey said imploring them.

"On one condition," Chili said, surprising the other two. "Look in this store window. I want one of those. For posterity."

The nearby storefront must have been illuminated by a million watts of blinding white light. On display were trashy souvenirs and cheap crap sure to catch the attention of suckers looking for a bargain or a few laughs back home in Banjo City. Chili walked over to the window and pointed at a pyramid of small boxes with a shiny object on top: a miniature camera modeled after a 35mm SLR.

"I want one of these, in case some day I ever forget this day, and I'll look at these pictures to remember it by, and remind myself why I should never, ever do it again!"

They went inside, passed the comic pornographic greeting cards, whoopee cushions, bobbing glass bird that seemed to drink red liquid, $1.99 transistor radios, and stopped at another pyramid of the tiny replica cameras with ARROW written over the faux SLR lens and MADE IN JAPAN printed underneath. An Indian-looking man with a turban stood behind the counter.

Fallout Shelter

"How do you get the film developed?" Chili asked politely.

"All de instructions are inside de box, all guaranteed!" he said joyfully.

"I'll take it. The film is included?"

"Oh most definitely!" he said, taking a box off the pyramid and ringing it up. "Would you like for me to load de fil-em for you?"

"That would be great!" Chili said handing him a five-dollar bill.

"It will just take a moment. And when you remove, do so in a darkened room. You will have a better chance of a proper development of de fil-em."

Chili watched carefully as the man loaded the tiny film into the miniature camera. Mikey and Angel perused the store's tourist bait and soft-porn merchandise; Sexy Suzy in the Bathhouse where a plastic nude girl is behind a door.

"I wonder what this is?" Mikey said, picking up a pink box with FOR THE GIRL WHO HAS EVERYTHING printed in script on the lid. Angel smiled with glee as Mikey opened it, to reveal two nipple pasties over a drawing of breasts with the words NIGHTIE NIPPLE WARMERS.

"I don't need the box, just the camera and the directions, thanks," Chili said, putting the camera in is top shirt pocket, as they left the store.

Peep Land was between a movie theatre playing *The Filthy 5* and a Tad's Steak House where the red neon sign displayed the price of a steak: $1.99. They stood next to an overflowing wire mesh garbage can at the curb looking at Peep Land, as a few men wearing long raincoats went in one by one. "I wonder which of those three establishments really is the filthiest," Chili asked.

"It's now or never," Mikey said, retrieving the discount card out of his pocket. "Just do what I do."

Mikey led the way, with Angel and Chili in lockstep right behind him. The door opened and there was an immediate overwhelming smell of bleach mixed in with cheap perfume spray. Chili did a fake gag as Mikey placed the card on a plywood counter painted red. A single bare low-wattage light bulb dangled from a wire. Behind a dingy plexiglass barrier sat an older man with a greasy comb-over. Behind him, a small black & white television with tin foil wrapped around a bent coat hanger flickered as *The Million Dollar Movie* began on WOR channel 9.

"Look at the TV. It's *The Giant Behemoth* again!" Angel whispered to Chili.

"We have a coupon," Mikey said in his deepest voice. "Three adults please."

"Fifteen bucks," the sweaty man said, chomping an unlit cigar.

"But we have a coupon…," Mikey said before he got cut off.

"Fifteen bucks or get out!"

Angel and Chili hurriedly dug deep into their pockets and forked over two fives. Mikey shoved the fifteen dollars through the opening, and the man snatched them up quicker than a snapping turtle going for discarded hot dog. "Go through there and up the stairs."

They pushed through a beaded curtain and walked up a narrow stairway that creaked with every step. At the top there was a large sign that read ENTER BOOTHS. NO MORE THAN THREE TO A BOOTH. DO NOT REACH THROUGH FENCE. NO SHOUTING. CLEAN UP ANY MESSES. NO PHOTOS.

The first five doors were shut and locked, but the sixth was open. They stood at the entrance of the broom closet-sized booth with a bench, a garbage can, and a roll of paper towels on the floor. There was a chain-link fence that covered a large opening that looked out to a performance area, which consisted of a red carpet and a stool. They shuffled inside and closed the latch on the door.

"I don't know about this," Chili said in a quiet panic.

"Just get your camera ready," Mikey said staring ahead.

Fallout Shelter

A monotone male voice came over a tinny loudspeaker: "Ladies and Gentleman, welcome to Peep Land for the finest in adult entertainment. Sit back, relax, and enjoy the show with Honey Velour." Followed by the song "Soul Finger." A door squeaked open and a voluptuous woman wearing a fringed vest entered. She sashayed to the middle of the red carpet, then paraded by each booth, and as she did fingers protruded through the spaces of the chain link fence. She was only inches from their fingertips.

Chili leaned forward, snapped two pictures and shoved the camera back into his pocket before she got to their booth. "I've had enough. I'll meet you guys at the Nathan's across the street." Chili was gone before Mikey or Angel could say a thing. Besides, Honey was just about to do her thing so close to them, he could smell her.

Chili went two steps at a time, holding his breath until he was back on the sidewalk. He took a deep breath and even with the bus exhaust, gutter sludge, and sidewalk slime it smelled better to him than the inside of the sex cage in Peep Land.

One could go inside Nathan's and grab a seat, or stand on the sidewalk at the outside counter, which is where Chili planted himself. It was dark outside and the neon signs, ginormous electronic billboards, and movie marquees gave everything a multi-colored shimmer, especially the stainless-steel counter where he stood. It reminded him of the midway at Playland in Rockaway beach on a crowded Saturday night, but with none of the joy. Whereas Rockaway's lights were from carousels, a fun house, the Tilt-A-Whirl, the Ferris wheel, zeppole stands, and Kill the Kat, the lights here were from dirty-movie marquees, neon boobs, and leftover burlesque and vaudeville signs over the entrances to peep shows and dildo shops.

"Waddyuh want, pilgrim?" A middle-aged Black man with a paper Nathan's hat asked.

"Um, I'll have…let's see…."

"I ain't got all day. Our menu ain't exactly the Oyster Bar in Grand Central. Dogs, fries, knish?"

"I'll have a hot dog with mustard and sauerkraut, French fries, a knish, and a cream soda."

"Good, you could use a few extra pounds."

Cars, taxis, buses, guys pushing huge hand trucks loaded with boxes and crates, bicycle messengers, hot dog and pretzel carts, and pedestrians all jockeyed for position on Broadway in a chaotic ballet that ignored traffic lights and DON'T WALK signs. Bums, hookers, cops, hustlers, tourists, and working stiffs each had their clearly defined destinations and goals.

Chili took it all in. Times Square was always considered the bulls-eye of New York. The crossroads of the world. He remembered his mom telling stories of seeing Frank Sinatra at the Paramount Theatre just down the street. And how she and her girlfriends would take the subway down here and walk the streets without fear of being mugged or hassled. She said that men would even tip their hits, and always gave up their seats of the subway for them. But now, Time Square seemed more like human waste circling the cosmic drain.

"Here ya go, pilgrim. Buck seventy-five. Why you hanging out down here by yourself? You look like a nice Catholic school kid. Am I right?"

"Yes, I go to Catholic school in the Bronx. I'm waiting for my two friends to... um, meet me here."

"I'm working nights down here to pay for my kids to go to Corpus Christi grammar school uptown. Don't do nothin' that you wouldn't want your momma to see!"

"Yes sir."

That was all Chili had to hear. He knew all about guardian angels, and how they appear from anywhere at any time. They can even be real people, like this Nathan's worker, who are full of grace, and open to God's love, and suddenly say and do things to help others, sometimes in small ways like this gentleman just did, or in superhuman ways, like when a man can lift a car off an injured person. They don't even know that for a moment they were used by an actual angel.

"Chileeee!" Mikey and Angel shouted as they grabbed him from behind mid-bite.

"You don't know what you missed!" Mikey said in a husky voice.

"No, Chili," Angel added. "You don't want to know."

Angel and Mikey ordered some food, and tried telling Chili what went on just beyond the cage that kept Honey Velour, Tasty Van Dam, and Vanilla Creamed inches away from them and the other paying customers.

"I wish we knew you could slip them dollar bills for extra action," Mikey said, chomping on a hot dog. "I only had loose change."

Chili laughed, smiled, and nodded, but every time he saw the Nathan's guy wipe the counter, serve a drink, or take an order he thought of the counterman's words of wisdom.

The ride home on the subway was a quiet one. Oh, the train still rumbled, squealed, and rattled from 42nd Street all the way to 238th Street, but the three of them didn't even talk to each other. Chili remembered the camera in his pocket, and patted it to make sure he hadn't lost it. He didn't know why, but he felt it was important for him to keep that camera, even though the images on there weren't something he'd want his momma to see. He watched Mikey and Angel slightly rocking and swaying along with the motions of the iron horse and wondered if they too were reflecting on what they had just been through.

"You guys," Mikey said over the subway noise, "next time, remind me to bring some singles."

Chili felt a sigh of relief when the train screeched to a halt at their home stop, West 238th Street. When the car doors opened, instead of the grime and putrid filth of Times Square there was a heavenly aroma of Anisette Toast biscuits being baked by the railroad-car load at the Stella D'Oro cookie factory right next to the el. It was always the strongest when Anisette biscuits were baked. If the wind was blowing right, you could smell them from the 225th Street Bridge by the Manhattan-Bronx border all the way up to the city line with Yonkers at 261st Street. There were also days when coconut macaroons, Swiss fudge, or Italian shortbreads were being processed, but those wafting aromas weren't nearly as strong. Mixed in with the delicious Stella D'Oro air were the spores and pollens from thousands of trees, shrubs, wetlands, and grasses emanating from the nearby 1,100 acre Van Cortland Park. It was almost as if one could subsist on this air infused with the molecules of butter, sugar, flour, Anisette, coconut, and vanilla combined with the oxygen generated from the woodlands and swamps of Vannie.

"Smell that?" Chili asked, happily jumping the last three subway station steps onto the sidewalk. "Anisette. That's my favorite. You guys going to mass tomorrow? I'm serving with my brother at the one o'clock."

Mikey and Angel looked sheepish as they pondered Chili's simple question for a Saturday night as they had asked each other too many times to count. With all the antics that the three had been through together, tonight seemed different.

Angel kicked a dried bubble gum blotch on the sidewalk. "I guess, I'll go to the one."

Mikey shook his head and after three attempts to get a word out said, "Yeah, I guess."

"What's with you guys?" Chili asked, sensing their reluctance to commit. Then it hit him. He had no idea what went on after he left that porno snake pit. Mikey and Angel's guilt was smeared all over their faces. "Oh, now I get it. I think you better be at mass tomorrow! See you then," he said, smiling and heading up the block.

"You going home?" Mikey asked Angel.

"Yeah."

"What are you gonna tell your parents?"

"I'll say I was with you guys and we were hanging out by the benches and went to Carvel's and Sam's Pizza on 231st. What about you?"

Fallout Shelter

"Ha, as if my parents will even ask. See ya at mass."

"Yeah, see ya at mass."

They headed in different directions; Angel up the hill to his roomy private house with a yard, and Mikey to his four-story walk-up railroad flat right next to the el.

Chili knew his father was at work. He wondered what would have happened if he met him in the subway at Times Square, and it made him fell anxious. He has never seen his father at work. Some kids, like Angel, actually work with their dad. Mikey's father drives a cab, so has definitely seen his dad on the job. But how would Chili even see his father at work? He'd probably be in a subway tunnel somewhere working on the tracks and ducking into those little alcoves where the workers stand when a train passes by.

He turned the keys on the four locks on the door and tried to be quiet as to not wake Jamie, but with four heavy-duty locks, that was like trying to be quiet when you open and then slam shut a jail-cell door. He immediately headed for the bathroom to wash the day's events off himself. He took the miniature camera out of his coat pocket and held it up, while he looked in the mirror. Without smiling, he snapped a photo of himself by pointing it at his reflection. He doubted he'd ever get the film developed, knowing full well he would probably try to forget the images that were forever etched into his brain and on the tiny, cheap, roll of film.

He gingerly opened the bedroom door. The streetlight's harsh beams of light sent slashes of white across the room through the venetian blinds, which were vented open on the hot summer night. He looked at Jamie to make sure he was asleep. Chili opened the closet, and reached all the way to the right, half of his body disappearing into the hanging clothes, piles of sneakers, baseball gloves, old toys, footballs, Spaldeens, roller skates, and old notebooks. He fished around and pulled out a small steel safe, which had a slot on top to deposit money. It was about as secure as a shoebox with tape closing it shut. He dialed the combination 2, 4, 6, opened the tinny door, and placed the camera inside under some baseball cards, photos of his mom, some holy cards, his birth certificate, and every report card since kindergarten. He didn't know it, but Jamie was watching his every move.

One o'clock mass in the summer was usually a low-key, sparsely attended gathering. Many of the families were on trips to the beach or away on vacation. And in the summer the nuns weren't pressuring kids to attend the nine o'clock mass, so there were a few more kids in attendance.

Chili made Jamie do all his own altar boy preparations on this day. He watched him like a hawk on a wire looking for mice. Jamie picked a cassock from the closet, put it on, and began to button it up. Chili didn't tell him it was obviously way too short. Jamie finished buttoning it and looked down at his feet.

"Is this too short?"

"Yes."

Jamie picked another and this time held it up against himself to check first if it would fit properly. After buttoning that up, he picked a white surplice from the closet and put it on over the black cassock. Chili noticed a dark stain on the back.

"The people in the pews are going to see more of your back than your front. Always check for stains all around."

Jamie took it off, and placed it in the laundry hamper. He chose another and examined it front and back before putting it on. He then filled a cruet with water. "Where's the wine?"

"Mrs. Madigan will bring that in a minute. Get the bells out of cabinet. Keep them quiet."

Jamie carefully opened the oak door of the cabinet where the bells were kept. Just as the door opened and Mrs. Madigan appeared, he dropped the bells with a loud clatter of all four bells against the marble floor.

"Cheese and crackers!" Mrs. Madigan said. "You'll wake up the devil with that!"

Fallout Shelter

"What is going on in here?" Father P. shouted as he pushed open the door to the altar boy's room. "William, you're in charge. Be in charge!" But his tone changed when he saw Mrs. Madigan half-hidden behind the ironing board. "Oh, excuse me. Hello Mrs. Madigan. I didn't see you there. I'll meet you boys in the sacristy in five minutes." He quietly left the room.

Mrs. Madigan studied the faces of Chili and Jamie. "Has Father been yelling at you boys or... or anything else I should know about?"

"Not to me. What about you, Jamie?"

"No."

Mrs. Madigan, placed the lint brush on the counter and approached Jamie. "Jamie, I want you to tell me if anyone, whether an altar boy, or anyone else, including grown-ups, all grown-ups, even priests, say anything to you that doesn't seem right. Or asks you to do... something without my permission. I am the one who gives permission involving all altar boys. About everything. Do you understand me?"

"Yes, Mrs. Madigan."

Mrs. Madigan looked at Chili and somehow Chili got the message she meant business. And she meant some kind of business with Father P.

On the altar, Jamie watched Chili's every move, from his eyes to hands, to head nods for his cues. It was easy for Chili to see if Mikey and Angel were in attendance because there weren't many people in the church. And there they were, not in the many empty pews, but standing in the back against the wall. Chili saw that they weren't even kneeling on cue, but just standing there with their hands lazily clasped in front of them.

Luckily, Jamie performed just fine, and Chili was confident that he'd be able to serve with another lower-grade altar boy without causing too much disruption. It was Chili's job to make sure all the younger altar boys were ready and today he started with the one who needed the most assistance. He knew he had to watch out for Jamie at home, in the street, and here in the sacristy.

❧ Chapter 5 ❧

The summer was speeding away faster than an express subway train passing through a local station. John's Bargain Store windows were stacked with the cheapest "made in Japan" back-to-school notebooks, pencil cases, and vinyl book bags. Alexander's was having end-of-the-summer sales to clear out all the bathing suits, shorts, and water pistols to make way for jackets, corduroy pants, and football equipment. The signs that school was approaching fast were apparent everywhere. Especially on Chili's dresser, where he kept the books on his summer reading list for freshman year at Archbishop Corrigan High School, of which the number he had read, or even started, was zero.

All Quiet on the Western Front by Erich Maria Remarque, *The Jungle* by Upton Sinclair, *Beowulf*, *Moby Dick* by Herman Melville, *The Catcher in the Rye* by J.D. Salinger, and *Wise Blood* by Flannery O'Connor loomed large in the fears that began to infiltrate Chili's conscious and unconscious mind. It wasn't that Chili didn't enjoy reading. He had read whatever books the nuns had assigned over the years, which were few and far between. And those were all biographies of prominent Catholics like St. Theresa, Elizabeth Seton, and his favorite, St. Francis of Assisi. From the looks of the books that beckoned him morning, noon, and night since the day he purchased them at Robert's Book Store with a 20 percent discount from school, he knew there were more to these tomes than self-sacrificing saintly souls who cared for all God's creatures great and small. He even saw the word *fuck* in *The Catcher in the Rye*, and *nigger* in a short story by Flannery O'Connor when he scanned them.

Day camp was ending this week, so kids had two weeks to prepare before returning to school just after Labor Day. It was even more depressing than usual because not only was everyone–campers and counselors alike–dreading the end of summer and returning to school, it had been raining the whole week. That meant, no swimming at the ocean or state park pools, no trips to amusement parks or swimming and rowboating in lakes. The entire week was spent in the auditorium having dreadful talent contests, bingo, and watching corny movies like Fred McMurray in *Follow Me Boys* on rickety projectors that broke down every 15 minutes. In fact it was raining so hard for so long that most of the highways had flooding problems so they couldn't even go to museums in Manhattan on the camp buses. By the last soggy day of camp, there were a handful of kids there to receive the silly end of the summer awards like "Best Guppy," "Camp Clown," "Perfect Attendance," and "Camper of the Year." It looked like summer was a sinking ship. But the last few kids put on their raincoats and galoshes and the counselors cleaned up the flotsam and jetsam of a week's worth of indoor boredom, there was the happy occasion of being handed an envelope that made it all worthwhile: cash money.

Chili went into the boy's bathroom and into a stall to count the loot. "Wow. One hundred sixty dollars!" he whispered to himself. That meant he received $20 per week pay for eight weeks instead of the $15 he thought he was going to receive. Just as he was exiting the bathroom, Mr. Black, the camp director, was entering.

"You got a little something extra in your pay packet, Chili. You did a good job. We hope you'll be back next summer."

"Yes, Mr. Black. Thank you. I'll be back!"

"You're going to Archbishop Corrigan, right?"

"Yes, sir."

"Work hard. Have fun. It's a big school. Always watch out for yourself."

"Yes, sir. Thank you."

Chili ran up the steps, grabbed his umbrella from the stand, and started walking in the rain. He thought that was a strange way for Mr. Black to send him off to high school. "Watch out for yourself?" Not too subtle. He headed to

Snookey's corner candy store for a celebratory chocolate egg cream, and from outside the window, he saw a welcome sight already seated on red stools in front of half-empty egg cream glasses: Angel and Mikey!

"Hey guys!"

"We thought you'd pop in here before heading home," Mikey said, holding his glass as if toasting Chili.

"Sit down, we got some plans for the rest of vacation!" Angel said, a pretzel rod in his mouth as if he was smoking a cigar. "Chili, did you hear about the vision?"

"The vision?" Chili asked putting his coins on the counter and counting them out for his egg cream and pretzel rod. "Who's vision? Rod Carew? I hear it's better than twenty-twenty."

Mikey gets all serious and leans in. "You know the Vitolo house on the Grand Concourse. Where the kid saw the Virgin Mary in 1945. We hear she's back."

"Don't kid around," Chili said, losing count of his coins. "My mom took us there when I was five and Jamie was in a baby carriage. We walked the whole way. There were hundreds of people lined up blocking the sidewalk and the street at the grotto."

The vision they talked about was when a Bronx boy of nine saw the Virgin Mary appear in 1945 in the rocky backyard of his home just south of Van Cortlandt Park on the Grand Concourse, the Bronx's main north-to-south boulevard. It happened just months after World War II ended, and jubilation was still in the air. *Life* magazine called it the Bronx Miracle. At one time 30,000 people gathered there to see what little Joseph Vitolo and three little girls saw one October night: the Virgin Mary floating above the rocks in his backyard. People gathered for days and weeks, and still go on the anniversary to pray there. Even Frank Sinatra visited and gave Joseph a statue as a tribute to this Lourdes of the Bronx.

Almost 30 years later, only the most devoted still remember the incident and visit this now-decaying corner where a grotto with a statue of the Virgin Mary still stands, visible from the sidewalk if one knows where to look.

"Why are you bringing this up now?" Chili asked, dead serious.

Chili's mom was a devout Catholic. A scholar might have described her as a Catholic Mystic, someone who has ecstatic visions of the soul's mystical union with God. She always told Chili and Jamie about her own dreams and visions, and the signs she received from Jesus and the Blessed Mother. From a young age Chili remembered her telling him about Guardian Angels and the Devil doing battle. She also told a story of how her own mother died of a sudden heart attack the day after her three sons were sent off to Europe to fight in World War II. And a day later, her mother appeared in a dream to tell her she passed away so that she would be the guardian angel for the three boys in the war. All three returned home safely, without a scratch.

"I heard some people talking after mass that they were going to the Vitolo shrine because there was gonna be a sighting," Mikey said, trying to be a little too serious. Angel was giving Mikey an eye roll over Chili's shoulder. "It's happening tonight. Are you in?"

"Yeah. I'm in," Chili replied, wondering if this was the right thing to do.

Angel put his hand on Chili's shoulder. "Meet at eight at the benches in the park. We'll walk across the park, then down the Concourse."

"Oh, I might be a little late," Mikey added on cue. "I'll meet you there if I'm late. I told my… brother, I'd help him clean out a closet."

Chili sipped his egg cream and nibbled on his pretzel rod without any expected enthusiasm for meeting the guys and hanging out after the last day of camp, complete with a packet of twenties in his back pocket. As happens so often, when his mind is led to thoughts of his mother, he becomes almost lost in a state of unreal reality. He knows she is dead and buried. He saw her in the coffin. He threw dirt into the grave and heard the awful sound of pebbles banging against the wood of the casket.

But sometimes she seems more alive now than before. He hears her voice. All his senses seem to feel her, hear her, even smell her. Like the counter man at Nathan's, who was an older Black man with a gravelly voice and razor burn on his face, he heard his mother speaking to him, through him. Sometimes he thought he was going kind of crazy.

"I'll meet you guys at the benches later," Chili said, leaving half a pretzel and half an egg cream behind.

Mikey and Angel watched him cross the street and enter his building down the block.

"Mikey, are you sure about this?"

"Oh, it'll be a goof," Mikey reassured him. "I mean if you can't take a joke, how are you going to handle high school? Guys are always pulling stuff on freshman. It'll get him prepared for the shit he's about to go through from jerks in high school."

"Maybe we're being jerks," Angel shot back.

"We're his friends!" Mikey implored, an egg cream mustache outlining his smiling face.

"Okay, let's make sure we remember that."

As Chili walked from his building over to the park benches his mind bounced around like bingo balls in a cage. Should he go through with this? His mom would want him to go, right? Is it safe walking through the park and down the Concourse to a different neighborhood? Mikey and Angel wouldn't have them doing this unless they knew it would be worthwhile.

It was unusually warm and muggy even for a summer night in the Bronx. As he passed apartment buildings, windows were wide open and the noises from each individual household from the ground-floor apartments to the ones on the sixth floor spilled out and created cacophony of city sounds. Televisions blasted *I Love Lucy* reruns, local news stories detailing out-of-control crime, random acts of murder, and the South Bronx burning. Latin music mixed with the Irish Rovers and the

Fallout Shelter

Rolling Stones as they melded into a sidewalk symphony. Kids played on fire escapes while mothers watched carefully from adjacent windows in their housecoats with buttons undone. Teens chased each other with water balloons, darting through traffic and ducking behind parked cars. Under the old oak tree at the end of the Review Place, eight beach chairs were lined along the fence with elderly couples watching the goings-on as if watching a parade by go. Stella D'Oro wasn't baking anything this evening, so the prominent smells were garlic from the pizza place, grease from the vent by the Chinese take-out, and overwhelming fumes of toxic hair permanent chemicals and hair spray from the beauty parlor. Of course there were the piles of dog poop you had to watch out for, since nobody bothered cleaning up after their pets, whether a Chihuahua or a Doberman Pinscher. Dented overflowing garbage cans with ill-fitting lids lined up in the alleyways between buildings added to the aromatic assault on the senses, which one learns to ignore over time.

It was getting dark so Chili was scanning the park for trouble as he entered through the gate. Some were playing basketball in what was left of daylight and the nearby street lamps. Older teens were sitting on the grass smoking pot while one of the guys was playing guitar. One kid with no shirt and gym shorts was doing pull-ups on an overhead fence railing. So all looked pretty normal.

There were about a half-dozen park benches just outside the fenced-in softball field usually occupied by families on warm sunny days. But at night they were sometimes occupied by kids and even weird adults drinking, smoking, sniffing glue from brown paper bags, or even shooting drugs. Luckily at this early evening time, there was just one kid sitting there and it was Angel.

"Where's Mikey?" Chili said, sitting next to him on the creaky wooden bench.

"Like he said, he had to help his brother move some stuff."

"He's gonna meet us over there?"

"Yeah. He told me. Hey, um, Chili, um, I got these…," Angel said struggling to pull a plastic baggie out of his out of his pocket, "…and wondered if you wanted one?"

Inside the baggie were two squares wrapped in tin foil.

"What are they?" Chili, asked.

"Homemade brownies," Angel replied, pulling one of them out of the bag.

"Yeah, I'll have one," Chili said enthusiastically as he grabbed it, tore off the foil and began eating it with gusto. "Mmm. Good."

Angel watched as Chili devoured it. "Do you want the other one? I, um, had one at the house and have to watch my weight."

"You don't have to ask me twice!" Chili said, eagerly unwrapping the second brownie.

Angel waited for Chili to finish, and watched him carefully. He had just given Chili two hash brownies. Mikey got them from his brother, who said they were a good way to experiment with hash before smoking them. Having no experience with hash or pot or anything stronger than fortified wine, Angel didn't know what to expect.

"Should we get going?" Chili asked. "I want to get to the shrine early so we get a good look at it."

"Yeah, let's walk through the park. It's shorter." Angel subtly suggested.

"Okay."

They took a path that went through a heavily wooded section of the park. Giant oak and elm trees created a tunnel of trees as they walked uphill in the quickly darkening night to the eastern edge of the park that eventually led to the Grand Concourse. As Yogi Berra once said about right field in Yankee Stadium, "it gets late early out there" when the sun dips below the apartment buildings to the west. Here the park becomes thick with ancient trees that provided shade for soldiers commanded by General Henry Knox in the Revolutionary War as he placed a battery of cannons by what is now known as Gun Hill Road. Any park in the Bronx can be a dangerous place, especially at night. Danger lurks wherever perverts, rapists, sadists, thieves, psychos, or just plain old neighborhood kids are hanging out in the dark, high on cheap booze or drugs. Under the cover of darkness, they are free to prey upon the old, the weak, the unsuspecting, and the stupid people who don't know any better.

"I don't think I was ever in this part of the park at night," Chili said, eyes darting to the source of every rustling branch in the wind.

"You've been here a million times during the day time walking to the number 4 train to go to Yankee Stadium with me," Angel said reassuring Chili at first, but then his attitude changed. "But I know what you mean. I've heard stories of strange things happening over here. They say that there are lots of Indians and slaves buried around here."

Chili noticed Angel's tone transitioning from Mr. Rogers to Rod Serling, but of course said nothing.

"Just look at all the names of streets around here. Gun Hill Road, where the Revolutionary War cannons were placed. Gates, Rochambeau, Knox, were all Revolutionary War generals who came through here and left trails of blood and guts of dead soldiers on both sides," Angel said, pouring it on really heavy. "And to think this is close where that kid saw the vision."

Angel strained to see if the brownies were taking their effect yet.

Now it all clicked in Chili's mind. Of course! The park ended at Jerome Avenue where the elevated number 4 train is, but this entire area must have been a forested war zone during the Revolutionary War. "You're right! Battles must have been fought here and they'd just bury them in mass graves. I know about the slave and Indian burial grounds in the park. I remember seeing the faded tombstones before the kids from Bailey Park destroyed them one night. It was in the Riverdale Press with a little history lesson of who was buried below the

Van Cortlandt's burial vault on the top of the hill." Chili was picking up his pace, speeding a few steps ahead of Angel.

"Slow down a little, Chili! What's the rush? Hold on, I need to stop and take a leak. At that big tree there that looks like it has a face on it."

Chili stood in a small patch of light that came from a lone lamppost about a hundred feet away up the path. It was hard to see where Angel was going into the blackness of the many enormous trees converging at the spot where he was pissing. Angel finished and walked over to the center of the dirt path. "Come over here, Chili. I thought I heard something weird."

Chili took baby steps out of his little patch of light and into the pool of pure darkness where Angel stood. "Like what?" Chili asked.

Angel noticed a change in Chili. His eyes were darting from side to side. He began licking his lips. Then he held his hands in front of his eyes, as if he was seeing something in the palms of his hands.

"I think I hear a strange, rustling wind noise, but it's not exactly like the wind. Almost like a voice."

Chili licked his index finger and held it high. "There's no wind tonight"

"I know. That's what's so weird," Angel said, doing the same. "How are you feeling, Chili?"

"I don't know. I think I'm a little queasy and kind of weird...," Chili said, with the brownies definitely kicking in.

"Wait. Don't move. Look. Over there," Angel said as he put his hands on Chili's shoulders from behind and steered him so he directly faced a trio of very large trees growing behind a five-foot high clump of thick bushes and shrubbery.

Chili stared in disbelief as a very faint light flickered about ten feet high between some branches thick with overlapping limbs and leaves.

"What in God's name...," Chili whispered loud enough for Angel to hear him.

In the faint light Chili could see something was beginning to appear. It was difficult to see in the dim light but started to take shape. It seemed to be glowing from within, and levitated higher and higher. It was a female figure with a blue hood and robe, and in her folded arms, she held something. An infant.

"Christ almighty! It's the Blessed Mother!" Chili said, stunned, and dropping to his knees. He covered his eyes and started to recite the *Confiteor* prayer in Latin.

Angel bent over and saw tears begin to stream down Chili's cheeks as he knelt there trembling.

What the fuck? Angel thought to himself. He looked up in the tree and saw that the light on the large lawn Nativity scene "Mary Holding Jesus" lawn figure was glowing, and was being lowered down into the thick bushes where Mikey was hiding, holding the fishing line that was attached to it. The sobs became louder as Chili struggled to say the prayer.

He pounded his chest with each line growing louder, "*Mea culpa, mea culpa, mea maxima culpa.*"

There weren't many lines from Latin prayers that Angel remembered, he sure remembered what these words meant: *Through my fault, through my fault, through me most grievous fault.* Angel knew he and Mikey should have been saying those words, not Chili.

"Chili, are you okay?" Angel asked when the prayer ended and the sobs quieted down.

"Yeah, I'm okay," Chili said weakly as he rose from his knees on the rocky path. He wiped the dirt from his knees and wiped his face with the bottom of his shirt. "You saw that, right Angel? I'm not seeing things. I saw that. You did, too, right?"

"I saw… something. I'm just not sure what it was."

"I know what it was. It was what we came over here to see. It was just a few blocks away. In terms of heaven, earth, hell, and the universe, it was almost the same location as the Vitolo vision. They say not everybody sees a vision. You have to be in the state of grace and open to receiving a message from the

Lord. Not everybody saw the visions at Lourdes or the visions on the Concourse," Chili said, arms flailing and stutter-stepping in circles.

"That explains why you saw it clearly and I didn't. I guess I wasn't in the proper state of mind, or grace, or something. Do you want to keep going to the Vitolo shrine to check it out?"

"Of course. We told Mikey we'd meet him there. We can't leave him flat."

Angel and Chili continued up the path until it put them by a hole in the chain link fence next to Mosholu Parkway, which led to the Grand Concourse. Mikey was still struggling with the four-foot-high plastic nativity scene Mary lawn figure that he and Angel snuck out of Angel's garage. He hoped he could hide it adequately in the thick bushes, so he could retrieve it later that evening and return it to its off-season resting place in the rafters of the garage. He was sure the three of them would have a good laugh over it later that evening. He hoped the hash brownies did their job.

The crowd filled the sidewalk and the spaces between the parked cars in front of the yard where the grotto that contained the statue of the Virgin Mary stood, on the site where the boy saw the vision thirty years earlier. It was a gathering of mostly women of every race and nationality. Almost all of them had their heads covered with scarves on the warm evening, in the same way they were required to wear them inside a Catholic church. Many held rosaries, missals, prayer books, and small statues of Mary and Jesus. There were also many children of all ages with some in wheelchairs or with crutches. A few were obviously blind or mentally handicapped, but all were respectful and pious. Very few groups of teenagers were present. Especially boys.

Just as Angel and Chili turned the corner and began pushing their way through the throngs on the street, a very elderly nun in a similar habit to the teachers at St. Gall's Grammar School appeared in the backyard grotto where the vision originally took place. She carried a large bouquet of white roses, which she placed at the feet of the three-foot-tall statue of the Virgin Mary. A man of about forty came to her aid when she bent her knees to kneel, bless herself, and then rise again. A gasp went through the crowd and whispers of *that's him, he's the one, it's the boy who saw the vision.*

Angel was discreetly watching Chili's every move. Chili seemed on the verge of something, but he wasn't sure what. Would he shout something? Was he thinking of pushing through the crowd to front? Maybe he should have given him just one hash brownie.

Angel once had a great aunt, Tia Rosa, who visited from Puerto Rico when he was around five years old. She wore black from head to toe not unlike the nun who just presented the roses to the statue. Angel's mom took Tia Rosa and Angel to a church in upper Manhattan that gave Angel a memory he will never forget until the day he dies. The church is the home of the Mother Cabrini Shrine. But Angel's understanding of a shrine was something completely different as a young boy. He had heard Yankee Stadium was a shrine to baseball. And that Grant's Tomb was a shrine to a great Civil War general and President. He had no idea that when he entered the ornate church that the glass case on display would hold the actual hand of Mother Cabrini, an American Saint. Not a model or reproduction but the actual skeletal hand itself propped up in a graceful position under a spotlight. His eyes were so transfixed on this bony display that it took a few moments for him to realize that his Tia Rosa was having some kind of seizure on the floor, flopping around like a flounder on the sand, and speaking, what he later found out, "in tongues." There are images and experiences that are forever seared into a brain so deeply that no amount time passing or self-medication can keep them buried. They come to the surface sometimes on occasion and the experience can be re-lived. Angel was watching Chili to see if he would suddenly become something like Tia Rosa.

An elderly priest shuffled through the gravel surrounding the statue grotto. He held a large golden bucket with a golden wand inside. In a thick Italian accent he murmured, "Issa here dat dissa man assa boy was blessed to see Mary, the Mother of Jesus, righta here inna da Bronx. Issa no accident dat happened justa aftah the world war was over and da boys come home. Dosa boys dey comma home because you prayers to Mary the Mother of Jesus, protecta dem. In facta, I know dat some you mudders anda you grandmudders, they die and go to heaven during da war so dat dey along widda Mary can protect da boys in da war. Dassa a facta. Now I wanna saya prayer and blessa you all who believe and want to protect and save da people who love Mary and Jesus."

Out of the crowd, Mikey appeared and slapped Angel and Chili on their backs, and just as he did, Chili started shaking uncontrollably and shouted, "My mother told me my grandmother died to protect her sons in the war. And my mother died to protect me and my brother. And I saw a vision...." He then began to shake, and drool, and say gibberish words that sounded like some kind of foreign language like you hear the Greeks or Lebanese speak in their Fordham Road ethnic restaurants.

"Give him room. Let him breathe!" Mikey said, pushing away some lookey-loos.

The elderly priest walked over to the chain link fence, interested in the commotion. "Hey you boys. Bringa dat boy over here. Quick! Over here!"

Angel and Mikey got Chili up and helped him over to the rocky wall where the grotto and the priest were a few feet above them.

The priest stirred the wand around in the bucket, pulled it out and began to shake holy water on the three of them as he recited a prayer in Latin that they didn't recognize from their altar boy days. Chili was getting splashed in the face by holy water and came to.

"Are you all right?" Mikey asked, helping Chili to his feet along with Angel.

"Yeah, I'm a little woozy. I think I want to go home." The crowd parted for them like the Red Sea and the trio headed north on the Concourse to return to the neighborhood.

"Let's not go through the park. Let's just go down snake hill," Chili suggested, still getting his bearings straight.

They walked past DeWitt Clinton High School, the all-boys public high school, where Mikey would be attending in the fall.

"I'm glad I can still walk to school when I'm in DeWitt C. You chumps will be riding the shitty subway to get to school," Mikey said jovially trying to change the mood.

Neither Chili nor Angel had a comeback line. They knew that Mikey didn't have the grades to get into a Catholic school. And that even if he did, his family couldn't afford even the cheapest Catholic high school, like Archbishop Corrigan, which was only about twenty bucks a month. Chili could pay almost the whole year's tuition at Corrigan with just his earnings from day camp. Angel didn't have to worry about money.

"I'm really looking forward to high school. I'm not going to fool around anymore," Chili said, finally starting to feel like himself as they walked down the steep snake hill, which led back down to the comfort of their own neighborhood. "I hear they have some great after-school activities there."

"Yeah, I hear they have a ham-radio club, a rocket club, even an ice hockey club," Angel added.

"I'm going to do everything. Especially the vocation-prep program," Chili said with confidence. "I wasn't sure about it, until tonight."

Mikey and Angel looked at each other like they just heard aliens had landed on Van Cortlandt Lake. "Um, tonight?" Mikey said, innocently.

"Yup. After seeing my vision, I know I was chosen by Jesus and Mary tonight. Everything came together on this night. I think I've had an an...."

"Epiphany?" Angel asked, with a sinking feeling in the pit of his stomach.

"Yes. An epiphany! Like Saint Paul on the road to Damascus!"

"Are you sure what you saw was… real?" Mikey asked. "I mean you did faint at the grotto. Maybe you were having like a fever dream or something? Or from something you ate?"

Angel nudged Mikey with a sharp elbow.

"I know what I saw. I'm not gonna blow this. I've been praying for a sign. And I got it."

There wasn't another word said all the way down Bailey Avenue to where the three of them took different directions to their homes. It was just weak, *see ya's*, *later*, and *ciao* as they went their separate ways.

Chili opened the locks to the apartment. He immediately smelled the alcohol fumes that his father was exhaling on the living room couch as he snored. He snuck past him and saw that Jamie was fast asleep. After washing up, Chili prayed with a rosary in his hand and thanked Jesus and Mary for the sign they gave him

A few blocks away, Mikey and Angel stared at their own ceilings and wondered what the hell they just did and how the fuck were they ever going to tell Chili?

Mikey knocked on Angel's front door at nine the next morning, despite the misting rain, occasional heat lightning and distant thunder. Mrs. Rodriguez was surprised to see Mikey so early. They usually worked afternoons in one of the bodegas.

"I think Angel is still in bed, come in," Mrs. Rodriguez said, motioning Mikey into the enormous living room with large picture windows and a vaulted ceiling with exposed wooden beams. It reminded Mikey of a ski lodge he once went to as a Boy Scout, but was unlike any other house he had ever seen. The view out the windows, which were towards the east, provided a nice view of his and Chili's neighborhood. It looked quite

Fallout Shelter

picturesque from a distance. The 238th Street elevated subway train station looked quaint with its red faux New England-style covered bridge architecture. When the station was built in the early 1900s it didn't look so out of place, as it was surrounded by bucolic wetlands and natural beauty with only a few homes and an apartment building or two sprinkled throughout the area. Now, however, this neighborhood and just about every other neighborhood in the Bronx was a different sort of urban swamp. From this far, you couldn't smell the gutters, doorways, or subway cars. One couldn't see the faces of the struggling families crowded into railroad-flat walk-ups. Or the young people under highway overpasses and in apartment building cellars drinking fortified wine, sniffing glue, or shooting up. Only when a subway car went by in the distance, covered from top to bottom in graffiti, were you reminded of the state of the neighborhood that looked unchanged from afar.

"What gives?" Angel said, descending an oak staircase, still drying his hair with a towel.

"Oh, I just wanted to get an early start on the day, since it looks to be rainy outside," Mikey said, careful of his words, knowing Mrs. Rodriguez was in the adjacent kitchen. "Maybe catch an early movie, or go to the bowling alley."

"Good idea," Angel said sitting right next to Mikey on the plush sofa. "What's really on your mind?" Angel whispered.

"Where can we talk?" Mikey responded softly.

"Come up to my room, I'll show you my new baseball cards," Angel said loudly.

Angel had his own room, which in itself was a reason for envy. But he also had his own desk, bookshelves, TV, stereo, chest of drawers, view, and window air conditioner. A far cry from what Mikey was used to. Angel closed the door behind them.

"What are we gonna do? We have to tell Chili what we did!" Mikey said, holding his voice down.

"I don't think we can. He'll never forgive us. Plus what difference does it make? You know how religious he's been since his mom died. He was gonna join something like the vocation club at Corrigan anyway. I mean he's still an altar boy for crissakes. He said he wanted to be a priest."

"We all said we wanted to be a priest in the third grade!" Mikey said loudly. "We outgrew that. He thinks he's like St. Paul, or St. Francis, or St. Michael, or one of those other saints on the stained-glass windows in church who saw the light or a vision and started slaying dragons or snakes or some other crazy shit! And in reality he was just blasted out of his mind on my brother's psychedelic brownies!"

"Psychedelic? I thought it was just hash?" Angel asked, concerned.

"He said it was hash with some special fairy dust or something."

"Keep your voice down, Mikey. Damn. Let's just think about it for a while. He might forget all about it, like we forgot about building a raft to cross the Hudson River, and running away to California, and wanting to be rock stars."

"Wait a minute, Angel. I still might have a shot at being a rock star."

"You can't even play guitar!"

"I can learn! I'm not even in high school yet!"

"Neither is Chili!" Angel said emphatically. "He always wanted to go that route. Yeah, he's been our partner in crime, but only up to a point. Maybe we just helped him along with his decision."

"Do me a favor. Don't help me out with any decisions like that," Mikey replied. "Let's go to the bowling alley. We can call Chili from there and hang out."

The bowling alley wasn't a new hangout for the guys on a rainy day. Fieldstone Lanes, next to the No. 1 train subway yard at W. 240th Street and Broadway has a bowling alley upstairs, busy with families, leagues, and teens who enjoy bowling. But downstairs, below the bowling alley, was where guys went who didn't care much for bowling. You had to be 16 to even enter the pool hall, where mostly males, young and old, chain-smoked, gambled, and made connections for nefarious underground activities ranging from pool-hustling, loan-sharking and drug-dealing to fencing stolen goods. Mikey and Angel figured they wouldn't get carded during the late morning, before most of the regulars showed up, and they were right.

"I've only been in here a few times, and never played pool here before," Angel said, putting two dollars on the counter for an hour of play. "I only played on our table in the basement when my dad says it's okay. I spilled a soda on it once."

"I hope none of my brothers see me here," Mikey said, scanning the few players in the large room with around 15 pool tables.

"No drinks around the tables. If I see you drinking near the table, you're outta here with no refund," a crusty old man with an unlit cigar in his mouth croaked. "Go to the table all the way in the back. Don't be more than an hour from now or you get charged for a whole hour."

They took the rack of balls, picked their sticks off a wall, and set up in the rear of the hall. There was a black payphone right next to them.

"I'll call Chili," Mikey said, gathering some change from his pocket and dialing. "Hello, Chili. Hey, me and Angel are in the pool hall. Come on down. We're at a table in the back. They don't care if we're underage because there's hardly anybody here. Okay." He hung up the phone. "He says he'll come."

They played a game of eight-ball, with hardly a word between them. It was obvious they were both more interested in trying to pick up on the conversations on the other side of the room, where some tough-looking greased-back-hair guys were giving some long-haired hippies a hard time. Except for the differing styles of clothing and hair, the two groups were speaking the same language when it came to cursing, betting, and talking about sex in crude terms.

"Can you believe what those guys are talking about out loud?" Angel asked Mikey in a low voice.

"It sure is different from the bowling alley upstairs," Mikey replied. "Here comes Chili."

Chili looked as if he was walking through a Halloween haunted house and a guy with a chain saw might lunge at him at any second.

"I've never been in here before. Is it safe?" Chili said, putting his umbrella under a bench.

"Sure it's safe," Angel replied reassuringly.

It took two games of eight-ball before anyone even made reference to the night before, and that was just to mention that how much they walked last night, going all the way to the Concourse. The chatter between the greasers and the hippies was getting louder and more coarse. The crusty counter guy even yelled at them to hold it down a couple of times. Through the thick cigarette smoke it was evident a fight could be brewing.

"Can we go somewhere else?" Chili asked, after knocking in the 8-ball early and losing the game.

"How about the fallout shelter?" Mikey asked.

"I guess," Chili said, trading his cue stick for his umbrella. "On second thought, I think I'm going home. I'm not in the mood today."

"Yeah, same here. Me too." Mikey and Angel said, as they returned the rack of balls ten minutes early and exited.

It was drizzling and the rain seemed to be muddy when it passed through the No. 1 train tracks above as subway cars rumbled overhead. Chili peeled away from the other two with a weak "see ya" and disappeared around the corner. After a few paces, Mikey motioned to Angel to follow him as they both headed to the corner where Chili was headed. And just as Mikey thought, Chili was walking up the steps to the church.

"Maybe he's going to confession." Angel suggested.

"Maybe that's just what we need to do. Let's go back to the pool hall."

Chili liked being home alone, which wasn't very often. His father worked long, unpredictable hours, not to mention his many

Fallout Shelter

excursions to the local gin mills. But Jamie was almost always at home when there wasn't school. *Perhaps he was finally hanging out with some friends*, Chili thought to himself.

It was definitely a day of reckoning and self-reflection. His ten-minute trip to the church earlier in the day was just another in a series of recent signs and efforts for him to figure-out his path. The images inside the church, where his parents were married, he was baptized, and his mother had her funeral, were seared into his unconscious mind. The wounds of Christ on the life-size crucifix on the side-wall. St. Michael the Archangel slaying a dragon with a sword in a giant stained-glass window. The Blessed Mother, Mary, calmly lording over churchgoers from her pedestal in the front. The Stations of the Cross, with its familiar tableaus of Christ's torture on display 365 days a year, not just on Good Friday. All reminders that suffering and guilt were ubiquitous and one needed to be proactive in order to attain some kind of earthly perfection.

"The camera!" Chili said aloud as he remembered the night he and the guys went to Times Square for some debauchery and laughs. He went to the bedroom closet and reached under the pile of laundry and sports equipment to retrieve the safe and the camera with the dirty pictures inside. "Holy shit!" he whispered upon opening the flimsy tin door. The camera was gone. He knew his father was always rooting around for extra money hidden by his mom, or anyone else. Did he find it, and throw it out? Or did Jamie? Either way, he couldn't mention it to them, just in case they ever actually got the film developed. As quiet as Jamie was, Chili knew he was a sneak, and a clever one at that. All Chili could do was wait and see if the camera was ever mentioned again, and accept the consequences no matter what they may be. Now or sometime in the future.

∽ Chapter 6 ∾

Mrs. Madigan seemed to be everywhere on the church and school property, whether it was at the altar, in the altar boys room, the sacristy, the rectory where the priests lived, the convent where the nuns lived, the school, the auditorium, or anywhere else. Having been there for decades, she was the one constant and had outlasted nuns, priests, and pastors.

To most parishioners she was merely the older lady who flitted around and kept things clean and shiny. But altar boys knew her as someone not to mess with. Even more-so than some of the nuns and priests.

Mrs. Madigan was busy in the sacristy ironing the priest's garments when, out a side window, she caught a glimpse of a boy entering the rectory from the back entrance by the parking lot. She put the iron down, turned it off, and rushed to another window where she could see the back entrance to the rectory more clearly. But by the time she got there, all she could see was the back door closing and no sign of the boy she was certain she saw.

After locking the door to the sacristy, she exited the church and walked the fifty of so feet to the entrance of the rectory where Monsignor Shannon, the pastor, and Father P. resided. The Monsignor was a busy man, and sometimes Mrs. Madigan didn't see him for days. He had many relatives and friends, belonged to a country club in Westchester, and owned a fishing boat, which he kept on City Island on the other side of the Bronx. Father P. was relatively new and she was unsure of his habits and whereabouts most of the time.

She unlocked the front door to the rectory and made sure the door didn't slam shut behind her. Very quietly, she went through the reception area, looked into the two ground-floor offices the priests used, and the kitchen, which were all empty. She then ascended the stairs, careful not to let them creak under her feet to the second level where the priest's quarters were.

Fallout Shelter

There were four bedrooms up there, but only two were currently being used. It was getting harder and harder to find parish priests to take up residence. Pausing in front of the closed door to Father P.'s room, she listened and heard Father P. talking to someone. She knocked on the door. A few seconds later it opened wide, revealing Father P. at the door and Jamie Manzilla sitting on a wooden chair.

"Oh, hello, Mrs. Madigan, how can I help you?" Father P. said smiling too broadly.

Mrs. Madigan stepped inside and approached Jamie. "Jamie, go downstairs, and sit in the reception room and wait for me. Do you understand?"

Jamie stood up, nodded, and walked out of the room.

Mrs. Madigan closed the door behind her. "Have a seat, father."

"This is highly insulting–"

"I said have a seat," Mrs. Madigan said, pointing a stiff finger at the chair where Jamie was sitting earlier.

Father P. sat in the chair. Mrs. Madigan stood in front of him.

"You don't know me very well, Father. And I don't know you. But let me make myself clear. I know everything that goes on here, on this property. And I have many eyes. Eyes and ears that can't be seen."

"Excuse me but I have every right–"

"Listen. I'll only say this one time. During the war, my husband parachuted behind enemy lines, and may God forgive him in his infinite mercy, he learned the art of stealth termination. There was a priest who violated more than one child, I won't say where he lived, but the priests downtown did nothing–"

"Don't you–"

"When he was confronted, he was so distraught, he committed suicide, by hanging. It was very sad. We prayed for him. As we shall pray for you. God bless you, father."

She exited and quietly closed the door behind her.

Father P. sat in stunned silence. He remembered hearing about a Bronx priest's suicide when he was in the seminary.

There were whispers and rumors going around, as the church usually keeps those things quiet. In fact he learned of many things in the seminary that were kept quiet. They said it was necessary for secrecy to protect the Mother Church. Outsiders wouldn't understand the nuanced vows and customs of the inner workings of the brotherhood of priests dating back centuries. Priests were human. And all humans have animal behaviors and desires. The seminary was where one learned to control those animal urges.

Father P. picked up the telephone book, searched for a number, and dialed. "Hello, do you have microfiche of *The New York Times*, going back say, 15 years? Oh, you do. What are your hours tomorrow? And these *New York Times* files are accessible to the public all day? Thank you."

He stood up, went to a drawer, and retrieved a small prescription pill bottle. He walked into his bathroom, lifted the lid, dumped the contents of the bottle into the toilet, and flushed it.

Mrs. Madigan approached Jamie who was sitting in the reception area's overstuffed dusty chair reading a copy of the *Irish Echo* newspaper. "Come with me, Jamie."

Mrs. Madigan led Jamie out of the rectory, through the parking lot, and around to the other side of the church. Just as she was about to turn the corner she glanced up at the second floor of the rectory, where she could see someone peering through the slats of a venetian blind. She crossed the street with Jamie and sat on a bench in a small park with a few benches. "Why were you in Father P.'s room?"

"He said he was going to tutor me on my Latin."

"Did he?"

"No."

"What did he do?"

"He showed me a magazine."

"What kind of magazine?"
"It was just...."
"Go on."
"It was muscle men. Lifting weights and stuff."
"Did he do anything else?"
"He said we were going to have refreshments and you knocked."
"Is that all?"
"Yes."
"Look at me, Jamie. This is very important. Is that everything that happened?"

Jamie paused. His face twitched slightly with thoughts bouncing around. "Yes, that's all."

"Don't ever go to the rectory again, okay? And if Father P. ever tries to talk to you alone again, you let me know. Promise?"

"I promise."

"Make the sign of the cross and promise."

He made the sign of the cross and kissed his hand upon completion. "I promise."

Father P. was at his desk, writing a letter on formal stationery. It was to the Archdiocese headquarters downtown, requesting a transfer to reside at the residence on the upper floor of Archbishop Corrigan High School for Boys, where he taught, instead of the rectory at St. Gall's parish. This, he explained, was due to the transportation difficulties during weekdays. Of course, he could still continue to say mass at St. Gall's on Sundays.

Jamie was scared of Mrs. Madigan. She made him walk with her to his building and brought him to his front door. She knocked hard. Chili answered.

"Oh, hello Mrs. Madigan. Is everything all right?"
"Is your father home?"
"No."
"May I come in?"
Chili motioned for her to enter. "Sit here on the–"

"No. I'll be brief. Jamie, go to your room."

Jamie did, and they waited for the door to click closed.
"Jamie was in Father P.'s room at the rectory."
"Was he stealing something? I'll beat the hell out of the little—"
"No, he was invited there by Father P."
"Okay. So what's the problem?"
"William, you are going to high school soon. You are becoming a man. There are things of this world, sinful things, you will see. You will be a witness to. You must bear witness, no matter what the consequences. Keep an eye on that boy and don't let him visit the rectory under any circumstances. Goodbye and may God bless you and your family."

Chili watched as she exited, dumbfounded. What was she saying? Was she saying what he thought she was saying? It had to be. Suspecting a priest? Of … that?"

Like many things that went on in the Manzilla household, the topic of Jamie alone in Father P.'s room would never be mentioned again. Whether it was a coping mechanism for survival, or just an avoidance of reality, denial and secrecy were as vital to life in these streets as were the overflowing bars crowded from breakfast to nightcaps after the graveyard shift. Peaceful family gatherings could only exist if scars from the past were ignored. On occasion the code of silence was violated and that's when switchblades and broken bottles on sidewalks outside bars settled old scores from decades or minutes ago. An utterance of simmering grievances at Thanksgiving or a christening party would mean overturned tables of cold cuts and over-mayonnaised deli salads. But sometimes black eyes, face scratches, and stab wounds were the outward physical manifestation, not of wrongdoing, but of a wrong finally being confronted and being exposed once and for all, the consequences be damned. Yes, there could be irreparable damage to family, neighborhood, and work relationships, but a hidden cancer has to be revealed if a remedy is at all attainable. When night falls and lights begin to appear in the cityscape windows, every single occupant has mothers, fathers, daughters, brothers, cousins, neighbors, fellow parishioners, or even "trusted" teachers and priests who they are no longer on speaking terms with. They are no longer discussed and the mere mention of them triggers anxiety, fear, or rage. Or worse yet, even deeper, more complete silence.

All the barber chairs were full. Louie the shoemaker was working overtime repairing heels and soles and polishing dress shoes. John's Bargain Store was out of loose leaf, pencil boxes, and cheap vinyl book bags. The only kids on the block that didn't have the white of their scalps showing above their ears were the kids going to public school, where there weren't hair codes, dress codes, or behavior codes. Similar misbehavior in a Catholic school could mean a close-fisted punch in the face from a hungover Irish Christian Brother with anger-management issues.

This first day of school for Chili, Angel, and Mikey would be unlike any other. Yeah, they were meeting in Chili's cellar fallout shelter, and yes, they'd have a few laughs and bitch about school. But this was the first time they'd meet and then separate, as they each went to different schools. Mikey would be walking up snake hill to attend DeWitt Clinton, a huge all-boys public high school, once known for its famous alumni Burt Lancaster, Sugar Ray Robinson, and Fats Waller, but now was more renowned for its race riots, gang fights, and muggings in the hallways. Angel would be taking the bus to Fordham Prep, an expensive all-boys Catholic high school that was a pipeline to law schools and M.B.A. programs. Chili would be riding a bus and the subway to the bargain-priced Archbishop Corrigan High School for boys in the South Bronx, which was also known as "the factory" for its resemblance to a massive industrial building, and also for the strict discipline fostered upon similarly groomed and dressed students by an army of iron-fisted priests and brothers.

"Are you gonna let your hair grow at Clinton?" Chili asked Mikey, offering him half of his package of Twinkies, which Mikey gladly accepted.

"Hell yes! I'm gonna grow my hair down to my ass, if it goes that far! I don't want to look like a boot-camp little soldier ever again. I hear they don't even care if you smoke in the halls. In Corrigan you get in trouble if you smoke in your neighborhood and somebody rats you out. I don't know how you guys are gonna deal with all that crap."

Chili used his chewing of the Twinkie as an excuse not to say anything.

"Fordham isn't as bad as Corrigan. I hear some of the brothers at Fordham Prep have long hair, and you're allowed hair over your ear and touching your shirt collar," Angel boasted.

"Well, Corrigan is pretty strict, but it's supposed to have really good academics for the top students and great extra-curricular activities. Discipline keeps the trouble makers under wraps," Chili added. "I like to keep my hair short anyway."

Chili knew that was a lie. Nobody wanted short hair anymore if you wanted to fit in with the cool crowd. Even baseball players had long hair, mustaches, sideburns, and oversized Afros. Politicians, TV news anchors, even cops and firemen were letting their hair grow. But Corrigan still had weekly surprise haircut inspections, and a dress code that brought to mind bankers and businessmen of the 1950s.

"I heard at Corrigan they busted kids for wearing black arm bands to protest the Viet Nam war," Mikey said, white Twinkie cream lingering on his lip. "That's bullshit. At Clinton they had a walkout to protest the war. I would've done that."

"I don't know. Isn't that unpatriotic?" Chili asked earnestly.

"Unpatriotic?" Angel added. "My dad says that protests are everybody's right."

"I don't know, guys, I think it's my country right or wrong, isn't it? You know, love it or leave it!" Chili replied.

Fallout Shelter

Mikey and Angel didn't jump on Chili. There were a lot of things on TV and in the newspaper front pages lately. There were huge protests against the war, for civil rights, and riots and assassinations. It seemed like everybody was more divided than ever and you didn't know what or who to believe.

"Well, all I know is when we turn 18 in a few years, I don't want go to war in a jungle on the other side of the world," Mikey said with sadness in his voice. "My cousin came home in a box. Or what was left of him. He looked like a mannequin in Alexander's window in the coffin. I gotta get going."

They walked out of the room and when Chili locked the padlock, he wondered if it would be the last time he would do it.

Father P. looked like any other commuter on the No. 1 train as he stood and waited at the 242nd Street station platform, the first or last stop of the train, depending on how you looked at it. He wasn't wearing his priest collar. In fact, he wasn't wearing anything that would reveal he was a priest. He was wearing blue jeans, a blue-collared shirt with the top button open, and tennis shoes. He was carrying a very businesslike hard-shelled briefcase and had a copy of *The New York Times* under his arm. He nervously stood there, knowing he probably would be recognized if a parishioner spotted him. He already had his alibi ready; he'd tell them he was meeting a college friend downtown for lunch.

The doors opened and as soon as he sat at the end of the car, he opened *The New York Times*, held it up to his face, and began reading, which provided good cover for the rest of the 45-minute or so ride to the New York Public Library at 42nd Street.

As the train entered the tunnel at Dyckman Street, the breeze of fresh summer air that had been blowing in the open windows quickly disappeared. The train made stop after stop with many more getting on than got off, and the lack of air conditioning became more apparent with wafts of unpleasant body odors. Even Father P.'s copy of *The New York Times* just inches from his face couldn't offer any protection.

The train dumped him right in the middle of Times Square and he made his way east along 42nd Street to the majestic main branch of the New York Public Library. He was pretty sure he was less likely to be noticed here in this massive building in mid-town Manhattan.

He approached the information desk in the periodicals section. "May I have the files for *The New York Times* from 1969 to 1971?" The clerk handed him a wire tray with boxes of microfilmed copies of the newspaper and he took a seat at a viewing station.

He was almost certain he heard whispers of a priest committing suicide while he was in the seminary, but he didn't recall any news articles. But facts, motives, and details were usually scarce when it came to suicide. Families, businesses, and—yes—religious orders, regularly suppressed the specifics of the self-destruction sometimes at the expense of important facts that could help the living.

It was hard to stay focused on the small screen with article after article whipping by as he tried to concentrate on seeing certain key words in headlines: *priest, death, suicide, hanging.* But after an hour and a half of bleary eyes and a sore wrist spinning the reel, he backed up the reel on a headline: A PRIEST COMMITS SUICIDE. His pulse raced and the research room seemed hotter than the packed subway car he rode in that morning. Yes, it was a priest who had served mass at St. Gall's. But he didn't live in the rectory, but resided in an apartment at a seminary in Westchester. He was also a teacher at a Catholic high school for boys in Yonkers. His body was found by a fellow priest and ruled a suicide. No mention of hanging, slit wrists, overdose of pills, gunshot, knife wounds, drowning, or asphyxiation. Just a body found, dead.

He returned the microfilm to the desk and went to the men's room where he entered a stall. He sat on the toilet, opened his briefcase, and began his transformation: fake mustache, oversized owl-eye dark sunglasses, and a Boston Red Sox baseball cap that he pulled low. With his disguise complete he exited the building and slowly walked down the many steps back to street level. He went to a Chock Full o'Nuts down the block, sat at the counter, and ordered a cup of coffee and a donut. *Mrs. Madigan must be bluffing,* he thought. *How could her husband sneak into a seminary residence, violently murder someone, and not be noticed? It's impossible. But she did say he went behind enemy lines in the war. They are trained in those things. No. It's preposterous.*

Nevertheless, his mind was made up. He would still request a transfer out of the St. Gall's rectory and into the residence on the top floor of Archbishop Corrigan High School to play it safe. The fact that there were no details of the suicide leaked to the *New York Times* actually made him feel even more secure. The diocese knew how to keep a secret.

He left the coffee shop and headed west on 42nd Street, back towards the subway entrance in Times Square. But he didn't enter the first subway entrance, or the second. He continued up Broadway where the sleazy theatre matinees were just starting. He wasn't wandering aimlessly. He had been here before and headed directly towards a sign for Howard Johnson's. He didn't enter there, but took an adjacent darkened doorway that led up to the Gaiety Theatre. The smell of the HoJo fryers churning out the all-you-can-eat fish and chips special gave way to the stench of dirty carpets, body odors, and stained seats as one pushed open the swinging door entrance to the theatre. He took a seat in the middle of a row and waited to see what sort of excitement might develop.

In three days, the Tuesday after Labor Day, school would start for Jamie. Chili worried that Jamie might not get to school on time because he wouldn't be there poking, prodding, and threatening him every step of the way to get up, get washed, wear clean clothes, straighten that tie, eat the cereal, brush your teeth, comb your hair, where's your homework, get to school on time, and pay attention in class. That was his job every morning since their mom passed away, but now since Chili had to leave an hour earlier to make it all the way to the South Bronx for school, Jamie would be on his own.

But besides worrying about that eventuality in three days, another fact of this holiday weekend was that the kids who are lucky enough to go away for the entire summer return home. Oh, Chili will be happy to see Buzzy Fraser and Mondo Monahan after their three months at the beach in a Rockaway bungalow. They will probably have grown a couple of inches, their hair will be bleached a few shades lighter from the sun, and they'll have more freckles to count. But his anticipation on seeing those two suntanned pals paled in comparison to finally seeing Pamela Hinderlap after her summer in Mattituck, Long Island with her family. As much as the physical features of two boys could develop during the steamy summer months after eighth-grade graduation, the effects on a girl could be astounding.

And when Chili walked to the benches next to the basketball court in Van Cortlandt Park, he was stunned. There she was. Pamela Hinderlap in short-shorts and a buttoned red-and-white checked shirt tied together just above her belly button, playing basketball with a few girlfriends. The summer salt-air breezes and hot white sands had melted away whatever remnants of baby fat lingered on Pamela's body. Three months of volleyball, swimming, and surfing had chiseled her soft childhood flesh into the toned shapes of an athletic woman.

Chili took a spot behind the fence under the shade of a tree where he thought Pamela wouldn't notice him. He couldn't believe that this amazing, graceful, dynamic female was the same person who he made out with next to Indian Pond just a few months ago. He knew she had outgrown him.

"Chili! Is that you?" Pamela shouted, taking the ball out of bounds in order to pass to a teammate on the court. "The game's almost over. I'll be right there!"

"Okay!" Chili said, waving. Was this possible? Would they pick up where they left off? Chili was terrified.

Fallout Shelter

The game ended, and the girls sat on the sideline drinking their sodas, passing around bags of chips, and turning up the sound of WNEW 102.7 FM on a boombox. Pamela was headed through a hole in the fence walking straight for Chili.

"Hi, Chili! It's good to see you! You look good!"

"You too. Um, you look... different."

"No braces!" Pamela said with a huge smile revealing gleaming perfectly straight teeth.

Chili could smell her sweat, but it was sweet and moist. Not like a guy's stinky BO sweat. Her face glistened, as if she had microscopic glitter on her, but he knew that was also perspiration.

"So are you starting at Corrigan next week?"

"Yeah. But I'm going all alone. Nobody else in class is going there."

"Really? Me, Cathy, Diane, and Rosemary are all going to Spellman. I'm really looking forward to it. I'm going to try out for the volleyball team."

"You look really good... in basketball, too."

"That's all we did all summer was play volleyball, basketball, and we even learned how to surf at the ocean. We met some really cool new kids from the East Bronx. In fact I'm going to visit them this weekend."

"Oh, some new girlfriends?" Chili wanted to pull the words back. He shouldn't have said that. And he knew by the look on Pamela's face, she wishes he hadn't asked it either.

"Well, yeah, girlfriends. And um, boyfriends. I've got to get back to the game. See you around, Chili."

"Yeah, see you around, Pamela," he said, dejectedly as he turned away. But quickly stopped and walked swiftly after her. "Pamela! Um, do you think I could see you later? I know it's a big weekend coming up and you're probably busy...."

"Okay, meet me outside my building after dinner at around seven-thirty."

Pamela smiled broadly and caught a basketball that was thrown with some oomph right into her breadbasket, which she handled and transitioned to dribbling like a player.

Chili couldn't believe what he was seeing. The more he watched her in action, just playing a three-on-three game with some neighborhood girls, he could tell she wasn't the same from a few short months ago. As far as he could tell, he looked exactly the same. He hadn't put on an ounce, still 129 pounds soaking wet. He hadn't grown an eighth of an inch. And he still had the same shoe size as before the summer. Mentally and spiritually, he did feel changes coming on. A trip to a peep show, a couple of punches in the face, and seeing the Virgin Mary rise out of burning bush would tend to do that to you. That's to be expected. But watching Pamela stirred something in him that he had never felt before: lust. Oh, yeah, they made out a couple of times and pressed their lips together with their heads rotating around like a bobble-head doll on the dashboard of a '65 Rambler American, but this was different. Boys and girls have been making out like that since about the third grade, when daring kids peeled away from pin the tail on the donkey in the living room, grabbed a Coke bottle out of the trash, and started up a game of spin the bottle in the bedroom. When Chili was at the peep show, and saw a strange nude woman in front of his cage, he had no sexual desires whatsoever. There was curiosity and amazement that an out-of-shape female writhing around naked on a dirty rug was something men would pay for. But Pamela's lithe body with large breasts bouncing with every dribble and jump shot aroused in him a feeling so strong, it made him frightened. It was indeed an animal urge that was difficult to suppress even here, in a park in broad daylight, with toddlers and strollers and old people walking with canes, and ice cream bells jangling nearby, and a baseball team doing calisthenics before a game, and the elevated train rumbling by. He wasn't aware of any of those things. All he could see and hear were the sights and sounds of Pamela Hinderlap that made every sense in his body tingle with desire. And he was going to meet her in a few hours. How could he possibly control himself?

Father P. sat on the subway car, sans mustache and hat, holding the *New York Times* close to his face again as the train rattled under Times Square, the Upper West Side, Harlem, Washington Heights, and Inwood, then ascended from the tunnel onto the elevated line that would bring him to the end of the line; home to the rectory. He had been scanning headlines the entire way, looking for current events to use a "hook" for this week's sermon at mass. He learned that in the seminary, among many other modern maneuvers, to keep up with the times.

The train screeched to a halt at the last stop and Father P. exited the car. He always enjoyed looking into Van Cortlandt as he descended the stairs. It was so far from the filth of Times Square. He was eager to take a shower and wash the grime off his body. He was careful to examine his pants for stains before putting them in the hamper. Mrs. Madigan had a habit of snooping everywhere, even the laundry baskets.

The sun was setting noticeably earlier and the evenings were finally cooling off. Chili ironed a just-washed long-sleeve shirt. If he didn't sweat it up, he could wear it next week when he started high school. Pamela only lived a couple of blocks away, so he hadn't much time to talk himself out of going to meet her. He was terrified that he would say something stupid or not be able to control himself if he was in as close proximity to her as he had been just before she left for summer vacation. And on top of that, Pamela didn't mention meeting new boyfriends from the East Bronx for nothing. He had to toughen-up and be ready for the big letdown.

He stood next to the stoop of Pamela's building on Bailey Avenue. There were two large white concrete lions on both sides of the stairway entrance. It was one of the few remaining clues that the neighborhood was once considered a tony enclave of luxury apartment buildings mixed with private homes in a leafy urban suburbia. When the elevated line opened in the early 1900s the neighborhood looked like a rural resort area with woods, horse stables, an amusement park, and public swimming pools. But after 70 years, almost every patch of green is gone, and what was initially upscale has been downgraded to barely livable. Working-class people of every ethnicity battle landlords and supers for heat in the winter, toilets that flush, and some sort of assistance to keep away the roaches, rats, mice, and human vermin that populate the cellars, hallways, elevators, dumbwaiters, and adjacent apartments. But they still consider themselves lucky to have escaped the hellscapes of the South Bronx, Bushwick, or the Lower East Side.

"Chili!" Pamela shouted from her second floor apartment window in the courtyard. "I'll be right down!"

Chili took a position next to one of the lions and girded his loins. And there she was, resplendent in wide striped hip-hugger bell-bottoms and a sleeveless paisley blouse coming down the stairs. As beautiful as she appeared on the basketball court, she now looked like a fashion model on the cover of *Seventeen* magazine.

"Sorry I'm late."

"I don't mind."

"Want to walk down to Carvel? I didn't have any desert."

"Sure."

Chili felt like he was a bodyguard for a Hollywood starlet. Every male from the age of seven to seventy took notice of Pamela as she walked by, and probably wondered what she was doing with a shlub like Chili, he thought to himself. Fortunately, the last couple of blocks to the Carvel soft ice cream stand were dark streets with no one hanging about, which made Chili feel a little more comfortable.

"You must have really enjoyed being near the water all summer," Chili said fishing for conversation. "We spent a week at Rockaway once. I think I got three shades darker."

"Didn't you get a tan this summer working at camp?"

"In the beginning a little. Then it rained a lot."

Chili ordered two brown-bonnet cones and they headed down the street towards Van Cortlandt Park as they licked their cones. Chili couldn't help but notice that Pamela's tongue seemed inordinately long and muscular. He thought hard, and realized he never noticed anyone's tongue ever in his life, except maybe for Red Skelton who seemed to stick his out a lot.

"Want to sit on the benches over there? It's probably not a good idea to go too far into the park since it's getting dark," Chili suggested.

"Good idea," Pamela responded just before she pushed the last inch or so of cone into her mouth.

They sat on the bench in silence, watching the people descend the stairs as they got off the train at the 242nd Street station. People who were working late in Manhattan waited for buses that would take them to the suburbs in Westchester. Across Broadway, the bars and pizza places started to fill up with college-age kids.

"So you had a good summer?" Chili finally asked, knowing this would begin the conversation that would probably determine the fate of his social life the next few months.

"It was great. I met some great new friends. They're from Throgs Neck by the bridge."

"I heard of lot of guys at Corrigan are from Throgs Neck. They go to Saint Benedict's."

"Yeah, in fact, one of my new friends is going to Corrigan. He's really nice. His name is Billy Santini. You'll really like him."

"Yeah. I'm sure I will. Maybe we should head back."

They walked down some dark tree-lined streets, but Chili was afraid to try and hold her hand like he did at the beginning of the summer. And just like that they were back between the lions.

"Chili?"

"Yes."

"I think I should tell you something...."

"Go on."

"That boy, Billy."
"Yes."
"I kind of went out with him this summer."
"Oh."
"But we didn't go steady or anything."
"Okay."

Pamela grabbed Chili's hand and squeezed it. Then she pulled him closer to kiss him. Chili complied and began the ritualistic bobble head circle kissing session, until Pamela shoved her tongue deep into Chili's mouth and gave him a sensation that sent blood coursing into every extremity of his body from his head to his toes, and particularly what was in between. When she pulled her tongue out and stepped back a little, she gave Chili a knowing smile.

Chili looked into her eyes, ignoring the fact that a drunk was less than twenty feet away peeing between two parked cars. "You know that was the only time in my life that I saw stars that weren't caused by a punch in the face."

"Chili, I know we're going to different schools, but let's keep in touch. No matter how many new friends we make."

"I promise."

Pamela turned and walked back up the apartment stairs. From behind, she looked so grown up. She wasn't a girl at all but a woman. Chili hoped she'd wait until he felt like a man.

Mikey and Angel knew they had to do something about the epic prank they pulled on Chili. The guys were used to giving and receiving practical jokes, from simple "kick me" notes slapped on backs, to elaborate Rube Goldberg types, like digging a deep hole, throwing dog shit in it, camouflaging the top of it with twigs and dirt and leading somebody to fall into it. But the level of this prank was elevated to a cosmic plane with the help of hash-laced brownies and imagery that Mikey and Angel both knew went beyond the conscious mind of Chili. They had an unfair advantage, knowing the innermost fears and weaknesses of their good friend.

They sat under the multi-colored lights in Angel's backyard, which his father would be taking down right after their Labor Day cook-out.

Angel fidgeted with some leaves on a bush. "We have to tell him."

"No way," Mikey said adamantly. "We can't tell him. First of all, he thinks he saw an actual vision of the Virgin Mary. It has more than likely changed his brain chemistry or something! He might believe he's on a divine path to sainthood. We can't tell him it's nothing but a stoner hallucination."

"I don't know. What do we do?" Angel said, now convinced by Mikey. "How about this? We tell Chili that we're gonna have a pact, and we'll do like a blood-brother thing and swear on our mothers that we'll never tell another soul about the vision from that night."

"Yeah, that's a good idea. If he really believes the Virgin Mary made a special trip to the Bronx just to visit him, maybe it'll make him feel like one of the chosen ones. Maybe that's a good thing?"

"Yeah. Right," Angel said, knowing there were no other options that didn't involve losing Chili as a friend forever. "Let's have one more meeting in the fallout shelter before school starts on Wednesday."

Chili was still in an altered state after Pamela's tongue awakened his animal spirits as if she unplugged a drain stopper next to his tonsils that kept his hormones under wraps. And it terrified him. He had erections in his life since he grew hair under his armpits. But mostly it was a reaction to something random, like seeing Betty Boop do a topless hula dance with a lei covering her nipples. Or the most embarrassing random-erectile reaction, the dreaded wet dream. The subsequent race to the washing machine in the basement at 6 a.m. is an added post-adolescent predicament. He was unprepared for his passionate petting with

Pamela. And now he felt… guilt. Of course! After year after year of *mea culpa*s, confessions, bless me father for I have sinned, impure thoughts and impure actions, Chili was programmed to believe that what he felt was so fucking good it had to be bad! Wasn't sex forbidden until one was married, and then only allowed if you are trying to make a baby? Sex was so taboo in the vast majority of circumstances that nuns and priest had to take sacred vows to never ever do it. Ever. It went beyond a promise. It was tantamount to what it took to be nun or a priest. Priests didn't even have to take a vow of poverty, like most nuns did. They could stand at their pulpit on Sunday and browbeat struggling fathers and mothers trying to put food on the table for their families to put more of their hard-earned money into the collection basket while they themselves ride their Cadillacs to the fishing boats on City Island and take a weekend cruise to the Hamptons to dine on clams on the half shell and lobster. But sex? Nope. Not allowed. Zero tolerance. They had to take a vow of celibacy. That means, no sex at all with a woman ever. Maybe they could whack off, but that was it. It's in writing, for chrissakes!

Chili got a call from Angel that he and Mikey wanted to meet early Tuesday morning before they started the first day of high school. It would be a very early morning, since each had an extra hour of commuting time to add to their morning. They would never again be the three musketeers, meeting before school, walking to school, walking home for lunch and hanging out in the schoolyard, and meeting right after school. Now each had to go their own separate way in their journey.

    As soon as Chili reached to fallout shelter doorway in the cellar he knew it was over. There was a brand-new padlock on the door, and no other way to gain entry. He had no choice but to wait in the dank, dark cellar hallway until Mikey and Angel arrived. He heard there was a new porter in the building, hence the change in security on that door, and the door on the other side of the hall. He heard footsteps approaching and hoped it was the guys. It wasn't.

A rotund figure shuffled around the corner and paused. Chili assumed he was being watched, but it was hard to see in the near darkness of the basement. The man walked towards Chili.

"Who are you?" The portly Hispanic man asked. He had a thick mustache, a thick head of salt-and-pepper hair, and wore a one-piece overall with buttons in front.

"I'm William Manzilla. We live on the third floor."

"Are you the one who used this room as club house?"

Chili paused. Should he tell the truth? "Yes."

"Okay. I put a new lock on there. I see you're dressed up with a tie and jacket. You're going to Catholic school?"

"First day of high school."

"My kids just got into St. Gall's. I just started as custodian here in the building. We got the basement apartment. I work in the garment district."

"We clean up after ourselves. It's just a meeting place."

The porter took off the new lock, reached into his pocket and pulled out the old lock. "Here. No noise. No parties. You clean up. No drinking or drugs, okay? If I see one beer can, I put the new lock back."

"Yes, sir. I promise."

The porter turned walked away and Chili entered the room, which looked the same. A few moments later Mikey and Angel appeared, Angel in a tie and jacket and Mikey in his normal street attire of jeans and a short-sleeve shirt.

"Who's the guy we passed by the elevator?" Angel asked.

"We have a new porter. We were locked out at first, but he said he'd let us use it as long as there's no drinking or drugs."

"Even the porter is out to get us!" Mikey said, pulling out a small mini bottle of Southern Comfort.

"Are you nuts?" Chili asked. "On the first day of school?"

Mikey looked at Chili and Angel in their neatly ironed shirts and ties and creased pants. "Yeah, maybe you're right. I'll save it. I've got to get going soon. I have a long walk. I think we need to talk, Chili." Mikey looked at Angel and gave him a knowing nod.

Angel stiffened himself. "We've been thinking about what we saw in the park, Chili. Mikey and I think it's a good idea if we make a pact. We have to swear on our mothers that we'll keep it a secret and never tell anyone what happened that night."

Chili seemed perplexed. He rubbed his cheek and felt a slight bit of stubble. Maybe he should have shaved that morning. "I was thinking the same thing. Let's spit and shake on it."

Each one spat into the palm of his right hand and then shook forcefully with each other. They had only done this ritual one other time. It was when Mikey took out the chocks from a large wooden cable spool, about four feet in diameter, causing it to roll down a hill, where it crashed into a storefront window. It was a spectacular prank gone wrong, that would've been a great story to brag about. But they decided it was better to keep it a secret, as the police were looking for the perpetrators according to the *Bronx Home News*.

"Well, here we go," Angel said, knowing this was the end, and the beginning. "My father told me last night, that we're starting high school as boys, but we'll go out as men."

Mikey added, "Yeah, you can go from getting your high school diploma to becoming fertilizer in a rice paddy in 'Nam."

"You guys want to say a prayer?" Chili asked tentatively.

Mikey and Angel looked at each other. This was a first. With his newfound extreme piety, maybe not telling Chili about the fake Virgin Mary vision was a monumental mistake.

"Uh, sure," Mikey and Angel mumbled.

Chili bowed his head in silence for several moments and said, "Amen."

"Was that it? That was the prayer?" Mikey asked incredulously.

"Yeah, didn't you guys say a prayer in your head?" Chili asked. "I think we better go and I'll lock up."

Mikey and Angel watched as Chili put the old padlock back on the door. They didn't say anything, but they knew. It would never be the same again. Once out on the sidewalk, Mikey started going one way, Angel another, and Chili another.

"See ya."
"See ya."
"See ya."

⋖ Chapter 7 ⋗

Jamie struggled to find two of his own clean socks that matched. He and Chili shared the same sock-and-underwear drawers in the dresser. Usually Chili would throw clean socks and underwear at him while he was still in bed. He went over to the list Chili left for him. He had checked off almost everything, and took the house keys out of the Freedomland ashtray on top of the dresser and stuck them in his pocket.

Having an empty home in the morning made him feel grown up. Nobody yelling at him to get dressed, brush his teeth, eat something... but then he realized he would be late for school if he didn't leave immediately!

There were fewer kids walking to school at this time because it later than usual for him. When Chili walked with him, there were lots of kids on the way to school. Jamie liked the way Chili had multiple conversations with all the kids, no matter what their ages. Sometimes he'd even kid around with parents and the crossing guard. But Jamie was mostly listening.

He just made it into school before the bell and entered his new classroom for sixth-grade. St. Gall's only had one class for each grade. His new teacher was Miss McArdle, who had been at the school for as far back as anyone could remember. In fact, she had been there since the school opened in the early 1950s, and was as much a strict disciplinarian as any of the nuns.

Jamie considered the first day of school a huge success. He didn't raise his hand or get called on once. The only time he talked in class was for attendance and saying the morning prayers. Some of the kids in the class really grew over the summer. Since it was still hot out, the boys were allowed to wear short-sleeve shirts. He noticed that a few of the boys had hairy arms. A couple of them were even showing off their newly developed muscles on their arms.

On the way home after school, Jamie walked by himself and felt very alone, not having Chili chattering and goofing around the whole time. He walked slowly and groups of loud kids passed him by. He could hear them making plans for meeting in the schoolyard, on the stoop, or in Vannie for games or just to hang out. Then there was a tug on the back of his shirt.

"Hi, Jamie."

It was a girl from class, Gerty Greeley.

"Where's Chili?"

"He started high school today."

Now they were walking side-by-side, but silent for twenty or so paces.

"What are you doing after school?" she asked.

Although Gerty wasn't overweight by any means, she did have a very round face and chubby cheeks, which many adults considered very cute. But to kids in her class, she was called fatso, or teased for looking like a chipmunk, or Lucy in *Peanuts*. But never by Jamie.

"I don't know," Jamie replied dryly.

"I have a new Chinese checkers game. You could come by my courtyard and we could play. Do you know how to play Chinese checkers?"

"Yeah."

"I'll see you later in my courtyard."

"Okay."

Jamie fumbled with the four keys that unlocked the four locks on the front door. No sooner did he unlock one, he'd lock another by mistake, and have to start all over again. Then the four locks swiftly were unlocked from inside and the door swung open.

"Goddammit, you woke me up! Get your ass in here and be quiet!"

Mr. Manzilla was in boxer shorts and a T-shirt and had been sleeping on the living room couch.

"Okay. I'll be quiet."

His father was snoring again within a few moments, and almost just as quickly Jamie was in dungarees, a T-shirt, sneakers, and out the door.

The courtyard of Gerty's building wasn't like the others in the neighborhood. This courtyard was a common area for several interconnected apartment buildings that was more like a park. It had benches, hedges, even flower beds. The buildings totally surrounded the courtyard from the street, so kids passing by couldn't see them, which made Jamie feel more comfortable. Unlike the apartment buildings down the hill on Bailey Avenue and Review Place and along West 238th Street, these buildings had mostly old people and not many kids playing. And they were known to house mostly Jewish families.

Jamie knew Gerty lived in the building because he saw her many times walking into the arched stone entrance. But he had never been inside the courtyard referred to other kids as "the maze" because of the expansive network of paths and hedges. He sat on an unoccupied bench and watched as elderly couples shuffled by, some with two-wheeled shopping carts, and some with canes. It was quiet there, unlike the stoops and sidewalks outside rife with buses, cars, the elevated train, and mobs of kids everywhere.

"Hi, Jamie." Gerty said, holding her Chinese checkerboard inside a cardboard box. "I got this for my birthday. You should see the marbles!"

"Hi. I used to play this when we had a board, but I don't know what happened to it," Jamie said, knowing full well that his father destroyed it after stepping on some loose marbles.

Gerty carefully removed the board from the box and placed it between them on the bench. Then she took from the box a fancy-looking cloth bag. "My mom made this bag for the marbles so they don't get lost or loose in the house. You know the rules, right?"

"Yes," Jamie replied, admiring the methodical way Gerty put out the marbles in their proper slots for both of them.

Fallout Shelter

There were many times that Chili tried to get Jamie involved in the many street games he and the boys played each and every day. Curb ball, stickball, king-queen, scully, johnny on the pony, call ball, ring-o-leavio… he didn't like any of those games. They were games where boys cursed, screamed, got into arguments, and many times fist fights over where the ball went or didn't go, fair, foul, late, early, on the line, or over the line. Plus, many times, there were painfully severe stakes on the line for losers: moons up. The losing players would have to bend over with their ass, or "moon," up in the air, and each winner would get three chances to throw the rubber ball called a Spaldeen at the target from about twenty feet away.

Jamie and Gerty sat mostly in silence as they played game after game, keeping note of how many wins each had. Sometimes an elderly person would pause and smile as they observed the two children carefully move their marble to the next position.

"Do you like being an altar boy?"

"I guess so. It was hard to learn everything. And sometimes you get yelled at if you do something wrong. It was easier when I said mass with my brother, but he's in high school now."

"I can't wait for high school," Gerty said, looking to heaven. "Even eighth grade seems so far away."

"I don't like school either."

"Oh, I like school. I just can't wait to go to high school and college. I'm going to be a doctor."

"Can girls be doctors?"

"Of course. My mom is a nurse. And she says they have lady doctors at the hospital. What do you want to be?"

"I don't know. Maybe a priest, like my brother."

"Chili is going to be a priest?"

"I think so."

After almost two hours, Gerty packed up her marbles and they said goodbye with plans to do it again the next day. Maybe she would bring Parchesi. It had been a while so Jamie had such a good time playing with a kid. That was why he mostly stayed home and just watched television. He just didn't like playing those games with the boys on the block.

He again fumbled with his keys at the door locks, but finally got them open. He was relieved to see that his father had already left for work. Chili wasn't home yet, so he just waited for him in front of the television to come home from his first day of high school, so he could have dinner.

Chili could barely contain his excitement as he hung onto the subway car strap with one hand and tried reading a pamphlet with the other as they rocked and rolled up Jerome Avenue on the No. 4 elevated train. There were so many activities to get involved in after school. Today was the day when each club had an open house to showcase their activities. Chili knew he couldn't do everything, so he had to narrow it down to three. Or maybe four. In the lead were the rocket club, the ham-radio club, the poster club, and the one club he knew he would partake in, the vocation club. Each club had a pamphlet prepared with the rules and requirements. It all seemed so professional compared to the rinky-dink activities in grammar school, which consisted of a yearly field day and maybe a school play every three years.

As he read the final paragraph of the pamphlet for the vocation club, his excitement came to a grinding halt, just as the train did, pulling into his stop. The moderator for the vocation club would be Father Palmer. He felt odd thinking that it would be Father P. guiding students to a higher calling, after knowing him the way that he did. I mean, he saw him barfing on the altar boy outing, and acted kind of like a jerk trying to fit in with the guys. Not to mention that Mrs. Madigan pretty much put out a red flag to keep an eye on him around the altar boys. He figured it was because Father P. was probably the youngest priest on the faculty there and would attract the younger generation. Some of

Fallout Shelter

the priests at Corrigan looked like they might have known Christ personally. He had heard from kids who had attended Corrigan that for priests it was the last stop before St. Michael's Nursing Home. Many of the priests who taught at Corrigan lived above the school in small apartments, which made it convenient for older priests who had trouble commuting. But if he wanted to get a head start into making a serious commitment about the priesthood he'd have to sign up for the vocation club to get a leg up on being accepted at a seminary. It just seemed like everything was aligning for his becoming a priest.

It didn't take long for the initial excitement of high school to give way to the harsh reality of academics. Chili had a ninety percent average all through grammar school without much studying. Oh, he paid attention in class and took notes. And he handed in his homework assignments. But basically he cruised through all eight grades without his brain breaking a sweat. That wasn't at all the case in Corrigan.

Every single subject required attention in class, careful note-taking, reading assignments, and written homework to be handed in on a daily basis. Homework was even handed back with red pencil marks throughout with warnings about having to improve fast or else. These weren't just psychological mind games from nuns who needed mental warfare to control classes. Chili had already seen two boys given slaps in the face, with the guarantee that next time, they wouldn't be slaps, but closed-fisted punches.

Compared to the older iron-fisted priests, Father P. was like a rock star. Students flocked to him in the halls and in the cafeteria. When he made an appearance in the vocation club, it was standing-room only that day. Oddly, Father P. didn't pay much attention to Chili, even when Chili went out of his way to be friendly to him. The vocation club only met once a week, and after several months, Chili knew for certain that Father P. was ignoring him as much as possible, and giving him the cold shoulder. Father P. didn't even respond when Chili asked him how Jamie's altar boy skills were progressing. After all, Jamie told him more than a few times he had served as his altar boy. And Chili began to feel that the coolness Father P. was sending his way, which was rubbing off on the other kids in the group who were treating him like an outsider.

As the semester wore on, homework became oppressive, midterms loomed, and the bus and subway commute was brutal. The vocation club became a fan club for Father P. and another youthful Christian Brother whose hair was also slightly over his ear and touching his collar. Chili was so anxious to beat rush hour that he dropped out of the vocation club and was part of the student stampede racing out of school at the bell to catch the first subway car or bus back to their own neighborhood.

Chili's fantasy of high school bliss didn't last any longer than the Thanksgiving leftovers. Chili discovered if he left the house a half hour earlier in the morning he could get all his reading and homework assignments done on the bus and on the subway, and then finishing them off in home room before morning prayers.

Mikey, on the other hand, had no illusions of grandeur about attending DeWitt Clinton, so heading back to the neighborhood minutes after the last school bell of the afternoon was a welcome sight for Chili.

By Christmas vacation, Mikey and Chili were mostly back to the same routine as when they attended grammar school together. Angel, however, apparently had new plans.

Angel was in an advanced placement pre-law program at Fordham Prep, which left little time for socializing. At least as far as Mikey and Chili were concerned.

The fallout shelter didn't seem the same with only Chili and Mikey. They had given up calling him on the phone. He never answered or returned calls after they left messages. They even stopped going over to his neighborhood to call on him after they saw some kids going in the front door, dressed in Fordham Prep sweaters and hats. But they weren't mad at him.

Fallout Shelter

They figured he'd be back soon, and things would be like the old days: The three musketeers!

Jamie and Gerty saw a lot of each other. He had been to her apartment on rainy days, and met her little sister, her mother, father, and even her grandmother and grandfather who lived in the same building. He wished his father was like Gerty's father, and thought that if his mother was alive she might be like Gerty's mother. Although her parents sometimes were loud or even yelled, they were funny when they were doing it. Grandma, grandpa, and the kids would be laughing along. Jamie tried to forget the bad memories of his mom and dad fighting. And whenever his dad got angry, he still couldn't help but re-live those awful feelings. There were days at Gerty's when girlfriends of hers from the building would come by to hang out. He enjoyed the way the girls played Parchesi or Monopoly or Clue. They weren't mean about winning or losing.

Chili made Jamie's favorite meal: breaded chicken cutlets, just the way their mom used to make them. It was a Sunday "go to" meal that he, Jamie, Mikey, and Mr. Manzilla enjoyed the most, even though dear old dad wasn't there most of the time, including tonight.

"Pass the mashed potatoes, please," Jamie said.

Chili was glad to pass the mashed potatoes. Jamie seemed to be eating more, and even may have put on a few pounds and grown an inch. He hadn't gotten any complaints from any teachers, and his grades had improved to mostly B's.

"Is everything going well in school, Jamie?" Chili asked.

"Yeah. I made some new friends."

"Who?"

"Gerty Greeley and some friends from her building in the maze."

"The maze?" Mikey asked. "You go to the maze? Aren't there a lot of Jewish people there?"

"Yeah," Jamie said. "Some of them are Holocaust survivors."

"Who told you that?" Chili questioned him.

"Mr. Greeley. You can even see the tattoos the Nazis put on some people. I looked it up in the encyclopedia and it's true. I took a picture of one."

"With what camera?" Chili asked.

Jamie's eyes bugged out. "Um, Mr. Greeley lent me his camera when we were on the bench and some friends of his dropped by from the building. They showed us their tattoos and said that we should 'never forget.' I asked if I could take a picture and Gerty's father had his Kodak Instamatic, so he let me take a picture. He said he would give the photo to me when he got it developed." He paused, and waited to see Chili and Mikey's reactions. To Jamie's great relief they just nodded their heads in acknowledgement and kept shoving chicken cutlets and mashed potatoes in their gaping mouths.

Jamie didn't take the picture with Mr. Greeley's camera at all. He took the picture with the camera that Chili hid in his safe. From the moment Jamie first saw that miniature camera he was obsessed with it. He was amazed at how such a tiny replica of a full-size 35mm camera could look so authentic. He marveled at its small viewfinder, the texture of faux black leather that covered the body of the camera. The printing on the front of the lens. The knob to advance the film. And it all worked! He hoped. Yes, he took it and he intended to keep it for himself. He even had a super top-secret hiding place for it. Maybe one day he'd return it Chili. But in addition to keeping the secret of the stolen miniature camera safe, Jamie discovered something even more important: he was a good liar. He thought up story about Mr. Greeley lending him the camera on the spot, and embellished it to perfection.

Mrs. Madigan finished unpacking the last box into the dresser drawer formerly used by Father P. in his old room at the St. Gall's Church rectory. It took months, but the Archdiocese finally found a priest that could reside there full-time and perform all the duties of the second-in-command under the

Fallout Shelter

monsignor, which would mean doing almost everything since the monsignor was about 26 rounds of golf from retirement.

    Father Robert LaVerne had bounced around the entire New York Metropolitan area. For a man of forty-five years old, he had more transfers than a commuter on a crosstown bus. From Yonkers to Babylon to Bay Ridge to Harlem he taught in grammar schools, then high schools, then went from parish to parish. He hoped he had found a home, here in a small parish in the Northwest Bronx.

    Mrs. Madigan had already gone through his file when it came in the mail for the monsignor. She opened all his mail for him. And she knew exactly what his itinerant journey meant. She'd have to also keep a keen eye on this one. He wasn't a rookie like Father P., who was an attention-getter, dressing like a teenager and thirsty for attention and acceptance from the young people, with long hair, sideburns, and bell-bottoms. Father LaVerne looked the part of a traditional middle-aged priest. Slightly overweight, black horn-rimmed glasses, never seen without his collar, short hair neatly parted, clean-shaven, polished leather shoes. Yes, she'll have to observe his every move.

    Father LaVerne missed teaching high school. He missed the camaraderie. Not of his fellow teachers, but of the students. Especially the older students who were discovering themselves. It wasn't like when he was in high school, where a boy who knew he was different was afraid to be himself. It was the only aspect of the "now generation" he thought had any redeeming value whatsoever. He longed for the days when mass was in Latin, and it was the priest who influenced young minds, not degenerate folk singers like Bob Dylan.

    Father LaVerne's first formal meeting with Monsignor Shannon went extremely well. He looked forward to taking on many of the administrative duties of the parish when the monsignor retired probably within a year. They sat going over budgets, bank accounts, the Liturgical Calendar, fill-in priests, and other nuts-and-bolts business. There was not a mention of

Father LaVerne's transfers, except for small talk about assignments and priestly name-dropping. The monsignor didn't like getting involved in matters that were strictly under the purview of the Archdiocese and were none of his business. He had a retirement and pension to think about.

"Oh, one last thing, before we wrap things up here, Robert," Monsignor Shannon said, waving to Mrs. Madigan in the adjoining room, "please meet the most important person in the parish, Mrs. Madigan. She's been the heart and soul of St. Gall's Parish since the cornerstone was laid in 1949. If you have questions about anything, she's the go-to person, down to the color of the vestments on the third Sunday of Advent and where to get the best deal on sanctified wine."

"It's a pleasure to meet you, Mrs. Madigan. I look forward to working with you," Father LaVerne said with as much warmth as a wilted flower.

"I'm here to see that you and the parish get everything needed for the Mother Church," Mrs. Madigan replied with a wink and a nod, as she glanced over to the monsignor.

After she left their sight, the monsignor whispered, "She can be a bit harsh at times, but she does more for the parish in ways we don't even know about."

"I'll keep that in mind," Father LaVerne said, getting up.

"By the way, any visitors to the rectory have to be cleared through Mrs. Madigan."

"Even personal guests?"

"Yes, and also for any, um, late-night-outs or overnight excursions."

"Really."

"I'm afraid so, yes. It makes things easier for me. And for Mrs. Madigan. When you put in your notification for guests, she'll prepare anything you may need as far as, um, refreshments and things of that nature."

"Of course. Thank you, Monsignor."

Fallout Shelter

Father LaVerne wasn't upset about the house rules. In fact, he knew he was going to change his ways and this was the perfect opportunity. He needed guardrails in his personal life, just as the regulations of the church provided direction in his spiritual life. The past was the past and he was grateful to the Archdiocese for understanding his predicament and adjusting his duties accordingly. When he got that woman in trouble he merely *helped* her take care of it. It was her choice to terminate it. He only *paid* for it.

He looked forward to working on the new plans the church had for a bell tower, and remodeling the interior with new pews, tapestries, and statuary. He'd be working with an architect, interior decorators, and making important decisions with a budget of at least a hundred thousand dollars.

He pulled the files for the remodeling project out of a drawer and laid them out in his desk. *I think we'll need an extra collection during mass for this*, he thought to himself.

Thanksgiving, Christmas, New Year's, and midterms came and went. Chili never worked so hard for a B-minus average. And his fantasy of a transformation once high school kicked in was already as dead as the Yankees' hope for another world-championship team, heading into spring training of 1973. In fact Chili's net worth was about as bad as the neighboring Yankees, who were just sold for three million clams less than they were bought for almost twenty years ago! His day camp earnings and other savings from odd jobs had run dry. Chili knew he needed a job. Bad. He hated asking his father for money. It was always a battle trying to explain that he and Jamie needed food, shoes, clothes, and other "luxuries for spoiled kids," as his father put it. But between bar tabs from Times Square to the 242nd Street terminal and gambling losses to bookies in every one of those gin mills, Mr. Manzilla needed a ten-way parlay at Belmont to get back on his feet. And a few more long-shot misses could mean a couple of broken legs. Chili needed a job and Angel was his best hope.

The February snows were almost gone, exposing the trash and dog poop that were hidden below. Chili knew if he waited long enough outside Angel's house he'd eventually meet up with him. March came in like a lion, and Chili stood across the street feeling like limping gazelle as his worn sneakers took on melting winter waters flowing down the sidewalk. Finally, there was Angel, coming up the city steps and heading for home.

"Yo, Angel!" Chili yelled crossing the street, hands shoved in is corduroy jacket pockets.

Angel stopped and looked at Chili, but wasn't smiling or waving. Chili took note of that, but continued on to greet him warmly.

"Hi, Angel, long time no see. Or hear."

"Chili? What are you doing standing in this crappy weather?"

"Oh, I was in the neighborhood and...."

"Let's go inside. We'll get some hot chocolate."

It was warm and toasty inside Angel's. Chili took off his wet sneakers and was embarrassed that his big toe was sticking out of a sock.

They sat at the kitchen table and Angel warmed-up some hot water for instant hot chocolate. Chili studied Angel's every move and expression. He knew he was deep in thought and worried what might be on his mind. Would he shut him out, like he has been doing?

"What have you been doing?" Chili blurted out.

"Oh, man. I'm sorry, Chili. I've been meaning to call you guys. I'm studying like a monk! I'm in several advanced-placement classes, I joined the debating club, and I started dating a girl I met at a dance."

"I wouldn't call me either if I was that busy! Who's the girl?"

"Actually, she's in school with one of our old classmates, Pamela Hinderlap."

Fallout Shelter

Chili was stunned. He forgot about his cold toes and his empty pockets. He hadn't heard from Pamela, and was afraid to call her for fear that she'd have a new life and no time for him, just like Angel. "Oh, how is Pamela?"

"I have no idea. She just mentioned that she knew her from class. Her name is Linda Piscotty. She lives in Throgs Neck so it's a schlep to be able to see her."

"Sounds like you are really busy. Are you working?"

"At the stores? No. My dad wants me to concentrate on school."

"Angel...."

"Is something wrong, Chili? I know I've been a jerk."

"No no. I hate to ask you, but...."

"What? Anything you want. Except Linda's number. Shoot."

"Could you ask your dad if I could work in one of his stores?"

"Done. What else? Does Mikey need a job?"

"I think so."

"Done. And you can have Linda's number if you really want. Hey, maybe we can double date or something!"

"Yeah. Maybe. Let me talk to Mikey. Can we call you or your dad to set up the jobs?"

"Call me, and I promise I'll take care of it. Maybe we should do a fallout shelter powwow like old times."

"That's what I'd like!"

Chili had a bounce in his still-damp socks and sneakers as he pondered his immediate future possibilities. Getting the old crew together and Pamela too! And spring training would be soon starting, where every team in baseball goes in thinking they have a shot at a winning season. Players that had miserable years get a new shot at redemption. Teams that finished at the bottom, make changes and think new, untested players can miraculously go from the minor-league sensations to becoming superstar major leaguers. But the majors are not the minors. And high school is not grammar school.

The fallout shelter get-together was impossible to arrange. Angel kept changing his mind with different excuses. Chili can take a hint. But Angel did come through for him and Mikey with jobs at the Inwood bodega his father owned. It was only a few train stops away, and when the weather improved it would be an easy bike ride down Broadway.

Mikey was busy cleaning the back-room toilet while Chili was mopping the floor in the stock room after the store closed at ten. Mr. Rodriquez would come by a half hour or so after closing to inspect the cleanliness and preparations for the next day, and collect the day's receipts.

"Mr. Rodriguez isn't exactly Mr. Rogers when Angel's not here working with us," Mikey said, cleaning the bowl with a brush. "He used to cut us all kinds of slack."

"I'm just glad to have a job. My father's tighter than Jack Benny shopping at John's Bargain Store for Christmas presents," Chili said, squeezing the dirty water out of the mop head.

"Yeah, I shouldn't complain. It must be nice not having to worry about money," Mikey said, dropping his toilet brush into his sudsy bucket. He went over to the walk-in refrigerator, entered, and came out with a can of Pabst Blue Ribbon.

"You better watch out. Mr. Rodriguez is coming any minute."

Mikey removed the pop-top and gulped the beer in one long swallow, finishing off the contents. "That was less than a minute. So no harm, no foul, and *buuuurrrrppp*."

"That was disgusting," Chili said, laughing.

"But it felt good. I better hide the can in the trash."

Mr. Rodriquez arrived, thanked them both, and locked the door behind them as they headed for the train home. It was always too noisy to have a conversation while riding the train, so they sat in the deafening silence together.

Chili hoped his father was either asleep or not home. It was almost eleven and he still had some homework to do. And

Fallout Shelter

he knew he had to attend to Jamie in the morning. He had barely seen him for days.

While half asleep, Chili heard the sound of the front door shutting and the locks being locked from the outside, which meant his father had just left for work. Chili liked getting up at five-thirty after his father left because it gave him some time in a quiet house before he had to get Jamie up and ready for school. Coffee was made, toast buttered, and orange juice downed, while WINS news radio recounted every murder, fatal car crash, subway mugging, and tragic house fire from the night before. The bedroom door opened and a sleepy Jamie shuffled to the bathroom for a tinkle. The door reopened and Jamie was headed back to bed.

"Hey!" Chili shouted. "I didn't hear a toilet flush or a faucet run to wash hands!"

"Huh?" Jamie said, pausing, still half asleep. Turning his head, he reached up to his eye and winced in pain, revealing an ugly shiner.

Chili rushed over to examine it up close. "What happened to you?"

"Um, nothing."

"Don't bullshit me. What the hell happened?"

"I fell."

"On your eye?"

"I hit a...step. On a stoop."

"I said don't bullshit me!" Chili said, grabbing him forcefully by the shoulders.

"I got punched in the face."

"By who?"

"Some kids I didn't know. When I was playing in the maze with Gerty and her friends."

"Why did they punch you? What happened? Tell me."

"We were playing Chinese checkers and these boys came and they knocked over the board. They were yelling stuff and I told them to shut up and one of them hit me when I wasn't looking."

"What were they yelling?"

Jamie pursed his lips in defiance and scowled, lowering his head.

"Go ahead."

"They called me a faggot sissy."

"Let's go back to bed. You've got another half-hour to sleep," Chili said, patting him on the head and leading him to the bed. "You got sucker-punched."

"What's that?"

"That's when a coward hits you when you're not looking. There's nothing you can do about that. But in the future, you've got to put your hands up and protect yourself. And fight back!"

"I don't know how."

"I'll show you. I don't know much, but I'll show you what I know. Get some rest."

"Chili?"

"Yeah," Chili said turning around just before he exited the room.

"What's a faggot?"

"It's like, the same as a sissy."

"You mean like somebody who plays with girls?"

"Well, something like that. I'll get you up in a little while."

"Oh, and Chili, one more thing."

"What?"

"I didn't cry. They couldn't make me cry."

Chili knew what it was like to be bullied. And he knew Jamie might have a harder time with bullies than he did. There were always kids around who didn't play sports, or take part in roughneck street games where moons-up for losers or fistfights among friends were everyday occurrences. Some kids were just different. They sometimes played with girls, stayed home a lot, or were rarely seen without their sister or their mom. And they were very well-behaved in class. Those kids may have been called teacher's pet or mamma's boy, or worse. But in high school, you started to hear new a new word whispered instead of sissy: *homo*. Chili had just discovered that it was short for *homosexual*. And that was something Chili didn't know much about. Kind of like some other sexual terms he was starting to hear, like *blowjob* and *sixty-nine*, which he wasn't quite sure about either. So there was more to being a sissy than just being "a fairy nice boy" and playing mostly with girls. He was shocked to learn that guys actually did it with guys. They had no sexual desires for females. In fact, he heard in the locker room at Corrigan that you couldn't always tell if a guy was a homosexual by the way they spoke or carried themselves. Some were athletes, actors, rock stars, and even priests.

PART TWO
3 YEARS LATER
∽ Chapter 8 ∾

In most high schools, senior year was a welcomed goal for the vast majority of students. The classes were a little bit easier, the fashion and grooming regulations less severe, and the teachers more forgiving. But that wasn't the case for Chili at Archbishop Corrigan.

He had sweated it out for three and a half years of haircut inspections, watching kids get their heads slammed into blackboards for talking back to priests who had liquor on their breath, and struggling to keep up with an academic curriculum which seemed more in line with the previous century. Four years of Latin, three years of French, Western Civilization I, II, and III, advanced Algebra and Calculus, Business Law I and II, Chemistry, Physics, English, and American History made him feel like he was drowning in a sea of outdated textbooks. And senior year was no better. Another year of Latin and French, Fortran programming, Trigonometry, and World Religions kept his eyes glued to the pages as they bounced off his knees on countless subway and bus rides.

Chili welcomed his after-school job at the Rodriguez bodega, which kept his mind off Latin verb conjugations and on the proper way to season a rump roast before putting it in an oven. The one class that kept Chili interested from freshman year and into senior year was Religion I, II, III, and IV. Yeah, there was memorization, and complex Bible history to understand, but each year seemed to be slowly building towards a climax. Freshman year began with a repeat of Catechism as taught by the nuns with question-and-answer sessions memorized out of the *Baltimore Catechism*, first published in 1885. But by the end of freshman year, the class was analyzing popular song lyrics by Bob Dylan, Pete Seeger, and The Beatles, and revealing their significance to popular culture, politics, and spirituality.

One seemingly simple chart drawn by freshman-year religion teacher, Brother Dodge, was an eye-opener for Chili. So much so that he wondered why in all the years of going to Catholic school, being taught by dozens of priests, nuns, and brothers, with Catechisms, Old Testaments, New Testaments, and religion textbooks, no else ever presented it in such a way. On the top of the blackboard in middle he wrote *The Catholic Church*. Underneath on the left he wrote *Institutional*. Underneath on the right side he wrote *Spiritual*. With easy input from this class of 14 year olds he began adding to the *Institutional* column. He wrote *Vatican, Churches, Golden Chalices, The Pope, Sunday Mass, Christmas, Easter, Cathedrals, Priests*. When it was time to write under the *Spiritual* column, the students were a little bit slower with suggestions. Then he wrote, *Love they neighbor as thyself, Feed the Poor, Clothe the naked, Give to the poor, Thou shalt not kill, Pray to Jesus*. Of course, the *Pray to Jesus* was forever close to Chili's heart, as they were his mom's last words.

By sophomore year, the lives of the saints, such as St. Francis of Assisi, St. Paul, and St. Joan of Arc were studied. Of course most kids slept through class, but to Chili this was part of his own journey. Ever since he promised his mother on her deathbed he would always be a good Catholic he did all he could to keep his word. And of course, seeing a vision of the Virgin Mary made him believe there was more expected of him than just attending mass on Sundays. Religion class provided context as they went from the Old Testament to the New, and studied the words of Jesus.

But at the same time in sophomore year, there were whispers in the halls and in the locker room during gym. Some priests were rumored to be doing more than just being friendly with students. There was talk of drinking, drug-taking, and even orgies. All within the confines of this all-boys high school. In Chili's mind, Father Palmer was suspected to be one of those fallen angels, but Chili had no evidence. And since his brother, Jamie, was a freshman now, he tried to keep a close eye on him and his interactions with the priests and brothers he had as teachers.

    Jamie had grown into a normal, quiet, average student at Archbishop Corrigan, and seemed to be fitting in. He even found an interest as a photographer on the school newspaper. Chili was unaware of Jamie having any disciplinary problems, and he made a few friends whom he even got together with on weekends.

    The moderator of the school newspaper, Father O'Brennan was one of the most popular priests in the school. He was also a full-time guidance counselor. Father James O'Brennan had the map of Ireland across his slightly pudgy middle-aged face. Laughing eyes, freckles that were turning into age spots, oversized teeth that gleamed with his ear-to-ear smile. Chili was glad that a guidance counselor was a constant presence at the newspaper. Jamie needed someone like that. Father O'Brennan always had a following of kids whenever he was spotted in the cafeteria, hallways, or at a game. He could tell a joke and have a good laugh, but when it came to schoolwork and respect, he was no-nonsense. He was firm but fair. Or so he said. Chili got a taste of his "firm" side one day when he dared go to his locker when he wasn't supposed to. Without warning O'Brennan pushed his face hard into the steel locker door. Chili's jaw felt the firm steel, but didn't think that was at all fair.

By senior year, the three musketeers had gotten back together. Mikey, Angel, and Chili had made new friends in high school, but after almost four years of hanging out with new kids in new neighborhoods, from Throgs Neck to North Riverdale, there was nothing like the kids you grew up with. And working summers together in the bodegas made those bonds even stronger. They had fought off shoplifters, junkies, and drunks

Fallout Shelter

together. Provided underage friends with cases of beer for parties in the park. Gone to concerts in Central Park and Madison Square Garden and attended funerals of relatives and even some friends who fell victim of youthful indiscretions such as car accidents, drunken mishaps, drug overdoses, and booby traps in Viet Nam.

Chili found it hard to believe that the guys were getting together in the fallout shelter to talk about graduating high school. It seemed like yesterday that they snuck beer onto the boat ride for their graduation from grammar school. But here they were. This time would be different. Chili would be making an announcement about his future. Mikey had been giving hints that he was looking into taking the firemen's or police test. Angel was on a fast track to law school. But Chili had kept mum about his life plan: the priesthood. He knew all along it would put a damper and their good times together. Drinking, dating, attending rock concerts, smoking weed, and X-rated discussions about sex weren't exactly conducive when one of the participants would soon be on a lectern giving a lecture about those very things.

"Just like old times," Mikey said, pulling a six-pack of Pabst out of a paper bag as he entered the musty meeting place.

"At least you're of legal drinking age now," Angel said, offering a Marlboro to the others.

"This place smells worse than I remember," Chili said, pulling down spider webs. "I wonder if the saltines and water will keep 85 families alive after a nuclear bomb falls on the Bronx."

Angel took a drag on his cigarette and popped open a Pabst. "Have you seen the news? I think a nuclear bomb has already fallen on the South Bronx."

Mikey was already downing the last few gulps of his can of Milwaukee brew. "Yeah, I figure if I'm a cop or fireman, I'll have enough to keep me busy 'til I'm ready to collect my pension. Hey, are you guys going to your prom?"

Angel nodded in the affirmative. "I am. I'm bringing this girl I just met in a corporate law class. She's a freshman at Fordham University."

"A college girl? Oh man, you better make sure you have some protection when you take the limo out to Rockaway to watch the sun rise on the beach!" Mikey added. "What about you, Chili? Are you taking Pamela Hinderlap?"

"Pamela? I haven't heard from her since she moved out of the neighborhood a few years ago. Nah, I'm not going. It's too expensive anyway."

"I thought you two might be a thing freshman year," Angel said.

"Yeah, me too. I just gave up trying to find her," Chili said, with regret in his voice.

After small talk about school, working at the bodega, and neighborhood gossip, Chili used a lull in the conversation to drop his bombshell.

"Guys, I have an announcement to make."

"An announcement?" Mikey said, befuddled. "What is this? Homeroom?"

"I made a decision about…my future. I'm going into the seminary."

Mikey and Angel looked at each other sideways, with worried expressions.

Angel was the first to speak up. "We sort of figured that might happen. Was there… something that kind of… sealed the deal for you?"

Chili went into deep thought. But Angel knew exactly what Mikey was thinking: Was it because he was "chosen" to be a priest by the hash-brownie Virgin Mary hoax they perpetrated on him all those years ago?

"Not exactly one thing. But sort of a promise I made to my mom. She said I should always look for signs."

Mikey snuffed out his cigarette under his foot. "And… did you see many of these… signs?"

"Oh yeah. Mostly little things. And some big ones."

Mikey and Angel didn't want to press the issue and just shook their heads.

Changing the mood of the room, Angel chimed in, "I have an announcement, too. And in light of Chili's announcement, I think it makes even more sense."

"Shoot," Mikey said, welcoming a direction far from dashing the dreams of his friend with a confession of a cruel prank.

"I got a car: a 1966 Volkswagon Squareback. And right after graduation, I'm planning on a cross-country trip, and both of you have to come with me! My dad said we can have as much time off as we want. He'll even give you guys two weeks vacation pay as a bonus. We can camp out every night, and split the expenses three ways. It'll cost hardly anything. I'm buying the tent and all the camping gear. It'll be the trip of a lifetime!"

Mikey opened another beer. "I'm in!"

"I'm not sure, guys. I have to report to the seminary in late August."

"Even if we go for six weeks, we'll be back way before that," Angel said enthusiastically.

"I'll have to check with my dad and Jamie, but I think I'd like to do it."

Slaps on the back and high fives went around as the excitement grew. Yellowstone, the Grand Canyon, Zion National, Vegas, L.A., Hollywood, San Francisco, Haight-Ashbury all were mentioned with great anticipation and excitement. Even by Chili.

"Yeah, the more I think about this," Chili said, finally taking a Pabst from the bag. "The more I think it's something I need to do."

Chili took a few sips of his beer without much guilt because his eighteenth birthday was only days away. He'd be able to drink, vote, and have to sign up for a draft card, but without the fear of being sent off to the jungle to kill. The Vietnam War was winding down and so was the dread of signing-up for selective service. Chili had already decided that if called, he would go. That was the law and he would follow it. He knew there was at least one, and possible two or three, Brothers at Corrigan who used their vocation to avoid the draft. Chili couldn't reconcile the fact that they were advocates for following the rules of the school and church, but not adhering to the rules of the government. And if they were avoiding draft, shouldn't they be instructing their students to also avoid the draft? But as far as he could tell, they didn't utter a word against the war in class. Maybe they were afraid that the ultra-conservative priests in the Corrigan administration wouldn't like it, and blow their own cover.

    As the three musketeers sat there, smoking, drinking, talking about their summer's big adventure, Chili couldn't help but reflect on how his two best friends had changed. Mikey was always such a daring class clown, willing to risk the wrath of weaponized measuring instruments wielded by enraged nuns for the payoff of a roomful of laughs. He also had no fear when it came to risking a punch in the face whether it was from a fellow wise-ass teenager, or an adult asshole, even if it was a family member. Chili had been worried that in attending DeWitt Clinton, where there is virtually no discipline and not much structure, that Mikey would fall through the cracks and wind up like one of the pool room bookies, druggies, or violent blowtop alkeys. Whether or not it was due to lower expectations at Clinton or not, Mikey had a solid B average all four years and seemed on track to be a cop or fireman, both highly honored positions for anyone growing up in the city in the sick Seventies and wanting to make a difference.

    The South Bronx was literally burning, weekly murder stats outdid 'Nam fatalities, and crime was so out of control, merely going out was accepting the fact that there was a 50-50 chance you'd be faced with loss of life, limb, or property. And the subways? You had no choice but to sit in the urine-soaked, floor-to-ceiling graffitied cars with fellow travelers hoping the psychos, perverts, and common thieves wouldn't pick you. Yet, Mikey was ready to jump into the belly of the beast to get the bad guys or run into burning Bronx buildings to save babies. His lankiness and boney physique had developed into a muscular, yet lean athletic body which, given the proper coaching and training, could probably play college basketball, baseball, football, or track. Mikey had other priorities.

If Chili had to guess in eighth grade what would become of Angel after high school, he would have thought he would study business in college and eventually take over his father's bodega business and transform them into a successful chain of supermarkets. And like Mikey, Angel found a new focus in high school. His plan to become a lawyer, and eventually become a prosecutor, also meant immersing oneself into battlefield of New York City. The courts were constantly mentioned as one of the columns of civilization that had collapsed, allowing crime and depravity to rule supreme in the streets. The revolving door at the courts was allowing crime from the gutters and corruption from the highest levels of government and corporate penthouses to run rampant. Not to mention the vast networks of the Italian, Black, Puerto Rican, Russian, and Chinese mobsters that supplied the prostitutes, drugs, and weapons that kept the working classes under siege.

And the fact that Chili had also made a choice to also take on crime and corruption in their most primitive form, i.e. sin, he felt that somehow the three of them had in fact come to the same conclusion about how to deal with the mess that New York had become: Take it on directly and try to do something about it. The fact that all three had such different home lives and attended separate high schools, yet somehow landed on similar life paths, made him think there was more to their grammar school education and friendship that he ever realized.

"I'm going to have to run this cross-country trip past my dad and Jamie before I commit," Chili said, "I think they'll go along with it, now that Jamie's been a little more responsible."

Mikey placed the empties in the brown bag. "Chili, you didn't finish your beer? Okay, I will. How did Jamie do freshman year? Corrigan is a big sports school. Did he find somewhere to fit in?"

"He did. He took up photography with the school newspaper. Sometimes he comes home from school pretty late."

"Shit," Angel said, "that little kid riding the subway late at night. That's not even safe for the undercover cops."

"On the really late nights, he gets a ride home from one of the priests. The moderator of the paper, Father O'Brennan."

Mikey and Angel looked at each other, as if Chili just said Jamie got a ride home from the headless horseman. "Do you know this Father O'Brennan?" Angel asked, sounding like a future prosecuting attorney.

"Yeah, I know him. Everybody knows Father O'Brennan. He's very popular. Very upbeat."

"Did he ever drive you home?" Mikey asked, adding to the mood of interrogation.

"No. What's with you guys? I never was in one of his clubs or activities."

Angel followed up. "Are you familiar with all of his activities?"

"That's it. No more joking. Let's get out of here."

Angel and Mikey dropped the subject, and they walked to the usual corner where they split in different directions for home. But Chili couldn't help but wonder about Father O'Brennan. He thought he lived above the school in the priest's residences. So why would he drive Jamie all the way home? That's like a half-hour drive to and a half-hour drive back to the school. Chili had heard rumors about certain priests, but never about Father O'Brennan. A priest so outgoing and extroverted would have to be extra careful if he was involved in any *shenanigans*, as Father McGoldrick, the dean of discipline, might refer to some sinful behavior.

Jamie was sitting at the kitchen table going over some papers when Chili entered the sweltering apartment. Every window was wide open, and the breeze buzzed through the venetian blinds, sounding like a rattlesnake. The overhead multicolored plastic lamp with a single light bulb created almost the same effect as a stained glass window in a church.

"Oh, Jamie, I'm glad I caught you. What are you doing?"

"I've got a form for daddy to sign. And I need forty-three dollars. The school paper staff is going on a retreat up in the Adirondacks."

"A retreat. That sounds good. Who are the chaperones?"

"The senior student council members and Father O'Brennan."

"Oh. Father O'Brennan. We were just talking about him. Me, Mikey and Angel."

"Why?"

"Just that it's so cool of him to give you a ride home sometimes when you are working late at the school paper."

"Yeah."

"He's a good guy?"

"Yeah."

"Where does he sleep?"

"Huh?" Jamie said, with umbrage.

"Where does he sleep? Where does he live, actually?"

"He lives partly at the school residences and partly at Mount Angel Seminary in Yonkers."

"How do you know?"

"Everybody knows. Can I have the forty-three dollars?"

"Yes, you can have it. But you better find a job this summer. Do you know where dad is? I need to talk to him."

"He went to the deli and said he'd be right back."

Chili went over the forms, flyers, and pamphlets on the Formica table. The high-glossy, full-color brochure of the Adirondack locale featured a resort with a lake, a pool, nearby horseback riding, and challenging hiking trails. "This looks great! I've never been to the Adirondacks. I hear they're magnificent."

"It's a retreat, so we'll also have mass and prayer sessions."

"I didn't think you went for that sort of thing."

"Well, all the guys on the school paper are going. Father O'Brennan said it would be good for me to go, so I can advance on the staff. I'm only an assistant photographer, and I do mostly filing."

"That's one way to get ahead."

Jamie and Chili turned their heads like dogs hearing a firecracker. It was the locks being opened on the front door.

Mr. Manzilla entered with a doubled brown paper bag that fits four quarts of Rheingold perfectly.

"Hi. I have to leave for work in two hours," Mr. Manzilla said, putting one quart on the kitchen table and the other three in the refrigerator. He set down put a large tumbler, filled it, and drank most of it in one gulp. "What's all this?"

"Jamie needs your permission to go on an overnight school trip...."

"How much?"

"It's forty-three dollars, but I'll pay for it."

"Gimme a pen," he said, and scribbled his signature on the form.

"And I wanted to make sure if it was alright with you and Jamie, if I went on a trip for a month or so."

Jamie was stunned. His eyes bugged out, and his jaw dropped so quickly you could almost hear it crack. "A month?"

"I don't care. As long as your brother can take care of himself and not let this place go to hell in a handbasket," Mr. Manzilla said, finishing off his beer, grabbing the bottle, and going toward the bedroom. "I'm taking a nap. Keep it down."

Chili studied Jamie, who was fingering through the papers and pamphlet on the table. "Jamie, are you sure can handle everything? Finishing up at school, shopping, cleaning the house?"

"Yeah, I can do it. I'll be fine. A whole month?"

"Maybe a little more."

"Where are you going?"

"Me, Mikey, and Angel are going cross-country in Angel's sixty-six VW. We're gonna see America, and camp out every night!"

"I should be all right."

"If you're worried about something, let me know. I don't have to go."

"No. You should go. When are you leaving?"

"Probably in a week or so."

"I'll be fine," Jamie said, with a hint of sadness in his voice and on his face.

Chili gathered dirty laundry from the hamper in the bathroom and assorted piles of clothes in the bedroom. He was stuffing them into a couple of pillowcases for the trip to the laundry room in the basement. Just as he was shoving the last bit into a pillowcase, it fell to the floor. When he stooped down to pick up the clothes that spilled onto the bedroom floor, he noticed a balled-up towel under Jamie's bed. But he didn't recognize it as one of their towels from home. In fact, it looked like one of the cheap, thin towels from gym class at Corrigan. He unrolled the towel and found a pair of what had to be Jamie's underpants. *What the hell?* Chili thought to himself. The seat of the underwear was stained with a large blotch of blood. Chili heard Jamie walking towards the bedroom. He quickly rolled up the underwear back into the towel and put it in the pillowcase.

"I'm going to do some laundry. Do you have anything else to go?"

"No. Nothing," Jamie said, barely above a whisper.

"Okay," Chili said, carrying the bags over his shoulder like a sad Santa on the way to the laundromat.

The next day, Chili stood by the window, looking down the street as he waited for Angel and Mikey to pull in front with the VW. Angel limited each guy to two medium-sized bags. It was a hot, muggy Wednesday morning with the sun barely above the apartment buildings to the east. It had rained the night before, so the street had a clean sheen to it, for maybe the next half hour. That is if you ignored the trash in the gutter, the overflowing garbage cans blocking the sidewalks, and the graffiti painted on the side of the building. And there it was. The 1966 Volkswagen Squareback was VW's attempt to build a car that would be an upgrade to the Beetle. And by upgrade, that meant about twenty more horsepower, or enough to go up a hill with three adults instead of two, and have more room for humans and cargo. The engine was in the rear, which allowed for a few items to be placed in the front trunk, where usually a normal-sized engine would go. But the geniuses at VW placed the engine under the rear deck of the vehicle, the "square back" part, so that all the noise and fumes from the engine compartment can easily enter the passenger compartment. Naturally all the windows had to be opened at all times, regardless of the weather. Air conditioning? You're kidding, right?

But to Chili, as he raced down the stairs with his two bags and a paper sack with three baloney sandwiches, it might as well have been a brand-new Cadillac with all the extras. Even though he was soon turning eighteen, he could count on his fingers the number of times he had even been in a car. And most of those were with adult relatives. Having a father who worked for the transit authority, meant *why get a car if you can get train and bus passes for free?*

The car rumbled with that familiar oversized-lawnmower VW engine sound as Chili put his bags in the front trunk. Angel was in the driver's seat, and Mikey in the shotgun position, with road atlases, unfolded maps, and a compass on his lap. Chili sat in the back seat, in the space that was available next to a Coleman stove a sleeping bag, and a cooler piled on top.

"Do we have everything?" Angel asked, his unshaven face beaming with pride and anticipation.

Fallout Shelter

"Co-pilot says yes!" Mikey exclaimed, holding up the compass.

"Co-co-pilot agrees!" Chili said, grabbing the top of the front seats with both hands and leaning in between.

Angel revved the engine, put it into first gear, and with a transmission that sounded like it had a rinky-dink chain drive instead of a driveshaft, they were headed to the George Washington Bridge, which led to all points west.

"We're off!" Angel said, gunning the engine up the ramp to the bridge.

"I hope the semi on our ass doesn't push us off the freakin' bridge!" Mikey chortled.

Chili turned around as they crossed the plaque that marked the border between New York and New Jersey. He hadn't seen the skyline of Manhattan from this perspective since Uncle Joey drove them to Aunt Dotty's house in Hackensack. That was his mom's sister. He hadn't seen them since the funeral. He knew things would be different since she passed, and God bless it, they were different. And he hoped this trip west would open his eyes to the world out there. His father once told him New York died when the Dodgers and Giants both deserted the city for the West Coast.

"What street was the Polo Grounds on?" Chili asked.

"Around 150th Street," Mikey replied. "But you can't see it from here."

"Yeah, especially since it's been gone since the early Sixties," Angel said, maneuvering between diesel-belching trucks, jockeying for position on the Jersey side of the bridge.

The beginning of the New Jersey Turnpike took them through a toxic cloud of fumes, some invisible, some so thick you could taste it. Mixed with the heat and humidity it created an atmosphere that might be similar to what the road to hell might be like if there actually is one.

But soon enough, the refineries, junkyards, sewage-treatment plants, and natural gas tank burn-offs were far away in the rear-view mirror. They had decided that they would try to drive straight through across the country and do their sightseeing on the way back. That way they could make sure they gave themselves enough time to get from San Diego up the Pacific Coast Highway to Seattle. California held the most intrigue for the three Bronx boys. They were especially interested in seeing San Francisco, Haight-Ashbury, and the redwoods of Northern California. A college kid who worked with them at the bodega told tales of hippie communes, tan and blonde California beach chicks, music in the streets, and pot smoke in the air.

The Turnpike led them through a never-ending megalopolis, which eventually went to Philly and Baltimore, where Mikey took over the driving. From there they hooked up to the I-70, which would get them all the way to Denver. "You guys ever read Jack Kerouac?" Mikey asked, chomping on a salami sandwich.

"No." Angel and Chili said in unison.

"Oh, come on! This is our *On the Road*. Kerouac and Neil Cassady went blazing across the country in a forty-nine Hudson Hornet and got into all kinds of mad adventures and mayhem from Harlem to Frisco. And Kerouac wrote about it in *On the Road*. They discovered jazz dives. Wild women. Crazy drug-fueled all-night parties. It inspired the beats. Allen Ginsberg?"

Silence overtook the whine of the engine briefly.

"Maynard G. Krebbs?" Mikey asked, exasperated.

"Him I heard of!" Chili said assuredly. "But the only blazing across the country we'll be doing in this thing is when we need to find a bathroom, which is now!"

I-70 rest areas, cafeterias, and gas stations were the only sights they would see until the setting sun and the blinding lights of on-coming traffic convinced them to follow the signs off the highway for a campsite somewhere in the darkness of Indiana. For three dollars, they could pitch a tent, use the bathrooms, and in the morning feed coins into a box that showered one with almost warm, more than just a trickle, of welcomed water.

Deli salami and Italian bread were devoured for breakfast, and they were back on I-70. The rush of the first day's excitement on the road was as much a thing of the past as were burning tenements, abandoned cars, and middle-of-the-night police sirens. The rolling hills and farmlands of Indiana, Illinois, and Missouri were only occasionally interrupted by big-city slowdowns. But soon, the non-stop, almost monotonous rural scenery rushing by reminded one of the repeating backgrounds that whizzed by as Ranger Smith chased Yogi and Boo-Boo through Jellystone Park. Corn fields, cow pastures, wheat fields, unknown vegetables sprouting in rows from here to infinity unrolled out the windshield, both sides, and the rear window. The smells changed along with the scenery. Passing through miles of cornfields actually smelled like corn. Fields dark with steers smelled like manure. Sprouting vegetables smelled liked... vegetables.

"So this is America," Chili said, gazing from left to right.

"Just think," Angel said, wistfully, "almost everything we sell in the bodega comes from all the way out here. Meat, corn, bread, milk, bacon, asparagus...."

"I know something that doesn't come from here," Mikey interjected. "Weed! That comes from Northern California!"

"You *would* think of that," Chili said, as if Mikey said there was no Easter Bunny.

A couple of hours of darkness down the road meant another search for a campground, somewhere in western Kansas. This location had a "rustic latrine" as listed in the campground guide, which meant basically an outhouse with a wooden toilet seat over a hole in the ground. There was water available with an old-fashioned pump that shot delicious cold water out with great force after a couple of pumps on the ancient cast-iron lever.

"I wonder what this place looks like?" Angel asked, as Dinty Moore beef stew warmed up on the Coleman stove. "It's weird how we can pull into this place in pitch-black darkness and have no idea what the surrounding area looks like until the sun rises."

Their small campfire crackled, as the tin-foil-wrapped potatoes baked in the red-hot embers. The flames barely illuminated their faces, giving them each a devilish glow.

"Just like life," Chili said, stirring the large pot of stew. "You're in darkness, thinking you know what's going on, where you're headed, but really have no idea until there's light."

"Then you find out if the light at the end of the tunnel is a train coming straight at you," Mikey said, jabbing a potato with a knife to see if it's done.

"Look at that sky. I never knew there were so many stars," Angel said, sweeping his arm towards the heavens.

Chili tasted the stew. "It's hot enough now. My mom told me when I was around three or four that I said that heaven must be on the sun because it makes us warm and nobody can go there except God."

"You were spouting crazy religious shit even as a toddler? You are one strange cat!" Mikey said holding his foil wrapped potato high in the air. "The potatoes are done, too."

The canned stew and potatoes tasted better than a fifty-dollar steak at Peter Lugar's to them on this second night of camping out.

Dawn brought an unveiling of the current landscape. To the west one could see the beginnings of more rugged terrain, and the tips of mountains. Without showers available, they hit the road sans breakfast, anxious to see what the way ahead would offer.

As the hours passed, and the car rolled over the undulating highway ribbon, in the distance mountains began to appear as farms disappeared. Fields of wheat transformed into trees, then forests. Hills black with steers and cows were replaced by giant boulders and rocky terrain with pine trees reaching to the sky. The highway itself went from a civil engineer's dream job of a straight-as-an-arrow path, to a windy, curving road that needed to blast through solid rock and transverse rivers, streams, and lakes. It was easy to see they weren't in Kansas anymore.

Fallout Shelter

They weren't planning on stopping in Denver and wanted to power through to get as far up the Rockies as they could until darkness set in. But when the carburetor started gasping for air and a sign read ALTITUDE 6,000 FEET, powering through one of the world's great mountain ranges was not in the cards for a sixty-six Squareback. They chugged along, and had to downshift to keep traveling up the continental divide.

"Can you believe people went over these mountains in covered wagons?" Angel asked, hoping he didn't have to go all the way down to first gear, with his left hand white-knuckled on the steering wheel, his clammy right hand loosely grasping the stick shift, and his left foot at the ready, lightly tapping on the clutch. "It must have taken months."

"We'll be here for months if this cockamamie engine conks out on us," Chili said nervously leaning in between the two front seats.

"Ah, what's to worry about?" Mikey said, studying his unwieldy map flapping around in the breeze. "In another fifty or so miles we'll be rolling downhill all the way to the Pacific Ocean."

Sedans, station wagons, vans, motorcycles, semis, even Beetles were passing them by as the vehicle lurched in spurts past signs that boasted 7,000, 8,000, 9,000, 10,000 feet.

"Holy shit! It's freakin' snowing!" Mikey said, pushing the maps to the floor. "There's a turn off up ahead! Let's go!"

They took a turn off the highway and continued up an even steeper road. In addition to all the other mechanical concerns, snowy conditions made their journey even more treacherous. They followed a sign to a SCENIC VIEWPOINT, which led them to a parking lot filled with out-of-state license plates. The temperature was in the 40s and it was snowing hard, but the couple of dozen people who were having snowball fights and frolicking in the snow were all dressed for summer. The vast majority of the wintry revelers were young people in cut-offs, sandals, and T-shirts. And more than half of them seemed to be attractive females.

"Look at those babes!" Angel said, pulling into a parking spot, facing all the action.

"This looks like a commercial for a Swedish singles ski resort! Mikey added. "Let's get out there and have some fun in the snow!"

"Guys, I'm gonna hang in the car for a few minutes...," Chili said out the car window.

Angel shouted as he jogged toward a group of college-aged girls, "I know! You're chilly!"

Without any invitation, Mike and Angel started making snowballs and offering them to the girls. They started throwing them at their friends, and then all five of the girls started throwing at Mikey and Angel. Then it was a total free-for-all, with other groups of kids joining in faux battle.

After a flurry of activity, the kids all took a breather and started with some small talk. One group of kids was from Chicago, another from Toledo, and another from Indiana University. But Mikey and Angel were more interested in a group of three girls, sitting on the hood of their 1972 Delta 88 red convertible.

"Look at those three on that convertible!" Mikey said, leading Angel across the parking lot in their direction.

They approached the girls, with snowballs in hand.

"We come in peace!" Angel said, squashing his snowball.

"Make love not war!" Mikey said, throwing his snowball into the ground.

"We won't fall for that trick!" A short red girl said as she threw a snowball at Mikey hitting him in the chest.

"I guess that was an ice breaker!" Mikey said laughing.

All five began small non-stop small talk. They were freshman at Iowa State going cross-county to visit some friends. Mikey and Angel lied and said they were freshman at Fordham University. Mikey gravitated toward the tallish blonde with flowing hair and jean cut-offs. Angel was trying to get on the good side of the smallish redhead. Mikey and Angel thought for sure that Chili would go for the third girl, a raven-haired beauty who looked Italian.

"Come on over here!" Angel shouted across the parking lot to Chili.

Chili sauntered over with a jacket zipped up tight. "Hi, I'm Chili."

"We're kinda cold, too!" the dark-haired girl said, to much laughter.

"That's my nickname. *Chili.*"

"That's cute," she replied. "I'm Sophia. And I really am freezing. We better hit the road. I'll warm up the car."

Much to the chagrin of the guys, the girls were in the Oldsmobile and headed west.

"Well, that was close. We almost got together with some babes," Angel said starting up the VW.

"There will be more. Guaranteed. Did you see those tits on the blonde? And the cold sure made the raisins stand out on those cupcakes! Man I'm getting horny just thinking about her," Mikey said, opening up the map book again. "Follow that red convertible!"

Chili was surprised at Mikey's language. Sure they talked about sex in lurid ways before, but now for possibly the first time, they were actually in a position where they could act on their lusty desires.

They continued to make their way up the mountain with the gray sky opening up as the sun set. And like a page being turned in a magnificent full-color coffee table book, as they reached the apex of the mountain and began their descent on the other side, the road dried, the sun created a golden glow across the horizon, the car began to hum again, and it felt like they were gliding into a vast bowl of America.

"We better find somewhere to camp out before it gets too dark," Mikey said studying the map. "Pretty soon we'll be going through some unforgiving territory. We've gotta be prepared for when we travel through the desert."

"Saint Paul's famous last words, I think," Chili said. "A little biblical humor before we start hallucinating in the desert, that's all."

Mikey and Angel glanced at each other with expressions that said *oy vey*.

When they woke up the next morning in the campground, there was no sign of snow, and in the distance there were no more mountains to climb. Only a massive carpet of forests sloping downward with a band of gold at the bottom. They rushed to break camp, load the car, and continue down the slope knowing that beyond that sliver of golden desert was their ultimate goal: the West Coast.

Just as Angel was about to shift into first gear, he noticed a note on the windshield. "What the hell?" He reached out the window, retrieved it, and read it aloud. "*You guys are sleepy heads! We're already on the road. If you're in Northern California, we're at the Trinity Lake commune, from August 1st through the 8th. Ask at the Family Tradition General Store on Route 299 outside of Eureka where it is. Love, the Iowa girls.*"

"Let me see that!" Mikey said, grabbing it from Angel. "Oh my my! Is this for real? Can it be? Have my prayers been answered?"

"How do we know this isn't some kind of set-up?" Chili said leaning back, arms folded. "It could be a trap. This is like that episode of *The Untouchables*, where the Bugs Moran gang were lured...."

Mikey whipped around in his seat. "Chili, come on! Leave your big-city mobster scene paranoia back in Little Italy. We're not going to the Saint Valentine's Day massacre! We're gonna meet three corn-fed American beauties in a goddam hippie commune in the mecca of marijuana! This is an invitation to Nirvana!"

"Mikey's right, Chili," Angel said, steering the car out of the campground, heading for the highway. "You might live to a hundred, and not get an invitation on a silver platter like this one."

"Yeah, well, we'll see," Chili said, foraging through the cooler for a granola bar. "If it looks shady, I'll drop you guys off for a week, and find a minor-league baseball park to squat in for a while."

"Forget the minor leagues!" Mikey yelled, "We're in the majors, now! I've been in the minors my whole life! I want some major-league action! I'm sick of sandlot ball. I want groomed infield grass. A perfect mound. Or maybe two mounds. My bat has been factory hardened. My balls have been rubbed with clay...."

"Alright already!" Chili screamed. "What are you, the Howard Cosell of the porn play-by-play announcers?"

"Gentleman, please," Angel interrupted. "We'll jump off that bridge when we get to it. We've got a couple of weeks and many miles to explore before we get to Eureka."

"I'll be screaming *eureka* when I get that blonde into my sleeping bag!"

Chili rolled just rolled his eyes and bit his tongue. There was a long way to go and anything could happen between now and then. There was a saying that one doesn't really know someone unless they live or work together. But he was adding to that, *or get crammed into a '66 VW for thousands of miles together.*

The Squareback back was able to go much faster on the downward side of the Continental Divide, sometimes a good forty miles per hour faster than when it was crawling and sputtering up the steepest inclines of the 15,000-foot elevation. At this pace, they might reach California before the next sunrise, if there were no hidden landmines on the golden road stretched out before them.

They headed south off the I-70 and thanks to Mikey's magnifying glass, included as a prize in a box of Cracker Jacks, after studying the maps they meandered through an otherworldly landscape unlike anything they thought possible.

Chili squinted at a sign in the distance. "What? We're going through Candy Land? The board game is a national park?"

Mikey almost got whiplash with a head-jerking guffaw. "That's Canyonlands National Park!"

"Oh, I know about this! It's like dinosaur land! They shot movies here. And further south the road goes to Monument Valley," Angel said, excitedly.

"Monument Valley," Chili added, "That's one of John Ford's favorite movie locations. They shot *Stagecoach* there with John Wayne. I saw that like ten times on the *Million Dollar Movie* on channel 9."

The three Bronx boys gazed in wonder as they drove past the massive red, brown, and golden spires, arches, and canyons.

"The Empire State Building seems like an Erector Set knockoff compared to these things. That one looks like a giant dick!" Mikey said.

"How you can look at God's creations," Chili said, shaking his head, "and say something like that is beyond me."

"Come on, Chili!" Angel jumped in, "Even a dick is one of God's creations!"

They traveled for hours, and the scenery just kept coming at them like some Cinerama film loop with more and more bizarre shapes, sizes, colors and textures. There were fewer and fewer cars on the road, and the temperature was rising as was the dust in the air.

"See! Look where we are!" Chili said excitedly. "Valley of the Gods. I'm not the only one who makes the connection."

Monument Valley seemed even more spectacular. One could easily imagine John Wayne leading a stagecoach through here. And like a stagecoach, they were traveling as fast as they could, but unlike a stagecoach, filling up with gas at every opportunity and eating salami sandwich upon salami sandwich. They had five huge salamis that can last up to 40 days once cut without any refrigeration, which happened to be the number of days Christ spent alone in the desert. Monument Valley also had an increase in tourists on the road, which continued steadily until they reached one of the landmarks they had to stop for: the Grand Canyon.

Fallout Shelter

They followed tour buses, school buses, station wagons, and motorcycles towards the wondrous hole in the ground, got out of the car, walked twenty yards, and stopped.

Mikey pulled out a Kodak Instamatic and snapped one picture. "Got it. Let's go."

Knowing it was best to travel through the infamous Mohave Desert at night due to daytime temperatures that could be the hottest on planet earth on any given day, they were gassed up, water containers filled, and ice in the cooler. If they could get through the desert without blowing a rod, a tire, or a head gasket, they'd be in California before sunrise. And soon the sand of the desert would give way to the sand of the Southern California ocean beaches from the Tijuana border stretching to Ocean Beach, San Diego, L.A., Big Sur, Frisco, and then Eureka, where perhaps the girls of Iowa just might become their California girls in every sense that Brian Wilson intended.

A sign declared they had entered California. And another sign soon after announced they were in Needles, perhaps named after what it felt like they had been gargling with for the past several hours. But Needles had a gas station, a convenience store, and a neon thermometer saying it was one hundred five degrees at 2 a.m.

There weren't many options for a campsite at that hour, so they headed for the Needles KOA. Kampgrounds of America, aka KOA, is the 7-11 of campgrounds. They seem to be everywhere there's a patch of dirt or gravel available and there's usually a line to get in, even at 2 a.m. Sometimes the locations are on the main highway between a K-Mart and a car dealership and you might have to set up your tent about three feet from pop-up camper-trailer filled with five screaming kids and two drunk parents. But there's always bathrooms with flushing toilets, showers with hot water, sinks to wash your Dinty Moore encrusted pots and pans, and if you are really lucky, washing machines!

Unfortunately they had to set up the tent next to the "doggie walk," so the night's hot breeze had a certain stench reminiscent of Bronx sidewalk. After several days stuck in a tin can with a belching internal combustion engine underneath, the discovery of the on-site washing machines was met with the kind of appreciation one might have finding a pearl at the bottom of the Harlem River.

"Come now!" Chili chirped, adding his laundry into the washer. "We've showered in hot water. We've got toilet paper that doesn't feel like sand paper. And our clothes will no longer smell like the bottom of a subway elevator shaft. Who's better than us?"

"We should make a reservation at the KOA north of Eureka now," Mikey added, "so that when we meet those three Iowa State Fair beauty queens, we are squeaky clean and lubed for love!"

"We've got a lot of miles to go boys," Angel said, scrubbing the funk off the stainless steel Army-Navy surplus knives and forks in the adjacent slop sink. "Anything could happen between now and then. We might even find something better along the way."

The roads south out of Needles went from smooth concrete to bumpy old asphalt and eventually gravel and dirt. They had tied bandanas around their faces to cover their noses and mouths, but the dust was finding its way around the cloth and also going into their eyes.

"Are you sure this is the right way? I thought California was a great big freeway?" Chili asked nervously.

"Hey, we made it to California," Mikey said, Cracker Jack magnifying glass in hand. "We're here now so it's time to see some sights. First stop, a UFO hotspot called the Integratron."

"The Integra-what?" Angel asked. "You didn't tell me where you were taking us into outer space when you were giving directions!"

"Simmer down," Mikey said coolly, "our real journey has only just begun. There's a turn-off coming up for Old Woman Springs Road. I'm taking us on an unforgettable adventure."

Angel and Chili looked at each other to gauge the other's reaction, which quickly transitioned into laughter for all three, until a deep pot hole caused a horribly loud bang, followed by the unmistakable sound of air rushing out of a tire and the flopping of rubber collapsing on a road. Angel slowed the car down, and steered it off to the side of the road, next to large cluster of cacti.

"Let's hope this *On the Road* adventure doesn't end with a broken axle, Jack Kerouac," Angel said to Mikey, exasperated.

Chili discreetly clasped his hands on his lap and began ten Hail Marys in his head. He hoped this was the last time he had to resort to this tactic on their trip. But he doubted it.

"Let's unload the vehicle and see what our options are," Angel said, mostly directed at Mikey. "And get a real fucking magnifying glass so we can see where we're going on that goddamm map!"

Looking like a scene from *The Grapes of Wrath*, everything was unloaded from the vehicle and piled in the dirt next to a ten-foot-tall spindly cactus.

"My guidebook says this is called a Joshua tree," Chili said, sitting on an ice chest. "It was named that because when explorers saw them for the first time, the trees reminded them of the passage in the Bible where Joshua extended his arms to heaven to pray for help in the desert."

Angel slid under the front of the car, "Well, so far our prayers have been getting through because the axle isn't broken. It looks like it's just a flat tire. Mikey, you can do the honors."

"I ain't complaining. I'll pull my weight. But remember it's somebody else's turn when the next disaster strikes," Mikey said, grabbing a rusty jack out of the front trunk and then holding it up high. "This rinky-dink thing is gonna lift the car?"

"Let me do the heavy lifting here," Chili said, taking the jack from Mikey. He placed it under the car and began pushing down on the tire iron that was inserted into the jack mechanism. He had to exert force with both hands to lift the tire off the ground inch-by-inch.

"I'll take over from here," Mikey said, removing the flat and replacing it with a spare.

Thankfully, the spare tire somehow held, and they were back on the road headed for something called The Integratron.

"Listen to this," Mikey said, reading from a guidebook, "The Integratron was built to attract alien visitors from other planets. It is said to be built over a convergence of earth and universal energy vortexes that intersect at the exact center of the structure. A network of cables produces a field of frequencies that can rejuvenate physical bodies and reverse the aging process. Although built by humans it was designed by Venusians."

"Venusians? What the hell does that mean?" Angel said, studying the rocky road for holes or obstacles.

"Beings from Venus," Mikey said, matter-of-factly. "Where have you been?"

"I know where I've been. I'm just not sure where we're going," Angel said, stepping on the gas.

Chili's hands were stinging slightly from his efforts jacking up the car. When he turned his palms towards him, he studied the center of his palm and discovered two distinct half-dollar-sized red spots. Putting his hands on his lap, palm side down, he thought to himself, *stigmata*.

Chapter 9

Jamie sat by himself in the back of the bus in the last row by a window as they cruised up the New York State Thruway towards the Adirondack Mountains. He had borrowed the worst camera available from the Corrigan school newspaper. The upper classmen, especially the seniors who were on the student council, got the best cameras and preferential treatment. But Jamie didn't mind being alone, or having the dinged-up Minolta camera. It was a 35mm, had a decent lens, and was issued a free roll of black & white film. Looking out the window at the passing scenery he was amazed at endless forests and majestic mountains as they headed north, the Bronx city line a distant memory.

This was his first trip alone, without a family member, and would be the furthest he had ever been from home. He imagined himself living somewhere like within these forests. Somewhere away from traffic and sirens and elevated trains screeching. Away from shouting and yelling and kids bothering you for no reason. Just someplace where you could be left alone.

Father O'Brennan was holding court in the front of the bus. Jamie couldn't hear exactly what was being said, but there was uproarious laughter. He did pick up enough to know that there were some jokes being told that had curse words in them. *Dick*, *tits*, and *ass* were definitely mentioned more than once. Father O'Brennan seemed more exuberant than ever. His laughs were the loudest, his slaps on the back the hardest, his punch lines, apparently, the funniest.

Jamie didn't get the choice assignments on the school newspaper. He was relegated to taking the crappy Minolta with a mid-range lens and taking crowd shots at games. But he was pleasantly surprised when one of his photos of some overzealous fans was printed in the school paper. He actually preferred the candid style of photography rather than staged shots or action of the games. He enjoyed being an invisible observer. Which is why he brought along his super top-secret possession: the miniature camera he absconded from Chili. It was only the second time he had taken it from the perfect hiding place to use it outside the apartment. After all, this trip was a first, and he thought he might encounter a situation where a tiny hidden camera could come in handy.

It was dark when the bus pulled into the mountain resort. There was an A-frame lodge made from logs where everyone checked in and received their room assignments. Jamie wound up with a sophomore named Alfredo Jefferson as a bunkmate in the small log cabin bungalow. Once they were settled in their bunk beds at around midnight, the only sounds they heard coming into the room were from buzzing insects, hooting owls, and the occasional coyote howling in the distance. Jamie's roommate mentioned that the sounds were freaking him out, but to Jamie they were the most beautiful sounds he had ever heard. He couldn't wait for sunrise and for the morning hike he signed up for.

Morning prayers led by Father O'Brennan and breakfast were first on the morning's itinerary. The hike up a mountain trail was led by a long-haired male college student who worked at the resort. And Jamie was surprised that he was the only Corrigan student among the five who was taking the hike. The other four people were two older couples, probably in their sixties.

They headed out to a trail head for a steep trek up a mountain closest to the resort. Jamie watched as the Corrigan group went into the recreation hall for a morning meeting. He was surprised he was allowed to go off by himself, but he was happy to do it.

It only took twenty minutes of hiking on a dirt trail through a canopy of massive trees for the wonders of the Adirondacks to be revealed. The path through the forest led to a trail that followed a cliff along a river probably a hundred feet below. Looking down into the chasm made him feel uneasy knowing that one slip could mean a plunge to the death.

Fallout Shelter

In the distance, there was mountain after mountain layered one upon the other that seemed to go on forever. There were bald eagles in trees, and eagles gliding upwards in thermal drafts until they were small dots in the sky. Stealthy animals could be heard scampering through the brush as the hikers advanced higher and higher, the vista becoming more dramatic with each step. A doe and her fawn watched them from behind a group of trees.

Jamie had his Minolta around his neck, but was so immersed in the moment, he didn't want to pause to take any photos for fear he would feel removed from being part of this extraordinary moment in time and become an observer instead of a participant.

They took a lunch break at a shaded picnic area. While the others were eating their provided box lunch, Jamie decided to take a walk into the woods. He took a trail that wound through brush and giant trees. After only a few minutes, the only sounds he heard were his sneakers stepping on a carpet of dried pine needles and soft dirt. He stopped and slowly rotated 360 degrees, listening to the silence, breathing the air infused with pine, beech, and spruce trees. It was the quietest moment of his life. Only an unseen chirping bird, or rustle in the bushes broke the complete and utter quiet.

Jamie knew he was the opposite of Chili. He was well aware how Chili saw religious signs everywhere he looked, from a bearded God in the clouds to Christ on burnt toast. Jamie thought it was all bullshit. Yeah, he was an altar boy in grammar school, did his due diligence to memorize and repeat to nuns, priests, and brothers what they wanted to hear. But he did so to remain anonymous. To do otherwise would make him stand out and attract attention. He knew he was different, but it was important to keep it a secret. He heard too many mean comments and received more than his fair share of noogies, water balloons in the face, and black eyes. He knew how to keep his mouth shut.

But for perhaps for the first time in his life, he thought he felt the indescribable power of something that maybe was similar to what Chili felt when saw what he thought were signs from God. Jamie felt the overwhelming feeling of belonging to something all-powerful. As he gazed upon the mountains through the treetops in the distance he felt small, but also connected to the unbound natural beauty of all that surrounded him. From the tiny barely visible insects that buzzed past his ears, to his footprint that left an impression not only on the path, but on the earth itself.

In the distance he heard his name being called, so he knew lunch break was over. He returned to the group where they continued on their way up the mountain trail. But Jamie felt different. Something changed him in those twenty or so minutes. And somehow, he felt he understood his brother more than he ever did before.

As dinner in the dining hall was winding down, Jamie noticed that members of the student council were going over to certain students, and whispering in their ears. His bunkmate, Alfredo Jefferson, and he, were not included.

"What do you think that's all about?" Jamie asked Alfredo.

"I don't know. But I've heard rumors," Alfredo replied.

Alfredo was a big kid for a sophomore. He was a big kid for any year of high school or college. Well over six feet and probably close to two hundred fifty pounds, he looked every much the center on the varsity football team that he was. That was in addition to being an honor student, the president of AFRAM, the African-American student organization, and an assistant editor of the school newspaper.

"Do you know what a 'Joe' club is?" Alfredo asked, wiping the last bit of gravy off his plate with a slice of buttered white bread.

"Nope. Never heard of it."

"I heard somebody mention it. And I don't think it has anything to do with the Joe DiMaggio fan club. Do you know how to play chess?"

"Nope."

"Wanna learn?"

"Definitely!" Jamie said, as they took their plates to the dirty-dishes counter.

The rec-room was quiet as Alfredo patiently taught Jamie how chess works. Jamie paid close attention as Alfredo's ham-sized hands delicately handled the chess pieces and gracefully demonstrated how each one moved across the spaces.

Alfredo had a Puerto Rican mother and a Black father. Although only fifteen years old, he had achieved the height and weight of a full-grown man. His mustache was on the verge needing a shave, but months away from having enough of a mustache to get busted for violating Corrigan's strict facial hair regulations. His monstrous size, which leap-frogged him from jay vee football to starting center on the varsity, gave cover to his mellow demeanor. Jamie appreciated Alfredo's quiet strength and felt a certain comfort being with him. Some of the older student council members could be real threatening assholes. At least to the smaller guys, such as himself.

This "retreat" was supposed to be a practical and spiritual getaway as described by Father O'Brennan's flyer. But so far Jamie hadn't seen any scheduled activities except for swimming and rowing on the lake. Father O'Brennan was the faculty moderator for the drama club and the school newspaper, and from what Jamie could tell, every one of the kids on the trip belonged to one of those two groups. Plus the senior student council members who went around wearing huge "Corrigan HS Student Council" buttons on their stupid striped beany hats.

"Where do you think they're going?" Alfredo said, looking out the window, observing a group of about six students walking down a gravel path towards the larger bungalows.

"Maybe they're the planning committee. I mean there have to be some school activities soon."

"I guess," Alfredo agreed.

After a long chess lesson, Alfredo and Jamie shot some hoops at an outdoor basketball half court at the end of the property. Jamie needed some instruction there too, with Alfredo more than happy to oblige.

The next morning Jamie awoke alone in the room, but thought nothing of it. He went to have breakfast, and still no sign of Alfredo. He finished breakfast and went back to the room, where Alfredo was on his made bed, staring at the ceiling.

He told Jamie he got up early to go to the head, and ran into the tall blond senior Randy Appleby. Randy told him that Father O'Brennan requested him for a special meeting that evening with some other chosen lower classmen who could go on to be leaders at Corrigan.

"What did you tell them?" Jamie asked, wondering why he wasn't one of the chosen ones.

"I said I'd go. But I have a feeling I'm gonna find out what that Joe club is all about. The meeting is in Father O'Brennan's bungalow at ten o'clock tonight."

"Ten o'clock?"

Alfredo stroked his budding mustache. "Yeah, doesn't sound like a student council meeting to me. I'll report back what I find out fer sure."

"Be careful, Alfredo," Jamie said, dead serious.

"Be careful? What's that about?"

"Father O. is…," Jamie paused.

"Is what?" Alfredo asked.

"He's a sneak. You think he's a friend, and he turns on you. And threatens you."

Alfredo stood up. "Yeah, well let's see if he has the balls to threaten me!"

Jamie went to bed just after Alfredo left for the meeting and quickly fell asleep.

He was deep into REM when he was shaken violently. He could see in the darkness, it was Alfredo.

"Wake up, Jamie! I gotta talk to you!"

Jamie sat up in his bed in the darkness, with barely enough light from an electric alarm clock to see Alfredo. "What's up?"

"You're not gonna believe what I just witnessed. First of all, the room was as dark as this room, and first thing, they have me take an oath of secrecy."

"An oath? That's creepy."

"Yeah, well listen, *creepy* doesn't come close. So then, that Randy dude has three small bowls of what looks like pills. And he says, pick one and eat it. So I pick one, put it in my mouth, slip it to the side and take a sip of wine from a freakin' chalice like you do at mass! So when he's not looking I spit out the pill."

"This is sounding like something out of *Rosemary's Baby*," Jamie says clutching his throat.

"I never saw that, but I'll take your word for it. Then the six of us have to sit, in the dark, in a circle, with a red silk cloth in the middle of the circle."

"Where's O'Brennan?"

"I'm getting there. Then Randy announces, take off your shoes and socks. So the other five do it on command, so I follow. He then says, take out your cocks! And I swear on my grandma's grave, the five pull out their johnsons and start wiggling 'em. Then Father O'Brennan comes out in red silk robe, squats, and watches the action with a smile on his face like the Joker on *Batman*."

"What did you do?"

"I shot out of there, like so fast, they probably didn't even see me leave."

"Then, I snuck around and peeked in a window, and as God is my witness, O'Brennan picks up the red silk cloth, passes it to the kid to his right, and the kid starts jerking off into it. That was all I could stand so I split. Father O'Brennan! He's my freakin' guidance counselor!"

"Mine, too. Don't be surprised if you have a special meeting scheduled tomorrow after your session was cut short," Jamie said, knowing O'Brennan's tricks. "Did he ever... act weird to you as a guidance counselor?"

"Nah. Just that he knew my parents were divorced and I lived with my mom, and things have been rough, and he was kind of treating me real nice, and offering to take me places and stuff like that. But come to think of it, I did think it was kind of weird to offer help outside of school."

"What are you gonna do? Are you gonna tell anybody?"

"For now, no. Just you. I need to go to sleep. If I can. Well, now we know what the Joe club is," Alfredo said, reaching for his toothbrush and mouth wash.

"What?"

"Not *J-O-E*, but *J-O*: jerk-off club."

"I guess O'Brennan's the moderator for that club, too," Jamie said, drolly.

Jamie heard voices out the window just as the sun was rising. It was Randy and Alfredo having a conversation, although he couldn't make out what they were saying. He did hear the name O'Brennan a couple of times.

Alfredo popped his head in the door. "I'm going on a hike with Father O. and some others at 7 a.m." he whispered. "Get your camera and see if you can follow us. You might get the picture of a lifetime."

"I'll do it. But be careful," Jamie said, worry in his voice.

Jamie guessed right. They met at the same trail head he went hiking on the day before. He kept far behind with his camera in hand, and at the ready. Alfredo was met by Randy first, then Father O'Brennan. They started the hike and from the cover of the thick brush, Jamie took a photo of them embarking on their walk up the trail. Knowing the path, he was able to circle ahead, to get some shots as they ascended the mountain path. When he arrived at a higher point, he noticed Randy was no longer with Alfredo and Father O'Brennan.

The two were going way beyond where Jamie had hiked the day before. The trail was following a canyon with a small river probably two hundred feet below. Jamie kept his distance in the shrubbery, trying to get shots. He could see that Father O'Brennan was tiring, at least a half-hour past where his hike ended the day before.

Father O'Brennan took a seat on a rock, and looked winded. The location of the trail where they were taking a breather afforded them a spectacular view of an emerald valley, which seemed to glow in with the morning dew. It reminded Jamie again of the power of nature, and how he knew it was what he wanted to surround himself with for the rest of his life.

Alfredo was at the edge of the trail, which was literally next to a sheer cliff of hundreds of feet. Jamie positioned himself, crawling through the thickets to get as close as possible for some photos, which was necessary since the lens on the Minolta 35mm was so short and didn't have a zoom.

Father O'Brennan stood up from his seat on a boulder and approached Alfredo from behind. He got close to Alfredo. Very close. And whispered in Alfredo's ear, which caused Alfredo to wince and turn around. He faced Father O'Brennan, with a scowl that was probably the same scowl he had on his face when he was center and facing middle linebacker. Then suddenly, in a quick karate-like move, Father O'Brennan pushed Alfredo with great force on both shoulders, sending Alfredo plummeting off the cliff. Alfredo yelled for a second. Then nothing but deadly silence. Father O'Brennan turned around, facing the forest and made the sign of the cross.

Jamie froze in terror. He was trembling uncontrollably trying to command his legs to run. But he couldn't. Did he really just witness this heinous act? Could he still be asleep? This couldn't be happening. He turned, took thirty fleeing steps, and right on front of him, blocking his way, was Randy. He grabbed Jamie around the neck as if he was going to strangle him.

"Give me that camera," Randy demanded with controlled fury.

Jamie handed him the Minolta, which Randy immediately opened, and pulled out the film, exposing and ruining any images that were on it.

"I'll say this once. I know who you are. I know where you live. If you say anything about this. Your father will be dead. Your brother will be dead. You will be dead. Understand?"

"Yes," Jamie said, no longer trembling. He was beyond that. He was numb. He had no feeling in his body. All he could see was Randy's chiseled features, blond hair, blue eyes, like some rabid Nazi Hitler youth with a stupid Corrigan beany on his head.

"Get out of here. Now."

Jamie ran as fast as he could back to his bunk, got back into bed and waited. He looked at Alfredo's bed, which he made perfectly before he left. He wouldn't let himself cry. Not then. Not ever again in his entire life. But he should have said more to Alfredo about Father O'Brennan. Maybe he would still be alive.

The retreat ended early. The news had spread quickly. The story was that while on a hike with Father O'Brennan and Randy, Alfredo Jefferson slipped and fell to his death. They recovered his body, and it was being transported back to the Bronx for burial. Father O'Brennan didn't ride the bus back with the students. Nor did Randy. They said they were too upset and said a fellow priest would take them home.

The bus ride was a somber one. No one uttered a word. They were dropped off in front of the school, and each went their separate way. Jamie hopped on the No. 4 train, which is how he usually went home. But instead of walking past DeWitt Clinton high school, he went inside to the registration office and obtained the necessary forms to transfer there next fall. His textbooks, notebooks, photographs, scrapbooks would remain in his locker. He would never step foot back into Corrigan for as long as he lived.

The next day, while picking up the *New York Daily News* for his father, he noticed a copy of the *Bronx Home News*. A small paragraph on the bottom of the front page had a headline, *Student*

Fallout Shelter

Dies in Freak Fall on Class Trip. Jamie didn't bother reading the story.

All the forms were in order. All that was needed was for his father to sign them, and bring them back to the registration office at DeWitt C. He could request his transcripts from Corrigan by mail.

Jamie had picked up enough about cooking from Chili and had the dinner table set for two; he and his dad. Like all the other dinners, family events, gatherings, trips, visits with relatives, and merely sitting around the house, anything involving Mr. Manzilla was like playing Russian Roulette. Especially since his mother passed away.

The marinara was ready, as was the rotini pasta, the sweet sausage, and the salad. Out of the bedroom came Mr. Manzilla, looking about as good as he ever did. Hair parted neatly, shaven face, neat clothes, eyes only slightly red and puffy.

"What's all this? Looks like a Sunday dinner layout. How was the retreat?"

"It ended early. A kid… got killed… in an… accident."

"Holy jumpin' shit. Did you know him?"

"I had only just met him, but he was my bunkmate."

"That's terrible. You never know when your time is up. Could be me, could be you, could be your brother. What's these papers?"

Jamie handed them to his father. "Transfer papers to Clinton. I don't want to go to Corrigan anymore."

Mr. Manzilla glanced at the forms, and studied Jamie's face. "Because of the death?"

"Yeah, and other stuff. It's just not right for me. I don't fit in there."

"Did you tell your brother yet?"

"No."

"Well, talk to him first. Then I'll sign. It'll save us twenty three bucks a month, anyway."

Dinner was being eaten in an unusually civilized manner, when the phone rang. Jamie picked up the receiver.

"Hello, Chili! How is your trip? Good…I'm leaving Corrigan…a guy I knew…got killed on our trip by falling off a cliff….yeah, I know…it's something I need to do…." Looking at this father, "He wants to talk to you."

Mr. Manzilla dropped his fork and picked up the phone. "How are you? Good…yes, I think it's okay if you do…when are you coming home? Okay…be careful out there…bye." He put the phone down and picked up his fork. "It's okay with him if you transfer out. He'll discuss it with you when he gets back in a few weeks or so. I'll sign the forms right after dinner."

Jamie managed a weak smile. They weren't perfect, but they were a family. He knew that deep down inside they loved each other, and they were all they had.

Chili walked from the gas station phone booth on a two-lane desert highway back to the VW as Angel finished topping off the tank.

"Everything okay at home, Chili?" Angel said, noticing the sullen look on Chili's face.

"Not quite."

"What is it?" Mikey said, pushing his seat forward so Chili could get in the back.

"Jamie was on a retreat with his school up in the Adirondacks and a guy he knew fell off a cliff or something and got killed."

"Holy fuck!" Angel said. "Was he with him? Was he friends with him? How did it happen?"

"That's all I know. And he wants to leave Corrigan and go to Clinton."

"I don't blame him," Mikey said, "I'd want out, too. I liked Clinton. It's mostly mooks, but if you show up you're gonna pass. And if you show any effort at all, there are some good teachers and classes."

Fallout Shelter

"I'll get more information. They were in the middle of dinner. Let's just keep going," Chili said, staring out the window gazing at the Joshua trees reaching up to the heavens.

"That's it? That's the earth's answer for attracting intergalactic space travelers?" Mikey asked, stepping out of the car on a dirt road in the desert community of Landers, California, about 150 miles from San Diego. The three of them leaned against the Squareback in the hundred-degree heat and gazed upon the structure called the Integratron. Mikey opened a guidebook and read from it. "George Van Tassel was contacted telepathically while meditating under the Giant Rock, a sacred Indian site, by aliens from Venus to construct this building. Then he was given plans by Venusians in person. It is not yet completed, but eventually will attract advanced civilizations throughout the universe. It is built over a vortex of global and universal energy fields and will also rejuvenate cells, which may reverse the aging process. It is a work in progress and should be completed soon."

"I'm in!" Angel said, squeezing through a hole in a chain-link fence, "I want to go rejuvenate my cells and maybe lose twenty pounds' worth."

"I think he was doing more than meditating under the Giant Rock," Chili said, following both guys onto the property, "Indian peyote may have been involved."

"Yeah, those hallucinogenics can cause strange illusions," Mikey said, immediately getting the stink eye from Angel.

They walked around the structure, which resembled a geodesic dome and had a system of wires and cables strung from various points, all connecting on the tip of the roof, which appeared to have a lightning rod in the center. A look through a dusty window revealed an empty interior paneled from floor to ceiling with wood, and more wires strung along the walls. There were piles of construction material consisting of cables, gears, plywood, bags of cement, and barrels.

"You'd think Venusians would be a little neater," Chili said, kicking a rusted spoon.

"Well, this was all they had to work with here on earth," Mikey said, picking up a handful of sandy dirt. "It takes time to construct an intergalactic space station using materials from Virgil's Lumber Yard and Hardware Emporium."

"Maybe they just needed more peyote," Angel said, heading back to the car. "Let's get out of this dirt and hit sand at the beach. It's only like two hours from here."

Soon the dirt roads led to a two-lane blacktop, then a four-lane blacktop, then an eight-lane super-duper freeway where even the semi's seemed to be going eighty miles an hour or more. The Squareback was sputtering and gasping again, not because of climbing mountains, but trying to keep up with the flow of traffic in the slow lane. More than one car that came up fast behind them and then swerved around to pass gave them the finger.

"Did you notice that they give the finger differently here?" Mikey asked. "The middle finger is extended the same, but the other three are only half-bent. Like this." He said demonstrating. "When we give the finger, the three other fingers are all the way down, like this." He said, holding up both hands, giving the middle-finger salute just as a California Highway Patrol car slowly passed them. The cop driving immediately motioned for them to pull over.

"Thanks a lot, Mr. double-fisted fuck-you to the cops," Angel said, downshifting and steering onto the shoulder. "Do we have any beer or anything in the car?"

"Shit. We have a couple of empties in the cooler," Chili said.

"Great," Angel said rolling down his window.

"License and registration please," the officer said politely, while looking inside the vehicle. "Everyone please keep your hands where I can see them. Is that how you New Yorkers greet your law-enforcement officers back home?"

"No sir." Angel said.

"Officer?" Mike said to the cop. Angel kicked him in the ankle. "I wasn't directing that to you. I was demonstrating that the

New York finger style is different from the California technique. You see, we've been obeying the speed limit, and some of the California drivers didn't seem to appreciate that as they passed us by."

The cop shook his head and laughed. "Really? Let me see how that works."

"See, Californians do it like this… and New Yorkers do it like this." Mikey said, straight faced, right at the cop.

"You learn something new every day on this job," the highway patrolman said. "Welcome to California, and I wouldn't advise demonstrating that to any more passing cars."

"Thank you, officer," Angel said, as he pulled back into the freeway lane. "You dumb shit! You're lucky you flipped off a nice cop and not some Hell's Angel lunatic."

"Signs, signs, everywhere signs," Chili said. "There are signs, gestures, and symbols everywhere. Be careful how you interpret them or be prepared how others interpret them."

Angel and Mikey just rolled their eyes.

Back on the road they watched as the scenery transitioned from stark rocky-brown mountains to hills with green patches of trees and shrubs. Then as the homes they passed appeared in clusters, closer and closer together, the humidity of the ocean could be felt and one could even smell the salt in the breeze. They were traveling due west when they saw the sign they had been anticipating for hours, days, weeks, and months: END OF HIGHWAY 1,000 FT.

"This is it and there it is!" Mikey proclaimed triumphantly. "The Pacific freakin' ocean! And who navigated us across this vast country with a road atlas from 1960 and a Cracker Jack toy magnifying glass?"

"I think having a vehicle also had something to do with it," Chili said, patting both guys on the shoulders.

They made a right turn and headed north through San Diego. Mikey guided them to Ocean Beach, a hippie and biker neighborhood in the city confines.

Angel turned onto Newport Avenue, which headed right to the Ocean. "Oh my God! Guys! What does this remind you of?"

Both Mikey and Chili shouted, "One Hundred Sixteenth Street in Rockaway!"

"No wonder Maguire and Muldoon are hiding out here. It's like living in Rockaway with a summer that never ends."

Maguire and Muldoon were two small-time neighborhood dealers who sold pot in the pool hall in order to make enough money to keep themselves in pot. But when the cops and the higher-up drug dealers came after them, they hitch-hiked cross country to Ocean Beach a few years prior to hide out.

"Let's call Maguire and Muldoon," Mikey said, digging a matchbook cover from out of a bag. "It could be our first West Coast connection. And our first night sleeping under a roof."

Mikey stood in the phone booth, which was next to a public bathroom and a beach volleyball set-up just yards from the surf. He dialed one set of numbers, then two, three, four, then returned to the car. "No good. Disconnected. And not listed."

"Drug dealers rarely have their numbers listed," Chili said. "Who knows with those guys? Plus I'm not sure we want to hang out with two guys wanted by the F.B.I. and the Mafia."

Angel turned to face Chili. "The F.B.I. and the Mafia? They sold nickel bags!"

"So! It's still against the law! And you don't cross the mob, either! They'll get you one way or another!"

After a pit stop, they were back on the road, going north on whatever street was closest to the ocean. They were amazed how the beach towns never ended, but just melded into each other. Mission Beach, Pacific Beach, La Jolla, Del Mar, Oceanside, one after another, sometimes separated by gorgeous parks, lagoons, and wetlands in a medley of Beach Boys lyrics with California girls, surfers, hot rods, palm trees, and bushy-bushy blonde hairdos.

But as they ventured north through San Diego County along the spectacular coast, the roads became more crowded and it was necessary to get back onto the I-5 freeway. In Orange County the ocean was nowhere to be seen from the freeway, and traffic resembled the Long Island Expressway as they advanced northward.

"Are we ever gonna stop and see anything for more than ten minutes?" Mikey said, exasperated.

"If we keep going," Angel said, concentrating on the speeding highway traffic flow, "we can hit Hollywood just before dark."

"Hollywood," Chili said, wistfully. "The place where dreams are made. Jimmy Cagney, John Wayne, James Stewart, Fred Astaire, Marilyn Monroe, Bette Davis...."

Mikey shook his head and scoffed. "Come up with some names from today. That's the past. Come on, Chili! Get with it! That was then. This is now!"

The neat suburbs of Orange County ended, and the industrial areas of L.A. County were almost as ugly as the New Jersey Turnpike. Cars, trucks, and busses were inching along bumper-to-bumper, and occasionally a motorcyclist would zoom between cars, long hair flowing, with no helmet.

"That's freedom, right there!" Angel said, admiring the hippie biker cutting lanes. "That's today. That's now!"

"I'm not sure *now* is better than *then*," Chili whispered to himself.

"What was that?" Angel said, over the roar of a truck's diesel engines a few feet to his left.

"Nothing," Chili responded.

As the song goes, L.A. was a great big freeway, and with Mikey trying to make sense of a spider web of intersecting highways, boulevards, and streets with a plastic magnifying glass on a map of Los Angeles that was about six inches by six inches.

"Well, I'm pretty sure I can get us to the Hollywood Bowl, so that should get us close to Hollywood," Mikey said, squinting with one eye.

Little did they know that there was a performance that night by a symphony orchestra and they were caught in a traffic jam that made gridlock in mid-town Manhattan seem like the Autobahn. Busses, taxicabs, limousines, station wagons, vans, and cars wound through adjacent hillside Hollywood neighborhoods with cops everywhere, forcing cars to follow the traffic flow. After an hour of traveling maybe ten blocks, they found themselves at the entrance to the Hollywood Bowl parking lot.

"Excuse me sir, can you tell me how to get out of this mess, and get to the part of Hollywood where the stars are on the sidewalk and the footprints by the theatre?" Angel asked as politely as possible, hoping the attendant didn't make him pay the ten bucks parking fee just to make a U-ey.

The attendant laughed and stooped down to look at the week's worth of mess and stink piling up around them. "I didn't think you were here for Mostly Mozart! Turn around here, and just go down the hill. When you go about a mile, make a right on Hollywood Boulevard and if you see a parking spot, take it. The Chinese Theater and the stars on the sidewalk are right there."

"Thank you, sir!"

Traffic was heavy-going toward Hollywood Boulevard, but moving fast. "This is like driving in the Indy 500," Angel said, grasping the wheel with both hands and shifting gears when necessary descending the winding hill.

There were no parking spaces on Hollywood Boulevard, so they cruised the side streets looking for a spot.

"This reminds me of Times Square," Chili said as two street hookers walked down the sidewalk in the opposite direction. "Do you think it's safe to park here?"

"Hey, we're New Yorkers! We know what we're doing," Mikey said, ready for anything. "There's a spot!"

The available space was in front of a dilapidated three-story apartment building that looked like Joe Friday might have found a dead body in a stairwell after a drug deal had gone wrong.

"Are you guys sure about this spot?" Chili asked—no, *pleaded*.

Fallout Shelter

"It's a tourist area. It just looks bad," Mikey replied assuredly.

"I'm taking some of my stuff just in case," Chili said, filling a paper bag with his camera, a transistor radio, his Swiss Army Knife, and a notebook.

They locked the car up, and headed down to the boulevard. Like Times Square, it was a neon glittering cesspool of hustlers, druggies, hippies, bums, hookers, and wide-eyed tourists. Yes, there were gold stars embedded in the sidewalk with movie stars' names, but they were covered with cigar butts, squashed chewing gum, and standard issue city filth.

"Oh no! Look at Jimmy Cagney! It's got dog shit on it," Chili lamented.

There wasn't much room on the sidewalks for gawking, and the courtyard of the Chinese Theater was wall-to-wall with tourists sticking their paws and sandals in the concrete impressions made back in a time when Hollywood did have legitimate glitz and glamour.

"Let's get out of here," Angel said, obviously disgusted.

They were a couple of cars away from the vee-dub when the awful reality of being stupid tourists with no street smarts bit them in the butt: the Squareback had been broken into.

"Holy jumpin' shit," Angel said as he approached the broken rear driver's-side window that was smashed. "Well, they got the big stuff. Sleeping bags, bags of clothes, the Coleman stove."

"The stove? Good! It wasn't even cleaned yet!" Mikey said. "Do you guys have your wallets and cash?"

"Yeah," they grumbled.

"Let's get the hell out of here," Chili said, climbing into the back seat. "I knew something bad was going to happen. We're surrounded by sin."

"Okay, Saint fuckin' Francis, spare us the goddam sermon!" Mikey shouted. "Let's find a freakin' Sears that's open late!"

Mikey steered them out of Hollywood to Santa Monica where they found a Sears that was indeed still open, and they stocked-up on camping gear, underwear, and a few items of clothing.

"Well, there goes the hope of staying in any motels for the remainder of the trip," Angel said, as they stood on line at the cashier and took turns handing over most of their cash. "Let's keep our heads screwed on straight for the rest of our travels. No stupid moves!"

"Killjoy," Mikey muttered. "Hey look, two blocks from here is Highway 1! That's the start of the Pacific Coast Highway! P.C.H.! It's one of the most beautiful highways in the country! And it goes to all the way up along the coast to San Francisco, Eureka, and beyond!!"

"What are we waiting for?" Angel said. "To Eureka and beyond!"

⚜ Chapter 10 ⚜

The Carpinteria State Beach campground was about two hours north of Los Angeles and the nighttime ride to it certainly wasn't beautiful. It seemed rather treacherous with its winding hills and low wooden barriers separating them from rocky cliffs plunging hundreds of feet below. They could hear the roar of the ocean as they set up their new tent on a patch of dirt and got some sleep.

As dawn approached, Chili was the first to notice a glimmer of light through the mesh tent window. Mikey and Angel were snoring in tandem like two small outboard motors hitched to a rowboat. There was a chill in the air and Chili draped his sleeping bag over his shoulders and stepped outside. There was a cool breeze that carried the scent of the ocean through the morning mist. Salt, seaweed, fish, wet sand, were all welcome fragrances for a Bronx boy used to smelling the garbage cans lined up outside his window on the sidewalk. There was a red glow behind them as the sun began to rise over the hills east of them. He could see the mist actually falling through the air in waves of miniscule water droplets smaller than any raindrops he had ever seen.

There was a wood-plank path a few yards away that led through some thickets and brush and landed on the wide beach. The sand wasn't that superfine white sand like one might find in Jones Beach or other Long Island beaches, like processed and refined sugar. The sand here was multi-colored, ranging from light brown mini pebbles to black marble-sized rocks. It was as if the beach on this side of the continent hadn't been beaten by the Pacific Ocean for as many millennia as Atlantic beaches. There was still a raw roughness to the coast that was primitive. A Jones Beach pavilion with showers, lockers, and hot dog stands would be totally out of place here.

The fog was lifting slightly as the sun peeked over the hillsides. Chili took off his sneakers and walked barefoot on the barren beach, not a soul in sight. There was driftwood and assorted chunks of formerly living things strewn about like broken seashells and fish spines. In the distance he saw a large dark object near the high tide mark. He thought it may have been a log or a boulder and walked toward it. He saw it move slightly, with it still about fifty yards away. He kept going towards it, and as he did, an odor similar to the barrels of garbage outside a fish store got stronger and stronger. Now at about ten yards away, he couldn't believe his eyes. A massive creature, probably fifteen feet long was lying in the sand. It must have been two to three feet high and possibly weighed as much as a small elephant.

He stood silently in awe and wondered if it was dead or alive. He took a step closer and suddenly the creature lifted his head, turned around, made a sound like a wounded hippopotamus, and then went back to its previous position.

"Sorry pal, I won't come any closer, don't worry!" Chili said to the giant creature.

He stood motionless and thought how this scene hadn't changed on this location probably for a million years. A pristine rugged coastline, rough sand, and an animal that appears it could have been roaming the oceans and beaches since the before the dawn of mankind.

He almost jumped out of his skin when he received a tap on the shoulder. He turned around to see a park ranger. In fact a young, beautiful female park ranger with her Smoky Bear hat and all.

"Sorry if I frightened you. But you are a little close to him."

"I guess I frightened him."

"Yeah, you don't want to do that. That's an elephant seal. If you're near one of the babies, he'll chase you and it won't end well."

"Are they here a lot?"

Fallout Shelter

"Not a lot, but sometimes. Consider yourself very lucky to be part of nature in this way. Not a lot of people get this opportunity to commune with such a wonderful creature."

"It's almost like a sign… or something. About the wonders of nature and God."

She smiled and nodded. "One could say that. I think maybe you might want to leave him alone for now. I have to put a rope around the area to keep the tourists away."

"Thank you, Ranger…?"

"Smith."

"Ranger Smith. Just like on…."

"I know, Yogi Bear."

"Bye."

Chili couldn't wait to get back to the tent to tell the guys about what he saw. But the part about being a sign from God, well he figured he'd just keep that locked away with all the others. He was beginning to realize that seeing symbols and signs in almost everything was not sitting well with his vehicle mates. But isn't that how mysticism works? Only the chosen are able to see signs that others can't or choose not to see. It was becoming clear to him that his visions, his perceptions, his senses were witnessing things that others were missing. Didn't many of the saints have epiphanies and revelations that only they were witness to? Saint Paul on the road to Damascus, Saint Francis of Asissi, Saint Theresa, Saint Pio all had visions whereby their lives were changed.

On the other hand, Chili also realized that hearing voices and seeing things that others didn't see were not only signs of going bonkers, but pretty ordinary stuff with half the crowd at any rock concert tripping their brains out on acid, mushrooms, mescaline, pot, hash, and any number of combinations of pills washed down with Boone's Farm Apple wine.

When he arrived back at the tent, Mikey and Angel were sitting at a picnic table boiling water for instant coffee and eating Moon Pies. The fog was almost completely burned off and the view of the ocean was laid out before them in all its raging majestic beauty.

"You guys won't believe what I just saw!"

"Don't tell me! The Virgin Mary on a half shell," Mikey shot back.

"An elephant seal," Chili said, grabbing a mug and a Moon Pie.

"Well which was it? If it was an elephant, let me know what drug you're taking," Angel said grabbing another Moon Pie.

"An elephant seal is this freakin' huge seal, like ten feet long and weighs tons. It was only a couple of hundred yards down the beach. This cute chick, Ranger Smith, told me about it. And what a stink."

"That's no way to talk about a cute ranger!" Mikey said.

"Ha ha. Very funny. He's probably still there if you want to go see it."

Angel put some instant coffee in their cups and poured in the hot water. "We better hit the road. I want to spend a little time in San Francisco. And then I definitely want to spend some quality time with the Iowa girls above Eureka."

Even though they had been on the road for over three thousand miles, there was a vibe in the vee-dub that the trip had just started. Every turn on P.C.H. seemed to reveal another breathtaking vista of a rocky coastline with an ever-changing scene where the forest and rocky cliffs seemed to go right to the breaking waves. Blasting through the turnpikes of New Jersey, Pennsylvania, and Ohio seemed like a drive that was in some long, distant past. The endless miles of terrain so flat and boring that a lone pine tree in a field was something to take note of were long forgotten. The fear of not making it over the Continental Divide, then choking on superheated air in the Mohave were already hidden memories. Now they were in California, cruising in the exhilarating cool ocean wind rushing into the passenger compartment thanks to the dual triangular vent windows turned inward. The miles melted away as they made their way past Pismo Beach, Morro Bay, and Cambria.

"Hey, Big Sur is coming!" Mikey said, peering through his cheap spyglass. "That's the name of another Kerouac book. If we stay there, San Francisco is two and half hours away."

"What's that one about?" Chili asked, leaning in. "I want to read some of his books."

Mikey was eager to share. "I wouldn't start with that one. It's basically Kerouac trying to go cold turkey from alcoholism in a small cabin in the woods. It doesn't have a happy ending to say the least. The last chapter is psychotic gobbleygook and hallucinations. It was kind of a sign of what was ahead for him in the next few years."

"A sign?" Chili whispered.

"What happened to him?" Angel asked.

"He drank himself to death at the age of forty-seven. A broken man."

"Ah, the noble life of an artist," Angel said shaking his head.

"I say let's plow through to Frisco," Chili suggested. They all agreed.

It was after ten o'clock by the time they rolled into the North Beach section of San Francisco.

"This looks just like Greenwich Village," Chili said as they rolled past hippies playing guitars on the grass in a park. "And it looks like it's right up against Little Italy and Chinatown. Just like New York."

"Should we park and walk around? I think with the New York plates we're a target just like in Hollywood," Angel said, with a worried frown as he scanned the area.

They decided to drive around until they found a deli or pizzeria where they could keep an eye on the car.

"Well, there's a chop suey joint right over there," Mikey noticed. "We could even get it to-go maybe."

As they parked the car, they noticed that right across the street from the row of Chinese restaurants and curio shops was a spicy addition to the neighborhood.

"Holy crap. Three strip clubs, right in a row!" Mikey said, gleefully.

"They don't have that in Chinatown in New York," Chili added. "I'm starving and if I have another can of Dinty Moore beef stew I think I'll barf every time I see a red can for the rest of my life. Can't we just get some Chinese food to-go and find a camp site?"

They found a campsite about a half-hour outside of San Francisco, and devoured their Chinese food as if they hadn't eaten since they crossed the George Washington Bridge. After Angel and Chili fell asleep, Mikey was busy mapping out the next day's activities in San Francisco. City Lights Bookstore and the Vesuvio Café would suffice for the beat and Kerouac connection, and Haight-Ashbury, ground zero for West Coast hippies, was a must-see for anyone who considered rock music part of their upbringing.

City Lights bookstore was just that: a bookstore. Mikey was aware of the history of the place and absorbed every dusty shelf and aisle with glee and wonder. But to Angel and Chili, it was just another musty old store that had seen better days.

The Vesuvio was a not much better for Angel and Chili. Yeah, they knew that Jack Kerouac, Allen Ginsburg, and Gregory Corso hung out there, but that was over twenty years ago. And who wants to pay three dollars for a cup of coffee, when you could go to the donut shop down the street and get one for fifty cents? So it was agreed they'd spend the rest of the day in Haight-Ashbury.

They knew that the Grateful Dead, Jefferson Airplane, Janis Joplin, Steve Miller, and Creedence Clearwater Revival either started there, lived there, or hung out there. It was to the West Coast what the East Village was to the East Coast. This was their

Fallout Shelter

generation's mecca, not the beatnik-bongo hangouts of North Beach.

As they drove through the streets of the Haight, it resembled the streets of the Bronx more than Greenwich Village. There was graffiti everywhere, overflowing garbage cans, and dirty gutters. The parks weren't full of weekend hippies like in Greenwich Village, in their hundred-dollar fringe jackets. These hippies were hard-core street kids, high, drunk, and hustling.

They found a secure parking lot and paid five bucks to park the car for two hours, rather than risk another break in. They followed the foot traffic to a nearby park, and were offered pot, cocaine, and pills and asked for spare change every few feet by teens who looked like they were on the run for months.

"This is like Times Square for hippies," Angel said, keeping his hand on his wallet in his front pocket. "Let's hang in that park where the band is playing and see what develops."

It wasn't exactly a scene from *Hair* playing out in front of them with clean flower children spreading peace and love. It was more like a traveling band of pirates.

"I guess this isn't exactly the Summer of Love, like in sixty-seven," Mikey said, forlornly.

"Yeah, this is just the leftovers that went bad," Angel added.

"Guys, I got to find a bathroom. I'll be back in a few," Chili said, getting up from against the tree where they'd planted themselves.

After a week or so on the road, and not too many showers or shaves or clean clothes to his personal appearance, he fit in rather well. He invisibly walked among the throngs, observing and smelling their drugs, incense, and B.O. He was surprised how young so many of them were and assumed they were runaways from all over the country. Several were even asleep in sleeping bags under picnic tables.

And just as Chili was entering the Men's door of the public bathroom, a girl exited the women's door that sent a flash of recognition through Chili's brain. Could it be? Is it? He whirled around and shouted, "Pamela Hinderlap!"

She turned, and there she was. Pamela Hinderlap. The one girl that gave Chili the chills. The girl that made him feel mad passion for the first time. The girl who taught him what a French kiss was. The first girl who broke his heart. But she looked like all the other dirty, frazzled, drugged-out, lost hippies in the park.

"How do you know my name?" She asked, frozen in her bare feet. Wearing ragged denim short-shorts and a Lou Reed T-shirt with the arms cut off and tied to show her belly.

"It's me. Chili Manzilla."

"Holy fuckin' Christ," she mumbled, then stumbled.

Chili rushed over to help her get her balance, and led her to a tree in the shade where they could sit.

"What in hell are you doing here? And how did you even see me?" Pamela said, slurring her words. "I don't go by Pamela, so don't call me that. Call me *Sunshine*."

Chili noticed she had small spots on her arms and immediately realized it was from shooting drugs. His heart sank. How could this person even be the Pamela he knew?

"Are you all right? Do you live here by yourself? Is there anything I can do for you?"

Pamela tried getting up, and needed Chili to help her. "Can you give me five dollars? I haven't eaten in two days."

Without hesitation Chili gave her the money. "Can I tell anyone anything back in the Bronx? Like your parents?"

Pamela's mood went from spacey to angry. "Don't you tell anyone you saw me! This is our secret." She began to walk away, but turned around. "Chili. I always liked you. You were always so nice to me. I really liked you. But things happened. Nobody knows I'm here. Please come closer."

Chili stepped forward, stopping just inches from her. He looked in her eyes and could still see that Pamela the girl he loved was still in there. She leaned forward and kissed him briefly and softly on the lips. Chili smelled and tasted tobacco, onions, and other things that weren't pleasant.

"I want you to have these," she said, reaching into her pocket and taking out a small plastic bag. "This is ten hits of acid. Take them. I don't want them. Do what you want with them," she said, waking away briskly. Then turned one last time and from ten paces away said, "I'll always remember you, Chili."

"Pamela, if you ever want…help, or anything. I'm still at the same apartment. Just write to me and I'll be there for you. I'll pray for you."

Pamela covered her nose and mouth with both hands as she cried, and disappeared into the crowd.

Chili was rushing back to tell Angel and Mikey about Pamela, but they were now sitting with two girls who looked like they were barely out of grammar school. He stopped short, ducked behind a tree, and decided to take a walk on the streets of Haight-Ashbury.

Once he got out of the madness of the park and walked through the neighborhood to head for the famous intersection, he realized that it was pretty much another urban neighborhood, not that much different than his Bronx street. Although many of the storefronts were adorned with psychedelic murals, they were still mostly neighborhood stores. There was Wong's Chinese Hand Laundry, Jamie's Barber Shop, and the Brooklyn Bagel Shop. Of course mixed in with the dry cleaners, the bodegas, the taco stands, and pizza places were the Free Medical Clinic, the Tibetan Gift Corner, The Hungry Head Shop, and the Hare Krishna Temple. There were hippies, hipsters, and run-of-the-mill, walking-around, scratching-and-spitting people of every age, ethnicity, and gender, walking the streets and just living their lives, just like back on 238th Street. There was even a small storefront chapel with a courtyard that had some shade and some benches. Chili went through the gate and noticed a bulletin board with what looked like a wanted poster. It read, *Wanted: Jesus Christ, Notorious Leader of an Underground Liberation Movement, Associating with known criminals, prostitutes, and street people. Feeds the poor and curses the rich! Claims to turn ordinary people in the Children of God! Appearance: Hippie! Extremely Dangerous! Still at Large! Come in for more information!*

The first thing that popped into Chili's mind was freshman-year religion teacher Brother Dodge's Catholic Church dichotomy: the institutional church versus the spiritual church, which he scribbled on the blackboard on the very first day of class.

"Signs, signs, everywhere signs," Chili said aloud to no one.

And as he walked back to the park he noticed that also like back in the Bronx, there were cops.

"Shit," Chili whispered. *I've got ten hits of acid in my pocket. I might look suspicious if I try to just dump them in the trash. There's probably undercover narcs all over the place*, he thought to himself.

Trying to look as nonchalant as possible, Chili whistled while he walked back to the park and found Angel and Mikey sitting alone. "What happened to the Mouseketeer Club you had here a few minutes ago?"

"You saw them?" Mikey asked. "They must have been thirteen years old and they were hitting us up for pot, pills, booze, anything. And when that didn't work, they begged us for spare change."

"Yeah, and when we refused on all counts, they cursed us out and gave us the California one-finger salute." Angel said, disgusted.

"Well you guys won't believe who I just met," Chili said sitting down.

"Grace Slick?" Mikey guessed.

"Pamela Hinderlap," Chili said slowly, his voice dripping with regret.

"What? Are you serious? No way!" Mikey and Angel responded.

"She looked like what those two little runaways you were talking to are going to look like after hustling on the street for four of five more years."

"That's sad," Angel said.

"That's worse than sad. That's fucked," Mikey added. "Should we go look for her and take her back with us?"

Fallout Shelter

Angel and Chili looked helplessly at each other, knowing that Mikey wasn't really serious.

"Oh, and she gave me these," Chili said, making sure they were hidden from any spies. He leaned in and whispered, "It's ten hits of acid. She said she didn't want them anymore."

"Put that shit away!" Mikey said sternly. "But they might come in handy when we go up north."

"You hold them then!" Chili demanded.

"Okay," Mikey obliged.

Angel shook his head. "Haight-Ashbury is already getting to us. Let's get the hell out of here."

It would be around five hours to drive up the coast to Eureka. Then there was the problem of finding the store the Iowa girls recommended they stop at for information on where they were staying. But thanks to some rather careful planning they would be in the vicinity exactly when the girls said they would be there.

As spectacular as the ride from L.A. to San Francisco was, this stretch of Highway 1 made it very clear why it had a reputation as one of the most scenic in America and on the planet. If not for this ribbon of concrete along the water's edge, it frequently resembled a time-machine look-back on when the West Coast was still forming, with the ocean pounding the shore right up to the giant redwoods where wooly mammoths roamed, and who knows? Perhaps some kind of dinosaurs roamed here, either on land or in the sea.

"If this was the East Coast there would be high-rise condos this entire way on both sides of the highway," Angel said in wonderment.

"It's just a matter of time," Chili said.

"Well our time is now!" Mikey said with enthusiasm. "And we're gonna meet three beautiful babes and spend some time in a hippie commune!"

"What exactly is a hippie commune?" Chili asked. "The only one I read anything about was the Charles Manson Ranch."

Mikey shook his head in disbelief, "Chili, you need to read more than the *Daily News* to know what's happening. You can get the kid out of the Bronx, but you can't get the Bronx out of the kid! It's not murder and mayhem everywhere. There's places where hippies get together and live in a communal setting where they share everything. There's peace and free love."

"Yeah, like Pamela Hinderlap got involved with," Chili shot back.

"Let's see what happens when we get there," Angel said, calming down the developing bad vibe.

As the hours flew by, so did the weather. They traveled through bright sunshine and literally through rain clouds, and back again to clear skies, over and over. Highway 1 turned into Highway 101 and traveled inland and the magic of the roaring coastline became the surreal spectacle of mile after mile of ginormous redwoods that turned daylight into a weird kind of twilight. Even the sun couldn't penetrate the ancient, endless forests of gigantic trees.

"Holy crap, we can drive through a tree!" Angel said, taking a short detour, then turning back onto the main road.

"Here's where it really starts, boys," Mikey said, looking through his plastic spyglass. "Route 299 turn off is just ahead, and then holy shit! Chili, get ready for this; Route 299 is also called Trinity Highway."

Chili bit his tongue. He wasn't going to say anything. But he couldn't hide the smirk on his face. And in his mind he sang, "Signs, signs, everywhere signs."

Mikey, not waiting any longer for Chili's response added, "And on Trinity Highway, in Blue Lake, that's where the store is where the girls said we'd get the directions to Nirvana!"

The Trinity Highway meandered eastward through thick forests of towering pine, oak, elm, and the occasional redwood. The coastal highway they had been traveling was blindingly bright from the morning fog burn-off until the moment the sun sank below the sea, whereas the road inland was almost like going through the Lincoln Tunnel, as it became a darkened tunnel of trees.

As promised on Route 299 there was the Family Tradition general store. It was a red-clapboard single-story building that appeared to be sinking back into the earth on one side. It had a screen-enclosed front porch that looked like a small bat could go through the holes, it was so badly in need of patching. They pulled into the empty parking lot, a patch of dirt in the midst of the woods in the front of the store. There was an old-fashioned Coke machine with a crank handle and wooden crate next to it to place the empties.

"I haven't seen one of those since they tore down Freedomland in 1964," Mikey said wistfully.

"I don't know how the owner of this relic is going to know about a hippie commune, but let's see if the Iowa girls have sent us on a wild-goose chase," Angel said, killing the engine.

The stairs creaked as they walked up the five steps and pushed through the screen door with an attached bell that tinkled announcing their arrival. There was a path on the sawdust strewn on the plank wooden floor in between barrels of grains, pickles, and nuts. There were tin signs on the walls for GREEN RIVER SODA POP, FLYING-A MOTOR OIL, VICTORY BONDS, and others that gave a clue as to when the last time the décor was updated.

"I think Sam Drucker from *Green Acres* is gonna walk out from that back room wearing a white apron and a bow tie, with Arnold the Pig and Mr. Haney right behind him," Chili said, taking in the ambiance.

Then another set of bells tinkled as a door behind the counter swung open and a guy about twenty years old, with blonde hair down to his butt, wearing a white apron with a white shirt and a bow tie.

"Well you got the apron and bow tie bit right," Mikey said.

"How can I help you guys?"

Angel stepped forward. "We're gonna pick up some stuff for our trip...."

"Oh, where are you from?"

"New York," Angel replied.

"Where in New York?"

"The Bronx."

"Where in the Bronx?"

"Near Van Cortlandt Park."

"You ever go to the pool hall across the street from there?"

Angel, Mikey, and Chili looked at each other in disbelief.

Mikey jumped into the conversation. "If you say you hung out there, I'm gonna bust a nut."

"No, but I was there once. My uncle lives in Riverdale and he took me there. Actually it was on the day John and Yoko were there. I just missed them."

"I was there that day, too!" Chili said, excitedly.

"Did you see them?" The counter guy asked.

"No, I was looking for my father. It's a bookie hangout."

"My name's Billy Crowe, cool meeting you dudes!"

"Hey, ah, Billy," Mikey said sidling up close to the counter. "We um, met these girls from Iowa in the Rockies...."

"Oh, yeah. They left me a note. Here's the directions to the Trinity Lake commune where they're staying. My cousin lives in their dorm. He says they are something else. Oh, and there's swimming there. But don't worry about bathing suits," Billy said laughing.

Angel took the directions from him. "We'll do a little shopping and hit the road. Hey, Billy, is it okay to just park anywhere and camp out if we want to on the way there?"

"Not with New York plates. The kids around here will push your car off a cliff for laughs."

"California has a lot in common with New York, we're finding out," Mikey said.

"Why is everything named Trinity around here?" Chili

asked.

"Well, there's Trinity Lake, Trinity Dam, Trinity Highway, I guess because we're in Trinity County."

"I see…," Chili said, with wheels spinning in his head. Angel and Mikey expected more from him, but were happy Chili left it at that. But in his head, Chili continued: *Here they are, zig-zagging across the country for three thousand miles going from the burned-out buildings of the Bronx to the burning gas fields of Elizabeth through the flatlands of America to the heap of earth known as the Rocky Mountains, to the rainbow-red canyons where John Wayne and dinosaurs roamed, to the UFO-baited deserts to the San Diego Los Angeles mega-megalopolis to the coastal cliffs into the redwoods, all leading to what? Trinity Lake, Trinity Dam, Trinity Road, Trinity County? Trinity! Of all things! Holy Trinity! How does the song go? They caught the last train for the coast! All the signs lead to this. But for who? For me? For Mikey and Angel?*

Trinity Alps Road started as a two-lane highway and became a single-lane dirt road between thick woods. They slowed down to read a sign on the side of the road, which read, THESE PROPERTIES PATROLLED BY ARMED COWBOYS. STAY IN YOUR CARS AND KEEP MOVING.

"I thought California was supposed to be laid-back?" Angel asked.

"It's a big state," Angel replied. "This is it. That gate is on the directions. We go through, then follow for exactly one-point-five miles, then turn left at a rusted tractor, and go exactly five miles to another gate that will be locked. The combination is 6650. Proceed along the road til you see the A-frame."

Chili noted the significance of the lock's combination, being the address of Corrigan high school, but said nothing.

Once through the gate, they drove another couple-hundred yards, past a small lake, a wide creek, some wetlands, and a field where several horses grazed.

"There's the A-frame. And you know what?" Angel said, slowing down as he approached the structure. "It's an A-frame, all right. Because that's all it is. It's an A-frame with no roof, no walls, and no windows."

"You're wrong. It's all windows!" Mikey said laughing.

Suddenly, in a cloud of dust, a horse appeared with a man riding it bareback. And the man was bareback also. Buck-naked as nature intended.

"What the hell?" Chili said from the backseat. "That guy is totally nude!"

"Oh my my!" Mikey said gleefully. "And here comes the best part!"

Around the corner of the A-frame came another horse with another rider: a beautiful young woman with long flowing blonde hair with cut-off denim shorts and a bikini top.

"Lady Godiva is for real!" Angel proclaimed.

"New York plates! Yeah!" the man shouted. "I'm from Connecticut!"

"Greenwich, no doubt. Probably a trust-funder. I'm not going out of this car and shaking hands with a nude guy. Who knows where his hands have been," Chili muttered.

"Oh, it's the Bronx boys!" the female yelled.

"It's one of the Iowa girls...," Mikey said, almost unable to speak. "Thank you, Jesus."

They both dismounted, and the guy gave both horses a slap on the butt, causing the horses to saunter away toward the field where other horses were grazing.

"I'm Stoney, and I think you already met my cousin, Karen. Pardon my outfit, but clothing is optional here at the commune."

Mikey and Angel exited the car while Chili stayed in the back seat, occupying himself by reading the road atlas. They both averted their eyes and tilted their heads upwards as they spoke small talk with Karen and Stoney. Chili listened from the car and picked up the fact that they could pitch their tent anywhere they wanted and stay for as long as they liked. There was an outhouse for number two, but they could pee anywhere. And there was a solar-heated shower behind the A-frame.

Fallout Shelter

Stoney was probably in his thirties, with long straight blond hair, his body all sinew and bone. He had some scarring on his arms and legs and facial features that reminded one of chiseled stone. "If you're shy, don't worry about leaving your clothes on. If you set up camp in the woods over there, you'll see a few tents, some lean-to's, and a couple of tepees. There's about ten people staying here on-and-off right now, including Karen and her two friends. There's a stream with a swimming hole. We have a pump for water, but we also use the stream. This is a commune, so contributing a little something is appreciated, whether food, labor, money, or whatever."

Mikey, still keeping his eyes above the shoulders of Karen and Stoney, reached into his pocket and pulled out the plastic envelope and dangled it in the air. "I think this might fit in the 'whatever' category. Ten hits of acid, if you want it."

Stoney threw his arms in air in a hallelujah gesture.

"Praise the lord and pass the ammunition! Wait'll I tell the rest of the clan the good news! We haven't had acid in months!"

A wave of guilt washed over Chili, as he now regretted not throwing the LSD in the trash immediately after Pamela gave it to him. But it was too late now, as Stoney ran around joyously spreading the word of the arrival of the psychedelic goodies.

Karen explained that she needed to tell her friends about their arrival, but had to go alone, in case they were nude sunbathing. "It's the first tepee on the right when you come down the trail."

Angel and Mikey rushed back to the car and jumped in the front seats. "Now *this* is the trip I've been waiting for!" Mikey said, elated.

"We have made it to nirvana, utopia, Shangri-la, and heaven all rolled into one!" Angel shouted.

"Heaven?" Chili asked. "I don't think so."

Mikey jerked his body completely around. "Chili, don't pull any holier-than-thou shit. This is our chance for some real…adventure!"

"Your chance," Chili said calmly.

"Don't ruin this for us, Chili," Mikey said, a hint of anger beginning to appear.

"Gentlemen, gentlemen, we've been here ten minutes," Angel said, calming the waters, "all we've seen is a hippie dude who likes to dangle his wedding tackle, and a college girl in a bikini top on a ninety-degree day. What's the big deal? Let's not get ahead of ourselves."

They parked the car, and began carrying their gear down the trail, settling on a spot not too close, but not too far from the first tepee on the right. They tried to look inconspicuous as they pitched their tent in a shady spot and attempted to see if the three Iowa beauties were indeed trying to get a tan from tip to toe and all the hot spots in between.

A spot for the Coleman stove and folding chairs was established as Chili took a walk down the trail to gather rocks that would circle the fire later that evening. Mikey tapped Angel on the shoulder. "We need to talk. Come over here," he said leading him to the other side of the tent. "Chili is acting weirder than normal, if you know what I mean."

"It's an oxymoron, but yes, I do."

"He's reminding me of that Alfred Hitchcock episode where the rape victim points out her rapist to her husband, so then he kills him. Then she says every man she sees on the street is her rapist. He's seeing signs and symbols, and I think he's hearing voices or something."

"You know Chili. He's…sensitive," Angel said, trying to be diplomatic. "He's always been the…cautious one. He's kept us out of a lot trouble a bunch of times."

"Yeah, but I don't want to be kept out of *this* trouble. Not here, with these gorgeous girls, and who knows who else is gonna come out of their damn tepee looking for some fun! I want in on it all."

Angel sighed. "Okay, let's just see what develops. Here he comes."

Chili arrived with an armload of stones and placed them

Fallout Shelter

in a circle about 10 feet from the tent. "I found that swimming hole in the creek. It's beautiful! There's even a rope swing you can jump off and land in the water! I'm gonna put on my bathing suit and head down there."

All three agreed and after all the miles, pit stops, countless bowls of Dinty Moore beef stew over Minute Rice, flat tires, car break-ins, and anticipation of what was around the next bend, it really, finally, once-and-for-all felt like vacation has started. The journey is over and they have arrived.

They cooled themselves in the swiftly moving waters staring at the white puffy clouds rolling against the crystal-clear deep blue sky. Each wore baggy bathing trunks with over-sized multi-colored flowers against an orange background, probably bought on a clearance table in Alexander's Department Store in 1967. Not much was said, as they enjoyed the complete solitude.

Then, in the woods, they heard some rustling of leaves and voices approaching. They turned their heads in the direction of the sounds and they couldn't believe their eyes. Two gorgeous women emerged out of the woods, wearing only sandals and a smile. They weren't teens or even college girls. These were grown women in their fully formed voluptuous beauty. Twiggy they weren't. Both raven-haired with a single French braid of hair hanging over one breast, they walked past them, waved, and said, "Hello. Beautiful day." That was it. They followed the creek for a few yards and followed the trail back into the woods.

"Did you see what I just saw? Or am I dreaming?" Angel asked.

"I know it's for real, because I have to go into the cold water to make my soldier go from attention to at-ease," Mikey said, going into the deeper waters.

"Guys, I'm sorry, but I don't know about this...," Chili said, standing and reaching for his towel. "I've been in the locker room with naked guys all through high school, but naked women? Whamming it out right in front of us like it's nothing?" Chili headed back to the tent.

"Chili...," Angel started.

"Let him go, Angel. He's a big boy. If he wants to sit in the tent and read the freakin' lost sea scrolls or some shit, so be it! I didn't travel three thousand miles to act like I'm still in sixth grade and go to confession if I see a picture of a topless chick. My father and mother got married when they were 18!" My oldest brother was born when they were 17 for chissakes!"

"You're right, he's on his own. Who knows? Maybe one of the Iowa babes is studying to be a nun or a therapist or something and they can pick each other's brains for the next week or so. I sure as hell am beyond trying to worry about what's going through that peabrain of his."

It was cooling off as the sun setting and the sounds of the evening were beginning to emerge. A coyote howled in the distance, insects harmonized in sync, and voices from nearby tents, tepees, and the A-frame got louder.

"Hey guys!" Stoney said, who was in evening dress: a loin cloth. "Go to the second tepee, just past Karen's, in an hour. We're having a yaby-yum with the help of your mother's little helper you laid on us! Be there or be square!"

"He sounds like Maynard G. Krebs. What did that mean?" Chili asked, pausing between spoonfulls of stew.

"My book knowledge for once is coming in handy! In Kerouac's *The Dharma Bums*, they have this thing called a *yaby-yum*, which is a traditional Tibetan ritual of compassion and togetherness, but the Americanized version is just a good old-fashioned orgy."

Chili froze with spoon mid-air. He waited for Angel to say something. Anything.

"And mother's little helper?" Angel asked.

"That's from the Rolling Stones song. It's a euphemism for drugs!" Mikey gloated.

Chili put his spoon into his tin bowl, rose silently, and went inside the tent.

"What are we gonna do?" Angel whispered to Mikey.

"We are going to a yaby-yum."

It was dark and in the not-too-far-distance from their tent they could hear squeals of ecstasy.

"I guess Stoney just pulled out the acid," Mikey said, as the three of them drank coffee by a small campfire. "Who's going with me?" There was a devilish glow on Mikey's face as the flames danced and popped.

Angel spoke up after a long pause. "I'm in."

They looked at Chili.

Chili put down his coffee cup. "I don't know what will be going on in there after this yaba daba doo party gets into full swing...."

"It's not the *Flintstones*. It's a yaby-yum party," Mikey interrupted.

"I'll walk down there with you guys just to get a flavor of what kind of hell you guys are getting into. I'll get the flashlight."

For three boys from St. Gall's grammar school, an orgy isn't exactly something that ever came up during grade school or in high school. Most dates were wrestling matches with similarly raised Catholic girls who knew when to say when, and throw a well-placed right hook as good as any nun. Orgies were the stuff of unattainable fantasy, on the same level as playing center field for the Yankees, or winning a Cadillac in a church raffle. It happens, but not to kids who grew up killing cockroaches in Bronx kitchens. Chili led the way down the trail as the voices grew louder with glee. The tepee where the party was taking off was twice the size of the one where the Iowa girls were staying. Chili pushed aside the leather cloth over the entrance and peeked in.

"Mazel tov, baby!" Stoney yelled, joint in hand.

Mike and Angel were right behind.

"These are the angels who brought us manna from heaven, everybody!" Stoney proclaimed, prompting hoots and hollers form the three Iowa girls and two other females, wearing cut-off shorts and bikini tops, and one other guy wearing gym shorts and no shirt. Stoney was the oldest at thirty, and all the others were college-age, not an unfit one in the bunch.

Stoney took out the plastic envelope. "Let the party begin! Line up!"

Each person stood in line and took position in front of Stoney with their tongues out. Stoney placed the hit of acid on the tongue and each person turned around as if in a sacred ritual and took a seat.

This was too much for Chili. The sight of tongues being extended looked just like communion when the priest places the wafer on the tongue at mass. "You guys have fun. I'll check back later to make sure you're all right," Chili said to Mikey and Angel, at the back of the line.

"If the tent is rocking, don't come knocking!" Mikey said with glee.

"I get it, Chili," Angel said, patting Chili on the shoulder as he turned to leave.

It took about an hour for the sounds of the party to go from ordinary party banter and laughter to outright insanity. Chili had been reading *The Dharma Bums* by the light of the flashlight, and was surprised at the parts that were spiritual in nature, and not a hedonistic bacchanal, but the noise coming down the trail from the tent might as well have been from a pack of coyotes after a kill, as from some kind of orgy. He could hear howls, screeches, wails, and yelps from males and females. Dare he go and try to sneak a peek at what was going on? Could it be as advertised on those Times Square marquees and sex shoppe storefront windows?

Chili walked gingerly down the path. The teepee seemed to be undulating and heaving. The candles inside were creating bizarre shadows of grotesque body part shapes on the exterior of the tee-pee. He snuck over to a vent window that had the cloth slightly drawn and looked in. And received the shock of his life. There they were the party-goers, Mikey and Angel included, in a lump of body-painted flesh on the floor of the tent in a sweaty, awkward ballet of tits, dicks, balls, asses elbows, and kneecaps. A few seconds was all he could take. He rushed back to the sanity of his sleeping bag in their tent and picked up his copy of *The Life of Saint Francis Assisi*.

One hour, two hours, three hours passed and Chili was in and out of consciousness in his sleeping bag as he worried about his fellow travelers. Chili was devastated. Could he possibly see his two best friends in the same light after witnessing their total disregard for morality? He understood the temptations of the flesh, and thanks to Pamela Hinderlap he knew how powerful lust and passion were. But an orgy? LSD?

Chili grabbed his flashlight and headed back to the teepee. Besides the devastating disappointment he felt knowing his friends took part in something so utterly contrary to his belief system, he felt an obligation to find out if they were safe.

It was eerily quiet at the tepee and only a dim flickering light was bouncing around the canvas exterior. Then suddenly, out of the darkness, came several lunatics screaming like wild Indians on a rampage. He shined his flashlight on them, and there was Angel and Mikey, and the three Iowa girls stark-naked with body paint smeared all over them. The screams turned to hysterical laughter as they collapsed on the ground around him.

"Have you guys gone insane? Look at yourselves! You're like wild animals. Worse!"

Mikey rose from the ground and turned off his laughter to dead seriousness. "You see a sign in all this? Well I see something! I see what you are! You are not even of this earth! You are a...some kind of a...you just don't understand!"

"You and Angel should probably come back to the tent with me...."

"No. We can't!" Mikey raged on. "We can't face you anymore. You think you see through us? Well we saw through you! You think we're hallucinating, huh? Well maybe you were hallucinating that night!"

Angel jumped up. "Mikey, no! Shut up!"

"You think you saw the Virgin Mary that night in the park! That was bullshit! That was us. We gave you hash brownies and you were tripping your brains out! And we rigged that stupid statue in the tree! We did it! You didn't see any vision! It's all a fake! You're a fake!"

There was total quiet. The girls covered their breasts with their hands and went inside the tepee. Angel went over to Mikey. "Shut up," he said calmly.

Chili said nothing. He wondered where he was and how he got there. *Naked people? Woods? A tepee? What did I see? A vision? Oh, yeah.* He turned and didn't look back.

At the tent, Chili packed his things and slept in the Squareback's rear seat.

The sun was rising and the fog and dew were still heavy. Chili left his sleeping bag and the copy of *The Dharma Bums* Mikey had given him. He took his two bags and began walking down the dirt road. He left a note that read, *I had to go home. I'll pray for you both.* He knew it was a few miles to the highway, and from there he would hitchhike back to the general store, or maybe all the way to Eureka. From there he could catch a bus to the nearest train station and head back to New York.

Chili had only stuck his thumb out on the Trinity Highway for about a minute when a van pulled over. Chili ran up to the driver-side window.

An oversized Black man with a large afro and a toothy smile was behind the wheel. "Where you headed, pilgrim?"

"I'm trying to get somewhere where I can catch a Greyhound bus or Amtrak?"

"It's your luck day, pilgrim. There's an Amtrak bus in Eureka that goes to the train station in San Francisco."

"Can you take me to Eureka?"

"Absolutely, pilgrim! Come on in!"

Chili was greeted by a van full of eight passengers and he squeezed into the rear row. There were three Black men, three

Fallout Shelter

Black women, and two Hispanic women. Chili noticed they were holding pamphlets and hymnals.

"Thanks for stopping. Is this a church group of some kind?"

There was no reply from the passengers, but the driver spoke up. "Yes we are, pilgrim! We're on a little missionary expedition up north here. We're headquartered in San Francisco."

"What the name of your church?"

"We're the Peoples Temple. You may have heard of our pastor, the Reverend Jim Jones."

"No, I don't think so."

"He's a great man. We live in a commune-type setting. We share everything. You know what a commune is?"

"Oh yeah. I know. I know."

The ride to Eureka was a quiet one. Chili tried making small talk with his fellow passengers, but would only get a one-syllable response, so he gave up trying. The van stopped right at the Amtrak bus station and Chili exited.

"Thanks so much for the ride!"

The driver handed him a pamphlet with a picture of Reverend Jim Jones on the front. He had a collar that looked exactly like a priest's collar. "Pilgrim, keep us in mind if you are ever lost on the road to salvation. Reverend Jones has big plans for our community. You're welcome to join us any time! Watch the news! He has big plans for us in a place called Guyana! It's gonna be a paradise!" He said joyfully as the van pulled away.

Chili stuck the pamphlet in his bag, and waited for the return trip back to the Bronx to begin.

Chapter 11

Jamie waited by the phone all day every day hoping Chili would call. He knew he wouldn't tell him about the horrors of what he saw. No one can ever know. He didn't care if he lived or died right now, but he would protect Chili and their dad until his last breath. He saw the lengths that Father O'Brennan and his followers would go to in order to protect themselves. He had no doubt they would follow through on their threats of killing all three of them if he squealed. He just wanted to hear Chili's voice.

He also needed to tell Chili about their dad. He seems different. He's coming home straight from work. And sober. But he's sleeping a lot, and not waking up or being disturbed by the sounds of normal household activities like dropping a pan while washing the dishes or having the TV loud when there's a western on. And he's eating even less than before. Jamie knows he's been to the doctor because he has scraps of paper in the garbage can with *Montefiore* and room numbers written on them. That's the hospital where Mrs. Manzilla died.

Chili had only been gone a few weeks, and Jamie was scared being alone for the two or so months Chili had planned to be away on his trip. What if their father got really sick? The money Chili left behind was running out. And what if Father O'Brennan's minions came after him? Staying at home seemed to be his best option.

All the papers to transfer from Corrigan to DeWitt Clinton High School were in order. There was no summer reading list. No dress code, haircut code, conduct code, or threats of detention or expulsion for code violations. Although he did see one warning: no knives, guns, or other weapons are to be brought into the school.

Mr. Manzilla was in the bedroom fast asleep since getting home from the night shift at 8 a.m. The apartment was stifling as usual, with windows wide open, and the sounds of the neighborhood reminding Jamie that he didn't live on a remote desert island. But the sound of the locks clanking open on the front door startled him from his Pop Tart. For a split second he thought perhaps one of O'Brennan's soldiers had gotten copies of the keys and were there to execute him. But an instant of terror gave way to jubilation when the door swung open and Chili stood there with two bags and a four-day beard.

In a display of uncharacteristic affection for his big brother, Jamie rushed to give him a bear hug. "Chili! You're home!!"

"Yeah, I had to cut the trip short. The guys wanted to go one direction and I wanted to go the other."

"How did you get home?"

Chili put his things down and headed for the kitchen. "I took the train. It was great. Four days staring out a window gave me a chance to really think about things. There's hardly anything in the fridge. Have you been shopping?"

"Yeah, I was gonna go this morning."

"I have some extra money since I cut the trip short. What's new? Where's dad?"

"He's been sleeping since he got home from work this morning," Jamie said, the excitement of the moment having already worn off.

Chili grabbed the last Pop Tart out of the box and popped it into the toaster. "Is everything all right around here?"

"What do you mean?"

"Just that. Is everything all right? Tell me about school. A kid got killed? That's horrible. How well did you know him?"

"We had just met at the retreat but we were roommates there."

"What happened?"

"He...fell off a cliff on a hike. That's all I know."

"That's so sad. Did you go to the funeral?"

"No."

"And is everything all set with you going to Clinton?"

"Yes. Did Mikey like it there?"

"He liked it. But I don't know if it did him any good."
"What do you mean?"
"Never mind."

Chili was happy to be home, seeing the normal neighborhood activities taking place as if he didn't miss a single day there. Louie the shoemaker holding court with the local *cognoscenti* in his store. The smell of the rotten fish barrels and sidewalk garbage cans camouflaged by the aroma of Stelllla D'Oro anisette cookies being baked by the truckload. Kids playing curb ball, old people sitting on lawn chairs getting some fresh air, the Good Humor man putting coins in his belt change-maker and clicking out the change. Despite all the sameness, the routine movements of life around him, Chili knew things were different. He was different. His world, his life, his very fate was intertwined with Mikey and Angel since he began to become self-aware as a human being. The three musketeers would hunker in the fallout shelter for comfort, for support, yes, for the love that sometimes wasn't found at home. And now that was gone. He felt betrayed by his two best friends. And now he was having a total break with his grammar school and high school playmates. He was taking his life seriously now. Enrolling in the seminary was no joking matter.

Mount Angel seminary in Westchester was only a few miles from the Bronx, but seemed a galaxy away. The rest of the summer Chili took three buses almost every weekday for the grueling application and approval process into the seminary to become a Catholic priest. His own failings, especially on his summer trip, would be left far behind. Even the words of the van driver from the People's Temple inspired him to remain steadfast on his spiritual journey. Was it a coincidence that such a man would pick him up, literally off the street, and show him the way back home? Of course not.

In two weeks, Chili would be packing his bags for a much different trip. The trip that has been on his itinerary since that first day of raising his hand in second grade to become an altar boy. With the milestones of each of the sacraments received, being promoted in the altar boys from server, to acolyte, to thurifer, to master. Then, to his mother's dying words about looking and listening for her direction and signs after she was gone. He was accepted into the ordination process and would begin his lifelong quest that he felt was pre-ordained for him.

Meanwhile, Jamie was overwhelmed beginning his new journey at the DeWitt Clinton High School for Boys orientation. With over 6,000 students it was three times the number of boys at Archbishop Corrigan and the building itself was three times the size and twice as old. It was also much more diverse than Corrigan, with more than half the student body Black and Puerto Rican. And with Jamie's dark features he could easily pass as Hispanic.

With all the usual babble about Clinton's history, famous alumni, opportunities for all who apply themselves, and fire exits, there was one shocking revelation that took Jamie by surprise. In gym class, when using the swimming pool, all boys must swim naked. It had something to do with hygiene, but the jarring announcement had Jamie in a state of panic. He recalled the first time he was in a group shower in gym class and that was enough to make him nervous. But swimming entirely nude for a class had him terrified. What if, by chance, he had an erection? It was easy to hide one in the shower if you were adroit with your towel. But how could you hide it going to the pool, swimming in the pool, getting out of the pool, and walking to the lockers? That would be another challenge as he grappled with the new directions his life was taking after the experiences he wanted so much to leave behind.

One good thing about going to Clinton instead of Corrigan was that he could walk there. No more buses and trains packed like sardines broiling in hot weather and shivering in the winter. Not to mention the awful smells regardless of the season.

You were pressed closer to every kind of stranger in these graffiti-festooned piss cars than you would be in any other circumstance except maybe some kind of disaster like an explosion or floor collapsing, when a mass of humanity would land on top of you. Hai Karate, Mad Dog 20-20, B.O., human excrement, and countless mystery odors mixed with the usual gastrointestinal fumes from cuisines ranging from China-Rican, Sicilian, Kosher, soul-food, and fermented food scraps picked out of sidewalk garbage cans were just something else one had to get used to. Just close yourself off. Don't look and for godsakes, don't ever stare! Staring can get easily get you a knife stuck in your neck. Sometimes it doesn't take anything to get a knife stuck in your neck. Or get bumped onto the tracks with the light coming down the tunnel. All one can do is isolate. Insulate. Hold your breath. Look down, but be aware. Who knows when danger will strike? Especially when you know that one wrong move can get you killed. Or your brother or your father.

    Sometimes in September, Indian summer would hit and the temperatures and tempers would rise. But this early evening, a cool breeze was blowing down the street and into the windows of the Manzilla apartment as Jamie watched the world go by his window. He saw a girl walking down the street toward the entrance to his building and he craned his neck out the window to get a better look. He was sure it was his old grammar school friend, Gerty. She looked so much more grown-up, gliding down the street in hip-hugger jeans and sandals. When she reached the front stoop just below his window, she stopped. She stood there, looked to the left, to the right, across the street, and then she shot a glance straight up at Jamie's window. Jamie froze. She waved.

    Jamie hadn't seen Gerty since the summer before freshman year of high school. They were still friends and had advanced from Chinese checkers to going to movies, walking to different neighborhood libraries, and even taking the subway downtown to museums. Once high school started, he at

Corrigan, and she at the Bronx High School of Science, they just lost touch.

Jamie finally waved to her.

"Wanna play some Chinese checkers?" Gerty shouted through her cupped hands.

Jamie laughed for the first time in a while. "I'll be right down!"

Up close, Gerty looked even better. The chubbiness in her cheeks was gone, but her still roundish face had a Linda Rondstadt cuteness. "Hi, Gerty! It's good to see you!"

"You, too!"

Jamie wanted to give her a hug, but instead reached out to shake his hand. Gerty pushed it away, gave him a wiggly hug, and kissed him on the cheek.

"Let's go for a walk," Jamie said.

They walked down the block, under the el, and up the city steps, which led to the suburban-like streets of Riverdale. There was much catching-up. Gerty was on the honor roll in her freshman year at Science, and looking forward to sophomore year. Jamie knew that being on the honor roll at the Bronx High School of Science wasn't like being on the honor roll in grammar school, or Corrigan, Clinton, or even some colleges. Science was the crown jewel of high schools in the New York public school system, based purely on academic merits.

"I'm transferring to Clinton," Jamie said, sheepishly.

"Public school is great! I think you'll love it."

"I've heard it's kind of dangerous."

"So is walking down the street. You'll do fine."

Gerty always made Jamie feel better. One thing that bothered Jamie was that as much as he liked her, and loved being around her, he didn't want to hold her hand. Or kiss her. Even now that she looked so adorable, he just didn't feel that way. Which made him feel even more alone. More different. Even ashamed.

"Clinton is really close to Science. We could even walk to school together some mornings," Gerty said, cheerfully, and brushing a little closer to Jamie as they strolled down the dark street with a the first leaves of fall under their feet.

"That would be great."

"Why are you leaving Corrigan?"

They walked about a half block before Jamie answered. "Something terrible happened."

"Oh no. I'm sorry. Can you talk about it?"

"A little. I was at a retreat with the school. And my roommate, who I just met…fell off a cliff and…got killed."

"Oh my God! That's so tragic. I don't blame you. A change will do you good. Get away from those awful memories." Gerty grabbed Jamie's hand for a second and looked him in the eye. She then gave him a tender, soft, slow hug, and put her head on his shoulder. Jamie could smell her shampoo, and even guessed that she was using Ivory soap to wash with by the fragrance. It was first time a female had hugged him in such a loving way since his mother was alive. And it made him feel kind of like that. It was a pure feeling of compassion and tenderness.

It seemed like Gerty was waiting for Jamie to do something. Something that would be obvious to a potential boyfriend. But Gerty was no fool. Science High School was known to be a progressive hotbed of protests against the war, and for women's lib, black power, and gay liberation.

"I understand, Jamie," Gerty said, sweetly.

There was a connection Jamie felt with Gerty like no other person alive. He would die for Chili and his dad, but he knew there were limits on what he could tell them. Only his mother had that deep bond with him where he could tell her all. He remembered the times when a snuggle, a stroke of his hair, or a shared giggle would make him feel whole. Complete. Nothing could ever come close. But he did feel a comfort with Gerty that he had almost forgotten about.

They walked all through Riverdale for more than an hour until they came upon the famous Wave Hill Estate overlooking the Hudson River. They stood across the street and gazed upon

Fallout Shelter

its opulent simplicity. Surrounded by manicured gardens, the fragrances from the flowers hung in the warm humid air.

"It's hard to believe that this only a walk away from where we live," Jamie said, admiring the grounds.

"Mark Twain lived here from 1901 to 1903," added Gerty. "We studied him in school. He was quite revolutionary for his time. You know he was very critical of religion. And some said he was anti-Catholic."

"Yeah, well there's still a lot of that going around."

"Science has a lot of Jewish kids. But nobody really talks about religion much."

"I've had it with religion I think. I've seen too much," Jamie said as they headed back towards their neighborhood. "I don't think I'll ever set foot in a church again. Not after…my Corrigan experience."

"That bad?"

"Maybe someday, I'll tell you about it."

They walked past Jamie's building, up the hill to where Gerty lived. In the courtyard, they passed the bench where they used to play together. Jamie remembered fondly how Gerty made him feel way back when they were just kids. And as she waved goodbye and headed into her building he was glad she still made him feel that way.

Chili knew something wasn't right with his dad. At first he thought it was just maybe the kind of hangover that lasts a while after a long bender. But after a few weeks the hangover didn't resolve back into its normal cycle of work, get drunk, eat, work, get drunk, ad nauseam.

But Chili didn't know how to talk to his father. Ever since just before his mom died, and Chili threatened to kick his father's ass, they would go days and weeks with only looks, grunts, and simple one- or two-word replies. However, his mother's final words haunted him. She said he had to look after his little brother *and* his father. She knew.

Sitting alone at the kitchen table while Jamie still slept, Chili heard the front door locks clicking open extremely slowly, as if it was an effort to do so. Chili leaned into the doorway to see his dad entering. He could tell it was time to have a conversation. A real one.

"Hi dad. How you doing?"

Mr. Manzilla looked surprised, as if he hadn't heard such a sentiment coming from Chili in a long, long time. "Not so good."

Those three nakedly honest words shocked Chili. Mr. Manzilla shuffled across the hardwood floor and sat at the kitchen table next to Chili. "I've been to the doctor. I didn't tell Jamie, but I had an episode while you were away. I was throwing up in the bathroom...."

"Yeah, all right. That's not a first."

Mr. Manzilla shot Chili a look as though he might have a cutting reply, but thought better of it.

"And I half filled-up the bathroom sink with blood. I made it to the emergency room and–long story short–I had a hemorrhage in my throat. I had to stop drinking. I find it hard to eat...."

"Do they say what else is wrong?"

"It was an esophageal hemorrhage but they're not sure what to do yet."

Chili had a pang of humiliating guilt as he collected his thoughts, because the first thing that popped into his mind was where would the money be coming from if he died?

"Does work know?"

"No. Tell Jamie to go sleep on the couch. I need to get some rest in the bed."

"Don't you want something to eat?"

"Nah."

Mr. Manzilla went into the bedroom and closed the door. Jamie joined Chili at the kitchen table.

"Dad's sick, right?" Jamie asked nervously.

"Yeah. It could be cancer."

"I thought so."

"All we can do is pray."

Jamie stood up quickly, pushing his chair into the stove making a loud *clang*. "Is that all you can ever think of? Pray? How about getting some expert medical advice! Maybe that's a better idea! Fuck your prayer bullshit. I'm gonna go for a walk," he said, storming out.

Chili was in stunned silence. He lost his mother. He was losing his father. And now Jamie was probably lost. Not to mention Angel and Mikey. How could it be that since graduation just weeks ago, that his entire world would be blown up? But his new life, his vocation, his lifelong ambition on the path to the priesthood was only days away.

Mikey and Angel had just driven two hundred miles without stopping and pretty much without speaking. Their goal was to see Mount Rushmore in the daylight. In the back seat of the Squareback there was a passenger where Chili sat for so many miles. It was one of the Iowa girls, Brenda. Like Chili, she was also appalled at the behavior of the acid-taking yaby-yum participants. And like Mikey and Angel, she was one of the willing participants. After the dust settled, she asked if Mikey and Angel could drive her home to Iowa. She had enough. So did Mikey and Angel. The three of them didn't remember everything that happened that fateful night, but what little they remembered was plenty.

Mount Rushmore was another sightseeing rush job. The plan all along was to speed across the country to maximize time spent on the West Coast and then enjoy the sights on the return trip that would fit into whatever time was left. Instead, the psychotic, cruel confession to Chili, revealing the phony vision of the Virgin Mary, took the luster off their journey.

They parked so they could view Mount Rushmore and all three hit the restrooms. They then stood in the parking lot and looked at the four towering figures of American history.

Angel stood between Mikey and Brenda. "I'll bet Chili would have had some insights about how the four symbols of American greatness were more signs of how he was destined to become a priest."

Brenda turned to Angel, nodding, "You didn't tell me that part of the story. Chili wants to be a priest? Now I know why he left in a New York minute. No wonder. You must have known he'd have a freakout when he saw Fellini's *Satyricon* meets Dante's *Inferno* play out in front of him."

"Yeah, well, that wasn't the worst of it," Mikey admitted, sheepishly.

In the vee-dub, Mikey went on to explain the twisted tale of that night in the Bronx when their devilish prank had unintended consequences.

"That's just terrible," Brenda said, more sad than accusatory. "Do you think your stunt could have made him even more determined to become a priest?"

"Yeah," Mikey and Angel said in unison.

It was about six hours to Sioux City, Iowa, where they would drop off Brenda at her home. Not much was said for the rest of the trip.

Brenda grabbed her bags in front of her long driveway on a typical suburban street. "Thanks for the trip. I mean…the ride. If you're ever in Iowa, give me a call. Let me write down your address and my number. I'd like to see what happens when you guys get together with Chili again."

She wrote down the information, waved, and was gone.

Angel started the car as Mikey used his plastic magnifier to find the nearest campground. "Do you think it will happen?" Angel said, going from first to second gear.

"What?"

"Do you think we'll ever get together with Chili again?"

"I think that's his call. Turn left here," Mikey said pointing, "Let's get some sleep."

"I hope I can." Angel replied.

∽ Chapter 12 ∾

For the first time since the very first day of first grade, he was no longer Chili. He was once again William from day one of moving into the seminary and from then on. He was surprised when he entered his shared room to unpack his things, and there was a middle-aged man already in the room, smoking a pipe, sitting in an overstuffed upholstered chair by the window.

"Am I in the right room?"

"If your name is William Manzilla, the answer is in the affirmative. I'm Andrew Clarke," he said rising up to shake hands. "I know you're wondering what's this old-timer doing enrolling in a seminary? I'm fifty-three years old, I have two grown children, retired from Wall Street, and I'm a widower."

"I didn't know you could do that," Chili said, putting down his things.

"Nor did I. But after three years of retirement, and wondering what my purpose in life was, I discovered there is a path to the priesthood."

"I guess these are my drawers here…did you have some kind of…sign?" Chili asked, filling his drawers with clothing.

"Signs? If you mean like a burning bush or something? No. Just many days and nights of prayer. I'll let you get settled in. Do you want anything from the cafeteria?"

"No, thanks, Mr. Clarke."

"Call me Andy."

"Andy."

Mr. Clarke left the room and Chili continued unpacking. He had been hoping to make a new friend with a roommate, but had no idea that he would be his father's age. At first thought he was disappointed. But not really having a relationship with his father for so long, there could be an advantage to having a man of that age as a friend and confidante. After all, he enjoyed hanging out with the older neighborhood men who sat in the rarely used shoeshine chairs in Louie the shoemaker's store. He learned so much about the history of the neighborhood, baseball, and what life was like during the Depression and World War II. Not to mention some dirty jokes that he never repeated, but certainly did laugh at.

The days and nights came and went with no time for idleness. College-level courses on Bible history, psychology, philosophy, English, public speaking, and even business management went from early morning to early evening. About half of the seminarians seemed to be Chili's age, the other half might have been recent college graduates. Then there was Mr. Clarke. He stood out, not only for his age, but being about six-foot-four, lean as a foul pole, and bald as a baseball. Even at fifty-three, he was the first pick for a three-on-three basketball game during gym.

Chili was wondering if sitting by Mr. Clarke during class, in the cafeteria, and of course chatting late into the evening with him was stifling his chance at mixing with others closer to his own age. But he didn't care. Mr. Clarke served in WW II, went to Columbia University on the G.I. Bill, married his high school sweetheart, raised two kids (the girl became a lawyer, the boy a doctor), and retired from Morgan Stanley at 50. He was a renaissance man who could take apart an engine, read Latin, explain *The Federalist Papers*, and play piano by ear, Hoagy Carmichael a specialty. He was the perfect studying partner. It was like rooming with your college professor.

But after the first few weeks, there was a change in Mr. Clarke. He was growing increasingly aloof, and would disappear for hours for what he simply called "meetings with higher-ups." He wasn't being picked for basketball pick-up games, and was even missing from some classes.

Then exactly three weeks to the day that Chili met Mr. Clarke, when Chili came back to the room after morning prayers in the chapel, he was gone. His bed was made, his drawers and his closet were empty, his trashcan was clean, and the ashtray was empty. There was no not a scintilla of evidence that he was ever there.

Fallout Shelter

Chili was dumbfounded. Troubled. Was he expelled? Did he quit? Was there a family emergency? With all Chili's time spent bonding with Mr. Clarke, he hadn't made any close personal relationships with any other seminarians, so he was reluctant to ask acquaintances if they had heard anything. He sat in the overstuffed upholstered chair where Mr. Clarke so often sat in contemplation in a fog of pipe tobacco smoke, like a spiritual Sherlock Holmes. He picked up his book, *The Life of St. Francis*, hoping for some kind of consolation, or sign. And upon opening it, there it was! And it wasn't a subtle sign. It was a note from Mr. Clarke: *William—I had to leave. Two things: Read St. Thomas Aquinas. Beware of Uncle Ralph.*

That presented two problems. Saint Thomas Aquinas had written much and had much written about him. And who in hell was Uncle Ralph?

There was a knock on the door. Chili crumpled the paper and stuck in his pocket. "Come in."

A blond-haired, blue-eyed young man who looked like he could still be an altar boy entered. "You must be William. I'm John McSherry. I understand we'll be rooming together."

Chili rose and shook hands. "Nice to meet you, John. Let me show where you can put your things."

Chili showed him all the spaces left vacant by Mr. Clarke. "Are you just arriving at the seminary?"

"No, I was instructed to move out of my previous room for some unknown reason. But you know how things are around here. Yes, sir, no sir, three bags full, sir."

"I never heard that before," Chili replied, pulling open some empty drawers.

"Oh it just means, do as you're told, or else."

"That I get. I'll let you get settled in. Do you want anything from the cafeteria?"

"No thanks."

Chili left the room, and headed for the reception area where the mail slots were. He was pleased to see a letter in his box. *From Mikey? I guess this is the day for cryptic notes,* he thought to himself.

He stepped outside to the park like grounds surrounding the one-hundred-year-old building and found a seat on a bench. He opened the letter. *Dear Chili, we left the commune shortly after you did. We even took Brenda, one of the Iowa girls, back home to Iowa. The return trip wasn't a fun one. The only stop we made was Mount Rushmore. That only made us feel even smaller as human beings. We fucked up. We're sorry. If you can forgive us, let us know. We can do a fallout shelter get together like the old days. Your ol pals, Mikey and Angel.*

Chili had mixed feelings about the apology letter. Tripping and doing something insane was one thing. But pulling a prank like they did on him and keeping it a secret for years was what was gnawing at his insides since that night of hippie-horror confessionals. It would take time for those wounds to heal.

Jamie felt like he was fitting in at Clinton high school. One revelation that struck him on the first day of classes was what it meant to have no dress or hair codes. At Archbishop Corrigan, everyone had to adhere to the same standards; suit jacket and tie, dress pants, no sneakers or suede shoes, short-cropped hair and no facial hair. Everyone had to look like little Wall Street robots in their bargain-basement blazers and attaché case-style book bags. Having everyone look so much the same may have been part of some master plan to make sure that all the students were put through the Catholic school blender and churned out looking and acting the same. Whether black, white, yellow, brown, or a mix of all four, at least they would all look something like a typical high school student body circa 1955. This was, of course, despite the fact that 1975 didn't look anything like 1955.

But from the first moment Jamie stepped inside DeWitt Clinton High School, it was as easy as spotting purple bell-bottoms or black-leather jackets or torn blue jeans or tailored slacks to get an idea of who you wanted to hang out with. Jamie had let his hair grow out, and it became what was known in the neighborhood as a Sicilian afro. And in his art class, the standards of dress and hairstyles were at their most extreme. It looked more like the green room at CBGB's than a Bronx high school classroom.

Jamie finally felt he could leave the Corrigan trauma behind. And he soon found friends who also enjoyed leaving things behind via marijuana, uppers, downers, cocaine, and speed. It only took a few glances and key words in small talk to figure out who the "heads" were. It wasn't long before joints were smoked before school, after school, and even in the boy's room. For the first time in his life, since playing Chinese checkers with Gerty, Jamie had found a clique of friends in art class. They had a look, a style, a manner of speaking that made Jamie feel like an outsider since kindergarten. But he fit right in.

This week, however, was the moment he dreaded: the first swim class in gym. He remembered his fear in the locker room at Corrigan. It seemed he was always the smallest one, surrounded by so many jocks from the football team.

Rules were rules, so Jamie left his clothes in his locker, and looked straight ahead, eyes high as he walked to pool bare-assed naked. He noticed two friends from art class were among the fifty or so kids standing poolside as the gym teacher announced it was a freestyle session and said "Everybody into the pool!"

Jamie jumped in, and doggy-paddled in the direction of the two other art class guys. And as he swam naked, he didn't feel afraid or ashamed. He enjoyed the feeling. It was liberating to him. And when he swam close to the two guys from art class, he couldn't help but notice that under the water, he wasn't the only one with a hard-on. And as much as it terrified him, he was elated by it.

As the weeks went by, Jamie met his art class friends at pizza places, in parks where he had never been before, even under overpasses by the railroad tracks. And there were other friends, female and male, dressed mostly in leather, torn jeans, and chains dangling. He soon realized that he was attracted to a girl. And also attracted to her boyfriend. He smoked pot with them. Went on walks with them. Even skipped school with them. And on one of those days when they ditched school, and the girl's parents were at work, they went to her apartment and took a new pill Jamie had never heard of: a Quaalude.

Sharing a bottle of Boone's Farm Apple wine, it took only two David Bowie albums for all three of them to be in bed together. It was the first time for Jamie. At least the first time he wanted to do it.

It was suggested that seminarians not leave for visits home at least until Thanksgiving. It was necessary to get into the routine of seminary life and not be distracted by what was going on outside of the walls of the campus. This was causing Chili much anxiety. His dad wouldn't tell him much about his medical condition other than, "he'll be fine." And when he could get Jamie on the phone he was even more evasive. And Chili was noticing a drastic change in him. He was mouthing off and even throwing F-bombs on the phone. He refused to answer how school was going, except to say that most of it was a joke, and the teachers didn't give a crap what students did in class. At least Jamie said he was still doing his artwork and photography in school.

When the long Thanksgiving weekend was approaching, his roommate, John, explained that he wouldn't be going home, but was going on a trip with another resident at the seminary. Chili thought it was strange that he didn't reveal the name of his fellow traveler.

Many of the seminarians had already left by the Wednesday before Thanksgiving, but Chili was still packing his things. He looked out the window and saw his roommate approach a Cadillac in the driveway. The driver went to the rear of the car to help him with his bags. It was Father O'Brennan.

Chili had seen Father O'Brennan around, but as he wasn't a faculty member, but a resident, he didn't have to interact with him. His roommate had never mentioned that he knew him, which is surprising because he knew that Chili went to Corrigan high school, and O'Brennan was still on the faculty there. There was a third person in the front passenger seat, but the window was up and it was hard to see inside. Then one of the monsignors walked over to the Caddy and tapped on the window. The window went down, and Chili couldn't believe his eyes. It was Bishop McQuirke. Bishop Ralph McQuirke. Could it be the "Uncle Ralph" that Mr. Clarke warned him about? Remembering Mr. Clarke's other directive from his letter, Chili went to the seminary library and picked three books about Saint Thomas Aquinas.

Chili didn't know what to expect as he rode the bus from Westchester to the city line, then transferred for the bus back to his Bronx street. Besides worrying about his dad's health and Jamie's mental health, there was the situation with Mikey and Angel. He was disappointed in their behavior on that night of drug-fueled debauchery, but after all, Chili was no immaculate goody two-shoes. He had a taste of sexual excitement with his short-lived dalliance with Pamela Hinderlap even if he never even got to first base. He was a willing participant on their trip to Times Square, where he sat in the booth at the peep show and enjoyed it at first, until the nudeness descended into explicit rudeness. He even took a picture of the peep show activities. And he was just as enamored with the Iowa girls when they seemed as pure as the Rocky Mountain snow where they frolicked. It wasn't until he saw them in a porno pile-up that he was shocked into revulsion.

But with Mikey and Angel, it wasn't the fact that they tripped their brains out and got it on with a bevy of college-aged beauties. He even couldn't say for sure if he wouldn't have jumped into the mass of seductive flesh if he had stuck out his tongue and received the tab of acid with the others. What continued to hurt was the fact that they didn't only dupe him by slipping him hash without his knowing it, and pulled a prank that preyed on his sacred sensitivities, but that they kept it a secret for several years between them. Nevertheless, Chili decided he would set up a meeting with Angel and Mikey in the fallout shelter.

    Chili entered the apartment, and was surprised there was no one home. He turned on some lights to see that the place was a mess. There was bedding strewn across the couch in the living room. The kitchen looked like it hadn't seen a sponge, dishcloth, or can of Ajax for weeks. Dirty dishes were piled high in the sink and on the kitchen table. The garbage can was overflowing and it stunk like a dumpster behind a vegetable stand. Chili got to work and began cleaning. And cleaning. And cleaning. All the time wondering if he was doing the right thing being away from home and leaving his brother and father on their own.

    Chili didn't hear the door locks opening over the roar of the vacuum cleaner. He turned around when the door closed. It was his father. Chili turned off the vacuum. Mr. Manzilla was in his work overalls, looked worn out, but looked better than he did the last time he saw him.

    "Hi, dad," Chili said, still holding the vacuum.

    "Well, hello stranger," Mr. Manzilla said sarcastically.

    "How did this place get to be such a mess?"

    "I told Jamie he had to keep house. That kid needs to learn a lesson."

    "What lesson is that? How to survive in a garbage can?"

    "I work hard. He needs to do some work. He's hardly ever here," Mr. Manzilla said, sitting on a rumpled sheet on the couch.

    Chili continued his cleaning, and was glad to see his father helping him. It took a while, but eventually it would probably pass a health department inspection. And just as Chili

Fallout Shelter

crushed the last remaining kitchen cockroach, the front door opened.
Chili couldn't believe what he was seeing. Jamie was nearly unrecognizable. His thick curly black hair had become a wild afro. He had dark circles under his eyes, and what appeared to be mascara or eyeliner. He had on a motorcycle-styled jacket with straps and chains dangling. And tight jeans with holes. He had a silver cross dangling from his right ear.
"Oh, hi Chili," Jamie said, as if everything was honky dory.
"Jamie, is that you in there?"
"Yes. It's me. Don't give me a hard time, please."
"Jamie, I'll ignore the Alice Cooper makeover. But how can you let this place become that Muppet on *Sesame Street*'s garbage can?"
"His name is Oscar the Grouch. And now you're being Felix Unger."
"And who are you supposed to be? Joey Ramone?"
"I'm me. That's all," Jamie said, going into the bedroom.
Chili turned to his father. "How long has this been going on?"
"Since he started at Clinton I guess. His grades have been good."
"Great," Chili said, putting away the vacuum.

Thanksgiving dinner wasn't awful. Chili prepared a simple meal, with turkey slices bought at the deli, and the usual trimmings. Jamie cleaned up, no eye makeup, no earing, and no tears in his clothing.
"I'll say grace," Chili said, folding his hands. "Bless us oh Lord, and these thy gifts, which we are about to receive from thy bounty and through Christ our Lord, Amen."
Mr. Manzilla made the sign of the cross, "Amen."
Jamie was silent.

"Can't you at least make the sign of the cross and say Amen?" Chili said.

"I don't believe in that stuff."

"Since when?"

"When you get something shoved down your throat your whole life, one day you are bound to just throw up," Jamie said, fiercely.

Chili and Mr. Manzilla had no response. The meal was eaten in silence. Afterwards Jamie went into the bathroom and the bedroom and reappeared with the outfit he wore the night before, complete with eye make-up, and left the apartment without saying a word.

Chili wasn't sure if getting together with Mikey and Angel was a good idea, but he was in his cellar opening up the fallout shelter like he had done so many times before, in good times and bad.

They arrived together. Chili noticed that Mikey looked filled-out. So did Angel, but not in the same way. Mikey was preparing for the police test, so he was working out lifting weights, watching what he ate, cutting down on his drinking, and he started running the trails in Van Cortlandt Park. Oh, and absolutely no drugs of any kind. Angel, however, was already feeling the pressure of a pre-law curriculum at Fordham University, and packing on the pounds while studying.

There was small talk, catching up, talking about sports and music, then when there was a lull, Angel went where they knew they didn't want to go, but had to.

"Listen, Chili we really need to talk," Angel said, his voice already cracking. "You have every right to never forgive us for what we did. We never thought it would go that far."

"Yeah, Chili, it was my idea, so if you want to freeze me out, go ahead. But don't take it out on Angel. We screwed up at the commune. We know it."

Chili paused, bit his lip, and shook his head. "How could you sink so low? I mean, I'm no prude, but an orgy with strangers?"

Angel and Mikey looked at each other.

"Orgy?" Angel asked. "There was no orgy."

"It's okay, I saw it through the window of the tent," Chili said, calmly.

"We were playing naked Twister," Mikey said.

"Yeah, then we went skinny dipping. There was no orgy for us," Angel added.

"Unfortunately!" Mikey said loudly.

"Really?" Chili asked, in disbelief.

"Chili," Mikey said, closing in on Chili. "I was tripping my brains out when I said those awful things to you, you know, about the vision, and all that stuff about you."

"Guys, it's over. It was a prank. When I came down from that brownie high, I knew something was going on. I went back to the park the first thing the next morning, and I found evidence that it was a prank. No harm, no foul."

That was a lie. Chili didn't go back the next day, but thought this was a good enough way for Angel and Mikey to stop beating each other up for what they did.

"So, the prank of the vision didn't influence your decision to...," Mikey said slowly.

Chili laughed. "To become a priest? Don't be silly. You both know I was on this path since I was a rookie altar boy."

Angel and Mikey knew this was an out for them, and didn't take it any further. "Ok, so the three musketeers are back. Like we were," Mikey said, holding out his hand for a three-way handshake.

"Yup, like we were," Chili said, with affection.

Even with all the drama, Chili was glad he went home for Thanksgiving. Despite the fact that it looked like Jamie was going through some serious growing pains, Chili knew just from being in the Bronx, riding the subways, buses, and walking the streets, kids that age are going through all kinds of changes. There are the "hitters" who go around looking to beat up Jews, hippies, Blacks, Puerto Ricans, or whoever doesn't look like them. Then there's the hippies who hang out in the park, smoking their weed and playing their guitars. Then there's the druggies who can usually be found under a bridge, on a roof top, or in the pool hall bathroom nodding out with a needle in their arm. Jamie seemed to be part of that group of artsy students who don't fit in with the usual groups but try to start their own brand of conforming to their own rules of non-conformity. At least according to his child psychology class instructor at the seminary.

    The weeks between Thanksgiving and Christmas always seem to go by in a whir. Especially if one is studying for the priesthood in a seminary and gearing up for the biggest event of the year: Christmas.
    Chili never asked his roomie about his Thanksgiving vacation with Father O'Brennan and Bishop McQuirke, other than, "How was your trip?" And the reply was "Fine."
    As the days got closer to Christmas, the seminary had fewer and fewer people on the campus. Chili had volunteered to stay, and only go home for a few days for the holiday. Many took almost two weeks off. Chili's roommate was gone the Monday before Christmas and Chili was enjoying the quiet and solitude of having his own room for the first time in his life, even if it was for only a couple of weeks.
    It was late one snowy evening, and Chili was deep into reading essays by Saint Thomas Aquinas. Although written over 700 years ago, his philosophies seemed contemporary in so many ways. In one of the books about him, there was an essay with the word *pederasty* repeated as being a mortal sin. Chili had to look it up in the Oxford dictionary. *Pederasty is the homosexual corruption of boys by men.* Even with all the rumors flying around Corrigan high school, he was shocked to see there was a term

Fallout Shelter

for it that was more specific than *pedophilia*. Not the sexual abuse of a child, but of a minor boy in his teens.

There was a knock on the door. Chili, looked at his watch. It was almost midnight. He went to the door and opened it. If he had been drinking anything, he would have done a spit take.

"Excuse me, is this the room of John McSherry?"

"Um, yes, Father, I mean, um, Your Excellency," Chili said choking on his words.

It was Bishop Ralph McQuirke. McQuirke was a sturdy man of about 60. Although not a familiar sight at the seminary, there were occasionally whispers when he was passing through.

"May I come in?" The Bishop asked.

"Yes. How can I help you?" Chili said, leading him to a chair. "I'm first-year seminarian William Manzilla."

"I know who you are."

Chili wasn't sure why that would be the case, but assumed he knew most of the first-year seminarians.

"Let me be candid, William. You have a brother named James?"

Chili's pulse began to race. He hoped it didn't show.

"Yes."

"It would behoove you to cooperate with me, if you want to continue your path to the priesthood. And it would be good for James, too."

Chili was sweating now. All he could think of was the movie, *The Godfather*.

The Bishop got up out of his chair and went behind the chair where Chili was seated. He put both his hands on Chili's shoulder, and began to massage him. "Don't be alarmed. You should be glad I'm here to help you," McQuirke said softly. He then leaned over and whispered a heavy, breathy garlic-soaked whisper in Chili's ear. "I need you to cooperate. It's important to your future. And your family's." He then began stroking Chili's neck and pushed his hand down the front of his shirt.

Chili shot up out of the chair and went across the room to the door.

"Goodnight, Your Excellency," Chili said, his voice trembling.

The bishop walked to the door and turned to Chili. "I think you should reconsider," he said as he exited.

Chili was numb. Did that really happen? Why? Of course! Father O'Brennan and he are close friends apparently. But what's the Jamie connection?

Chili double-locked his door for the rest of the week, and was home for Christmas Eve, midnight mass at St. Gall's. As he knelt in the pew, he couldn't help but think of all the years he served as an altar boy, all the sacred rituals of sacraments, first Holy Communion, Confirmation, graduation, his mother's funeral mass. He knew he had to say something about what happened and whatever happens, happens, come hell or high holy water.

He didn't know who he'd be meeting with, but he knew it would be with higher-ups. He sat in the outer room of the monsignor's office and felt like he was back in St. Gall's grammar school waiting to see the principal, Sister Agnes, for throwing a dead mouse at the girls in the schoolyard.

A nun at the large oak desk told him to enter.

The room is what he imagined a Wall Street boardroom would look like. Oak paneling, paintings of people dead for centuries, bookcases filled with leather-bound books, and at the center behind the desk a very large crucifix, probably five feet high with realistic blood and wounds.

Holy shit, Chili thought to himself. Sitting between two higher-ups at the seminary, Monsignor Gomez and Father Boyle, was himself, Bishop Ralph McQuirke. Chili was frozen with fear. All he could get out of his mouth once he sat down, was that he thought Bishop McQuirke coming to his room unannounced at midnight was an invasion of his privacy.

"I apologize, William. I only wish you had come to me first." The Bishop said, dripping with false sincerity.

"Can we consider this just a miscommunication and consider the matter closed?" the monsignor said, and waited for a reply from Chili.

Chili sat there. And sat there. He closed his eyes and bit the inside of his cheeks. He saw a vision. His mother telling him to be honest. Do the right thing.

"No. I'm sorry. There's more. Bishop McQuirke acted inappropriately. He touched me and made a not-so-subtle remark, no–a threat–about my future."

"Why that's ridiculous!" The bishop said, firmly.

"Do you wish to file a complaint against the bishop? That's a serious charge for a new seminarian to make," the monsignor said, in an intimidating manner.

Chili sat there in silence.

"No. I don't. But I suggest he read Saint Thomas Aquinas."

The bishop rose up, enraged and shouted, "If I hear one more fool bring up Saint Thomas Aquinas to me, I will lose my temper! I am sick and tired of hearing about Saint Thomas Aquinas!"

The monsignor and the other priest in attendance looked stunned as they watched Bishop McQuirke sit back down to try and compose himself as Chili quietly exited the office.

Chili called Angel and asked if he could come pick him up to take him home. He was through with the seminary. For good. A half-hour later, the Squareback pulled in front. Angel was behind the steering wheel, and Mikey was in the shotgun seat. Chili put his things in the back and jumped in the rear seat.

"Looks like we get to finish our trip together after all," Chili said smiling.

"Wanna stop for a nightcap somewhere?" Mikey asked.

"Yeah. Good idea," Chili replied.

The Terminal Bar is what the younger people in the neighborhood called an "old man bar." But in reality, it wasn't just old men who plopped down at the ancient wooden bar on crooked bar stools. There were mostly men over 50, but also a few women, and a smattering of young guys. What they all had in common was that they were there to drink cheap alcohol. There was no other reason to be in the dank tavern, established in the early 1900's when the elevated line was completed right above their neon sign. The jukebox was almost always on the fritz, and the latest hit record on there was "Sixteen Tons" by Tennessee Ernie Ford. The bar itself reeked of decades of spilled booze, beer, tears, and blood. You just hoped that you didn't have to use the bathroom for anything other than a quick pee, and that there would be a big pile of ice in the urinal to help with the smell. Don't even think about opening the door to the toilet stall.

They sat under the TV at the end of the bar and not trusting the sanitary conditions of a glass, ordered three bottles of beer.

"So what happened?" Angel asked Chili.

Mikey and Angel studied Chili's face as he prepared an answer.

"You're not gonna believe this. I was hit on by a bishop."

"Come on, really, what happened?" Mikey asked.

"I'm not kidding. Then he freakin' started saying something about Jamie and how I should look out for him. Then when I tried to complain they had kangaroo court in front of me with the bishop making me out to be a liar and a fool."

"Well, you're no liar!" Mikey added.

"Stop kidding around, Mikey," Angel said poking him hard. "I've heard rumors about this shit. Who was the bishop? McQuirke?"

"How did you guess?"

"Like I said we heard rumors about the guy in high school."

Fallout Shelter

"What's messed up, is I saw McQuirke with Father O'Brennan and my roommate get in a car together."

"O'Brennan's that teacher at Corrigan who used to drive Jamie home from school sometimes!" Mikey said excitedly.

"That fucker. Something's going on."

"Do you know what you're gonna tell your father? Because here he comes," Angel said pointing at the front door.

Chili positioned Mikey and Angel in front of him, and ducked under the TV. Mr. Manzilla went up to the bar and called over the bartender. They chatted for a moment, and Mr. Manzilla gave him a slip of paper. The bartender walked over to the cash register, took out a few bills, and handed them to Mr. Manzilla. No drink. No talk. Just a smile and a quick exit.

Chili went back to his position at the bar. "I guess he hit the number. For once."

"He didn't have a shot?" Mikey asked.

"I don't think he's been drinking since he had a health scare. He seems to be doing better." Angel smiled.

"Maybe those prayers are helping."

Chili stood outside his door, going over exactly what he would say to his father. And to Jamie. He mustered the courage, turned the locks, and entered into a dark apartment. His father was snoring on the couch, with the TV still playing an old *Honeymooners* re-run. He went to the bedroom, and Jamie wasn't there. His bed looked like it hadn't been made in days if not weeks. The explanation of why his life-long dream came crashing to a halt would have to wait until morning.

Jamie was still awake on the bare mattress in the basement of his friend Marty's house. His parents go to Florida for the winter, so they wouldn't be home for a few months. Marty and Phoebe, sharing the mattress, were fast asleep. All three were fully clothed. There was a red light bulb hanging from a wire, giving the room a hellish glow. Jamie hadn't been home for several days, ever since he found an envelope under the door.

He pulled the note out of his pocket and re-read it for the hundredth time. *James, You know we know where you live. Where your father works. Where your brother is. It would be helpful if you weren't heard from again. We really don't want to help you disappear.*

Jamie walked home from Marty's house, one of the few remaining private homes that hadn't been divided into tiny slummy apartments over by Fordham Road and University Avenue. Jamie knew he must look like hell, so he hoped his father was sleeping. He was confused upon entering when he saw Chili having breakfast. "Oh, you're home. I thought you were staying at the seminary until Christmas day," Jamie said acting as if he didn't look like a Twisted Sister reject.

"Christ almighty where have you been?"

"Oh, I've been staying with some…friends."

"On this planet?"

"Well what about you? You don't exactly look like somebody on a Wheaties Box. What are you doing here?"

"Well, I haven't told dad yet, but I quit the seminary. It's just not for me."

"I could have told you that when I was an altar boy."

"What's that supposed to mean?"

"Never mind. Is dad sleeping in the bedroom?"

"Yeah."

"I'm gonna try to get some sleep on the couch."

Chili closed the blinds and closed the drapes, darkening the room as Jamie prepared to crash on the couch.

"Jamie, is there anything you want to tell me? Are you all right?"

"I'm all right. I just been out with some friends. I'll be fine."

"I'll be back in a couple hours, I'm going for a walk in the park," Chili said, tucking in Jamie like he did when they were still in grammar school. "Don't forget, I'm your big brother. I'll do anything to help you. Anything."

Fallout Shelter

"Yeah. Me too," Jamie said, touching Chili's hand tenderly.

It was a bright, sunny, cold day in the park. There was some snow on the ground, which glistened in the early morning sunshine. Chili liked the park when it was empty. It was easy to think one was in the country, far from the Bronx. He liked walking up the old railroad tracks, which went past the lake where Canada geese floated on the patches that remained free of ice. And he chuckled when they slipped and slid as they scampered on the frozen chunks of ice that floated there. He walked along the tracks, and noticed a small sparrow that appeared to be dead. It was next to a mighty oak, so he assumed it had perhaps flown into the tree by accident. He reached down and picked it up. It was still warm. He gently poked the belly of the bird several times and paused. He poked a few more times and felt something course through his body. He cupped both hands, cradling the bird entirely. He suddenly felt the tiny feet of the bird kicking into his palm. He spread his hands apart and the bird flew away. *Could it be a sign? Am I on the right path, even though I've abandoned my vocation?* He thought to himself, watching the bird disappear into the sky.

He lost track of time as he walked up the railroad tracks several miles, all the way to Tibbets Brook Park in Yonkers. He could just barely see Tibbets Brook pool through the bare trees and decided to go explore.

The last time Chili was at the pool was when he was a day camp counselor. The pool would be teeming with kids, shoulder to shoulder, frolicking in the sparkling water on hot summer days. But today everything was empty, cold, lifeless. It was hard to imagine that the barren concrete and icy puddles would soon have barefoot kids hopping from towel to towel because of the hot foots they were getting walking on the super-heated poolside surfaces.

It had been over four hours since Chili started out on his contemplative outing and when he finally arrived back home, his dad was dressed in his work clothes, and having a sandwich.

"Dad! You're looking fine today! Where's Jamie?"

"I was going to ask you that. I haven't seen him for a few days. I guess we've just been missing each other. Oh, did he tell you about some guy from Corrigan who came to visit?"

"No. Who?"

"I can't remember, but he said something about Jamie leaving Corrigan and mentioned something about you."

That didn't sound right to Chili, as he finished unpacking his bags. When he opened a drawer there was a note. *Chili, I will be gone for a little while. Tell dad I'll be fine. I'm spending the Christmas vacation with some friends who have a cabin in Vermont. I'll call when I get there. Sorry for the short notice. Say a prayer for me. With love, James.*

That was very unlike Jamie to use *James*. Only his mom called him that. And *say a prayer for me*. And *with love*. Something was very wrong.

Chili told his father about the note just as he was leaving for work. He waited for the phone call from Vermont late into the night. And for days. Then weeks.

Chili tried to find Jamie with the help of Mikey and Angel and the police and by calling nearly every hospital in the city. He even tried calling morgues in New York, New Jersey, Vermont, and everywhere in between. But Jamie never called. And it got to a point where all Chili could do was to pray and pray and pray.

PART THREE
5 YEARS LATER
◈ Chapter 13 ◈

It was taking Chili longer than the usual four years to complete his degree from Hunter College in midtown Manhattan. Although tuition was extremely low for the public colleges of the City University of New York system in 1980, once you piled on school supplies, fees, and textbooks on top of regular household expenses such as rent, food, and everything else, Chili had to work a full-time job while he attended college. He was majoring in education with a minor in psychology and his job fit in perfectly. He was working part-time as a live-in counselor at a group home for boys run by the City of New York. A group home is where at-risk boys who are having trouble staying in foster homes with families can live in a supervised setting. Many have a history of emotional, behavioral, and even drug-abuse problems. Some are victims of violent or sexual abuse. Chili stayed at the home with two other "house parents" for three days and nights per week. Kids were expected to live under the house rules and attend regular junior high and high schools. There wasn't a day when Chili wondered if Jamie was lucky enough to have entered such a facility somewhere in America, if he was still alive.

Mr. Manzilla, whose health had deteriorated greatly, was out on disability, so his salary was greatly reduced. But once you factored into the equation that he was no longer drinking, smoking, or gambling, the money wasn't that much lower than when he was busting his butt slaving away in the subway tunnels. Chili worried about him the three days he stayed at the group home, but he was only about a ten-minute bus ride away in case of an emergency.

He had little time for socializing with his fellow musketeers, Mikey and Angel, who were also busy making their ways in their new lives. Angel had finished undergraduate pre-law school in three years, and was already two years into Manhattan Law School. Mikey was well into his career as a cop with the NYPD and was already two years "on the job," working the streets of the South Bronx as it descended into Dante's *Inferno*'s ninth circle of hell.

Being a city-run operation, there was no religious aspect to the supervision at the group home. That's exactly why Chili wanted to work there, and not in a home sponsored by Catholic Charities. He hoped his disillusionment with the church was only temporary, but after five years he didn't have much hope. He received nothing from the seminary after his departure. There was no *Was it something we said? Won't you reconsider? Can't we work this out? Are you happy with your current long-distance plan, auto warranty, and religion?*

And it was killing him. He wondered what his mother would think, knowing that he walked away from not only the seminary, but the church itself. Other than her, he really didn't give a crap what anyone else thought, from the pervy bishop all the way down. He debated the schism in his own head: *Question: When the fools at CBS and Mike Burke ran the Yankees into the ground from 1965 to 1972 didn't I stay a loyal Yankee fan? Reply: Yeah, but if Mike Burke had tried to tried to force me to rub his balls in the locker room, I would have become a Mets fan in New York heartbeat.* He kept thinking of that day in freshman-year religion, where Brother Dodge wrote on the blackboard comparing the spiritual church and the institutional church. Chili wasn't denying anything in the spiritual column, only the institutional. But he kept seeing his mother's face and hearing her words. Then he would think of the happy van driver that picked him up after his escape from the commune. The guy was certain that his spiritual leader, Jim Jones, showed him the path to salvation. Little did the driver know that all 918 of the People's Temple followers would commit mass suicide on Rev. Jim's instructions to drink the Kool Aid in Guyana, just because. That didn't stop Chili from continuing to pray and pray and pray, for his dad and Jamie.

As Chili got closer to finally receiving his college degree, his father's health continued a downward spiral. He knew he couldn't give his dad the type of care he needed and would have to place him in a nursing home. He dreaded that conversation. But after a fall in the apartment, a trip to the emergency room, hospitalization, and doctor's orders, it was time for Mr. Manzilla to go from his hospital bed to a bed in a nursing home.

Just the sight of seeing Montefiore Hospital brought a rush of unwanted memories back to Chili. That was where his mom spent her final days, and where Chili held her hand as she made her transition. Although it was over a decade ago, it hurt like it was happening all over again. Which, essentially, it probably was, with his dad.

Into the same entrance, the same gift shop, check in at the same front desk, and up the same elevator. Although there was a small hip fracture, they didn't want to risk surgery. It was time for the talk.

"Hi dad. How are you feeling?"

"Not so good."

"Are you able to eat anything?"

"A little."

"Can you watch TV?"

"Sometimes."

"You know the doctors are going to release you soon."

"Thank God."

"But you have to go to re-hab."

"What's that?"

"It's in a nursing home."

There was a long pause. Mr. Manzilla crossed himself. "I want to go to St. John's Home."

"Okay. I'll work on it," Chili said, gently stroking his dad's forehead.

Chili had to face the facts. St. John's Nursing home was where nearly all the Catholic parishioners from St. Gall's went. Despite his own reservations, he knew he had to fulfill his father's wishes.

It took non-stop phone calls, and all-day meetings, but finally Mr. Manzilla was admitted to St. Michael's Nursing Home and Rehab Center, not far from where they lived. It would be easy for Chili to visit each day. Run by the Archdiocese of New York, the nursing home had a stellar reputation. Upon entering most nursing homes, the first thing you notice is "the smell." Thankfully, at St. Michael's there was no mystery smell. The personnel were a mix of typical New York working class of every ethnicity. As Chili walked the halls to his father's room, he could swear he was seeing faces from his childhood come back to life. *Is that Mr. McCabe from the first floor of the building? I thought he died years ago. That looks like Theresa Traynor from first grade pushing that food cart. That can't be Sister Ignatius in that bed. She'd have to be 100 years old!*

He stopped at the nurse's desk. "Is that Sister Ignatius in that room over there?"

A nurse replied with a Jamaican accent. "I'm sorry, sir. We can't tell you patients' names without permission. But I can tell you that yes, we do have some nuns and priests as patients and long-term retired residents. And the name Sister Ignatius does sound familiar," she said, winking.

"Thank you. You're very kind."

Chili reached his dad's room and stood outside the open door. His father was sleeping with a game show playing on TV. In the other bed was a man, also sleeping, with his mouth wide open and his head far back in an awkward position. Chili stepped in and approached his father's bed.

"Dad. Hi, dad. Dad," he said softly, tapping his hands.

Mr. Manzilla opened his eyes and smiled. "Hi, Chili. Have you heard form Jamie?"

"Not yet. Maybe tomorrow."

"Oh, good. Let me know when you hear from him," Mr. Manzilla said as he drifted back to sleep.

Chili took a seat next to his dad. The room had a pleasant view with the woods of Van Cortlandt Park out the window. He then realized that just up from there was where

Fallout Shelter

Mikey and Angel pulled the infamous phony vision on him. At least now he could laugh about it.

The food cart rolled into the room and Chili was pretty sure he was correct. Pushing it was his classmate from grammar school, Theresa Traynor.

"I'll just leave the tray here, for when he wakes up," she said, putting the food on the side table.

"Aren't you Theresa Traynor?"

"Oh, Chili, right? Gosh, I haven't seen you since graduation. Is this your dad?"

"Yup. Just got here."

"Yeah, we'll all get here one day, if we're lucky. Hey, did you know Sister Ignatius is here, the poor thing. I don't know how she hangs on. You went to Corrigan, right?"

"Yeah."

"There's a couple of priests upstairs from Corrigan I think. Father…O'Brennan, I believe, had a stroke and is living here full time now."

"I think I remember him. A little after my time."

"Nice to see you, Chili," she said pushing her cart into the hall.

When his father awakened Chili helped him eat his meal, all the time thinking about how he would find Father O'Brennan, and what he might say to him.

The Riverdale Diner, under the el at 238th Street and Broadway, always had identity problem. It wasn't really in Riverdale, which was at least five blocks away. And sometimes you got the feeling that the owners wished the clientele *was* from Riverdale, and not mostly Kingsbridge people. But the Kingsbridge residents who always got first-class treatment there were the cops from the 50th Precinct just a block away, or any cop that stopped in for a nosh, especially late at night. And of course, they want the officers sitting as close to the windows as possible so any potential robbers or troublemakers can easily see them.

Mikey wasn't in uniform, but Julio, the manager, knew very well that he was a cop and sat him in a large booth by the front door. It wasn't easy to get the guys together, but it was a lot easier to meet here around 10 p.m. than in the old fallout shelter where three men wandering around a cellar could arouse suspicion, maybe even resulting in a call to 911.

Angel and Chili entered together, were greeted warmly by Julio, and seated with Mikey. It had been weeks since they were together, the last time being when Angel's father's store was robbed at gunpoint in Inwood. Mr. Rodriquez feared for his life with a crazed junkie nervously waving a .38 around as he grabbed the night's receipts out of the cash register.

"How's your dad? Did they ever catch the scumbag who robbed him?" Mikey asked, stirring his tea.

"Yeah, the jerk lived in the building above the store."

"How to rob a store," Chili laughed, "lesson number one: Don't rob a store in your building where everybody knows you."

"So how's your dad doing in Saint John's, Chili?" Angel asked.

"He's all right. I was with him until a little while ago. As far as nursing homes go, Saint John's is pretty good."

"I'd like to visit," Mikey said.

"Me, too!"

"Let me see how he's doing tomorrow and I'll let you know when a good time is. Oh, I forgot to tell you guys! Sister Ignatius is in there. She looks really bad."

"She looked bad when we had her in eighth grade!" Mikey said, pouring a half bottle of ketchup on his scrambled eggs.

"You want eggs with your ketchup?" Angel deadpanned.

"I gotta work tonight. You never know when it's gonna be your last meal, so enjoy! And how's law school, Perry Mason?" Mikey said, holding his fork up to Angel's face. "Send anybody to the electric chair yet?"

Fallout Shelter

"Watch out! I might become a D.A. and grill your ass on the witness stand one day!"

Chili thought about mentioning that Father O'Brennan was also at Saint John's but decided not to just yet. He first wanted to be certain that he was indeed going to find him, and consider what might happen afterwards. Instead, he just enjoyed being with his friends.

Chili opened the four locks on the front door and entered the dark apartment. The only sound was the rattle and hum of the refrigerator. It was an eerie feeling, being alone in the small apartment. It even felt like the apartment was cavernous with no one else there. When his mom was alive, and all four of them were crammed into that one-bedroom apartment, it didn't feel small. Yeah, everybody was bumping into each other in the tiny kitchen or waiting on the bathroom, but somehow with his mom's unbounding energy and joy filling the space it was fun. When she left this world, it was never the same. And then when Chili and his dad realized Jamie was never coming back, it felt as though the walls were caving in on them. And now, it was just Chili. Maybe his father was never coming home again either. It was overwhelming to think, that out of the four of them, he would be sole survivor.

Although Mr. Manzilla was improving, it was obvious that he wouldn't be going home. As his hip healed somewhat and his meds could be reduced, he was able to lead a more normal life as a long-term resident at Saint John's. There were the normal nursing home activities, such as bingo, sing-a-longs, and movie nights. Plus being a Catholic operation there were daily mass, prayer sessions in the chapel, rosary recitals, novenas, and even Holy Communion in the room for the bedridden. Chili felt an emptiness when he rolled his father's wheelchair to the chapel for mass but didn't stay himself. It was something that he thought might go away over time, but after five years, he had his doubts. As he bent down to pull the brake on his father's wheelchair, his dad turned to him and whispered, "I'll pray for you."

    While in the home, Mr. Manzilla was able to retire from his subway job, start his pension, obtain retiree medical coverage, and since he was eating regularly and no longer drinking or gambling his life away, his personality was even on the upswing. He could joke with the nurses, and laugh at Archie Bunker on TV. Chili thought it was time for Angel and Mikey to come for a visit.
    Sundays were always special days in the nursing home. Residents were energized after morning mass, knowing that there would be extra visitors on Sunday afternoon. Not just the spouse, or the one child who has taken on most of the responsibility for the parent. The extended families and friends usually show up for at least a quick visit to say hi to grandma just to get some face time in, in case there's still time to get in the will before she kicks.
    They wheeled Mr. Manzilla into the recreation room, which was set up with tables and chairs on Sunday to accommodate the additional guests. Mikey, Angel, Chili, and Mr. Manzilla sat at a round table. There were a few moments of awkward silence as the settled in, then Mr. Manzilla broke the ice. "Anybody got a deck of cards?"
    "You're looking good, Mr. M!" Mikey said, laughing.
    Mr. Manzilla didn't really look good. It was obvious that his health was declining fast. Sunken eyes, gray skin tone, trembling, and atrophy all signaling that that the exit ramp was fast approaching. Chitchat was mostly of the fun variety, which meant the good times before Mrs. Manzilla passed away. Cub Scout events, little league, day camp, and birthday parties from about age seven to twelve were all condensed into about fifteen minutes of fun highlights.
    "Hey, Mikey, could you help me with something, back in dad's room?" Chili asked. "We'll be right back."

Chili led Mikey back to his father's empty room and closed the door behind them. "Mikey, I want you to come with me upstairs."

"What's up?"

"You remember Father O'Brennan from Corrigan?"

"Oh yeah. He's the one we had suspicions about with Jamie...."

"Well they were more than suspicions, I found out at the seminary. He's living upstairs. He had a stroke a while back, and he's a full-time resident."

"Are you sure you need me to go with you?" Mikey asked, knowing that many times when friends, neighbors, and relatives ask him to escort them for some reason, it's because he keeps a badge and a gun discreetly hidden in his faded blue jeans.

"I'd appreciate it."

"Let's go."

They took the elevator to the top floor. It looked more like a floor in a college dorm than a nursing home. There was a large reception area with couches, upholstered chairs, a TV with the sound turned off, and a fireplace with burning gas logs. Several elderly, but certainly not sickly looking men, were reading.

Chili scanned the nameplates outside the doors, and nodded to Mikey that he found Father O'Brennan's room. "Wait outside the door. Just so you know, I'm going to see if he has any clues about what might have happened to Jamie," Chili whispered.

Chili knocked.

"Come in." A voice could barely be heard from behind the solid oak door.

Chili slowly opened the door, and there he was. Father O'Brennan sitting in a chair, watching television. He looked a lot older, but couldn't see any obvious after effects of the stroke.

"Hello, young man. And you are?"

"Manzilla."

O'Brennan's face looked as though he was going through a Rolodex of his sexual conquests in his mind.

"Manzilla! Yes! Come here! I want a good look at you. My eyesight isn't so great anymore," O'Brennan said slowly rising from his chair.

Chili took a few steps toward him, and then O'Brennan shuffled quickly to him, and gave him a strong bear hug with extra hand movements up and down his back. Chili pulled back.

"Come here. Manzilla. Yes," O'Brennan said, taking baby steps to Chili again. "You were one of my favorites. Come closer. I know what you like. I remember," O'Brennan said, then with a burst of energy, grabbed Chili's crotch, jerked him closer and tried kissing him on the lips.

Chili pushed him away with a degree of force, but not too much.

"Tell me what you remember about me," Chili said, stifling his anger. Hoping to finally get answers about Jamie.

"You fought me at first. Like now. But in time I won you over. I always do. And it makes it so much better. You? I remember well. So reluctant at first. A fighter. Until I tamed you like breaking a bucking bronco," he said, with spittle shooting out of his mouth as if he was getting excited. "But you were mine. There is nothing in this world like coming in a virgin. It's like heaven…."

Chili saw nothing but red. His brain was on fire. He reared back and with a haymaker slugged Father O'Brennan so hard he flew across the room and crashed into the television, knocking it and the metal entertainment center to pieces. O'Brennan was bleeding from his mouth and nose. But that didn't stop Chili as he continued to pummel him.

"I'm not Jamie, you motherfucking evil son of a bitch. You're going straight to hell!"

The door swung open. Mikey rushed over and grabbed Chili off of O'Brennan.

"What the fuck are you doing? You'll kill him!"

A crowd appeared in the doorway in total disbelief at the sight of Father O'Brennan unconscious and bleeding profusely.

"Call 911. Get an ambulance and request a cop car. There's been an assault," Mikey said, holding Chili, who was still seething.

A nurse rushed to O'Brennan to render aid to him. "He's still breathing. His pulse is racing,"

"Let's get out of here," Chili said, dazed.

"Chili, are you kidding me? I have to arrest you, you dumb fuck."

"Did I do that?" Chili asked, pointing to O'Brennan.

"You have the right to remain silent…," Mikey said, reciting the Miranda Rights as he escorted him out of the room, and out of the building, where they waited for the squad car to pull up. Mikey told a nurse to give a message to Angel that they had to leave because of an emergency but will tell him about it later.

Mikey held Chili by the arm at the end of the block, fifty feet or so from the main entrance where the ambulance was unloading the gurney as they waited for the squad car to arrive.

"Why didn't you just have me go in there with you, Chili?"

"I never would have gotten the information I went in there for?"

"What did he say?"

"I'll never tell. Never."

It was a busy night in the 50th Precinct. There were arrestees crowded into cells, and a few handcuffed to pipes. Some had bandages with Rorschach blotches of red blood oozing through. A janitor mopped the floor around everyone's feet while the chaos ensued.

Chili was booked on a *felony assault with intent to cause great bodily harm* charge, but that could change. He didn't use a weapon, but on a frail elderly man, even a fist could be construed to fit the bill to up the charge to attempted murder. And if he died, it would be murder.

Mikey knew Chili was in big, big trouble. Even in crime-ridden New York, where the justice system is described as a revolving door for criminals, this case was different. Once the tabloids and trashy "Action News" TV broadcasts got wind of a former altar boy attacking a priest in a nursing home, it would be plastered all over the newsstands and airwaves.

Chili was lucky he wasn't in a crowded cell with the dozen or so mostly inebriated Bronx miscreants. He sat in a corner on a folding chair, handcuffed to a pipe next to a radiator. That was about the only thing Mikey could do for him. Other than that, the system would take over and Chili was going along with it.

THE ALTAR BOY'S REVENGE, PRIEST ATTACKED BY DERANGED FORMER STUDENT, SEMINARY DROP-OUT GOES ON DEATH-WISH RAMPAGE were just a few of the next day's headlines. Chili was arraigned, bail set at $100,000, and he waited in a cell for something to happen. He had no idea what that something was. But then it happened. He was being released because someone posted bail for him.

Angel and his dad were waiting for him in the receiving area. Angel grabbed Chili by the arm. "Dad posted bond. There's a circus out those doors of TV cameras and photographers. We're gonna bust through and you'll stay with us. Let's go."

Like a mafia perp walk, Chili, Angel, and Mr. Rodriguez charged through the crowd and ignored the shouted questions from reporters, and the obscenities from bystanders calling him a Christ killer among other things.

There was silence in the car for blocks, until Mr. Rodriguez, behind the wheel, addressed Chili. "Are you hungry?"

"No, sir," Chili said, blankly staring out the window, seeing the sights of his childhood pass by.

"Chili, I have a lawyer for you. Don't worry about the money. It's pro bono," Angel told him.

"What does that mean?"

"He's doing it free of charge."

"Why?"

"He'll explain when we get back to the house," Angel said, from the front passenger seat as he and his dad exchanged looks of disbelief and worry.

They parked in the garage at the Rodriguez home and entered through a door into the kitchen. Mrs. Rodriguez unhesitatingly rushed Chili and embraced him. Sitting at the kitchen table was the last thing Chili wanted to see—a priest.

Angel went to the priest and stood behind him. "Chili, this is one of my instructors in law school. Father Martin Driscoll. He's a Jesuit."

"Hi, William," Father Driscoll said, standing, "may I call you Chili?"

"Is this some kind of bad joke? Because I can't think of what else it possibly could be," Chili said, backing away.

"Chili, Father Driscoll is one of the top faculty members at Manhattan Law School, and a highly regarded defense attorney," Angel said, inching towards Chili.

Father Driscoll addressed Chili and the others, almost as if he was addressing a jury. "Chili, of course you know who John Adams is?"

"Of course."

"And you've heard of the Boston Massacre."

"Yes."

"When the British soldiers were arrested for murdering the patriots in Boston, do you know who represented them in court?"

"No, I don't."

"John Adams. Perhaps the number-one patriot and revolutionary leader in Boston, signer of the Declaration of Independence and future President of the United States. He did that because he believed in the justice system. That everyone is innocent until proven guilty and they have a right to the best representation possible. Don't look at my collar and think I represent the Church. I will represent you."

"I don't know...."

Angel went up to Chili and put his hand on his shoulder. "Chili, we don't have a lot of options here. You're facing five to fifteen years in prison, and God forbid, if O'Brennan has permanent injuries or dies, it would be even worse for you. You've got to put your faith in me, and in Father Driscoll."

"Faith is what got me here," Chili said, sitting at the table and slumping forward. "Blind faith. But I guess I have run out of options. Okay, I accept the offer."

As the local TV news flashed the images of Chili's exit from the police station, with sensationalized descriptions of Father O'Brennan's brutal attack, Mr. Manzilla laid in his bed in a state of shock. In his right hand was a rosary and he mumbled through the rosary prayers until he fell into a deep sleep. And not just the local TV news programs were covering it. Each of the network TV broadcasts included a short piece on the horrors of the story, with the gist of the story being, *Yup, Catholics are one messed up group of whackos.*

The trial was weeks away, and it was decided it would be best if Chili moved everything out of the apartment and gave it up for good. His father was never returning home, and of course, neither was Jamie. And if Chili was convicted, he would go from the courtroom, onto a bus, and straight to prison.

Angel and Mikey helped Chili box everything up that was worth keeping. Going through the stuffed-to-the-gills closets and drawers was like digging through strata on an archeological expedition. The top layer being recent clothing and accessories, but by the time they dug down to the bottom there were the relics of days gone by. School notebooks, baseball cards and gloves, old missals, and other altar boy ephemera.

"Hey, look at me!" Mikey said, after donning a crumpled white altar boy's surplice that was once the prized possession of every altar boy, ironed and starched for every Sunday.

"Take that shit off!" Chili shouted from across the room and rushed to Mikey, pulling it off him. He then began ripping it to shreds and stuffed into a garbage bag. He then began going through every box, every drawer, every shelf, grabbing anything with a religious connotation and ripping, smashing, crushing, and stuffing them into garbage bags. Mikey and Angel stood by and watched in silence. Chili picked up a small item from his father's drawer and stopped dead. He knew what it was: his mother's rosary beads. Chili held them in his hand and looked over at Mikey and Angel. "I'm keeping this, but that's it."

"What is it?" Angel asked, softly.

"My mom's rosary."

Not much was said for the rest of the day as boxes piled up on one side of the living room, and furniture was pushed to the other.

"What am I gonna do with all this furniture?" Chili asked.

"Call the Salvation Army. They'll come and pick it up," Mikey replied.

Chili called and they said they would be there sometime the next day, but couldn't say exactly when, so it was decided that Chili would spend one more night in his apartment, so he could wait for them to arrive.

"We'll come back tomorrow for the boxes, and you can keep them in my garage for as long as you want," Angel told Chili as he and Mikey were leaving.

"Thanks, guys. I'll see you tomorrow."

Chili locked the front door and looked at his life laid out in front of him. Boxes were marked *Dad, Mom, Jamie, Chili*. So simple. So final. Each life reduced to a few boxes. Chili went to sleep in Jamie's old juvenile bed. They just never got around to upgrading it to the adult-sized one.

The next morning a knock was at the door at eight.

"Who's there?"

"Salvation Army."

Chili opened the door to see two young, slender, Black youths, one tall, one small, with pleasant smiles. "You're our first pick-up."

"Are you sure you two can load up all the furniture? Do you need me to help?"

"No sir. We'll take care of it," the short guy said.

In about an hour all that was left in the apartment were the boxes. "You guys were great!" Chili said as they each drank a glass of water after a job well done. "Here take this," he said, attempting to put a five-dollar bill in each of their hands.

"No sir, that's okay," the tall one said.

"Please, take it. Buy yourself lunch on me."

"Well all right," they said together.

Then the tall one pulled a flyer out of his top pocket. "Sir, here's some information about the services the Salvation Army provides. They helped us. Who knows? Maybe they could help you some day. Have a great day."

Chili stuffed the flyer into his pocket, and gazed at the apartment. He had never seen it so empty. He thought that this is what his parents must have seen when they stepped in there for the very first time when they got married. It seemed much larger when it was bare like this. They were probably about his age when they stood here with their lives ahead of them. And now Chili was facing his future. His possessions were being boxed away and soon he could be, too.

Chili and Father Driscoll had several brief meetings about what to expect once the trial started. It was mostly procedural details about how a criminal trial operates. But they hadn't the "the talk" yet. That would be where the lawyer and the defendant have the super-secret confidential meeting where the defendant is supposed to tell the lawyer the truth, the whole truth, and nothing but the truth, so help him God.

Chili sat in the guest room where he was staying at the Rodriquez home and closed the door after Father Driscoll entered. Driscoll took some books and a yellow pad out of his boxy case.

"Oh, now I see why it's called a yellow *legal* pad," Chili joked.

Father Driscoll smiled briefly. "Chili, you need to go through everything you did on the day in question. Leave nothing out. Even though there is no disputing the fact that you assaulted Father O'Brennan, there could be extenuating circumstances that can reduce the penalties down to very minimal for you."

"Do I have to call you Father?"

"No. Call me Martin."

"Martin, we can cut to the chase here. I'm not going to reveal what he said to me that caused me beat him up."

"You have to tell me. It will be kept secret, legally, in our lawyer-client relationship. It's sacrosanct."

Chili closed his eyes and lowered his head so his chin was touching his chest. He knew what he was facing: years in prison. But if Jamie was still alive, the attention on this trial would drag him back into something he was running away from. He looked his lawyer in the eye. "Sorry, Martin. I can't."

"Are you protecting someone?"

"Yes. Look, I watch Perry Mason and I'm pleading the Fifth."

"This isn't a TV show, Chili. I think you're making a huge mistake. The jury isn't going to buy that one bit, and our chance for a plea bargain goes out the window."

"I don't care."

"Are you protecting a family member?"

"No comment."

"All right, let's move on for now. Tell me everything that happened that day," Father Driscoll said, exasperated, as he took notes.

Chili went through everything in detail until the point where O'Brennan said the vile things about what he did to Jamie. "He said some things to me, and I began to beat him up, in a rage."

"What were you enraged about?"

"Martin, that's it. I'm not saying. I don't care if the evil prick drops dead and they sentence me to the electric chair, I will never tell what he said."

"It might help the person you're protecting if you reveal it."

"Help? Help? No. It wouldn't help."

"That's all for today. Thank you, Chili. Please think about this carefully and reconsider. It could be a matter of life and death."

Father Driscoll went downstairs to the kitchen where Angel and his parents were waiting anxiously.

"How did it go?" Angel asked, as Driscoll was barely in the room.

"As you know I can't reveal anything that was said. We're in that stage where everything said between us is completely confidential. All I'll say is I think that this may be even more challenging than what John Adams was up against."

The trial was perfectly suited for trashy TV news and the tabloids. The headlines, the sordid details, the Shakespearean themes of revenge, blind rage, mysterious motivations. Of course the more serious network TV anchors with their $400 haircuts and thousand-dollar suits made it sound like legitimate news with their "I'm from nowhere" accents and furrowed brows. But there was Chili and O'Brennan blasted across America's newsstands and airwaves for all to see, from coast to coast on the evening news.

As the prosecution laid out its opening statement even Driscoll knew this was a lost cause. Chili, a former student at the same high school, a seminary dropout, tried to kill a priest in a rage of revenge. Driscoll was thinking of how he might get

Chili five years instead of the maximum sentence of fifteen to twenty. Chili, listening to the prosecution lay out the devastating details of the case, caused a sudden change of heart. Chili whispered into Driscoll's ear, "Okay, I'll testify. I'll explain why I did it."

Father Driscoll's opening statement painted Chili as a troubled youth, former model altar boy, camp counselor and seminarian who lost his mind when he was expelled from the seminary and his lifelong dream, fulfilling him mother's dying wishes were forever dashed. Chili thought the insanity defense was close behind.

But as crazy as the press coverage was on the first day of the trial, the courthouse nearly levitated when the real shit storm hit.

Chili took the stand as the first witness for the defense. He was sworn in, and when instructed to tell his story of why he attacked Father O'Brennan, he went numb. Everything in the courtroom became a blur. A swooshing noise swirled in his head. He then focused on something hanging on the wall. At the rear of the courtroom was the Seal of the State of New York. On the left side of the seal was Lady Liberty, and on the right was Lady Justice. Chili wiped his eyes as Lady Liberty transformed into his mother, and Lady Justice became the Virgin Mary. They both put their fingers to their lips and went, "Ssshhhhh."

"Mr. Manzilla, tell the court why you attacked Father O"Brennan," Father Driscoll instructed him.

"No, I can't. I refuse to testify. I'm taking the Fifth."

Of course the press went bonkers with conspiracy theories: Who was he protecting? Was there a second person doing the attacking? Was it his friend the cop? Was there someone else in the room who escaped out the window?

Chili couldn't care less. If Jamie was still alive he wasn't dragging him into this mess and revealing to the world that he was groomed and raped by the priest who was supposed to be guiding and protecting him. Chili could lie and make something else up to protect himself, like he was raped by O'Brennan, but he wouldn't do it. Now was the time for only the truth, and the consequences be damned.

There was a delay in the trial because one of the jurors came down with an illness. It was expected to be a few days, plus a weekend. This gave the sleazeball news outlets even more time to play up the story with even more speculation, conspiracy theories, and outright falsehoods. Then there were the statements from the PR arm of the Archdiocese, who only expressed grief and sympathy for all those involved and hope that the justice system would be allowed to do its job.

Chili knew he was screwed. He stayed in his room at the Rodriquez home, and didn't even come out for his meals. He thought about running off to Mexico or Argentina, or even committing suicide, but didn't want to stick Mr. Rodriguez with the $100,000 bond he had to put up for him. It didn't even bother him anymore that suicide was considered a mortal sin, damning you to the eternal fires of hell, according to the Catholic Church.

There was a knock on Chili's door. It was Angel.

"Chili, I got a call from your dad, and he says he had some personal effects hidden in the apartment, and he wants to know if it's okay for me to take him there to look for them. He knows exactly where they are."

"Personal effects hidden? Like what?"

"Some small things like your mom's wedding ring, rosaries, stuff like that."

"Maybe I should go?"

"We think you should stay inside here. Father Driscoll says there are press guys hiding in the bushes."

"Yeah, no problem. Here's the keys."

"Thanks, Chili. Just call the home and tell them it's okay for me to take your dad out of the building."

"Sure."

Fallout Shelter

Angel picked up Mr. Manzilla at the home and they drove to the apartment Chili had already given up a few weeks earlier. Mr. Manzilla was confused when they pulled up in front of the building, and Angel retrieved the wheelchair from the trunk.

"Am I going home?"

"No, Mr. M. Chili forgot some items in the apartment and asked me to find them for him. We'll take the elevator up through the ground-floor entrance."

Angel pushed Mr. Manzilla into the lower floor of the building, which also had the entrance to the fallout shelter where so many of life's milestones were celebrated or commiserated.

They exited the elevator and rolled to the old apartment. There was a new name above the bell at the door: Davis. Angel rang it.

A female voice from behind the steel door could be heard. "Who is it?"

Angel answered, "It's the former tenant, Mr. Manzilla."

The locks began to click and then door cracked open, with the security chain allowing it only a few inches space. An elderly black lady's face appeared. "How can I help you?"

"Ma'am, my name is Angel Rodriguez, and this is Mr. Manzilla, who just moved out of this apartment before you moved in. He's in a nursing home now, but he says he left a few personal items hidden in the apartment that his son forgot to pick up. Would it be okay if we came in and got those items? They're purely sentimental. They were his wife's items. She passed away."

"Oh, dear, yes, come in," as she unlatched the chain and let them in.

"We really appreciate this, ma'am. It means a lot to the family," Angel said wheeling in Mr. Manzilla.

The apartment was neatly furnished, and there was a toddler quietly playing with some toys in front of the television with *Sesame Street* on. Mr. Manzilla smiled and waved at the baby.

"That's a cute baby," Mr. Manzilla said in a gravelly voice.

"Thank you. That's my daughter's baby. I'm the babysitter, pre-school teacher, cook, and head bottle washer around here. My daughter's at work."

"You said it was in the old milk cooler cabinet, right Mr. M.?"

Angel wheeled him into the kitchen, where under the window there was a door that had been painted over probably ten times in the past 75 or so years.

"Is that what that is?" the lady said. "I always wondered."

"Yeah, people would put their milk and dairy products in here to keep cool when folks only had small ice boxes."

Angel stooped down, took out a pocket knife, and pried open the door. He reached in, and with his knife, pulled back some wood slats and retrieved a small tin Cracker Jack box. He replaced the slat, and closed up the door. "Thank you, ma'am. This is it. I'm so glad he finally remembered where he hid it."

They walked to the door, and before they left, Angel took a bill out of his wallet. "Here ma'am, take this, please. We just won the lottery. Take it."

"A hundred dollars? I can't."

"Please. If you don't want it, give it to your grandchild. Start a college fund for her."

"God bless you!"

Angel and Mr. Manzilla were back in the car, returning to the home.

"That was a cute baby," Mr. Manzilla said. "I remember when William was born. Our first son. I haven't seen our second son, James, in a long time."

"You never know, Mr. M. Keep praying."

The No. 1 train is a graffiti-marred mess from the first car to the last. But there was no faster, more convenient way to get to midtown Manhattan from the West Side of the Bronx. Angel sat at the end of the car, keeping an eye on everyone who entered the train. It wasn't a good idea to read, because then you didn't have a constant view of who could be a potential problem.

He kept the precious item he retrieved from the former apartment of the Manzillas in his inside jacket pocket of his Yankee jacket. He'd sooner give up his wallet with several hundred bucks in it than the item in his pocket, which was worth five bucks at the most, but could make or break Chili's future.

He had the address written down of the location where he was to go, which was given to him by a mysterious female voice on the phone. He got off the train at 34th Street and walked west toward the Hudson River. It was an industrial building on west 32nd Street that was once probably a sweatshop for the garment industry, but was now divided into artists' galleries and lofts. He entered the small lobby and scanned the names on the directory. He pushed the button for PHUNKY PHOTOGRAPHICS and received the buzzer sound to enter. He walked up the three flights and knocked on the steel door, which was painted a glossy black with a white outline of a skeleton in the center.

The door opened and a woman in a white T-shirt and khaki pants spattered with different colored paints answered. Angel would describe her as drop-dead gorgeous except for the fact that she had haircut similar to Curly of Three Stooges fame.

"My name's Cat. Zowie told me to expect you. Have you met her?" She asked, leading him through a maze of paintings and photography setups. "I love California, there's such great art out there. She's in Joshua Tree. The desert is so magical."

"No we haven't met. She's just a friend of a friend."

"So she told me about this. Let's hope we get lucky. Was it stored in a cool, dark place?"

"Yes," Angel said, taking out the brown paper bag, which contained a tiny miniaturized version of 35mm SLR camera.

"I haven't seen one of these since I was a kid," she said, placing it into a black cloth bag and zipping it closed. "They used to sell them in those cheap junk stores in Times Square. They built giant pyramids of them in the front window displays! Let's hope this works. You stay here. I have to go into my dark room for this. Look around, if you'd like."

Angel looked at her ceiling-to-wall paintings, which reminded him of finger painting in kindergarten. But he was amazed at the beauty of her huge photographs that adorned the walls, including photos of some punk rockers, New York street scenes, and gorgeous city skylines.

After about an hour, the red DO NOT ENTER sign was turned off and she appeared with a large envelope.

"Are you a cop or FBI agent or something?" She inquired, seriously.

"No I work for a lawyer. This is important evidence in a criminal case."

"Are those stills from some movie or something? God, I hope so. I'll tell Zowie you got what you needed."

"Thank you so much."

"Aren't you gonna look at the photos?"

"I'll wait 'til I get home."

"I'll keep the negatives under lock-and-key in case anything happens to the prints. By the way, what's your name again?"

"Angel."

"Yup. Figures. Good luck."

Chili's attorney, Father Driscoll, and Angel had a lot of work to do if they were going to use the photos in court. They would also need affidavits from one or more individuals. They had lists of phone numbers and addresses, and hoped that the new evidence would help people to finally come forward.

"Thank goodness, somebody on the jury got sick, otherwise we'd be out of time," Angel said, fingering through a thick Manhattan phone book."

"You can thank goodness," Father Driscoll said, typing on an electric typewriter. "I know who I'm thanking."

There was a knock on the door.

"Who's there?" Angel asked.

"Chili."

"You can't come in here. We're working on some...legal things. We'll let you know. Hang in there."

"Okay." Chili said, weakly, and headed back to his room.

"Actually, Angel…."

"Yes, Father?"

"You need to leave, too, at this stage. This will be confidential attorney-client material and communications."

"Sure, Father. Good luck."

"We'll need a lot of that, too."

The phone rang. "Hello?" Angel said into the receiver. "Hold on." He handed the phone to Father Driscoll.

"Speaking. Right. Okay. Call me as soon as you hear anything else." Driscoll said, then hung up. "Bad news. Father O'Brennan took a turn for the worse. If he continues on this trajectory, he'll die."

"Then it's murder?" Angel asked in disbelief.

"Yes. I have a lot of work to do."

"Later," Angel said, leaving the room. He thought about telling Chili, and decided it wasn't necessary. Yet.

~§ Chapter 14 ~§

Chili, his attorney, Father Driscoll, and Angel pushed through the throngs of reporters and TV news crews into the Bronx Criminal Court House, positioned pretty much between Yankee Stadium and Archbishop Corrigan High School. When Chili was playing in little league, he had dreams of one day making it to Yankee Stadium. He thought it was funny that he came up a few blocks short and wound up in criminal court.

The courtroom was packed. The jury box was full, with two alternates sitting nearby. The gallery was full of journalists and the public. Chili took his seat and dared not turn around to see if he recognized anyone. This wasn't exactly like sitting in the kid's one o'clock mass on Sunday and seeing which friends were sitting behind you.

After the lawyers conferred in the judge's chambers for a while, and whispered to each other at the bench for another while, things looked like they were ready to go.

Driscoll leaned into Chili and whispered, "Keep your cool. Don't say a word, don't make a sound, don't make a hand gesture, don't move unless I ask you to."

The prosecution laid it on heavy, picking up where they left off before the delay of almost a week. Chili was a crazed, violent criminal seeking revenge against a frail, stroke victim who dedicated his life to helping young people until he was no longer able to and had to retire to a nursing home after a debilitating stroke.

In his head, Chili went over the entire rosters of the Yankees, from 1980 going backwards to 1973, the year Ron Blomberg became the first designated hitter in Major League Baseball history. That kept his mind active until lunch, so he missed all the witnesses for the prosecution reinforcing what a crazed lunatic he was. Oh, yeah, even Mikey the cop was part of that parade, describing the sounds and sights of that day for all

Fallout Shelter

to hear and forever part of the public record as the stenographer pushed her magic buttons non-stop.

Chili knew his days were numbered, but he had no idea when this would all be over. One day, two, two weeks. But he dreaded the thought of hearing the jury foreman say "guilty on all counts," going into the van, next stop Sing-Sing Prison, now called the Ossining Correctional Facility, where old Sparky the electric chair still resides. Chili figured that if O'Brennan kicks, there was a chance that he could one day meet old Sparky.

While eating lunch at a nearby diner, Angel rushed to the table where Driscoll and Chili were eating. "Father, I just got word, O'Brennan is doing better. He's fully conscious, eating on his own, talking, and able to get to the bathroom."

"How do we know that?" Driscoll asked.

"We have spies in the hospital, of the boys-in-blue variety."

"The D.A.'s office probably got the word out he was on the verge of death just to give us a scare."

"Thanks for telling me!" Chili said, eyes wide as saucers.

"See, we didn't have to tell you because it all worked out," Angel said reassuringly.

"Let's hope we get a few more lucky breaks," Driscoll added.

After lunch recess, Chili was attempting to go beyond the 1972 Yankees roster in his head, which is where things started to get a little hazy as he thought to himself, *Let's see in the outfield, Murcer, Felipe Alou, was Ron Swoboda on the Mets or the Yanks that season...?*

The prosecution did something, because Driscoll shot up out of his seat, startling Chili.

"You're honor, may I request a sidebar at this time?"

Chili watched as Driscoll and the prosecutor had heated exchanges while the judge alternated between listening and telling one or both to be quiet.

The lawyers went back to their chairs.

The judge struck his gavel, dismissed the courtroom, and said it would reconvene the next morning at 10 a.m. Chili turned around, saw Angel, and gave him a look like *What gives?* To which Angel responded by mouthing the words "I have no freakin' idea."

Father Driscoll called Angel over. "Angel, you escort Chili back to your place. I have business to take care of in the judge's chamber. Go out the exit that goes out the side of the building and maybe you can avoid the TV crews and photographers. Take a cab."

There was silence as they went right past Yankee Stadium, and hopped onto the Major Deegan Expressway in the back of the Yellow Checker cab, until Chili turned to Angel. "Was Swoboda on the Yanks or the Mets in 1971?"

"The Yanks. You're facing 15 years in prison and that's what you're thinking about?"

"What would you wanna think about?"

"You're right."

After dinner, Chili, alone in his room, stared at the ceiling like so many times in his life when things were awful. The night he had a fist fight with his father. The night he found out his mother was going to die. The night she died. But Chili wasn't alone those nights. He always had Jamie in the next bed. And even if they didn't know how to communicate the pain they were both suffering through, just hearing him breathe gave him comfort. But here he was alone, on perhaps the last night of his freedom. And maybe the next time he hears breathing right next to him at night it will be from somebody named Bubba.

Father Driscoll stood in court and announced, "Your honor, I have an affidavit from a woman who was a victim of a violent rape by Father O'Brennan.

The prosecutor jumped up so quickly it sent his heavy oak chair flying back three feet into the railing.

The room was loud with excitement and three people rushed out of the room.

"Order! Order!"

"I object your honor! This is an outrage!" The prosecutor said loudly. "Father O'Brennan has already sworn that he has never in his life, either before priesthood, during the priesthood, or after the priesthood, had sexual relations with any woman ever!"

"May I call the witness, your honor?"

"Yes."

"The defense would like to call to the stand Zowie Mandalay."

Chili watched in bewilderment as a slender young woman with thick blonde hair and deep dark eyes stood in the docket and swore the oath. She wore a plain blue woman's business suit, but had very large loop earrings, that gave her an exotic look.

Chili tried to ignore her and was working on the Yankees roster from 1971.

"State your name."

"Zowie Mandalay."

"Where do you live?"

"Joshua Tree, California."

"What is your occupation?"

"I'm a professional photographer and an artist."

"You stated in this affidavit that you were raped by Father O'Brennan. You understand this is a very serious charge?"

"I do. He raped me multiple times."

The prosecutor jumped up again. "Objection!"

"Overruled."

Chili was in another world, looking only at his hands. His fingers, counting players, infielders, pitchers, catchers, outfielders, third base coach, manager. What was their record?

He was having trouble fighting it. He had to look. Those eyes. Those lips.

"Ms. Mandalay. Did you ever go by another name?"

Chili's eyes widened, his heart raced, he had to control himself. He was told not to move. Don't move. Don't breathe.

"Yes. My given name was James Manzilla."

The courtroom erupted into frenzy! Several more people with pads in their hands went flying out of the room.

The judge banged his gavel a half dozen times. "I will clear this courtroom! Order! Order!"

"Are you related to the defendant, William Manzilla?"

"He is my brother," Zowie said.

Chili felt a rush go through his body, as if he had just gotten a jolt from Sing-Sing's Sparky.

"Please explain the name change for the court."

"I was a male at birth, but have transitioned to female over the last several years. I had to move to California to protect myself and my family."

"Thank you, no further questions for now." Driscoll paused while Zowie rushed out of the courtroom, looking straight ahead. He continued, "Your honor, I will prove not only that Father O'Brennan was a serial rapist of minor boys, but in fact, have proof that he is a murderer!"

"Court is adjourned for today! Clear the courtroom! Prosecution and defense see me in my chambers. Now."

The place exploded. People were running to the phone booths faster than Clark Kent after hearing that Jimmy and Lois were tied to the railroad tracks.

Father Driscoll went over to Chili. "We're not out of the woods yet. But I can see the highway from here."

Angel approached Chili who had his head down on the table in front of him, resting on his folded arms. He tapped Chili on the shoulder. "Let's go. We'll try to sneak out the side door."

They rushed through the courtroom door and pushed through a mob of press people shouting questions, and ran to the stairway. Out on the street, they grabbed a cab and were soon passing Yankee Stadium and onto the Major Deegan Expressway heading back to safety of the Rodriguez home.

It was not a time for celebration. Chili was in daze going over his relationship with Jamie as he stared out the window of his room, looking at the bare oak and elm trees in the yard and down the street. He thought back to all the signs of his abuse as an altar boy and freshman year at Corrigan. How could he not know? How could he not intervene? Then he remembered Mrs. Madigan. How she would burst into rooms and tell the priests what to do. Where to go. And where not to go. Perhaps she was the one doing her best to protect her flock.

There was a knock on the door.

"Come in."

Father Driscoll entered, with sadness dripping from his face.

"Is it bad news? Did O'Brennan Die? Am I a murderer? Chili said, panic stricken.

"On the contrary. O'Brennan's doing better than expected. You never would have made it as a boxer. He's got some bruises, needed a few stitches, but nothing broken."

"What's troubling you?" Chili asked, pointing to a chair.

"There are no winners here. One of my own, a fellow follower of Jesus Christ, who gave a sacred oath to serve the Lord and lead the most vulnerable to salvation has been exposed as pure evil. O'Brennan preyed upon young boys. He groomed the most susceptible to his so-called charms, then raped, sodomized, terrorized, blackmailed and yes, even murdered."

"You have proof?"

"Remember a miniature camera you bought years ago, that disappeared?"

"Yeah, of course."

"Jamie, being fascinated with photography, stole that from you. When he was going on the retreat with the Corrigan newspaper staff and some others, he took that little camera with him. He followed the boy who was murdered, with the school-issued 35 mm camera, but kept that as a backup in his pocket.

When he was hiding in the brush, he took out that camera and caught on film the moment that O'Brennan gave the boy a shove, sending him off the cliff to his death. He put it down his pants and fled. But a student accomplice grabbed him and the school-issued camera. In no uncertain terms he warned Jamie that if he ever mentioned anything about what happened, the same fate would befall you, your father, and him. By the way, that accomplice is now a priest also."

"What the fuck? Excuse me, father!" Chili blurted out. "So when Angel took my father to the old apartment to get mom's jewelry it was a ruse. The camera was hidden somewhere?"

"Yes, thankfully in a cool, dark place, sealed in a container that didn't leak any light. Angel was contacted, unbeknown to him, by Zowie. She instructed him where to find the camera, and where to bring it to secretly develop and print the photos."

The door opened and Angel stuck his head in. "May I come in?"

"Yes, I was just explaining the chain of events."

"Oh, and by the way, Chili for a holier-than-thou prude back in the day, you took a few pretty graphic photos at the peep show we went to in Times Square."

"Busted." Chili deadpanned. "What happens now?"

"I don't know for certain, but I'm thinking that the case could be dropped tomorrow, and O'Brennan and his accomplice will be arrested. I have to look at the statutes of limitations for the rape of a minor, which can be tricky depending on the circumstances, but as you know there's no limitation on murder."

"What does dropping the case mean for me?" Chili asked.

"That is unknown. But the D.A.'s office will look at the case, and decide if there should be another trial, or if they will drop all charges based on the new circumstances. I think your chances are pretty good for dropping the case entirely. By the way, we have affidavits from several other people you might recognize, Chili."

"Shoot," Chili shot back.

"Father Palmer from St. Gall's back in the day. He was raped as a minor by O'Brennan."

"The cycle continues. Did Palmer ever...touch Zowie, I mean Jamie?" Chili asked.

"No. But I'm sure he was grooming little Jamie. He showed Jamie some soft-porn gay magazines. Zowie said she listened through the door and heard Mrs. Madigan say something about her husband was a cop and would go after him."

"Her husband was dead at that time. Killed on the job as a cop," Angel added. "By the way, I heard Mrs. Madigan retired to Florida. I heard she volunteers at her new church."

"Well, whatever she was doing at St. Gall's it worked because Father Palmer left the parish shortly afterwards," Father Driscoll said. "Oh, and another person, Mr. Clarke, your roommate at the seminary, stated that O'Brennan and McQuirke tried to blackmail him with falsehoods after he complained about the orgies and sexual abuse in the seminary. And your other roommate, John McSherry, was raped and blackmailed by McQuirke and O'Brennan as a minor and at the seminary.

There was silence in the room, as Father Driscoll, Angel, and Chili stared at the papers on the kitchen table outlining the evil that had been hiding for so long.

"Will you both excuse me?" Chili asked, visibly shaken.

"Of course," they both said and exited.

Chili stood up, and dug into that little extra pocket on the right side of the Levi's dungarees, and took out his mother's rosary beads. He knelt and for the first time since he left the seminary, he prayed.

The next morning the courtroom was abuzz with spectators and the press. The judge was announced and he got right to the business at hand. "The prosecution has dropped all charges against the defendant at this time. Charges have been filed against Father John O'Brennan and Father Randy Appleby for second-degree murder and both have been arrested. Other charges are being drawn up for assorted sexual assault crimes against minors, blackmail, etcetera. This courtroom is adjourned. Everyone is free to go."

Chili stood and turned around to see Zowie in the last row. She stood and they stared at each other. Suddenly Chili saw something from a distance while looking into Zowie's deep dark eyes, the shape of her nose, the curve of her lips, the cheekbones, the slightly crooked smile. He saw his mother.

They slowly walked toward each other and stood just inches apart. They embraced tenderly. While still embracing, Zowie said softly, "I feel like I've come back from the dead."

"We've both come back from the dead," Chili said, touching Zowie's face.

"Can we visit dad?" Zowie asked.

"Sure. Maybe wear a hat. The blonde hair might throw him," Chili said with a smile.

Mr. Manzilla was fading away. He hadn't eaten in five days and was refusing water. Chili and Zowie entered the room and stood by his bed as he slept. Zowie was wearing a Yankees cap with her blonde hair pulled back. She had no make-up, no jewelry, and was wearing blue jeans and the man's motorcycle jacket she used to wear when she was attending DeWitt Clinton high school.

Chili leaned in. "Dad, look who's here."

Mr. Manzilla opened his eyes and looked at Zowie. "Jamie? Are you for real?"

Zowie, who had sworn to never cry in her life as Jamie or Zowie was in tears. "Yup, dad, it's me. I've been away, but I've come back for a visit."

"Where did you go?"

"California."

"Oh, I like California. It's warm there. Maybe I'll go visit you there."

"Anytime, dad. Anytime."

Mr. Manzilla fell back to sleep. He never woke up.

✥ Chapter 15 ✥

Zowie returned home after they buried Mr. Manzilla. Chili was trying to get his life back in order. He moved in with Mikey without having to pay any rent until he could find a full-time job. Although he was fired from his city job as a group home live-in counselor when he was arrested, he came across the Salvation Army flyer the worker handed him as they were taking away his furniture, and had an application in for their own group homes.

Mikey's apartment was in the basement of a private home on Corlear Avenue, about halfway between Angel's house and Chili's old apartment. It was decorated in contemporary thrift-store chic. The walls were adorned with assorted sports heroes, including Walt Frazier, Rod Gilbert, Sam Huff, and Yogi Berra. The only non-sports item on the wall was on the door to the bathroom. It was the familiar black-and-yellow sign that had been attached to a wall in Chili's cellar that read FALLOUT SHELTER, which Mikey borrowed for safe keeping after the Manzillas moved out.

"Angel's bringing over some of his mom's enchiladas in a little while," Mikey said, putting his badge and his gun in a drawer under the TV set.

"I love those! I could eat a dozen of them!" Chili said, reading the *Daily News*.

"Yeah, well, I've got to stay in shape for the job. You wouldn't believe the fat cops I see huffing and puffing trying to chase scumbags down the street."

"And then *you* have to chase them and cuff 'em? Maybe that's why they're fat."

"I never thought of that. Maybe I'll have some extras tonight."

There was a knock on the door. "Open up! It's the enchilada police!"

Fallout Shelter

Angel entered with bags of enchiladas, homemade chips, green and red salsas, and bottles of Yoo Hoo. "If we're gonna sit here staring at a picture of Yogi Berra while we eat, we gotta be drinking Yoo Hoo."

As they were feasting, Chili remembered something. "Oh, I forgot to mention, I've got an interview tomorrow at the Salvation Army headquarters down on 14th Street."

"Hey that's great!" Angel said. "Did Father Driscoll write you that recommendation letter? He said your expungement should happen soon."

"Yeah, I've got it. Tell your dad he may have to find another mop-up man at the bodega if I get the job."

"He'll be thrilled to hear that!"

Chili put on a tie, dress slacks, and a blazer that he hadn't worn since his days at Corrigan. Luckily they still fit. Mostly. He took the subway to 14th Street and walked to the address. He had been on 14th Street hundreds of times, but somehow never noticed the Salvation Army Headquarters building. He stood in front and admired the grand entrance, which resembled a church with its golden gate, and slabs of marble and granite.

Chili found the office and opened the door. An Asian woman sat behind a desk. "May I help you?"

"I have an interview for a job."

"Okay. Go through that door."

Chili went through the door and took a seat, while a female executive was facing the window and speaking on the phone. She turned and hung up the phone, immediately smiling broadly at Chili. She was a middle-aged Black woman wearing a dark blue outfit which a female executive might be wearing in a corporate setting.

"Pleased to meet you, Mr. Manzilla. I've been looking through your file. You did an excellent job filling out your application. And was impressed by the letter Father Driscoll wrote in your support. I'm Mrs. Viola," She said reaching to shake hands.

"Thank you for the interview, Mrs. Viola."

"In full disclosure, Mr. Manzilla, I'm well aware of your recent court case and appreciate you filling in some of the details of your circumstances…"

Chili froze. Was this the beginning of a lifetime of rejections for his actions?

"…but we at the Salvation Army believe in second chances. And third and fourth and fifth."

"I'm so pleased to hear that," Chili said, exhaling.

"I know you worked in a city run group home for young men. But until your record is expunged we can't have you in such a position. Is there a chance for that happening?"

"My attorney says there's an excellent chance."

"That's good news. In the meantime, do you have any other work experience?"

"I worked in a bodega for a couple of years. Doing cleanup, stocking shelves, making sandwiches, preparing salads."

"Well more good news! We have a position available in our cafeteria here in this building. It gets you in the door, and when a social services position opens up, in a group home for instance, you can apply."

"That would be great! When will you notify me if I get the job?"

"Consider yourself notified!"

Chili wanted to hug her, but just smiled and shook hands, biting the inside of his lip, trying to contain his emotions.

For the first few days, Chili was learning the ropes of the cafeteria and the kitchen. Many of his co-workers, male and female, had a hard look. Some had tattoos and scars and a tooth or two missing, but each and every one of them was friendly, polite, and eager to teach the new guy how to do the job properly.

By the end of the first week, Chili was positioned at the counter, dispensing assorted hot foods onto plates for customers. It was here that Chili saw the range of people passing through. He knew very well that this building was possibly the last chance for drug addicts, alcoholics, victims of physical abuse, ex-convicts, the homeless, and the mentally unstable. And he witnessed small acts of kindness from his co-workers to those on the other side of the counter with a smile, laugh, words of encouragement or simply a *have a good day*. The only thing he didn't like was that he had to wear a round white paper hat, not unlike the burger flippers in White Castle.

Lunch on this Friday was extra busy and it was hard for him to keep track of the orders as he dished out the mac 'n cheese, broccoli, mashed potatoes, and string beans. When they were swamped like this he barely saw the faces of the people he was serving. But as a female voice asked for broccoli and string beans, his senses went into overdrive. He put both veggies onto a plate but hesitated before placing it onto her tray. Directly in front of him, on the other side of the steam tray and just above the glass counter was a vison. Or was it?

"Pamela?" Chili asked, as though questioning whether a mirage was for real.

Her eyes widened like a rosebud opening in time-lapse photography. "William?"

There she was; Pamela Hinderlap! Not the Pamela Hinderlap Chili stumbled upon in Haight-Ashbury with torn and frayed clothing, needle marks, and tragedy dripping from her face. This was the Pamela Hinderlap who awakened Chili's inner most feelings and yes, passions as a young teen. And she was a vision, of beauty, once again.

"Oh, Pamela, it's so…great to see you. You look… so healthy," Chili said putting the vegetable plate on her tray.

Pamela looked at the short, elderly Asian lady next to her, "I'm sorry for holding up the line."

"No, no. That's Okay. This is more important," the lady said, obviously delighted.

"William, I'll sit over there. Can you come say hello?"

"Yes. I think. I'll have to check. But yes!"

Chili watched as Pamela continued down the line, paid, and went to a table off to the side. He served several more people and received permission to take a 5 minute break.

Chili approached Pamela's table and removed his paper hat, sitting down beside her. "Pamela Hinderlap! Well I never in a million years—"

"…Thought you'd see a burnt-out little drug addict in a Salvation Army cafeteria," she said grinning.

"I didn't mean…."

"When we bumped into each other in Berkley, I was so out of it. I don't even want to tell you how low I was. But somehow I hadn't reached rock bottom until I met you that day. It wasn't until I was confronted with someone who knew me when I was…not an addict, did I see what I had become."

"This is amazing. You look fantastic! Um, by the way, did you happen to see what I've been going through lately?"

"Yes. I have. So tragic. I'm so proud of you. So proud of Jamie, I mean, Zowie." Pamela looked down, and pushed her string beans on her plate. "Do you remember how you said goodbye to me in Berkley?"

"I said, I'll pray for you."

"I don't think you were the only one. I went through the Salvation Army drug rehab program. I come here for my recovery group, and I'm working at the retail store in Yonkers. This is my new life."

"I didn't know the Salvation Army did anything except sell junk and sing goofy Christmas carols on the street corner…oh," Chili said, catching himself. "I didn't mean to disparage…"

"That's okay. Most people have no idea what the Salvation Army does until there's no place else to turn," Pamela said, tenderly touching Chili's hand.

Chili looked at her hand touching his, and thought that the last time someone touched him that way, it was Pamela after eighth grade graduation, all those years ago. "I know exactly what you mean."

Several weeks later, Chili was proud to give Mikey his first rent payment from his new job. He was enjoying working at the Salvation Army cafeteria, making new friends behind the counter and in front of it. And now that Chili and Mikey's apartment was the new version of their fallout shelter, Chili was excited to call an emergency meeting there. It was arranged so Mikey and Angel could meet his new girlfriend– the only girl that ever truly touched his heart–Pamela Hinderlap. Well, except for his mom. And Zowie.

Steven Schindler

About the Author

Fallout Shelter is Steven Schindler's seventh novel. Born and raised in the Bronx, he has worked for several decades in television as a writer/producer/editor in many genres of TV programming. Credits include 4 Chicago Emmy Awards, a Journalist of the Year award, and many Emmy nominations in Chicago and Washington DC. for news, entertainment specials, and magazine programs. Highlights include exclusive interviews with The Who, *The Tonight Show with Jay Leno*, *America's Most Wanted* and a Chicago Emmy Award for Outstanding Achievement for a TV Entertainment Special, *Rock 'N Roll Legacy*, a program he created, wrote and produced.

Writing awards include Grand Prize Winner, *The Last Sewer Ball*, NY Book Festival and Best Fiction, *From the Block*, Hollywood Indie Book Festival. His novels have received praise from Jay Leno, Roger L. Simon (*The Big Fix*), the *New York Post*, and *Publishers Weekly*. Will Manus (*Mott the Hoople*) said about Schindler: "Faulkner chronicled the south, Updike the suburbs, Hemingway the expat life. Now the Bronx has its literary equivalent, its literary champion. Steven Schindler is his name."

He lives amidst the avocado groves of North San Diego County with his wife.

Steven Schindler